HOW TO
Seduce A Scot

WITHDRAWN

CHRISTY ENGLISH

sourcebooks
casablanca

Published by Sourcebooks Casablanca, an imprint of Sourcebooks, Inc.
P.O. Box 4410, Naperville, Illinois 60567-4410
(630) 961-3900
Fax: (630) 961-2168
www.sourcebooks.com

Printed and bound in Canada.
MBP 10 9 8 7 6 5 4 3 2 1

For my friends LaDonna Lindgren and Laura Creasy.
Thanks for hanging in there while I became a better writer.

One

London, 1820

CATHERINE MIDDLEBROOK SURVEYED THE BALLROOM at Almack's, looking for a quiet, biddable man to marry. She knew that she needed to focus her attention properly if she were to catch the interest of a suitable man before her one and only Season was up. But she kept being distracted by a dark-eyed, wide-shouldered Highlander staring at her from across the room—and by his sister, who was prattling in her ear.

"The problem with this hall is that there is only one way out," Mary Elizabeth Waters said.

"Indeed?" She needn't have bothered saying anything—the Scottish girl seemed to need little encouragement to expound on her wild notions. Catherine welcomed those wild notions, for they helped her forget that she had been in Almack's for over an hour, and so far, not one man had asked her to dance. Not even Mr. Waters, who seemed intent on memorizing the planes of her face since the moment she had saved his happily oblivious sister from another debutante's cruel snub.

Though he made no move toward her, her new friend's brother kept staring. It made her skin prickle with a strange awareness. It would have been uncomfortable had it not been so delicious.

Alexander Waters, a younger son from the wilds of Scotland, was not the kind of man Catherine needed to attract. He was too large, for one thing. Mr. Waters's shoulders were too broad—both for the black superfine coat he wore and for the room he lurked in. Though he stood silent across the length of the ballroom from her and his sister, he seemed to take up all the air between them with his presence. Catherine was not certain that she would have enough breath in her body to dance a set with him in the room, even if she were asked.

His dark-chocolate eyes hid depths that Catherine wished she might find the bottom of, and the sight of him drew her gaze no matter how she tried to keep her mind fixed elsewhere. Like all gentlemen present, he wore the requisite white breeches with knee buckles and polished slippers. He simply did not look at home in them, as the other men did.

But of all his stellar attractions, Alexander Waters's lips drew her gaze the most. There was a quirk of humor to them that made her wonder what he found amusing. She would like to have been let in on the joke.

Sometimes she felt as if *she* were the joke, and this evening was one of those times. Never had the task she had set herself seemed so insurmountable as it did that night. The ballroom was full of lovely young girls, none of whom were on the last desperate leg of their family's money. If by some chance Mr. Waters were looking for a bride, there would be no need to stare so fixedly at her, a girl with only her mother's good looks and five hundred pounds to recommend her.

She had to be mistaken. No doubt the handsome Alexander Waters was not watching her at all, but keeping a close eye on his little sister, still chattering away beside her.

"One would need a good stout rope of hemp to make it out of that window there," Mary Elizabeth was saying.

Catherine blinked, drawn away from her anxious thoughts. "I beg your pardon?"

"You are not attending, sweet Catherine. Pay attention. This is important. It may save your life someday. Say for example the English had cut off the staircase..."

Mary Elizabeth Waters paused for breath, and Catherine wondered if the girl realized the unsuitability of using her given name so freely. Perhaps such informality was common north of the border. Never having been further north than Mayfair, Catherine did not know.

She turned to survey the company, trying to see them as Mary Elizabeth might, taking in the London *ton* all around her: the tabby-cat aunts who stood as chaperones, the Almack's patronesses who deigned or refused to let various young ladies dance, the young lords who preened before girls just out of the schoolroom, and the debutantes in delicate white who vied for those young lords' attention. Most in that room, save Mary Elizabeth and her brother, were English.

Catherine's young friend seemed to realize her

mistake, for she began again. "Say for example the staircase had been cut off by some sort of ruffians, pirates perhaps—"

"Pirates in Almack's?" Catherine asked, keeping her voice free of the laughter that seemed to gather just at the back of her throat. It threatened to take her over in an unseemly bolt of hysterical mirth. Open laughter would be a true disaster, as no gentleman would approach her if she were to behave in such an unladylike manner. Catherine schooled her features into a semblance of calm, even as her heart lightened for the first time since she had arrived. And as she felt the hot caress of Mr. Waters's gaze on her skin once again, the notion of pirates skulking about did not seem so outlandish.

"Highwaymen, then," Mary Elizabeth said. "The type of ruffian doesn't signify."

"But the ruffians are definitely English," Catherine said, unable to suppress her smile.

Mary Elizabeth caught the gleam of humor in her new friend's eyes and smiled as well. "Ruffians are almost always English."

"I bow to your greater knowledge of ne'er-do-wells. Please continue."

"If pirates or highwaymen had cut off our escape, we would need a good sound hemp rope to descend the side of the building to the street below and to safety."

Catherine did her best to resist, even as her desire for propriety and good sense gave way to good fun. "But do you think it would be at all proper for a lady to climb from a window? Might all on the street below take note?"

Mary Elizabeth waved one hand in dismissal. "If the gents below want to get a glance at my undergarments, let them. Better to escape with my throat uncut, and let those below sort themselves out."

Catherine felt her telltale blush rise as it always did, and she wondered how to steer this bizarre conversation to safer waters. She looked around at the company and saw that not one soul was paying any attention to them at all, save for Mary Elizabeth's brother. She decided to let caution and prudence go, if only for the moment, and simply enjoy herself.

"I wonder if Almack's keeps such rope handy?" Catherine asked, joining her new friend in her outlandish speculations. "And if they do, would there be enough rope for all present to effectively make their escape?"

"Unlikely," Mary Elizabeth said. "But we keep a sound hemp rope ladder in every room on the upper floors of the duchess's town house. You look shocked, Catherine, but it is quite proper. Even my uncle, the Bishop of London, keeps rope ladders in the bedrooms of his home. Just in case."

Catherine blinked. Mary Elizabeth had mentioned that she and her brothers were guests of the illustrious Duchess of Northumberland, who was sponsoring Mary Elizabeth's debut. Catherine would never have guessed that a headstrong girl from the north would have such lofty connections, but in spite of them, Mary Elizabeth seemed completely unspoiled. Unfortunately, her alliance with the duchess had not drawn any men to her side either.

Catherine brought her mind back to their bizarre

conversation. "The Bishop of London keeps rope handy above stairs in case of pirates?"

"In case of fire. But it would work if pirates invaded as well."

"Or the English."

Mary Elizabeth laughed, the velvet tone far too confident for such a gathering of fops and young ladies. "We're in London, Catherine. The English are everywhere."

"I am sorry to bring up a sore subject," Catherine said, "but *I* am English."

"I beg to differ. You are a decent woman from the county of Devon. That's practically Cornwall. That's practically civilized."

Catherine was about to inquire as to Mary Elizabeth's standards of civilization when she noticed that Mr. Waters had vanished from his accustomed place on the other side of the dance floor. In the next moment, the mystery of his whereabouts was solved when she felt the gentle touch of his hand on her arm. The heat of his palm, even encased in a leather glove, drove all rational thought from her mind for the moment—and most likely for the duration of the night.

She would have to begin her husband hunt again later, once she retrieved her good sense—which had deserted her completely.

❦

Alexander Waters could not keep his mind on the task at hand—namely to ferret out a decent Englishman for his sister to marry. He found that he could not even plan his next sea voyage, the best refuge he knew from boredom when trapped in London. The girl who stood beside his sister took over all conscious thought, his gaze drawn back to her again and again like a lodestone.

She was a butterfly flown in from some summer garden. A butterfly with soft green eyes, blonde curls, and a body with curves made for sin.

No, Alexander corrected himself, she was not a butterfly. She was an angel, if such a celestial being might come to land among the heathen English. If such a gentle soul might sit still among the melee of the London *ton* and listen with patient serenity to his sister as she prattled on. About swords or fly-fishing, no doubt. No other lady present would have been as kind, he was certain of that.

Alex wondered if she smelled of sunshine. He had wondered all night, for her hair made him think of sunlight on the burn near Glenderrin. Now that he stood beside her, he found that she did not bring the scent of sunlight into that stale, stilted ballroom. Instead, she smelled of the hothouse rosebuds in her hair.

He had spent the evening watching as both his sister and the lovely girl beside her were ignored by every man present. He did not understand the English mind, why the men in that assembly room seemed intent on dancing with every girl but them. Mary Elizabeth did not give a fig for what the members of Almack's thought of her, but Alexander would have bet the contents of his brother's flagship that the angel beside her did.

Alex knew he should not touch a gently bred young lady without permission, but his hand found the soft skin of her upper arm on its own. The heat of her body burned through his glove, and he almost swallowed his tongue. Luckily, he had been raised to make polite conversation with ladies, even when his brain had shut down. He breathed deep, trying to set aside his own fascination with this girl, determined to bring her out of the shadows.

"May I have the pleasure of this dance?"

Alex was pleased that his tongue did not betray him by clinging to the roof of his mouth. Lady Jersey gave him the evil eye from across the crowded assembly room; he would bring her a glass of watered-down lemonade later, to sweeten her. He winked and watched as his mother's friend colored at his regard. Lady Jersey's hawk-like gaze softened, and her natural beauty rose to the fore as she gave a subtle nod.

"I have not yet received permission to waltz, sir," the young lady said, blinking up at him as if she were standing in the bright light of a small sun.

He turned his smile on her, nodding to Lady Jersey, who watched them from down the ballroom. "I think you just did," he said.

Alex did not wait for her to protest again, nor did he listen to the snide comments of his little sister as he left her, and the angel's mother, standing on the edge of the dance floor. Mrs. Angel was chattering away to the woman at her side and did not seem to notice that he had whisked her daughter away, leaving Mary Elizabeth frowning in his wake.

The waltz would not last long. When it was done, he would take his sister and the angel to meet Lady Jersey and to obtain a slice of dry cake. Such were the rewards to be found among the English elite.

He felt the heavy gazes of the lords and young

fops on him as he had all night. None of them had shown the sense to ask an angel to dance themselves, but now that he had put his filthy Scottish hands on her, they were ready to draw swords. Not that any of them would have the nerve to approach him. They all looked too inbred to be men of action. Perhaps they might hire it done, and have him stabbed in the street. He almost laughed at that thought but pushed it aside when the angel in his arms spoke.

"I beg your pardon, sir, but we have not been introduced."

It took Alex a moment to comprehend the statement, for he was too busy breathing in the scent of rose petals, with London and all its so-called men forgotten. It was not just the blossoms in her hair that entranced him. Her skin smelled of roses warmed by the summer sun. He wondered at himself. It was too cold to grow roses along the Glenderrin. Where had he suddenly acquired this fascination with their scent?

As she gazed up at him with clear green eyes— which filled with more genteel irritation by the moment—he knew that it was not the scent of roses in particular that fascinated him. It was her.

"I am Alexander Waters, brother to your new friend Mary Elizabeth Waters of Glenderrin. You are…?" Here he faltered, for he had no idea of her name. Michaela? Gabriella?

She smiled a little, then pressed her lips together as if to suppress it. She succeeded only in drawing his attention to her mouth, and to the fact that her lower lip was a plush pillow that he would like to take between his teeth.

"I am not accustomed to dancing with gentlemen I do not know."

"No one knows anyone at these things. Except for the bloody English, who have known each other since birth."

"As I have told your sister, Mr. Waters, I am English."

"You are an angel from heaven. I don't know why you've touched ground here tonight, but I am grateful to God you have."

"Now you are simply teasing me," she said. She did not look embarrassed, as any other young girl might, but she searched his face as if to find his motives reflected there.

"Far be it for me to ever mock a lady," he answered.

She smiled then, and Alexander found his heart lighten as her mossy-green eyes took him in, lit by a wry humor he would not have thought to find. He knew he had more than overstepped the bounds of propriety by foisting himself on her without even the semblance of an introduction. But there was something about this girl that drew him to her, a light in her eyes that made him want to know what lay behind them. As he looked down at the girl in his arms, he would have given half the gold in his family's coffers to know what she was thinking.

Her color rose to an even lovelier shade of pink, and he drew her a bit closer—too close it seemed, for he caught Lady Jersey's eagle eye. He felt her censure and knew it was deserved. These English did not seem to know what a waltz was good for—namely for a man to sneak a moment of warmth with the woman in his arms. He reminded himself that he was not at home in the Highlands, nor in Venezuela, nor in a planter's mansion in the West Indies, but in a staid London ballroom, and ought to behave as such. But Alexander clutched his prize for one moment more, breathing in the scent of her hair before forcing himself to relinquish her. The song ended, and his angel stepped away, but not before he caught her hand and laid it on his arm. Now that the dance was done, he would set aside his growing infatuation and return to his original intention.

There was one more way in which he might be of service to her. The fops that called themselves men at that assembly might not dance with her simply because he had done so, but they would have no choice but to accept her if Lady Jersey smiled on her.

"Please allow me the honor of presenting you to her ladyship."

His angel looked up at him as if trying to read his thoughts from his eyes. Her gaze was frank and unflinching, which only confirmed his suspicion that there was more to admire in this girl than her beauty and her sweetness.

"You cannot present me to anyone," she said. "You do not know my name, and I see no reason to give it to you."

Alexander smiled, reveling in the challenge she laid down. "Very well. Since you will not reveal it, let us see if I might discover it another way."

Two

As much as she enjoyed his touch and his fine, dark eyes, Catherine wondered if she should be annoyed with Mr. Waters's high-handed ways. But just when she thought to become irritated with him in truth, he took her, not to Lady Jersey as he had threatened, but directly to her mother.

"Catherine, there you are at last!" Mrs. Middlebrook said as Alexander Waters returned her relatively unscathed. "And who is this fine gentleman with you? A friend of Miss Waters's, no doubt?"

Mary Elizabeth frowned like thunder. "Ma'am, may I present my brother, Alexander Waters. Alex, this is Mrs. Middlebrook, sweet Catherine's mother."

Catherine prayed to the Holy Virgin that none of the people close by were listening to the belated introductions, but her mother's voice was a bit strident, and carried far. She felt her hated blush rise again, and wished herself anywhere but where she was.

Mr. Waters seemed to sense something of her pain, for he patted her hand once where it rested on his arm. She felt shored up by the gentle touch. The

Scots might not hold with all the proprieties that
her grandmother had drilled into her, but they were
warmhearted people who seemed genuinely to like
her. All of her own people seemed only to ignore
her—or to stare at her as if she were a bug on the
bottom of their shoe.

"Mrs. Middlebrook, it is an honor to make your
acquaintance," Alexander said. Catherine found herself distracted from her embarrassment once again by
the deep, honeyed tones of his voice. "Please forgive
me for squiring away your lovely daughter, but I
found myself overwhelmed by her beauty and could
not resist drawing her into the dance."

Catherine wanted to reprimand him for saying
something so improper, but had lost all ability to
speak. She breathed deep, and as her blush began to
subside, she sneaked a glance at the virile man beside
her. In spite of his audacious behavior and speech,
there was something about him that soothed her,
though he was truly too large for comfort. For the
first time that night, standing beside him, she felt oddly
sheltered from the dismissal of the people around
her, and even from her mother's haphazard care. She
wondered where she might have gotten such a wild
notion that she was being protected by a man she had
only just met. Perhaps Mary Elizabeth's taste for wild
speculation was catching.

"Oh, what is an introduction among decent people
of good fortune?" Mrs. Middlebrook asked. Catherine
cringed but her mother spoke on. "I am as pleased as
I could be to make your acquaintance, Mr. Waters,
and that of your lovely sister. We have only been in

London a fortnight and have had little society since we arrived. You and your sister are a breath of fresh air."

Catherine prayed for death, though she knew it would not come. For her mother to reveal their countrified unpopularity to near strangers was one thing, but her voice carried and revealed their situation to every man and woman within ten feet of them. Catherine was not sure, but it seemed to her as if those groups standing closest to her drew back a little, as if her mother's gauche impropriety was a disease that might be catching.

Before her mother could launch into an explanation of Catherine's intentions to marry for money within the next two months—or something else equally damning—Alexander Waters smiled. His masculine beauty was such that even her mother fell suddenly silent.

"With your permission, ma'am, I would like to present you and your daughter to Lady Jersey. She is an old friend of the family, and Mary Elizabeth and I have not yet spoken to her this evening."

Mrs. Middlebrook almost crowed with triumph. "Lady Jersey herself! How wonderful! I find that my dance card is filled for the next set, Mr. Waters, but if you would be so good as to escort Catherine without me, I would be ever so obliged."

Catherine's mother caught the eye of a man across the room and winked.

Catherine wished very fervently that the parquet floor beneath her feet would open and swallow her whole. It did not, but Mr. Waters's arm beneath her hand shored her up. He bowed to her mother, then offered his other arm to his sister.

With her mother's good-byes ringing in her ears, Catherine concentrated on walking as calmly as she might while Mr. Waters escorted Mary Elizabeth and herself across the ballroom to Lady Jersey's side. As they faced the august lady, Catherine was grateful that her mother had stayed behind. She straightened her spine and reminded herself of her grandmother's teachings. She was a lady, no matter how unguarded her mother's behavior. Her father had been a gentleman, and if he could glimpse her from his place in heaven in that moment, she would make him proud of her.

Mr. Waters was blessedly silent, not commenting on her mother's behavior as he led her across the room. Mary Elizabeth seemed to wish to distract her, for she did not stop speaking about her new favorite topic—fishing in the burn near her home—until they reached the seat of power and stood at Lady Jersey's feet.

"So, Mr. Waters, it seems you have grown." Lady Jersey perused the man before her with a smile that did not seem quite proper to Catherine. She was brought out of her own embarrassed misery over her mother's behavior to feel a strange stab of jealousy just below her spleen. But then the moment passed, and Lady Jersey talked of banalities. "I do hope your mother is well. It has been many years since last I had the pleasure of Lady Glenderrin's company."

"Since we came south when I was fifteen," Mr. Waters said.

"Indeed. Far too long ago."

"A mere moment, my lady. You have not aged a day."

Lady Jersey laughed, then seemed to dismiss him and all his dark-eyed charm.

"This is your sister, Miss Waters. And this young lady must be…"

Mary Elizabeth spoke up. "This is my friend, Miss Catherine Middlebrook. May I have your permission to waltz, my lady?"

Lady Jersey blinked at the sudden onslaught from a girl who should know better than to speak before being spoken to. Catherine held her breath. But the illustrious lady did not stare Mary Elizabeth out of countenance, though it was clear that she was not best pleased. "Of course you may dance, Miss Waters. Any young lady sponsored by the Duchess of Northumberland is a graceful addition to these halls."

"I thank you, your ladyship. Do you ever fish when you are in the country?"

Seeing Lady Jersey's smile waver, Catherine made her curtsy, tugging less than gently on Mr. Waters's arm. Mary Elizabeth did not pursue her line of questioning but curtsied as well, understanding without being told that in this instance, retreat was the better part of valor. All three stepped away from Lady Jersey, who turned to speak with the next eager girl and her mother who were waiting for an audience.

Catherine had no idea what to say, which was just as well, as Mr. Waters was too busy chastising his sister to notice her. "I thought we agreed that you would not mention fishing in company."

"Lady Jersey is not company," Mary Elizabeth said. "She is Mother's friend. Alex, take me to the cake before we go back to the dancing. I'm sure to be asked now that Lady Jersey has smiled at me. The English have their rituals, and God knows we must follow them."

"One of those rituals, as you put it, is not to discuss fishing in a ballroom."

"Why ever not? Fishing is one of the best sporting pastimes one might expect to find. Even the English fish, surely."

Catherine choked on a laugh she was trying to suppress. Mr. Waters caught her eye and smiled wryly, handing both girls glasses of lemonade and slices of dry pound cake. Catherine felt as if the entire room were watching them now. She felt her nerves jump beneath her skin and wondered how she was going to bear it if no other man asked her to dance.

She ate some cake and found that it was not as bad as she had heard it was. She had been on her best behavior before Mr. Waters had drawn her into a waltz, and no other man had approached. Maybe now that she had waltzed and had been presented to Lady Jersey, she might have a bit of success in catching her prey.

Namely, a gentle, titled husband who would take care of her madcap family for the rest of their lives. Her papa had left enough money for her to have one Season, but with her mother's spendthrift ways, that money was drying up already. Catherine needed to be engaged, as quickly as possible, to as gentle and decent a man as she could find.

She met Alexander Waters's warm gaze over her now-empty lemonade glass. The heat in his eyes was neither gentle nor decent.

She set her empty glass down and turned away from him just in time to see Lord Farleigh, a blond gentleman with well-shined shoes, bow low before her.

"Miss Middlebrook, your mother introduced us earlier, if you recall."

Her mother had all but throttled the gentleman in an effort to get him to dance with her daughter—an effort that had come to nothing.

Until now.

Catherine put Mr. Waters out of her mind and smiled at the man in front of her. "Of course I remember you, Lord Farleigh. Will you take a cup of lemonade with us? May I present my companions, Miss Mary Elizabeth Waters and her brother, Mr. Alexander Waters."

"Waters of Glenderrin fame? I understand your brother brought in quite a load of timber the last time he came into port."

Mr. Waters bowed as if the young lord had just offered him a compliment and not cast aspersions on his family's ties to trade. "Nova Scotia has been good to us, and to the whole clan. The lumber is just the beginning. It is the fur trade that really keeps us in gold and land." The Highlander spoke all of this as if he were proud of it, and accompanied his words with a bland smile. But Catherine saw that his eyes were gleaming.

"You still consider yourselves members of a clan?" Lord Farleigh asked. "How quaint."

"But true, my lord. No matter how many times the English come to burn the barley, the clans are in the Highlands forever."

Catherine felt her dread and horror rise up from the ground at her feet. She prayed that Mary Elizabeth would begin her usual talk about highwaymen or fishing—anything to break the silence that seemed to linger in her ears like a curse.

No one mentioned trade in polite society, and no one mentioned the old wars of the last century that had devastated Scotland and left the clans broken, the men who were not dead imprisoned or transported for life. How the Waters family had escaped such a fate, Catherine could not guess. She told herself that she did not want to know, but she felt the keen edge of curiosity slide into her thoughts like a blade. Once the opening was made, she found she could not turn away from her questions about Alexander Waters, his family, and his pride.

But in the next breath, the moment was over, and Lord Farleigh was bowing once more over her hand. "Miss Middlebrook, may I have the honor of this dance?"

A simple quadrille was forming in the center of the floor. Catherine took his hand as if it were a lifeline. She nodded to Mary Elizabeth, ignoring her friend's brother as she turned away. She smiled on the bland, quiet Lord Farleigh as he led her into the dance. Though she wished herself as far from Alexander Waters as she could get, she felt his eyes linger on her long after she had walked away.

❧

On the carriage ride home, Alex found himself brooding about the angel who had turned her back on him.

Though they had lingered another two hours, Alexander had not asked her to dance again. Instead, he had watched as all the fops and dandies who had been too cowardly or too blind to approach her before now came to her side, offering punch, cake, even to meet their mothers as if she had just appeared among them from her home among the clouds.

The rutting bastards had clearly only stepped up when they'd seen that a real man valued her.

Alex was not sure why, but he was bothered by that girl. She was lovely, but he had seen lovely women before. Her soft, blonde hair had been piled on her head in an unfashionable style, covered with pink rosebuds, a pink ribbon woven through the curls. He did not care for the new fashion of ladies shearing their heads as if they were sheep. When he was in bed with a woman, he wanted her hair covering them both like a curtain of silk, or laid out across his pillow like a spill of sunlight.

Alex caught himself, and realized where his thoughts were tending. He could not bed that girl. Angel or no, she was a virgin meant for marriage, and he was a rutting bastard himself to think of her in any other light but an honorable one. Now that Catherine Middlebrook was well launched among her own kind, his time would be better spent focusing on the task at hand, so that he might return to the sea. Once his sister was happily married to the best Englishman he could find, he would set sail for Antigua and forget for six months together that England even existed.

If he could only keep Mary Elizabeth from speaking too freely of her love of fishing, hunting, shooting, riding, swordplay, and archery, giving the game away before it had even begun.

Mary Elizabeth was a delightful sister, but she would make some poor bastard one hell of a wife.

"Did you see how many times I danced after we took lemonade? It was delightful! Say what you will of Englishmen, but they certainly know how to waltz." Mary Elizabeth sat smiling on her side of the duchess's coach.

"They had enough sense to value you once they decided your friend was of worth. The English are a peculiar people, but I am glad to see that the gentlemen you danced with made you happy. I don't suppose you want to marry one of them?" Alex asked hopefully, waiting for the usual gleam of irritation to come into his sister's eyes.

For once, she did not bristle at the subject, but sighed contentedly as she leaned back against the velvet squabs of their borrowed coach. "Oh, I won't marry any of them. That is why they are so pleasant. I don't want a thing from them. I'll enjoy myself here for a bit, and then go home."

Alex did not open his mouth to argue with her. She was in a sunny mood and he was not going to break it by telling her hard truths she already knew.

"Catherine Middlebrook is coming to tea tomorrow," Mary Elizabeth said.

Alex felt a strange sense of elation at the thought of seeing Catherine Middlebrook again. A simple family tea with a lovely debutante should not matter to him, but the idea of that serene angel in his home brought him simple pleasure, as if tomorrow had become suddenly brighter.

"Who?" he asked, feigning ignorance.

"The only girl you danced with tonight—the sweet blonde from Devon. She hardly has a thing to say, but

I think that's because she's been taught to mind her tongue in company."

"What an idea."

"Indeed." Mary Elizabeth nodded as if he had agreed with her on the foolishness of that. "I will have to train that out of her."

"Is she your new hound dog, then?"

Mary Elizabeth smiled at her brother fondly. "Alex, you know I don't hunt with dogs."

He was feeling oddly lighthearted now that her friend's name had been mentioned, and he did not like to think of why. His eyes were full of the sight of her back turning on him, just as his nose was still full of the scent of warm roses and sunlight. He tried to force himself to think of the cold running waters near Glenderrin, of the icy North Sea his brother often sailed—anything but that honeyed angel and her warm green eyes.

"I tell you that she is coming to tea tomorrow with her mother and her sister so that you and Robert know to be on your best behavior. She is my first friend in London, and I want to make a good impression."

"Will you serve her barley cakes and honey?"

"No, you rascal. The duchess's French pastry chef will come up with some comfit or other. Maybe a cake stuffed with cream. I'll bet Catherine would like that."

"Catherine, is it? You know her so well then."

Mary Elizabeth leveled a sharp look at her brother. "She is lonely and has no one. I am taking her in. I am going to help her find a husband who will love her all her life."

Something about his sister's simple, heartfelt words

made him catch his breath. He swallowed hard, a lump coming into his throat from he knew not where.

"And where will you find this paragon?" he asked.

"Among the English, of course. Catherine's from Devon, but she is willing to make do with what we have."

"Thank God somebody is," Alex groused.

Mary Elizabeth ignored him, happily humming to herself, no doubt thinking already of pastries and cream.

Alex raised his hand to push his hair back into its queue and saw that it was shaking. Too much talk of marriage, no doubt. It always made him nervous. Of course, spending any time at all among the English put him on his guard. He'd known the assignment of getting Mary Elizabeth married off would be a difficult one when his mother had given it to him. He just hadn't realized how difficult.

Nor had he thought to find any of the girls he met in London even remotely entertaining, much less entrancing. If he wanted to get back on the sea, he would have to keep his eye firmly on the prize, and he would have to stay as far away from Miss Catherine Middlebrook as possible. He could not be in the house when Angel Catherine and her mother came to call.

He also knew that he would be nowhere else on earth.

God help him.

Three

In spite of staying up late at the assembly, Catherine rose while the dew was still on the grass to cut lilac and thyme in her garden. They had been forced to let their Town gardener go after her father died, and did not have the funds to replace him. While Charlie, their boy of all work, did his best in the small, enclosed yard, Catherine enjoyed keeping up with the garden herself.

She loved their London town house, though it always made her think of her father and miss him. He had been dead over five years, but she could still remember the sound of his laughter and the scent of his pipe tobacco. She had an old handkerchief with his pipe wrapped in it that she kept buried under a pile of shawls. She rarely looked at it, but she knew it was there.

When she came back, the house was in an uproar, as usual. Instead of sleeping late as Catherine had thought she might, her mother, Olivia, was up with the dawn, shrieking in the breakfast room for hot water. Little Margaret, twelve years old now, was trying to quiet her mother down in a futile effort to spare the servants. Their butler, Giles, had broken his leg the month before, falling down the wine cellar stairs, and now reclined in annoyed splendor in his room at the top of the house. Catherine brought him fresh flowers every day and apprised him of the day's crises before teatime. In the Middlebrook household, there was always a crisis.

Catherine sighed at the thought of how quiet her own household would one day be. She would marry a sweet, genteel man who kept to himself in the library, save for dinnertime, when he would escort her downstairs to their own dining room with a little flourish of his arm. Over dinner, he would regale her with tales of the City and perhaps his favorite hunting sport while she listened in silence, nodding her approval, grateful to be happy and well cared for.

Of course, where her mother was in these scenarios, she was not sure. For Catherine would only marry a man who would take in her mother and her sister too, no questions asked. A kind man who would welcome them into his home, allowing it to be theirs as well. Catherine sighed as she laid her flower basket down on the hallway table and took off her gardening gloves and bonnet. No household would be quiet as long as her mother was present.

Still, a girl could dream.

Catherine had tried to be very strict with herself, fighting valiantly to keep her mind on Lord Farleigh and the dozen or so other polite gentlemen she'd had the pleasure of dancing with the night before. They had all been agreeable, very quiet, almost bland, like weak tea that was a bit too tepid. She did her level best not to think of Alexander Waters—a deep mug of the finest chocolate cut with heated cream. There was nothing tepid about Alexander Waters. Not in the least.

Catherine was about to step into the breakfast room to save the footman, William, from having to answer her mother when the door knocker sounded. She almost knocked her flower basket onto the marble tiles. She blinked, catching the wicker before the lilac and thyme could fall across her slippers. The door never sounded this early. She wondered for one horrible instant if someone was dead and a constable was bringing the bad news.

Jim, the tallest footman, had been promoted to under butler in Giles's absence. He stepped into the hall from parts unknown, his wig askew, his dark clothes coated with a thin layer of toast crumbs. He bowed to her in a stately manner before opening the great mahogany door.

A boy from the florist stepped in with three great bouquets that hid him almost completely from view. She should have sent him back downstairs to come through the servants' hall below, but she had never seen so many beautiful store-bought flowers in her life. Her garden was lovely but yielded nothing that could rival these.

Her mother flew in from the breakfast room, diving on one of the bouquets like a bird of prey. She slipped it out of the delivery boy's hands, carrying it to the center table in the hallway and giving it pride of place.

"Margaret! Come and look! Catherine has received her first bouquets of the Season! How lovely!"

Margaret ran pell-mell into the room then, her slippers sliding along the polished floor. "Mama, how beautiful. You say they are all for Catherine?"

"Surely not," Catherine replied. "There is no doubt some mistake."

"No mistake, miss," the delivery boy said. "They are for this household, and welcome."

Jim stood by in silent, crumb-laden glory, not moving to tip the errand boy. Catherine drew a six-pence from the lacquered box on their front table and slipped it into the boy's palm as she saw him out. "We thank you. Good day."

She closed the heavy door behind him with only a little difficulty. "You should let me tend to the door, miss," Jim said, his accent heavy with the sound of home.

Catherine sighed, and smiled. She would have to ask Giles to give Jim another lecture about the duties of an under butler. As it was, she did not have the time, nor could she hear herself think over her mother's latest shriek.

"Catherine, these lilies of the valley are from Lord Farleigh! My word, girl, you have made a conquest there."

Catherine felt a warm light come into her chest, and she smiled. But there was no exultation, no exuberance. She realized two things then: that she could one day marry Lord Farleigh, or a man very much like him…and that she would be disappointed to do so.

She pushed those nonsensical thoughts out of her head to better hear her mother read the card from the second bouquet. "These forget-me-nots and primroses

are from *A. Waters*. My word, the Highland gentleman who waltzed with you last night!"

Catherine felt her skin heat. The warm light in
her chest turned into a conflagration, and spread in
a blush up her chest and neck and into her cheeks.
She suddenly felt light-headed, though she had never
fainted in her life. Mr. Waters had not spoken to her
again after their dance and her presentation to Lady
Jersey. Surely, out of all the men she had met the night
before, those flowers could not possibly be from him.

She stepped forward and took the note in her hand.
The slanted *A* made her think of an eagle in flight, and
the terse *Waters* made her think of the burn behind
their castle in Scotland. Catherine wondered what a
burn was. Mary Elizabeth had mentioned fishing in it,
so perhaps it was some sort prehistoric stream that led
to wild delights, like the Loch Ness Monster or some
such fanciful creature. Mr. Waters had written nothing
but his name, but Catherine was certain that he had
written the note himself.

Before Catherine could completely lose herself to
giddy fancy, her mother cawed anew. Catherine saw
her brandishing the note from a third bouquet of deep
red roses.

"These flowers are for me!"

Catherine felt her color rise even as her stomach
sank. What gentleman would send vulgar red roses
to a respectable widow? She swallowed hard, trying
to hide her sudden nerves. Surely they had not run
across some unsavory cad in the middle of Almack's
who might prey on her mother's sensibilities? As her
mother was in raptures over the inappropriate flowers

before her, she did not notice Catharine's concern, but Margaret did. She sidled up silently to Catherine and took her hand.

Mrs. Middlebrook was still speaking, beginning to preen. "I am still an attractive woman, girls. I am not completely off the market yet." She tittered. "Perhaps they are from the Duke of Wellington. How romantic!"

"God forbid," Catherine murmured under her breath while Margaret laughed.

"The duke is married, Mama," Margaret said. Catherine herded both her mother and her sister back into the breakfast room, determined to get some food into them. Mrs. Middlebrook refused to relinquish her flowers, and brought the vulgar bouquet with her. Catherine wanted to bring Mr. Waters's flowers too, but that would have been foolish. She shut the breakfast door on the bouquets with a decided click.

"Of course the duke is married," Mrs. Middlebrook said. She took a large bite of buttered toast while Catherine poured her a fresh cup of tea, adding a liberal number of sugar cubes and cream, just as her mother liked it. "He took a wife for purely dynastic reasons, as all great men do. Our liaison would be pure romance, a love for the ages, like Tristan and Isolde."

"Or Romeo and Juliet," Margaret added, taking another dollop of blackberry jam.

Catherine shot her sister a quelling look, which Margaret blithely ignored.

"Those characters all ended up dead," Catherine pointed out.

"Your soul has no romance." Her mother sniffed, taking a sip of her fresh tea.

"I'm sorry, Mama. No doubt you are right." Catherine drank her own tea and watched as her mother dimpled, ire forgotten just as suddenly as it appeared. In spite of her advancing years of eight and thirty, her mother was still a lovely woman. Catherine said a small prayer to the Holy Mother to keep scoundrels and their ilk far away.

"I am pleased that handsome Scotsman sent those primroses for you, little miss."

"Yes, Mama."

For some reason, Catherine did not want to talk about Mr. Waters. She felt herself blush again and sipped her tea, trying to force her mind into the calm, bland waters of Lord Farleigh—and failing.

"He's a fine-looking man, but foreigners are never ideal. Still, he may be rich. I'll make inquiries among my acquaintances. Perhaps he is worth looking at."

Catherine choked on a bite of scone. Margaret hit her forcefully between the shoulder blades.

"I don't think Mr. Waters is appropriate, Mama," she managed.

Mrs. Middlebrook smiled, licking the butter off her lips like a cat just out of the dairy. "Indeed, my dear, I agree with you. There is little about Mr. Waters that is appropriate. Men like him, once tamed, make the best husbands."

"He is not a hound dog, Mama, or a spaniel."

"Heavens no, dear. But all men must be tamed before you let them in the house, or you'll have nothing but mayhem and trouble all your life. No woman of sense wants that."

"No indeed," Catherine agreed, trying desperately

to make her blushing stop. She had never learned to control her coloring, and she supposed she never would. She had better get all her blushing done and out of her system, for they were due to take tea with the Waterses at five o'clock.

She swallowed a sip of tea and this time did not choke. "Margaret will have a fine time meeting your new friend, Miss Waters, this afternoon," Mrs. Middlebrook said. "What a merry party we shall make!"

"Maybe they have a puppy," Margaret said.

"Scotsmen always keep dogs. No doubt they have a dozen." Her mother offered this sage bit of wisdom while adding clotted cream to another scone.

"I am sure only Miss Waters will be there," Catherine said.

Mrs. Middlebrook cut her eyes at her eldest daughter. "Are you indeed? We will see, little missy. We will see."

Four

CATHERINE SAT DRINKING TEA IN THE DUCHESS OF Northumberland's drawing room, listening to Margaret play Beethoven's *Appassionata* on a nicely tuned pianoforte. The duchess herself was not in residence, but Catherine's mother sat with Robert Waters, Mary Elizabeth's older brother, regaling him of tales of Devon and the growing of roses there—as if a Scotsman, or any man for that matter, might care about such things. It seemed Robert Waters was a gentleman, for he feigned interest so well that Catherine could not quite tell if he was really a secret gardener or not.

She listened with half an ear as Mary Elizabeth spoke beside her of the coming Season and all the dancing to be had among the *ton*. The other half of her attention was taken up with wondering at the most beautiful room she had ever entered in her life, much less taken tea in. The house was swathed in velvets at the windows, with no thought whatsoever to the fact that such expensive cloth would soon be ruined by the sun. The settee she perched on was covered in watered silk of a deep burgundy hue, a color a man might choose if he were left to his own devices and allowed to decorate a parlor.

Catherine found her mind wandering to the question of whether or not Alexander Waters might like it and where he might be at that moment. She tried to focus on what her friend was saying, but as she took a sip of the fine Darjeeling, she could not think of anything else but Alexander and the heat of his dark eyes.

She was brought abruptly back to the here and now when Mary Elizabeth spoke without preamble, changing the subject from the next dance they would both attend. "We must find you a good husband."

Catherine blinked. "I beg your pardon?"

"We are going to find a man to love you. He will have to love you all his life, and beyond. That's certain." Mary Elizabeth frowned, looking off into the middle distance as Margaret clanged on the piano, missing more than one note.

Catherine felt her blood rising into her cheeks, and she cursed herself silently. If she had a fairy godmother, she would not ask for gowns or princes, but for her foolish blush to be gone for life.

"Do you not seek a husband for yourself, Miss Waters?" she asked, trying to be polite while deflecting her friend's focused regard.

Mary Elizabeth's hazel eyes seemed to pierce her where she sat, like a butterfly on a pin. She felt exposed as she never was when her mother or her sister looked at her. Her father had seen through her, past her soft smiles, to the girl within. He had fed her hunger for botany and growing things, and had even paid for a Latin tutor to teach her the proper terms for the foliage on their estate. Her father had been the last person to truly know her.

As she sat, caught in her new friend's gaze, she wondered if Mary Elizabeth might also see behind her polite smiles to the self she tried to keep hidden. No man cared for her true self, nor would. Marriage was not an accommodation of souls but a meeting of two people who needed each other—for companionship, for children, so that they might not grow old alone. To wish for someone to see past her smile into her soul was to wish to hold the light of the moon in her hand.

"I need no husband," Mary Elizabeth said. "In spite of my brothers' scheming and my mother's insistence, Papa will allow me to hunt and fish on our glen for the rest of my life. There is no need to marry to do that. But you"—Mary Elizabeth's gaze did not waver, even as she blinked as if to clear her vision—"you shall marry for love."

Catherine found herself smiling then, and the smile was a true one. "There is no such thing as a love match that lasts."

"Of course there is. My parents have it. I think your parents had it, before your father died."

Catherine looked across the parlor to her strident mother, who had only become so after she had managed to crawl out of the chasm of her grief. It was almost as if, without her father present in the world, her mother was afraid of not ever being heard again.

"They did," was all Catherine said.

"And we will find it for you." Mary Elizabeth

squeezed her hand, and Catherine felt for one hideous moment as if she might weep.

She had not cried in years, not since the summer her father died. Tears were wasted salt. Her grandmother had taught her that a woman had better use salt at table and leave weeping to children, who could not help themselves.

"I have made you sad, and I am sorry. Come to the ballroom with me." When Catherine hesitated, Mary Elizabeth smiled and tugged her to her feet. "Your sister is happy and well banging that pianoforte until it's out of tune. Your mother is safe in Robert's care. He's not good for much, but he can chat with a woman until the sun sets and rises again in the east."

Catherine laughed a watery laugh, and blinked her unwelcome tears away. "All right."

Mary Elizabeth announced to the room at large, "We are going up to the third floor. Offer our guests another cup of tea, Robert."

Robert Waters glowered at his sister over Catherine's mother's head, but Mary Elizabeth only smiled at him sweetly. Catherine looked at Robert, trying to find in his blue eyes some of the warmth she had felt his brother direct at her. He was an attractive man, with curling auburn hair and shoulders as broad as his brother's. But there was nothing else between them. Only a kind regard on his part, coupled with his polite and distant smile.

Perhaps she had imagined the heat she had seen in Alexander's eyes. Perhaps he had simply been polite, as his brother was, and she had been overwhelmed by the excitement of Almack's, by the dancing and the company. It was her only Season, after all, a time for a girl to lose her head, if only for one night.

"What will we do in the ballroom?" Catherine asked as her friend drew her into the hallway beyond, closing the parlor door behind her. "Practice our dance steps?" Catherine could use a bit of practice on the quadrille. She had danced but rarely before coming to Town.

Mary Elizabeth's eyes gleamed with ill-concealed joy. "No indeed. I'm going to teach you how to throw a knife."

Catherine was so shocked that she did not even laugh. "I beg your pardon?"

"Don't be missish, Catherine. Every woman needs to know how to throw a knife in her own defense. Come with me."

෴

Alex was careful to spend the afternoon out of the house. He was acting like a fool, but better to play the fool in private than display his foolishness in front of his family. Mary Elizabeth might notice nothing, but Robert knew him better, and was a good deal sharper when it came to relations between the sexes. Robert would know as soon as he saw them in the same room that his sister's new friend had taken over too many of Alex's waking thoughts. Robert might have even been able to discern that Alex had dreamed of nothing but her the night before, just by looking into his brother's face.

So Alex spent the afternoon at his tailor. When he grew bored of fittings, he thought of getting a drink, but had no interest in drinking alone. Nor did he have any interest in sitting among the English at his father's club, swilling watered-down Scotch and missing home. So he walked the streets of London, almost hoping that some pickpocket might attack. Or that some ruffian might take him for a fop and bring out a knife, so that he might get some of his frustration out with a good old-fashioned rough-and-tumble.

Though, if he were honest, fisticuffs were not the kind of rough-and-tumble he was looking for.

He could go to Madame Claremont's. She ran a clean house, and her girls would be willing and able to take him into their beds for the turn of a coin. They would even pretend to care what he thought about the latest happenings in the world, as all good courtesans did. In his place, Robert would have bought himself a woman and not thought twice about it. But when Alex tried to walk to Madame's establishment, he found that his boots simply would not take him there. He found himself among the menagerie at the Tower of London instead, watching the squealing girls as they pretended fear at the old lion in his cage, their beaus manfully standing by before ushering them protectively away for ices at Gunter's.

Alex did not even feel amusement at watching the shenanigans of English courting. Instead, all he could think of was how much Catherine would like the Tower, as all the other young ladies seemed to, and how he should escort her there before the week was through.

When he caught himself in that thought, he cursed and headed home.

Of course, he had no home in London. His home was by the burn at Glenderrin, or on the open sea with his brother Ian. But knowing that even now Catherine Middlebrook sat taking tea with his sister, Alex turned like a homing pigeon toward the Duchess of Northumberland's town home. The Duchess of Northumberland's house, while grand, was far too fussy for his taste. If he took a house in London, he would not ruin its clean Georgian lines with velvets and tassels.

He caught himself thinking that and cursed again in silence. It would be a cold day in hell before he took a house in London Town.

Alex came into the front hall of Northumberland House, handing the butler his coat and hat. He carried no walking stick, though Robert thought he should obtain one. "What better way to conceal a weapon," his brother often said. Alex preferred to wear his weapons openly, just as he liked his whisky neat. Let a thing be what it was, just as he was always himself, with no pretense otherwise.

He stood like a green boy in the entrance hall, listening outside the parlor door while some benighted soul pounded out Beethoven very badly on the duchess's pianoforte. He waited until the noise had stopped before he stepped inside and found Robert trapped against the arm of one settee by Mrs. Angel herself. Robert shot him a harried look, and Alex smiled. Catherine's mother had clearly run the boy to ground.

"Good day," Alex said, bowing to the lady. Robert stood as if to be polite, barely masking his intent to escape the clutches of Mrs. Angel. A little girl waved to him from behind the pianoforte, before barreling into the same song all over again. Perhaps it was the only one she knew.

He scanned the room: the angel and his sister were not there.

"If you're looking for Mary Elizabeth, she's taken her quarry to play among the rafters on the third floor." Robert's brogue was thick, for he could not care less about the fashionable necessity to leave one's Scottish roots at home.

"Are the knives locked up?" Alex asked.

Robert frowned. "Aren't they always?" Before Alex could relax, Robert added, "Of course, Mary Elizabeth has the key."

Alex caught himself before he swore in front of Mrs. Angel. The lady stared at him, her blue eyes taking in every aspect of his person, as if he were a stoat on sale at market.

"Catherine went to the ballroom with her friend, Mr. Waters. Perhaps you may go and seek her there."

"I had better do so, madam. I do not trust what my sister may have gotten up to."

Mrs. Angel smiled blithely, as if she could see not only beneath his words, but beneath his very skin. "Indeed, you must. Catherine needs protecting, you know. And in case she forgets to say so, thank you for the beautiful flowers."

Robert's eyes were as sharp as a dagger on him, no doubt seeing everything his brother wanted to hide. Alex ignored him valiantly, though there would be hell to pay later.

The child at the pianoforte piped up then. "Catherine liked your flowers best."

"There were others?" Alex asked before he could stop himself.

The girl did not answer, but her mother did, her smile shifting to feigned innocence. "Indeed, our household received a great many bouquets this morning. Such a warm welcome for a young lady just up from the country. London gentlemen are ever so kind."

Alex could not trust himself to speak without cursing, so he did not. He bowed once, turned, and left the room. He thought he heard laughter in his brother's voice, as Robert said, "Shall we have another tune, then, Miss Margaret? Alexander may be a while hunting your sister and mine."

Alex closed the door on Mrs. Angel's pointed gaze and his brother's amused voice, and climbed the stairs to the third floor two at a time. There was only one room free of furniture where Mary Elizabeth indulged herself in knife play.

Pray God she had not stabbed their guest by accident already.

Five

CATHERINE HELD THE THROWING KNIFE IN HER HAND. It wasn't a long steel blade, as she had heard was used in the former colonies of America. It was nothing like a machete that she had read had been used to cut through the jungles of Africa. It was a deadly sharp blade, rounded along its edges, except for the tip, which was quick to draw blood. As she had discovered to her chagrin as soon as she handled it carelessly.

Mary Elizabeth had showed her how to dress her wound quickly with her own handkerchief, ripping it neatly into thirds and tying a makeshift bandage into place over her wrist where the shallow cut lay. She had never experienced a small wound with so little fuss made in her life. She savored her new friend's casual attitude both toward knives and the blood they drew. Catherine did not live in a world where such things as bloody knives existed, especially for a lady. To enter a world in which they did, even for the space of an hour, was the most exciting thing she had ever done.

Spending time with Mary Elizabeth would never be dull, it seemed.

The small blade in her hand was perfectly balanced for a woman's strength. It seemed that Mary Elizabeth's father had had them made for her, and her brother Robert had taught her how to use them. Catherine could barely imagine what it might be like to have an older brother, much less one who offered to tutor a young lady in the use of knives, but it seemed the Waters clan took self-defense very seriously indeed.

Catherine had been throwing knives at the wooden board set up for that purpose in the Duchess of Northumberland's ballroom for almost an hour. She had lost all track of time as she looked from the blade in her hand to the target before her and let her knife fly. Amazingly enough, she had discovered, much to her pleasure, that she was very good at it.

"Well done, Catherine. One more and then I will feed you more tea sandwiches. Or perhaps you and your family might stay to dinner. God knows the duchess keeps enough food on her table to feed an army."

Catherine smiled and did not reply. She cast her last knife at the wooden board, hitting the center of the bull's-eye, which in this case was the outline of a somewhat menacing ruffian. Someone, Catherine suspected Mary Elizabeth, had drawn a jaunty top hat on him to indicate his Englishness.

"I must applaud your efforts, Miss Middlebrook. It seems you have killed our pirate outright with a clean blow to the heart."

The hot, honeyed tones of Alexander Waters's voice seemed to caress her, and she felt her cursed blush rise into her cheeks unbidden. Her stays were too tight suddenly, as if she had run a mile, though she rarely walked anywhere in her life save to church when they were home in Devon.

"Don't devil her, Alex. She's a prodigy. It seems our girl here has a bloodthirsty streak."

Catherine swallowed hard in an effort to find her voice. "I am sure I would never be able to throw a blade at an actual person. I would be horrified to draw blood."

Mary Elizabeth dismissed those words with one wave of her hand, and went to collect the knives sticking out of the board. "Nonsense. You would kill a man to keep him from killing you."

"I am not certain I would," Catherine said. She felt Mr. Waters's eyes still heavy on her, like a warm blanket before a roaring fire. She was sure that in a moment she would begin to perspire from the heat of his gaze alone, and humiliate herself completely.

"I have seen you with your mother and your sister. If you'll marry to protect them, you'd kill a man to do so. Taking one more evildoer out of the world would be no great loss. Not compared to giving up the rest of your life to a husband," Mary Elizabeth said.

Catherine choked on nothing, unable to reply. She wished herself dead in that moment, or perhaps shrunk to the size of a mouse, that she might scurry into the wainscoting and disappear completely.

"Now you stop deviling our guest, Mary. You've made her blush and swallow her tongue both within the space of three minutes. You had best take yourself downstairs and leave the putting away of these knives to me."

Mary Elizabeth stared at her brother as if trying to discern something in his face. "You may lock them up again, but I have the key, you know."

"And I know a good locksmith. Downstairs you go."

Mary Elizabeth flounced to the doorway, and Catherine, still silent, moved to follow her. She stopped when she felt the heat of Alexander's leather-gloved hand on her arm.

"Catherine, you are wounded."

"I did not give you leave to use my given name." She heard the priggishness of her own voice, but she could not help herself. He was standing so close, she had almost lost all breath she needed to speak. "It is not proper."

"Says the girl fresh from throwing knives." She heard the laughter in his voice, doubtless at her expense. She kept her eyes down, but could not seem to move. The hand on her arm did not restrain her, but simply rested there, tempting her. She felt sorely tempted. If only she knew to what.

"Mary Elizabeth, see to your guests. Miss Middlebrook and I will be down directly."

Catherine knew that she ought to protest, but the thought of being alone with Alexander Waters for the space of only a few minutes thrilled her, just as throwing knives had. She had so little excitement in her life. It was delicious.

Before she could open her mouth to protest out of a beleaguered sense of propriety, Mary Elizabeth spoke for her. "I already bound her wrist, Alex. There's nothing in the world wrong with that dressing."

"Did you wash it with soap?"

Catherine listened as a new, uncomfortable silence spiraled around them. She heard in her friend's tone the first hint of chastisement. "No, Alex. You know that's just an old superstition Mama repeats ad nauseam. No doctor agrees with her."

"How many people do you know who visited a sawbones and lived to tell of it?" Alexander asked.

Mary Elizabeth grumbled but did not answer. Catherine assumed that meant not very many. How terrible were the doctors in the wilds of the north, that they killed their patients?

"Don't take too long, Alex. I want my dinner soon."

"You heathen, eating without changing your gown."

Catherine heard the teasing note in his voice and she looked up, expecting him to be looking at his sister with affection. Instead, she found him staring down at her, almost as if he were trying to memorize her face. This time, she did not blush, but stared back.

Mary Elizabeth did not seem to notice anything amiss, for she strode out of the room without a backward glance. "Come downstairs as soon as you can get away from this beast, Catherine. We've got fine beef pasties to eat this night, along with some roasted carrots and onions."

"Thank you," Catherine said. She was going to decline her friend's generous offer to dine with them in a duchess's house. They had certainly overstayed their welcome. At least, her mother and her sister surely had, even if she had not. But Mary Elizabeth was gone before she could finish her thought, and she was left alone with the hulking Scot beside her.

"So, Miss Middlebrook. Let's have a look at the wound you got from indulging in my sister's shenanigans."

"We are alone, sir. It is highly improper. I must go to

my mother." She forced the words from her lips, though for some reason it was Mr. Waters's mouth that fascinated her. There was a sensuous quirk to his lips that she had not noticed before—as if he were a man who savored his life, his whisky, his food, and, no doubt, his women.

She blushed hard at the thought and tried to pull away from him, hoping to put a distance between herself and her own wild imaginings. She had no idea what a man might do with a woman alone. She had only been told time and time again by her grandmother that she bloody well did not want to find out until a priest had blessed her union with her husband and there was a ring on her finger.

Still, as she looked into the heat of Alexander Waters's fine, dark eyes, she wondered.

He looked down at her, and this time, the heat in his eyes faded as if it had never been. "Miss Middlebrook, I give you my word of honor as a gentleman, you have nothing to fear from me, now or ever. I would defend you with my life. As long as you are in my presence, you need fear no man or beast."

She listened breathlessly to the most poetic oath she had ever heard a man take. He was very solemn, and for a long moment, she felt as if a spell had fallen over them, as if he had sworn more to her than just his respect. The silence spun out, until it seemed to hold a wealth of feeling that made no sense, a layered tapestry of emotion that it would take her a lifetime to understand. She had known this man less than one day. And yet she felt as safe with him as she once had with her own father.

His lips quirked, and the moment and all its import slipped away. "I will defend you, even if the beast in question is myself." He smiled, and she found herself laughing out loud.

"That is reassurance indeed, Mr. Waters. Still, I must go downstairs before your brother takes an ax to the duchess's beautiful pianoforte to save himself from further pain."

It was Mr. Waters's turn to laugh then, and as she listened to the deep warmth of it, she wished for an odd, wild moment that she might never go anywhere else. His laughter was food enough, bread and meat together.

She shook her head at her own strange turn of thought. His Scottish poetry must be rubbing off on her.

"Robert has heard far worse than your sister's playing, I assure you. When Mary Elizabeth was learning, we all thought we might go mad. My brother Ian fled to the sea to escape it."

Catherine drew away from him, and this time she forced herself to walk toward the door. "I had better get downstairs, so Mr. Robert Waters does not join him."

She had almost made it to the hallway when Alexander caught up with her and took her hand in his.

"You won't slip away that easily, my girl. Come with me. A decent cleaning and a decent dressing will take less than five minutes, and will save this from becoming infected. If you were to fall ill from a visit to my house, I would not forgive myself."

Catherine had never heard of the odd practice of washing a wound, but she did not want to give up his company just yet. She knew she was wicked and improper, and no doubt her mother would scold her roundly, as she deserved.

She knew all this, but she went with him anyway.

Six

THE SIGHT OF THAT ONE, SINGULAR WOMAN THROWING A knife had been the most erotic thing Alex had ever seen.

He almost could not speak a word of sense for five minutes after. He'd let his sister prattle on about preparing dinner and killing a man, neither of which she had any experience with, until he had regained his breath and some modicum of self-control.

The girl had been like a doe in flight as soon as she'd laid eyes on him—frozen before she ran from the hunter. He had been careful to modify his tone, to treat her as he might his sister, but still she would not look at him. He could not help but touch her.

Now, alone in his room, the most improper place to care for her—wounded slightly or not—he stripped off his black leather gloves. He spoke of the weather, of the ices at Gunter's, of the ball at Almack's the night before, all banal, urbane, pointless conversation. Which wasn't actually a conversation but a mono-logue, since Miss Middlebrook did not speak a word.

He knew better than to take her into his bedroom proper, for then his angel would no doubt fly back to heaven at once, never to be seen again. He brought her to his sitting room and fetched wash water for her wound himself.

She was still waiting for him when he came back. He had not been gone long, but part of him had been certain that she would disappear as soon as he was out of sight. Part of him almost hoped she would, because the tightness in his trousers was becoming uncomfortable from being near her for too long. Of course, it was a sweet discomfort, one he savored as he looked at her.

The slanting rays of the afternoon sun warmed her yellow hair. It was piled on top of her head as it had been the night before, only now she wore no flowers in it. Her girlish, light blue walking gown did nothing to camouflage the glinting intelligence in her green eyes. He wondered why she had bought such a simple dress, or if perhaps she had made it herself.

The thought of her tiny hands manipulating a needle and thread was almost his undoing. He had to breathe deep before he stepped into the room and let his presence be known. His angel sat and waited for him, as calm as a bishop.

"Thank you for indulging me, Miss Middlebrook. I would be deeply horrified if you left my house wounded, with no one to care for you."

"This is the duchess's house," his angel said. She smiled as she looked up at him with a sideways glance that on any other woman would have seemed coy. On her pure face, it only looked like harmless teasing. Still, that look made him want to touch her lips with his. "And my mother might look after me," she said.

"She might," Alex conceded, keeping his tone light. "Still, I would rather see you put to rights before you go."

"I will not keep my family here for dinner, in spite of your sister's generous offer. I think your brother has very likely had all of the Middlebrook family that he can stand."

Alex laughed. "My mother has forced him to sit with much tougher ladies than your mother and sweet sister. Put your mind at ease. I would be obliged if you would stay and eat with us. The duchess's cook keeps feeding us as if we are a standing army, and it would do us good if you took a bit of the pressure off Robert and me. We are always troubled to send so much food back to the kitchen untouched."

"Mary Elizabeth doesn't help with eating it?"

Alex laughed again, beginning slowly to unbind the makeshift bandage at her wrist. "She eats more than the two of us put together."

Miss Middlebrook did not laugh as he had intended, for though a small table stood between them where she sat in one armchair and he in another, his fingers were on her wrist as he opened the bandage for inspection. He was sorry that his touch left her silent, but he could not help her without touching her. He kept his focus on her arm, and did not look at her face, in case he embarrassed her further.

It was a shallow cut but long, reaching from the base of her wrist halfway up to her elbow. Even as he unbound the cloth, a bit of blood began to seep out again. He clucked his tongue as his old nurse had done every time he or Robbie came home with a scrape.

"That could turn nasty," he said. "I'm glad you're letting me have a look at it."

Miss Middlebrook spoke then, and her voice was soft. "Thank you for helping me. I did not think it would still be bleeding."

He cleared his throat. She suddenly seemed a good deal nearer than she had only a moment before. The skin of her arm was hot beneath his fingers—not feverish, but warm. He wanted to place his lips against the inside of her wrist. Instead, he washed away the blood with the soapy, clean rag he had brought from his dressing room.

"It is good that it bleeds a little," he heard himself say. He felt as light-headed as a green boy who had just kissed his first girl. He ordered himself to stay alert, and to hold to his word not to malign her, even with his thoughts. "A little blood keeps the wound clean." He opened the crock of honey at his elbow.

She jumped under his hands as he applied the first of it to her open wound.

"This will help the bleeding stop, and will help the cut heal."

"I've never heard that," she said, eyeing the crock suspiciously.

He almost laughed out loud at the wary look on her sweet face. He wanted to kiss it away.

He kept his voice light, though his tongue was growing thick with longing in his mouth. Her breasts rose and fell with her breath. He could see nothing else but the sweet mounds that called to him to cup them in his palms.

He should have gone to Madame Claremont's. No doubt of it.

"Well, now you've heard of it. You can spread the good word among the English that honey cures all ills. Well, most of them." He kept his movements brisk and his tone businesslike as he bound her wrist again and set his tools aside.

"You seem very prepared for mishaps in this household."

He smiled at the note of teasing in her voice, and looked into her eyes only to find her staring back at him, a little of his own hunger on her young face. She could not be a day older than eighteen, as innocent as a newborn lamb, and just as vulnerable. He remembered his oath to her, and his own honor. Still, he had never wanted to touch a woman so much in his life.

Her plump lips seemed to beckon him as she licked them once, though he knew it was his own lust that called to him and not the girl at all. She had no idea what she was feeling or why. She need not know until her wedding night.

Mary Elizabeth had told him of Catherine's plight. Miss Middlebrook had no father or brother left in the world to defend her. He was not a marrying man, and would not be for many years to come, but in that moment, he knew that he would look after her as if she were his own until she was safely wed.

He was happy to hear his own voice steady in his ears when he finally remembered to speak. His tone was light as he rose to his feet, offering her his arm.

"We must be prepared for anything. Mary Elizabeth has been known to cut herself simply slicing a loaf of bread at table."

Catherine Middlebrook laughed, and it was the

sweetest sound he had ever heard. He was growing fanciful in his infatuation with this girl, but there was something about her, something so unconscious and unspoiled, that made him want to wake her from her slumber of innocence. But he was no cad. When she laid her hand gently on his arm, feather light, he simply led her out of his sitting room and down the front staircase to meet her mother.

ভ্ৰত

"Your mother and sister just left."

Mary Elizabeth stood at the foot of the grand staircase, declaring to all and sundry who might be listening that Catherine had been effectively abandoned to her own devices among the Waterses, whom she had only known for one day. Had she not been a lady, Catherine might have cursed out loud. As it was, she pressed her lips together to suppress a sailor's oath, and tried valiantly to swallow her ire.

She could feel Mr. Waters's eyes on her, as she always could. It did not make her nervous now, only aware of a strange, new heat running beneath her skin. She could not blame it entirely on him. It was something odd, and it came from her.

Upstairs, alone with him as she should never be alone with any man save her husband one day, she had watched his lips as he talked. She had listened to the deep and even sound of his breathing when he was not talking. She had felt the steady heat of his hands on her wrist. And the strange heat had begun beneath her skin.

The same strange heat was with her still. It was not

a blush. She was used to those. It was something that seemed to walk with her like an old friend, though she had never experienced it before. It seemed to pool just beneath her stomach, making it uncomfortable to sit or to stand. There was a delicious heat that seemed to course through her blood, making her weak.

And now, as she was trying to keep breathing steadily and figure out what was wrong with her without making a cake of herself, her mother had abandoned her as if leaving her among family in Devon.

Catherine would not ever understand what that woman was thinking.

"If I may impose on your butler, might a hackney cab be called?" Catherine asked.

"As if we'd let you out loose among the English," Mary Elizabeth scoffed. "You'd get your throat cut."

"I'll see you home, Miss Middlebrook," Mr. Waters said before Mary Elizabeth could wax poetic on the perfidies of their neighbors.

"I could not trouble you." Catherine forced herself to meet his eyes. Their fathomless brown was calm, unreadable.

"No trouble at all. Mary Elizabeth, bring your best hooded cloak."

"Whatever for? It is balmy out there. It's spring, Alex."

"Bring your cloak so Miss Middlebrook can wear it. It would not do for us to be seen driving in company alone."

Catherine thought to suggest that they bring a maid along, as any decent English household would without question. She knew that she should correct them, and let them know that whatever a girl might do north of the border, in London, she must be chaperoned at all times. But as she stared up into the handsome face of Mr. Waters, she held her tongue. To take such a foolish risk with her reputation was madness, but as she stood close beside him in the Duchess of Northumberland's entrance hall, she found that she did not care.

The stately butler spoke then from his perch by the front door. "The duchess's carriage awaits you, sir."

They all waited a moment as a footman brought a deep woolen cloak from who knew where. Catherine stood still while Mr. Waters draped it over her shoulders. She caught her bottom lip between her teeth as he raised the hood to cover her hair and obscure her face.

He smiled down at her, and it seemed as if she caught a breath of heat on his gaze, as she had the night before. "Beautiful. We'll go then."

She did not notice if Robert Waters or his sister thought her odd, or a strumpet, to go off with their brother alone. She murmured her good-byes and let Alexander usher her out the door and down the duchess's town house stairs to the carriage waiting below.

Seven

CATHERINE COULD NOT FIND HER VOICE ON THE RIDE home. She lived close to the Duchess of Northumberland's beautiful town home, but the time seemed interminable as they rode to Regent's Square. She tried to focus her mind on the mischief her mother might have gotten up to in her absence, what delicacies she might have ordered that they could no longer afford. They had a little money kept for them by their solicitor in the City, but that money yielded fewer and fewer dividends each year.

In spite of her money troubles and her very real need to marry well within a month or two, she could not keep her mind on such grim realities. As she sat with Alexander Waters in the closed carriage, she could smell the scent of his skin on the air, a hint of cedar and bergamot that seemed to linger in her nostrils like a blessing. She wondered if she was going mad. Who would have bergamot in the Highlands, for heaven's sake?

She kept her hands folded demurely in her lap and tried to swallow the strange warmth that seemed to rise in her stomach at his nearness. He sat across from her, facing backward, as was proper, and she kept her eyes down in an effort to avoid his gaze, but that seemed to bring only more trouble. She could not help but look at his muscled thighs encased in his black trousers. No doubt his body would be beautiful beneath his clothes. He must be quite a horseman, to have thighs like those, riding to hounds, leaping over every barrier in his path. In her fantasy, he was not chasing a poor, benighted fox, but her. She was not sure what she wanted to happen when he caught her.

If he ever chased her, perhaps he would kiss her. And if he kissed her, what would that be like?

The carriage stopped abruptly as it drew up in front of her father's town house. She held herself very still as a silent Mr. Waters opened the carriage door without waiting for the duchess's footman. He pulled the stairs down himself, offering a hand so that she could alight in safety.

"Thank you," she said. "I should ask you in, but…"

"At this odd time of day, it would not be proper."

She raised her eyes to his at last, and saw that the warmth beneath her own skin was mirrored in the dark brown of his eyes. She wanted to drink that heat down as she used to drink her chocolate in the morning years ago, when they had been able to afford it, when her father had still been alive.

She offered him her gloved hand without thinking, and he took it. He bowed over it as if she were a princess in a fairy tale, and not some penniless girl from Devon. His lips were hot against the cotton of her glove, and she felt the heat of that kiss all the way down to her stomach, and lower. She shivered, but before she could take her next breath, he had dropped her hand and taken one step back.

"Good evening, Miss Middlebrook. I will see you again."

Catherine fought down the irrational need to ask him when, to ask if he would call on her tomorrow. But she remembered the lessons her grandmother had drummed into her about what was proper in a lady. A woman should never seem too eager to ever see a man again, if she actually wanted to keep him. Catherine knew that she could not keep Mr. Waters even if she wanted to. He was like some wild, beautiful beast that had stepped into her life with no warning, and one day would step out of it again just as suddenly. She knew without being told, as innocent as she was, that Alexander Waters was not the marrying kind.

She pushed the idea of marrying a foreigner from the wilds of the north away with her next breath. Even if Mr. Waters wished to court her, her mother would never move to the Highlands, away from all she knew and held dear. Her mother would want to rule in splendor over some calm Englishman's house, moving into her patient son-in-law's domain and making it her own.

Catherine had to marry a man who would take her family in, and care for them. Her mother would set up household with Catherine here in London, and once Mary Elizabeth was married, Mr. Waters would go home to the Highlands, where he so clearly belonged.

She did not speak to him again but climbed the stairs to the door. Jim was paying attention to his duty for once, and swung it open for her before she even had a chance to knock. He closed the door behind her, blocking out all sight of the street. She wanted to run to the window in the front parlor and stare down at the carriage below as Mr. Waters climbed in and rode away. But she held on to her good sense as her mother and sister closed in on her.

"I thought you would take supper with the Waterses," her mother said, coming to kiss her and take her heavy cloak. "Why on earth are you wearing this thing?" Mrs. Middlebrook handed the cloak off to Jim, who stared at it as if he had no idea what do to with it.

"I wore it to conceal from prying eyes that it was me riding alone with Mr. Waters in a closed carriage as twilight closes in. Why did you leave me alone there, Mother? That was highly improper, and you know it."

"What's proper is not always fun, now is it, pet?" Mrs. Middlebrook smiled like a cat that had eaten a low-flying bird. "Did you have fun with your Alex, then?"

"He is not my Alex, Mama," Catherine said. There was no reasoning with her. The woman simply wouldn't listen. She should have known that by now, but she still was vexed daily by her mother's complete lack of common sense.

"Well, it's neither here nor there, Daughter. Time will tell. He's a good-looking man, that's certain, and rich as Croesus for all that he stays as a guest in the duchess's house. Of course, who would *not* stay with a duchess, if asked?"

"Mama, I cannot marry Mr. Waters, even if he

deigned to ask me. You and Margaret would never live that far north."

"God in heaven, no! We'd freeze. You'd have to come south for visits." Her mother smiled, as if looking at a future that Catherine knew would never be. Catherine felt a strange longing for it, and thought of Mr. Waters's warm, dark eyes, and his steady, reassuring hands as he bound up her cut.

"Where would you and Margaret live, if I were in the north, Mother?"

"Well, here of course, pet. Your father provided for us amply, as you well know."

Catherine felt her stomach sink, and it did not rise to hope again. Her mother looked at the same figures she did, and saw their dwindling resources. She simply refused to believe them. She was certain, as she stated time and time again, that their holdings in the City would revive one day, and all would be well.

Not likely, the solicitor had told her. Still, her mother listened to no one but her own opinions, which were based on fancy rather than fact.

Catherine squared her shoulders. She would have to look after the family affairs well enough for both of them.

"It's time for supper, pet. Quit your fretting and come into the dining room. Cook has outdone herself again. It's roast beef and braised potatoes with onions tonight!"

"Beef," Catherine said with a heart that was sinking even further. They had not been able to afford beef in months. When her father had died, they had agreed to retain every servant they could, for the members of

their household were like family. With careful economy, the family had managed quite well in the country. But now that her mother had come to London,
she clung to every available luxury as if Papa still
lived, and money still flowed freely. Catherine was not
certain how to break her of her new spendthrift ways.

"The butcher had a fine cut all ready for us, and I
said, why not? My girl only debuts in London once.
Let us dine at home in style."

Catherine did not answer her, but Mrs. Middlebrook
did not seem to notice her sudden silence. "It's too
bad your Alexander could not stay to supper. Well,
we'll give a party and host him and his family another
time. Come, Margaret," her mother said, gesturing
toward the stairs where the dining room waited above.

"Yes, Mama," Margaret said. She stopped at her
sister's side and squeezed her hand. "Mr. Robert lent
me new sheet music. He said that Beethoven is fine,
but that it might be fun to learn a Scottish tune. What
do you think?"

"That sounds lovely, sweetheart. Go on ahead. I
have to speak with Mrs. Beam."

Margaret blithely lifted her skirts to her knees and
took the stairs two at a time, not noticing the grim
look on their housekeeper's face. Jim had disappeared
from the entrance hall, so they were alone.

"Miss Catherine, I am sorry to trouble you before
you've eaten your supper, but…"

"It's urgent," Catherine said. "What's wrong,
Mrs. Beam?"

The older woman had been housekeeper even
when Catherine's father was a boy. Along with the

rest of the household, Mrs. Beam had come up from Devon to take care of the family in London. Though Catherine's inheritance went far in the country, it seemed that London prices were eating it up almost as fast as Mrs. Middlebrook ate delicacies.

"It's the butcher's bill, miss. We've no money to pay it."

"The last of the quarterly allowance is gone already?" Catherine asked. Dread began to grow in her heart, making her stomach swoop within her like a bird in flight.

"It is, miss. I paid the baker for the next month ahead of time, so we'll have our daily bread, but your mother ordered the beef without mentioning it to me. I am very sorry, Miss Catherine."

Catherine ignored protocol and took her housekeeper's hand in hers. "Do not apologize for what you can't control, Mrs. Beam. I will speak to my mother again, and see if I cannot get her to economize. I do not want to fall into debts in London that my husband will have to pay."

Mrs. Beam's face lit up as with a sunrise. "You are engaged then, miss? God be praised!"

For a moment, Catherine feared the old retainer would weep with joy. She took her hand back. "Not yet, Mrs. Beam. But I will be. I promise you that."

The housekeeper schooled her face into a soft smile, but Catherine saw the fear and worry in her eyes as clearly as she felt it in her own heart. "Of course you will, Miss Catherine. A beautiful girl like you—who would not want to marry you?"

Catherine smiled grimly. "Indeed, who would not?

Meanwhile, I will write to our solicitor first thing in the morning asking for an advance on next quarter's allowance. He knows I am in the midst of my first Season. I am sure he will comply."

She did not mention, though she and Mrs. Beam both knew it, that this could be her only Season. She had only this one chance. Tonight had taught her once again that she must make the most of it.

Mrs. Beam stepped closer, lowering her voice in case someone else might be nearby to hear. "You'd best write to Mr. Philips this night, miss. Then, I can send Jim with it first thing in the morning."

Catherine's fear spiked, and she took a deep breath to tamp it down. "Yes, Mrs. Beam. I am sure you're right."

She headed upstairs to the dining room then, to eat a bit of her mother's expensive beef.

Eight

CATHERINE DID NOT SLEEP WELL. WHEN SHE FINALLY did doze a few hours before dawn, her rest was troubled. She did not see the beautiful Mr. Waters in her dreams even once. She dreamed only of a parade of ledgers and figures that did not add up, and once of a ship going down into a black ocean with all her hopes inside it.

She woke feeling bleak, but when she checked her appearance in the mirror, her looks seemed unaffected, save for a little tiredness around her eyes. She applied a cold compress while Marie, the upstairs maid, drew her blonde hair into the one design they knew how to affect, a pile of dainty curls on the top of her head, with a few tendrils left around her forehead and ears to soften the look. She wore pink that day instead of light blue, and made certain that she looked well in it, though she wasn't going out again until the next night, when she and her mother would be attending Lady Jersey's ball.

In spite of her success at Almack's, she had received no invitations save to take tea with the Waterses, which, while enjoyable, had mostly been a disaster. Her arm had already healed almost completely, as if Alexander's touch and his honey compress had worked some kind of strange magic. She had Marie tie a light dressing over it, in case it broke open and started bleeding again, but covered by her long, light muslin sleeve, the wound was not visible at all.

When she took the compress off her eyes, her sleepless worry had been concealed as well.

Her letter to Mr. Philips, their solicitor, had been written the night before and no doubt sent to Lincoln's Inn before the sun was up. Catherine was not sure what she was going to do with her day while she waited for his reply. She would do her best to avoid the Waters family, both for her own sake and for the sake of Mr. Robert Waters's musical sensibilities.

She took breakfast with her mother and sister as she always did, and saw that Cook had furnished the breakfast table with more beef from the roast the night before. Though it stuck in her throat, she ate it, for she could not bear the idea of it going to waste.

The morning passed in relative silence for their household, with her mother writing letters to friends and Margaret working diligently on her French verbs. Catherine sat in the window of the family sitting room at the back of the house, overlooking her flower garden. She might go down and weed it later, though Charlie seemed to keep up with their little patch of green well enough.

There was something soothing about having her hands in the dirt, though she could not fathom why. Of course, in Town, she had to wear gardening gloves, which took away half the fun. Still, the soil under her hands always brought her comfort. And there was comfort in knowing that both the town house and their small estate in Devon were free of mortgages.

Jim entered the family room without knocking and Catherine sighed as he addressed her mother. She reminded herself to speak to Giles about Jim's need for further instruction on how to behave as an under butler.

"There is a gentleman caller to see Miss Catherine," Jim announced, his Devon accent doing nothing to take away from the grandeur of his address.

"Did he leave his card, Jim?" Mrs. Middlebrook asked, laying her pen down.

"No indeed, madam." Jim stood silent then, not giving any further indication of who might be waiting for Catherine even then.

Mrs. Middlebrook went back to her letter as usual, not caring about the running of her household. Catherine suppressed a sigh of martyrdom and told herself to stop being a fool as she rose to her feet with a smile. "I will be happy to greet the gentleman, Jim, but please, in future, obtain a calling card before you announce a visitor."

"Yes, miss." Jim bowed low, as if this stricture were a revelation, though Catherine was quite certain that he heard it once a day.

Neither Mrs. Middlebrook nor Margaret took any more notice of the proceedings, so Catherine checked her hair in the mirror above the fireplace and smoothed her pink gown where it had wrinkled a bit at the waist. She stepped into the hall and made her way downstairs to the formal parlor, where her visitor waited.

She took deep breaths and tried to pinch color into her cheeks, her only thoughts revolving around Alexander Waters. So when she opened the door and discovered Lord Farleigh waiting for her, she lost her train of thought altogether. At least she did not lose the manners that her grandmother had drilled into her when she was only knee-high.

"My lord Farleigh, good morning." She left the door wide open behind her and curtsied to him prettily. He stood from his perch on the uncomfortable settee in the center of the room as soon as he saw her, and bowed with an elegance and grace she could not remember him displaying before.

"Good morning, Miss Middlebrook. Do forgive the early call, but as the morning sun rose, I found myself hungering for a bit of a ride in the park. I know it is not the fashionable hour, but it would be my honor if you would accompany me." His handsome features were schooled into a calm smile, which revealed nothing of his inner thoughts. As this was only proper, Catherine was surprised that she was disappointed.

Catherine blinked at him, and wondered for a fleeting instant if he did not want to be seen with her. Despite his remote politeness, she dismissed this idea as vaporish nonsense. He had taken the time and trouble to call on her, after all. "Thank you for the kind thought, my lord. I would love a ride in your carriage. Let me go and fetch my pelisse. May I call for refreshments while you wait? Some tea?"

"Perhaps another day, Miss Middlebrook. I find that the warm spring sun calls to me, and I fear we must take advantage of it before it is gone."

Catherine laughed. "That is true, my lord. So many fine days in the city seem to turn suddenly to rain. I will not be a moment."

She sent Marie for her pelisse and bonnet, and sent word by Jim to her mother that she was going for a drive in the park. It might have been her imagination, but she thought she heard her mother chortle from above stairs as she and Lord Farleigh closed the wide front door behind them.

Before she knew it, she was perched high on the seat of his curricle, the matched grays charging down the sedate street as if they were at Newcastle. She watched as Lord Farleigh brought them under control easily, and let them keep their spirit and their gait if not their speed as he turned the carriage deftly into Regent's Park.

She kept up an easy chatter with his lordship, all the while watching him surreptitiously beneath her lashes. Her bonnet blocked a good deal of her peripheral vision, but as she faced him, he kept his eyes on the road, as any wise driver should. That left her able to look him over with no concern for embarrassment or propriety.

He was a fine-looking man, blond and blue-eyed where Mr. Waters was as dark and swarthy as a pirate. His hair was neatly pomaded, but not overdressed, and his cravat was well tied without being officious. His address was polite if a bit distant, as he was fully engaged in keeping his spirited beasts from overturning them at every opportunity. Though his pantaloons were not as tight as Mr. Waters's, his superfine coat showed his shoulders to advantage. All in all, looking on him for the rest of her life would be no hardship.

This thought brought a pain into her heart, which

she ignored, the way she would ignore a stomach cramp brought on by too many croissants with jam.

They rode out for almost an hour before Lord Farleigh turned back and brought her safely home again. He called for a footman, and Jim deserted his post at the door at once and came down the front stairs to hold his horses. "I will see you indoors, if you will allow me, Miss Middlebrook," Lord Farleigh said.

"It would be a pleasure, my lord. Will you take a cup of tea?"

He helped her down from the high seat then, and she forgot her question, his gloved hands strong and warm around her waist. As he swung her gently to the ground and stepped decorously back, she found that she felt safe with him, as she had all morning long. Safety and pleasant conversation were no small things.

As they stepped inside, she forgot to renew her offer of refreshments. Her mother was holding court with both Mr. Alexander Waters and Mary Elizabeth, all three laughing uproariously at something which had already been said. The laughter died abruptly when Catherine entered the room on Lord Farleigh's arm.

Mr. Waters stood, as politeness dictated, but he rose from his chair with an air of menace that seemed out of place in a formal drawing room. Catherine felt her tongue threaten to cleave to the roof of her mouth, and she forced herself to speak. It was suddenly difficult, but she managed it.

"Good morning, Miss Waters, Mr. Waters. My lord, may I present my mother, Mrs. Olivia Middlebrook. You no doubt remember Miss Mary Elizabeth Waters of Glenderrin, and Mr. Alexander Waters, also of the same."

Lord Farleigh smiled his calm, warm smile and bowed to the two ladies, but when his eyes fell on Alexander, his bow turned to a simple nod, and his smile grew cool. "Good morning. I believe Mr. Waters and I have met."

"Yes," Mr. Waters said. "We discussed the fate of Scotland at Lady Jersey's latest soiree."

Lord Farleigh's smile did not falter, but as Catherine watched, the last of the warmth went out of his eyes. "Indeed we did. And came to no firm conclusion, if I recall."

"Oh, I don't know. I think one or two things were decided during that talk."

Catherine did not understand why two men would take such a sudden and intense dislike to each other, but it seemed that they had. Lord Farleigh refused her mother's offer of tea, and bowed to the room at large before taking his leave.

He raised Catherine's hand to his lips, but did not touch his mouth to her glove. Instead, he asked, "Will you and your lovely mother be attending the ball at Lady Jersey's home tomorrow night?"

Catherine felt a little breathless as one man held her hand while a large, hulking Scot stood staring daggers at him. "Indeed, we will, my lord."

"If I might be so bold, I would like to secure the first waltz and the second quadrille."

"I would be honored, Lord Farleigh."

She caught his eye, and for the first time, she saw a hint of the same heat that rose in Mr. Waters's gaze whenever she was near. She waited for an answering flutter in her belly, and was disappointed when none came. Still, such tender feeling no doubt grew in time, like good lavender, coming back year after year fuller and more beautiful with careful tending.

"The honor is mine," he said, relinquishing her hand.

He left then without another word, and Catherine sat down at once, for her knees were weak. She forgot, until she caught Mary Elizabeth staring at her, that she was still wearing her bonnet and pelisse.

"Eat something, Catherine, and then we'll go," Mary Elizabeth said.

"Go where?"

"To the menagerie, of course, and then on to Gunter's. Did Alex not ask you yesterday when he was driving you home?" Mary Elizabeth offered the sandwich plate as if it were her home and her parlor. Catherine's mother did not seem to care one fig, as she was busy contemplating Mr. Waters, who had sat down once more. The circle was complete, for it seemed that Mr. Waters was busy contemplating Catherine.

Catherine could feel the heat of his gaze but she did not turn to look at him. She refused to feel at odds for going out for a lovely carriage ride in an open rig in broad daylight with a man it seemed was courting her, an eligible gentleman with whom she would hopefully stand before a parson before the summer was over.

She took one look at Mr. Waters from beneath the rim of her bonnet. His eyes were as hot as melted chocolate, but for once, they did not seem welcoming, but irritated. She did not know why he was frowning at her as if she had just kicked his favorite spaniel. She ate her tea sandwich, and took a second when Mary

Elizabeth brandished the plate at her, but she did not look at him again.

"What do you think? Shall we see the lion in the Tower?" Mary Elizabeth asked, ignoring her brother completely.

Catherine managed to finish her second sandwich without choking, and she accepted a glass of lemonade from Mary Elizabeth's outstretched hand. "Sounds delightful," she croaked, turning her back on the man altogether. She noticed that her mother's eyes moved from him back to her. In spite of the young man's glare, or perhaps because of it, her mother simply smiled.

Nine

ALEX WANTED TO THROTTLE THAT ENGLISHMAN WITH one hand—his left, perhaps, so that his right hand would still be free to get at his knife if he needed it. He had always counted himself as a rational man, but something about that Englishman set his teeth on edge.

Lord Whatever-His-Name would be the perfect man to stand by Catherine for the rest of her life. No doubt he kept a decent wine cellar and went to church on Sundays. He might even keep country hours when at home, and no doubt judged the local roses with fairness and equanimity. His innate English assumption of superiority was simply part of his makeup, the way arrogance and self-assurance were part of being a Waters man. Alex told himself all these things, but as he stared down into his tiny cup of tepid tea, these attempts at rationality did not help in the slightest.

He knew now, with no uncertainty, that he had not begun to lose his mind. He had already lost it.

Catherine sat munching sandwiches, wilting under the heat of his stare as a hothouse flower wilts under the heat of too much sun. Alex tried to rein his irrational fury in, to contain it, to bottle it until he could thrash someone or something later. All this sitting in her mother's parlor, listening to his sister prattle on about the Tower and its long-ago-drained moat, was going to make him lose what was left of his control.

He felt a primitive urge to pick Catherine up, toss her over his shoulder, and make for the Highlands without looking back. He knew now that not only was he among strange people, but just as his sister always said, he was among the enemy. That blond English bastard was going to marry his angel, and there was nothing Alex could do to stop him.

Other than marry her himself.

He was too angry to see straight, and too angry to think wild thoughts. But for the first time, he wondered what his mother would say if he brought a slight, angelic blonde girl back to the frigid halls of his family's keep. How would this too-thin girl fare during her first winter in the Highlands, when even stout men sometimes caught a chill, fell ill, and died of it?

And what of his own ship, that in one month's time would have landed in Aberdeen, ready to take on luxury goods bound for the islands of the West Indies? What of his plans to see Mary Elizabeth wed, and then to return, as all sane men must, to the lure of the sea? He owned his own ship, not bought with the family's funds, but paid for with his own earnings. It had been his lifelong dream to serve as captain on it, and he had only done so once, a year ago, before his mother called him home to deal with his sister's lack of prospects. He had sworn that once Mary Elizabeth was settled, he would go back to the life he had built, the life he had always longed for.

He could not take Catherine to sea. He could not live here, among his enemies. And he could not marry her.

Still, for the first time since the Englishman had stepped into the room with Catherine's hand on his arm, Alex became calm and ready to listen to reason.

Catherine seemed sensitive to his moods, for as soon as the black cloud of his irritation passed, she smiled tentatively at him and offered the plate of tea cakes. Alex was not a man for sweets, or so he had always thought, but he accepted a sesame cake as a peace offering and made her blink by devouring it all in one bite, as he often wished to devour her.

She seemed to catch something of this in his gaze, for she blushed, a delightful, delicate pink rising to color her throat and cheeks to match her pretty, pink walking dress. He could have stared at the girl for the rest of the afternoon—indeed, for the rest of his life. But he could hear the impatient tone of Mary Elizabeth's voice, though he had long since stopped listening to her words. He had to get her out of doors and soon, before she embarrassed them both by proposing a knife toss in the front parlor, or a race up the staircase in the corridor outside.

Alex smiled at the room at large, turning on the charm he had in abundance but so seldom bothered to use. "Ladies, the afternoon draws on. Shall we adjourn to the Tower, to hear of the fate of the doomed wives of Henry VIII and see the great lion of Africa?"

Catherine laughed, and her laughter was like music. Not a high, tinkling sound as a pianoforte made, but a lower thrum, like a bass drum used to call men to war.

"Have a care with my girl, Mr. Waters. She needs protecting from prowling beasts, do remember," Mrs. Angel said.

Catherine finally spoke. "Mama, please."

Mrs. Angel did not acknowledge her daughter's protest, nor did she heed it, but kept her blue-eyed gaze firmly fixed on him. Alex bowed, and took her mother's hand.

"Catherine need fear nothing so long as I am with her."

Mary Elizabeth missed the byplay between him and Mrs. Angel altogether. She was not one for subtleties of any kind, as she found them a complete waste of time. "The lion is secure in his cage, and is no danger to anyone. Come, Alex, the Tower awaits."

Mrs. Angel only raised one elegant eyebrow at him. The Tower's lion clearly was not the first beast that came to her mind.

⤜⤛

The Tower was not quite as large as Catherine had imagined it would be. Nestled next to the bustling Thames, so close to the City, the noise of the streets was overwhelming as Mr. Waters handed her down from the duchess's open carriage.

She stood with her half boots touching the worn stones of the path that led up to the walls of the Tower of London. Somewhere in there were the black ravens that were said to keep England whole, and the king safe on his throne. She assumed that he and his ministers took great care that the ravens were well fed, and stayed close to home. It was only a superstition, but it didn't do any harm to look after a few birds.

She stood frozen in place, feeling overwhelmed both by the history of the place and the bustle of the street behind her, until she felt Mr. Waters's hand on her arm. Mary Elizabeth had forged through the crowd and had moved on ahead to the Tower's gate, where she had already struck up a chat with one of the yeomen. Dressed in the beefeater regalia of Henry VIII's reign, the man unbent enough to lean down and listen to whatever she was saying, and to smile at her. Catherine felt a surge of envy that her friend was so relaxed in such a strange place, and confident enough to speak with any man, about anything at all.

Mr. Waters drew close to her, shielding her from a group of lords and ladies who moved toward the gate. The moat was long gone and the water gate filled in with dirt, but many wanted to look at it and to speak of it, and of the doomed yet never forgotten queen, Anne Boleyn.

"It is a bit much," Mr. Waters said. "I did not realize it would be so crowded on a Tuesday. Please forgive me."

Catherine looked up at him, peering past the rim of her bonnet to see genuine concern on his face. He was watching her as if he feared she might faint right there. She laughed, and smiled at him. "I do not hold you responsible for the tourists of London, Mr. Waters. I am not quite as delicate as you seem to think."

"You are more so," Mr. Waters countered. "You are too good for this world."

Catherine felt her cursed, telltale blush rise as it always did, but this time, she did not look away from him. She kept her eyes on his, wanting to see whether or not she could do it, whether or not he might look away first. He did not, and she found herself caught in the snare of her own game. For as she stared at him, she noticed for the first time that his deep brown eyes were rimmed in a light gold, and that his dark hair, while long and tied back in a queue, had slipped its moorings and fallen a little over one eye.

Her gloved hand longed to push it back, to slide in behind his ear perhaps, or to bind it back in the leather thong he wore at the nape of his neck. She wondered suddenly if he wore it long because he was Scottish, or simply because he was old-fashioned. She couldn't touch him—certainly not in public, and certainly not with such intimacy, then or ever.

He pushed his hair back on his own and, without a word, took her to join his sister. They were at an impasse, it seemed. But at least he was no longer annoyed. And she was no longer afraid.

Catherine decided to go against her rules of propriety, and spoke of what was in her thoughts, in the hope that Mr. Waters might listen. "My father always said that he would bring us here," Catherine began. She had to swallow hard, for the very mention of her father, even five years later, made her feel melancholy. Mr. Waters's arm beneath her hand gave her strength, just as it had at the Almack's assembly. She wished wildly and without sense that he might stand by her for the rest of her life. She dismissed that thought at once, and returned to her tale. "Margaret was deemed too young, both for the journey to London and to take in the views of the Tower. Papa passed on before he could bring us."

She stopped speaking then, for her heart was bleeding, and she did not want that sorrow to make her cry. She breathed deep, and Mr. Waters pressed her hand once, gently, before he let it go.

"I am sorry for your loss. Perhaps we should turn back. I would not cause you pain for all the world."

His honeyed voice was deep and soothing, a balm for once instead of a temptation. Catherine drank it in, along with her next gulp of air. When she was certain she was in control of her emotions once more, she smiled up at him, tilting her head so that he might see her face.

"You do not cause me pain. I am glad to be here. I am glad to be here with you."

She blushed anew at that unguarded statement, and wished she had not spoken at all. But she saw no censure in his gaze, only kindness. He turned the conversation back to safe topics, letting her regain her bearings as they walked on. "We will have to bring Miss Margaret with us the next time we come. She will love the lion."

Mary Elizabeth had listened to their exchange in uncharacteristic silence. She still did not speak as she led them past the place for viewing the crown jewels, straight into the royal menagerie. The lion sat in his cage, just as Mr. Waters had said he would. Mary Elizabeth became bored with the king of beasts almost at once, and began to ask yet another beefeater how he would defend the Tower if London were invaded.

Catherine heard the question just as she caught Mr. Waters's eye. They exchanged a conspiratorial look, united in their effort not to laugh out loud.

With Mary Elizabeth in the care of the Tower guards, Mr. Waters brought Catherine closer to the lion, who did not seem interested in them at all. Catherine moved closer still, and knelt next to the cage. She had to resist the urge to reach out her hand and pet the beast inside.

"Don't get too close, Miss Middlebrook. He still has his teeth."

"The poor thing must be so lonely here, far from home."

"Lonely or not, step back, please, for my sake. His keepers must see to his comfort. I would rather bring you back to your mother with all your limbs intact."

Catherine smiled at him again and obeyed. "I'm not foolish enough to touch him."

Mr. Waters seemed to relax as soon as she stepped back from the cage to stand beside him.

She felt buffered by his presence, as though the rest of the crowd in the room simply did not exist.

"It is wise never to try to touch wild things."

She looked up at him and knew that he was no longer speaking of the lion. She felt as if she stood at the edge of a precipice. Never in her life had she been tempted to impropriety, but this once, she spoke. She leaped into the void, her pulse hammering in her ears. "Not even when those wild things are beautiful, and touch your heart?"

There was a long, stilted silence in which she wished very fervently to die. Mary Elizabeth was not just a terrible influence on her; she was also a force that might ruin Catherine's life. Catherine stood frozen, unable to look away from him, wishing that some kind soul might come to her side and distract them both, saving her from her own folly.

Sadly, no one came.

Mr. Waters spoke at last, and she could hear in the distant tone of his voice that he was not pleased that she had been so bold. "Especially then, Miss Middlebrook. Wild things are dangerous."

She had never felt so humiliated, or so unwomanly, in her life. She cursed herself for being a fool, for speaking of her infatuation with him so openly. He had looked away and was scanning the crowd as if searching for the door.

Maybe, if she waited, he would look back at her and acknowledge the truth of what she had spoken. There was something between them, something odd that seemed to grow of its own accord every time they saw each other.

She waited, but he did not look at her again. He simply offered her his arm and led her to Mary Elizabeth's side. His sister was regaling the beefeater she had cornered with a description of a stronghold in Edinburgh, one that had left her unimpressed, it seemed, in relation to the Tower.

Catherine could not listen but kept her eyes down, fighting off the blush of mortification that seemed to have permanently painted her cheeks. She had spoken of her nascent feelings for him, and he had given her a gentle set down, then ignored her, as any gentleman would when a lady forgot herself and overstepped the bounds of propriety.

She took a breath, and reminded herself of Lord Farleigh's regard. He was open about his interest, and would dance with her the following night. She must set Mr. Waters out of her thoughts, and out of her life, altogether.

Catherine was not sure how she would see her way through the rest of the afternoon. She thought of her grandmother, and of the pride inherent in the tilt of the old woman's head, in the way she carried herself. She drew her shoulders back, as her grandmother had taught her to do. She schooled her face into the hint of a smile that her grandmother had told her made men run mad, wondering at the mystery behind it.

But there was no mystery to her. She was a girl, a green girl from Devon, a debutante with only enough coin for one Season. She could not afford to feel affection for Highlanders who would never marry her. She certainly could not afford to express that affection openly, no matter if her heart was touched or not.

And how was she to know anything about her heart? She was a girl, searching for a husband who would honor and care for her, and her family, for the rest of her life. Her heart and all it contained simply did not signify.

She smiled her small smile at Mary Elizabeth, whose keen eyes clouded over at the sight of it. "Are you all right, Catherine? You look peaky. Did you eat a bit of bad cheese when you were out riding with Lord Farleigh?"

The idea of Lord Farleigh offering her a spoiled bit of Brie while they careened behind his matched grays in Regent's Park made her laugh out loud. So much for being a lady of mystery.

"We did not partake of cheese on our drive," she said. "Well, you no doubt need a bit of diversion after all of this lion gazing. Lord, but they should keep the thing outdoors! The stench alone is enough to make a woman swoon, if she were the swooning type."

Catherine laughed again, careful to keep her gaze on Mary Elizabeth's face and away from her brother altogether. "You would never swoon."

Mary Elizabeth took her brother's arm as he led them out of the keep and into the sunlight of what had once been the bailey. The clouds had cleared away entirely, and the sky was as blue as any in Devon. Catherine found herself tilting her face to the sun, drinking in the warmth past the concealment of her bonnet. She felt Mr. Waters's heavy gaze on her, but she knew by now not to look at him.

"I might swoon under some circumstance I have yet to encounter," Mary Elizabeth said as her brother handed her into the duchess's open gig. "Perhaps if I killed a man."

Mr. Waters spoke at last. "I would swoon if you killed a man, Mary, and Mother would have your hide."

Mary Elizabeth frowned at the mention of her mother, but shrugged off the thought with her next breath. "Mama is in the Highlands, and I am here. I might kill twenty Londoners before she could even ready her carriage to come and fetch me home."

"The English frown on killing in the public streets, Mary Elizabeth," Mr. Waters said. He sat between the girls, and the carriage, with its single large seat, could barely contain him and them both. His knee pressed against Catherine's through the thin muslin of her skirt, and his thigh distracted her, radiating heat like a hot brick in winter.

Catherine chastised herself for noticing and instructed herself to be a lady. She need not concern herself with Alexander Waters. She must forget him, even as he sat beside her, and keep her mind on Lord Farleigh—a marrying man, and her future.

Mary Elizabeth waved one hand. "Fine and dandy, Alex. I won't kill anyone. I'm just saying, if I did, I might well swoon." She looked at Catherine across her hulking brother. "Catherine looks as if she will swoon dead away right now in this bright sun. Get us to Gunter's, quick time, Alex. We've not a moment to lose. A strawberry ice is just the thing to fortify a young lady in the warmth of spring."

"Gunter's it is. We can't have Miss Middlebrook swooning on us. Her mother would not be pleased."

"You did vow to protect her, Alex. You always keep your word."

"That I do, Mary, that I do."

Catherine ignored this entire exchange as if it had not been spoken. She wished herself home, listening to Margaret play the pianoforte, or back in Devon, tucked away in the garden of her childhood, long before she knew Alexander Waters even existed.

Ten

His angel had spoken of her heart.

Alex had thought he would lose the last of his good sense when she'd said that he had touched her, not just her body, but her tender feelings. He had felt a welter of emotion rise when she spoke, a tidal wave that threatened to swamp the ship of his reason and drown him on the spot.

He could not trifle with a young girl from Devon. He would not. He was a man of twenty-five, sworn to guard and protect her, even from himself. He could not look into the soft green of her eyes, pools of burn water running over mossy stones. He could not take her away from this place and keep her from the lust-filled eyes of all those Englishmen, none of whom she noticed. All of whom wanted her as much as he did, no matter how decorous their outward regard. He was not in the south to marry among the English, but to see his sister married. He could not hurt this girl.

So in spite of the rising tide of his own emotions, he did not look at her again. He did not answer her save to warn her away. And when he had felt her flinch as if he had slapped her, he'd cursed himself for a cad and a bounder. He had let his own interests and flirtation interfere with a lovely girl no older than eighteen, a girl with no man to defend her.

She had closed up like a rosebud and would not look at him again. It was for the best. He had done as he ought, as any honorable man would do, but all the same, he was in the wrong. He did not know how to make it up to her, and heal the breach between them without giving the girl false hopes. It was better for her to forget him altogether, for her to marry her Lord Farleigh, or someone just like him. Alex would see Mary Elizabeth safely married; then he would go home to the Highlands, and all would be as it should.

And yet, he had offended and hurt her, and his own heart was bruised. He knew nothing about dealing with young girls, or honorable women. He always kept them at a decorous distance, dancing once with them but never twice, never fetching an unmarried lady punch at a ball, never looking at any decent woman for long, but looking only to keep his own sister safe. He had only known this girl a few days, but it seemed a friendship of sorts had sprung up between them, in spite of his lack of good sense, in spite of his lust. He had bruised that tentative friendship, if not cut it off completely, before it could become full grown.

He was being an ass. What man kept a woman for a friend? Women were family, they were lovers, or they were dance partners for one dance. That was all. He knew better than to trifle with this way of looking at the world.

He cursed himself as he climbed down from the gig

to fetch the girls' ices. Father had always claimed that women were trouble. Only now, for the first time in his life, was Alex beginning to see what he meant.

❧

Mr. Waters said little after the discussion of killing Londoners. He maintained a wary silence, bringing them ices and then standing outside the carriage, nodding to the fashionable women around them. They eyed him as if he were a delectable tidbit far more enticing than the sweets on offer at Gunter's.

Catherine cursed herself for noticing, and Mr. Waters for the fact that the *ton* ladies were right. She might take chocolate every morning for the rest of her life, and each cup would not be able to contain the decadence of one touch of the hulking Highlander's hand.

"You've been in a sour mood since we came out of the Tower," Mary Elizabeth said. "Are you feeling ill?"

"Just a bit peaky, as you said."

"Well, I've a bit of something that will cure your ills."

Mary Elizabeth looked toward her brother, and when she saw that Alexander had his back to the both of them, guarding them like a sentinel, she reached into her reticule and pulled out a silver flask with her initials on it.

"My father gave me this before I left home," Mary Elizabeth said. "He told me to keep it, and my knife, always at my side. One never knows when one will need it."

Catherine turned her back on Mr. Waters and looked at the pretty silver flask, intrigued. She wondered if she might get one of her own, and what it might contain.

"What is it?" she asked.

"Only a bit of the *uisge beatha*. It's good for all that ails you."

"Well, I'm not actually ill," Catherine confessed. "Just out of sorts."

Mary Elizabeth looked shrewdly past her friend at her brother's forbidding back. "Ah. An afternoon in that one's company will do that. Here, have a nip."

Catherine took the flask and drank deep, only to splutter at the heat and the bite of the drink. She did not know what it was, but it certainly bore no resemblance to lemonade. Still, she felt daring drinking it, and knew from the careful way Mary Elizabeth tried to hide it from her brother that whatever it contained would annoy him. She drank deep one more time, before handing the flask to her friend.

Mary Elizabeth laughed a little, but quietly, so as not to draw Alexander's attention. She poured liquid from the flask onto Catherine's ice. Catherine looked around to see if any of the fashionable people had noticed, but they were too busy preening and trying to be seen to pay any attention to what two lone girls were up to.

"Will it ruin the flavor of the ice?" she asked, suppressing her excitement, feeling a strange warmth beginning to creep over the edges of her mind.

"No, love, it'll just give it a kick. Eat up, then." Mary Elizabeth added a tot to her own ice, then slipped the flask back into her bag before her brother could see what she had done.

The liquid tasted strange, and a little off-putting, but as Catherine continued to eat, she found the taste not as strong, and a warmth spreading along her tongue. The heat of the drink and the cold of the ice pleased her immensely. She must find out what that stuff was, and get a bit for herself. Margaret might like it when she was feeling out of sorts.

By the time she had finished her strawberry ice, a lovely sense of well-being pervaded Catherine's whole body. She felt warm in her belly, but not too warm, and the whole world had taken on a sunlit cast in spite of the gathering clouds. She was not even embarrassed when she handed her silver cup and spoon back to Mr. Waters to be returned inside.

She smiled at him beatifically, feeling at peace with all the world and every man in it. Even him.

Mr. Waters hesitated at her smile. He looked into her face as if searching for the answer to a puzzling question. She saw the moment he found it, for his look turned thunderous.

"Mary Elizabeth Waters, what have you done?"

Eleven

HIS ANGEL WAS AS DRUNK AS A SAILOR.

Alex cursed, not bothering to do it under his breath. Mary Elizabeth ignored him, but Miss Middlebrook stared him down like a schoolroom governess.

"I beg your pardon, Alex, but I must insist you do not use that language in my presence." She looked at him imperiously from under the narrow brim of her white flowered bonnet. He was about to open his mouth to apologize when she laughed long and loud. The sweet sound echoed down the street in waves, and more than one gentleman looked over to see where the courtesan was sitting. When they saw only a little debutante dressed in pink muslin and silk flowers, they raised their eyebrows and turned back to their companions. But not before their gazes lingered for a moment, as if to memorize her face.

He returned the silver cups that had held their ices, not hesitating a moment longer before vaulting into the seat and drawing up the duchess's black geldings. The pair shook themselves awake and dove into the melee of the London street, as eager to get back to their mews as he was. Of course, he had a second stop to make.

Alex's stomach sank. Even their connection to the duchess would not be enough to smooth the way with Mrs. Middlebrook this time. One cut from a throwing knife was bad enough, but when he brought the eldest daughter of the house home intoxicated, there would truly be hell to pay.

He would probably never be allowed to call on her again, much less dance with her in company.

Alex turned his glare on Mary Elizabeth, who sat beside her friend, contemplating the sky that was turning gray above their heads. Catherine Middlebrook, sandwiched between them, hummed a lilting little tune he did not recognize. She leaned heavily on his arm, as if she were a vine that sought to grow there.

His body hardened at her nearness, as it always did, but this time there was a keenness to his appetite, for it grew by what it fed on. An almost constant diet of her presence had only made him want her more. And now she was warm and willing by his side, hanging on his arm, her breast pressed against his bicep.

He was a gentleman, and had to remember his oath. He thought of unpleasant things instead: the coldness of the burn when he tried to swim too early in the year at home, the icy slickness of the water he was obliged to break in his wash bowl every morning in the middle of winter.

All these thoughts did not cool his ardor in the least. For his angel was a warm burden against him, a bud ready to flower, and he was but a man—a man of honor, but just a man.

God help him.

"Alex," his sister said, as if she had not been wreaking havoc in her wake, "do you think it is going to rain?"

"We're in London, Mary. It is always about to rain. And do not speak to me. Your friend has had a bit of the whisky."

"She has." Mary Elizabeth kept her eyes on the sky, not looking his way at all. "Only a tot, just to sweeten her mood. An afternoon with you had put her in an ill frame of mind." She turned to him then, raising a pointed eyebrow. "I wonder why?"

"Do not speak, Mary Elizabeth. Your friend is drunk, we are ruined, and you are going home."

"To Glenderrin?" Mary Elizabeth asked hopefully.

"No. To the duchess's."

His sister slumped a little, sighing.

"Yes, it is such a burden to live in a princess's palace while all the swains of London leave you calling cards and flower bunches, each waiting to dance with you at the next ball."

Mary Elizabeth brightened and straightened her back at the mention of dancing. "That's right! Tomorrow, we dance! Alex, do you think these English know any reels?"

He breathed deep, working hard not to thrash his little sister with his buggy whip there in the street. He was overwrought, and overreacting, but as his angel pressed one lush breast tighter against his arm, he had all he could stand. It was high time Robert took over the business of marrying off their sister. Robbie need no longer wander among the whores of London, but stay home and squire Mary Elizabeth about Town while Alex drowned himself in a vat of cold water in the garden.

"I doubt it, Mary Elizabeth. Maybe you can teach them one."

"Maybe I will."

He drew the duchess's carriage up in front of her town house. "Why are we here, Alex? Aren't we taking Catherine home?"

"What happens to Miss Middlebrook is no longer your concern, Mary."

Catherine roused herself enough at this point to speak. "No, indeed, Alex. Mary is my best friend. I will see you at the dance tomorrow, Mary. You can teach me a reel."

"It would be my pleasure," Mary Elizabeth said, planting a kiss on Catherine's cheek before leaping down from the carriage, into the road. Lucky for her, and less lucky for him, no other carriage was barreling by to kill or maim her in that moment. His sister gave him a jaunty wave before blithely strolling into the house. The forbidding ducal butler shot him an evil look before closing the door behind her.

Catherine pressed harder against his arm to get his attention. His body was at full attention, but he turned his head at last to look down at her against his better judgment.

Her lips were swollen as they always were, as if someone had just been kissing her. The telltale scent of whisky lingered on her breath, along with a hint of strawberries from the ice she had eaten. She leaned closer, if that were possible, raising herself up to whisper in his ear.

"Alex," she said. "I think it is going to rain."

Catherine should be standoffish and ladylike around Alexander Waters, but ever since she had eaten her strawberry ice, she had felt at peace, at one with the world and every man in it. She could not quite remember why she was angry with him. She liked him. She knew he liked her. There was not much else to think about when it came to a man and a girl.

Her grandmother's strictures about proper decorum seemed very far away, as far as the river that ran by their house in Devon. As Mr. Waters drove her home in the busy traffic of the Mayfair streets, she leaned comfortably against his arm and looked at the sky. She could not see it properly, for her bonnet blocked her view, as it always did.

She pulled away from Alexander for a moment and reached for the ribbons of her bonnet.

"Miss Middlebrook, may I ask what you are doing? Please keep your bonnet on. We are almost at Regent's Square."

"Balderdash, Mr. Waters. I am tired of not being able to see properly. I want this bonnet off."

She fiddled with the tie that bound her until the bow under her chin finally came free, and she drew the hat off her head. She sighed, and tossed the bonnet at her feet, where the ribbons fluttered at her gaily. It seemed for a moment that the cursed hat might take flight, so she set her neat-booted foot on it. It was a bit crushed, but it would not flap out of the carriage and scare the horses.

"Miss Middlebrook, your lovely bonnet is ruined."

"I doubt that, Alex. May I call you Alex? I doubt that, but if it is, I have another at home that will suffice for everyday use, and one for Sundays."

Her hair suddenly felt tight on her head. The hairpins seemed to be sticking into her scalp more than usual, and she needed to loosen one or two. She reached up and drew out the two largest hairpins. A hank of curls fell across her shoulders and down her back. Alexander clucked to the horses and they picked up speed, bringing a lovely breeze against her heated skin and along her face. She drew two more pins out, and then two more, until her entire head of hair had fallen around her in a mass of curls.

"That's better," she said. Her reticule was caught under her thigh. It seemed she had sat on it. Rather than draw it out from under her in an unseemly show of maneuvering in the open carriage, she simply tossed the pins into the street.

"Miss Middlebrook, I beg you, please do not take anything else off."

"Alex, I must remind you that I am a lady. A lady does not disrobe on a public street, in an open carriage, in the full light of day."

Alexander seemed to blush under his tan, and she laughed in delight. Finally, someone besides herself was blushing! What a lovely change that made.

Emboldened by the heightened color on his handsome face, she leaned close to him again, sliding her hand up his muscled arm. His tight coat did not do him justice, it seemed. The muscles leaped beneath her gloved hand, radiating warmth and coziness and a tiny bit of danger. But his hands were occupied with the horses... What could one tiny bit of danger matter?

She took both of her gloves off and tossed them on the floor of the carriage beside her hat. Her hands free to roam unencumbered, she leaned close to Alex and slid one hand up his arm, past his elbow, to the bulge of his bicep.

She sighed. "It occurs to me, Alex, that a lady might indeed take off a few more constricting clothes, if she were driven in a closed carriage, in the dark of night. Perhaps that is why I am never allowed to go anywhere, save with Mama, once night has fallen."

Alex choked, and she looked up into his face with concern. It seemed he was not having an apoplexy like the one that had killed her father. Perhaps he was only trying very hard not to laugh.

"You may laugh, Alex. I will not be offended. I know that I know almost nothing about the world. I suppose I am a disappointment to a worldly man like you."

She felt a little of the happiness go out of the day, as he stopped the carriage by the curb. This time, Jim did not come out to hold his horses. Indeed, no one from her household greeted them at all.

He turned to her, not moving to hand her down from the rig. His dark eyes were serious, and seemed to be lit with an inner fire that she thought she should heed.

"You are far from a disappointment, Catherine. You are the most beautiful girl I have ever known, and the sweetest. You are wholly unspoiled and could never disappoint a true gentleman or a man of sense, this day or ever."

"Even with my bonnet off?" she asked, eyeing him warily.

"Even then."

She smiled at him, the day coming back to rights. She heard the distant sound of thunder and bent down to pick up her bonnet and gloves. Her reticule was indeed tucked under her derriere, and she held on to Alex's arm as she reached beneath herself to draw it out into the light.

"There that blasted thing is. What do I owe you for our ices, Alex? A Middlebrook always pays her debts."

He did laugh then, and raised his arms to help her down from the carriage. "You owe me nothing. A lady does not pay for her own ices."

He swung her down from the high seat and she clung to him like a limpet. Suddenly the ground seemed very far away, and seemed to sway a little as her feet touched the earth.

"Alex, I fear that bit of *beatha*...whatever it was, might have made me a little...odd."

He smiled and let her lean all of her weight on him. "Only a little. I must admit, Miss Middlebrook, I like you odd."

"Then you will like me forever, Alexander Waters, for odd I always am."

He helped her up the stairs to the front door, so she managed them without tripping once. For some reason, that simple fact made her inordinately proud.

Jim did not answer her knock, so she simply pushed the door open. The entrance hall was dark, for rain clouds were gathering and the candles had not been lit in the vestibule. Mrs. Beam had her work cut out for her, it seemed. But Catherine did not even care. She was too happy and warm and well to care about households and candles. Who could care for such trifles when a man like Alex Waters stood in the room?

"I must tell you a secret, Alex. And you must not tell a soul."

"What is that, Miss Middlebrook?"

"Call me Catherine." She leaned close to him, drawing him into the darkened hallway. She felt a tiny bit dangerous, a tiny bit wild, but she also knew that no matter what the provocation, he would always look after her, would always see to her needs and interests without her even having to ask. For all his good looks and non-marrying ways, Alex was a good man.

"Come close, and I will tell you."

He obligingly leaned down, and she raised her hands to settle on his broad shoulders. She knew that his horses would stay in place and not run away, as she had seen him tie them to the post by the road. So she closed the door behind him with a tilt of her hips, and stepped even closer in the dark.

"I like you too, Alex Waters. A very great deal. More than any man I have ever met, save my father. And he was a great man."

"I am sure he was. Miss Middlebrook—"

"Catherine," she corrected him.

"Catherine," he amended. "We are standing a bit too close. Someone might see."

She smiled at him then, and felt as if a little sun had risen in her heart. Even in that dark corridor, when any other man would have taken advantage, he was still trying to care for her. She leaned close, as if to whisper once more in her ear, but at the last moment, she turned her head, and brushed her lips against his.

Twelve

Her lips on his were like a bolt of lightning.

Alex had never been struck by lightning, for he still lived to walk the earth, but he had seen a tree that had been split in two by a blast from above. Now, he knew what that tree felt like. A fanciful piece of his mind thought of that tree as his angel kissed him. His life was now like that tree, divided into two parts: before she kissed him, and after.

Her lips were soft and warm, and more than willing. He tried in the first few moments to remember that he was a gentleman, that he was sworn to protect this girl, even from her own folly. But as she pressed her sweet, round breasts against his chest, winding her fingers into the long dark of his hair, drawing the ribbon out of it, he found that he forgot his oath. He had forgotten every oath he had ever taken, every breath he had taken before that moment. There was only that girl, and her soft sweetness in his arms.

She did not know how to kiss. He wondered if this might even be her first. That thought too splintered off from the main, and drifted away with the current of what he did not care about. He cared only for her, for her breasts against his chest, and the way she felt beneath his hands as he pressed them to her waist.

Her waist was reed thin, with no need for stays save to hold up the delectable weight of her bosom. She seemed interested only in pressing that bosom to him, so that all of his thoughts spun away on the current of his lust.

He gentled his lips and ran his tongue over her sealed mouth until she opened it beneath him. She gasped a little, and he pressed his advantage, sweeping his tongue into her mouth as gently as he might, so that he did not offend or frighten her. If this was her first kiss, let it be the best he could offer her, as it would also be their last.

For he knew well, even in the throes of lust, that he could not have this girl. She needed a husband, and he was not a marrying man. He repeated this mantra to himself, but somewhere he lost the thread of it. She began to learn what his tongue was teaching her, and her own tongue joined his in a mating dance.

It seemed she had a natural affinity for it.

She slipped past the last of his defenses then, as her tongue tangled with his, and she pressed her hips against his manhood. He would never think to bring himself against an untutored girl like this one, but she seemed to think nothing of it. She was not frightened or repulsed, but seemed to savor the contact as he did. She moved her hips against him, and his body became a white-hot brand, his mind and morals almost burned away altogether.

It was a sound from inside the house that saved him.

Somewhere within, above stairs, some ham-fisted servant dropped a bin of coal, and it rolled across a metal grate. The clatter startled him out of his sin, drew him back from the precipice that would have led him to his doom.

The selfish part of his nature rose to the forefront of his body and roared. She was his, and he would have her—there, against that wall if he willed, and damn the consequences. There could be no consequences that held any more weight than the weight of her breasts against his chest, than the heat of her flower pressed against his ever-tightening trousers. He shook with the need to claim her, to make her his. He felt as that lion must have done in its youth, on the precipice of an ever-ravening appetite that would take over his reason as well as his body, until his reason and his body moved as one.

But he was a man. He had given his word. And he would keep it.

His angel was in a frenzy by then, her body starving for she knew not what. She only clung to him, and moved against him, as if she might sate that hunger on his body with all their clothes on.

He could do that for her. She was close to the peak of pleasure, and he could take her there without even raising her skirts. He might offer his wide thigh for her to perch on, and show her how to move against him so that she might assuage her own lust, that she might shatter the quaking terror that filled her now, and find a modicum of peace.

The temptation beckoned, and he knew in that moment that he was too far gone. To think of doing such a thing with a gently reared virgin was simply not to be borne.

At every point in his life, at least once a day, the question presented itself: was he a real man, or a false one? Did he hold in his actions to the principles he claimed to bear as a standard before him, or didn't he? It was a simple question, with an answer of yes or no. For the first time in his life, he was tempted sorely to answer in the negative.

But he would not hurt her that way. He had too much respect for her. He had too much respect for himself. Whatever came, he would have to soothe her out of this, and find a way for both of them to live with it.

So he drew back, taking his lips from hers.

His angel whimpered when he pulled away, and tried to follow him with her mouth. He spoke to her soothingly, a little in Gaelic, a little in English, whispering softly, running his hands over her waist in an attempt to appease her need for his touch, even as he pressed his lips to her temple.

"*Leannan*, we must stop. Please, my angel, listen to me."

She seemed to hear him, for she stopped writhing in his arms. She froze, as a deer might before the hunter, and she opened her wide green eyes.

"Dear God," she said, blaspheming. "What have I done?"

❧

Catherine could still taste the sweetness of his tongue. She wondered at herself, at her behavior, at the wildness of her lack of decorum, at her complete disregard for self-preservation, for common sense, for the decency she had been raised to. Her grandmother would have had her beaten, eighteen years of age or no.

But he had tasted so good.

His body was even harder than it looked, harder than his forearm had been under her hand, than his upper arm had been against her breast in the open carriage. She had never been kissed before. She had certainly never kissed a man before, and never would again until she was engaged. But that kiss had been perfect bliss, a touch of heaven in the midst of her daily worries, her fear, and her helplessness. She had felt delicate and vulnerable in his arms. She had also felt safe, almost cherished.

She could not get the taste of him out of her mouth, no matter how hard she swallowed.

The earlier warmth brought on by Mary Elizabeth's odd drink had burned away in the heat of Alexander's touch. So now Catherine had nothing to dim her humiliation, nothing to draw her mind from her embarrassment as she stood and faced him in that dark-ened corridor. Catherine rallied, and stepped back, her eyes on his.

"I apologize, Mr. Waters, for my behavior. It was unconscionable, unthinkable to act as I have done. I can only rely on your discretion and your honor."

The handsome Scot drew himself to his full height, well over six feet. He had bent down to kiss her, had leaned down to cradle her between his hands like an egg that might break with too much rough handling. She caught herself looking at his large hands encased in leather gloves, and wondered what those gloved hands might feel like against her skin. She swallowed hard, and could still taste him.

"It is I who must beg your forgiveness, Miss Middlebrook. A true gentleman would ask for your hand in marriage this very moment. As I am not free to wed, I can only beg your indulgence in my folly, and confess that your sweet charms overwhelmed me."

All Catherine heard out of that pretty speech was that he would not marry her, then or ever.

Did he have a wife tucked away somewhere in the Highlands, some huge woman as hulking as himself, with dark red hair and a passel of children? She realized then that she did not truly know this man. She saw in that moment of cold clarity that she never would.

The pain in her heart was like a blade tearing her chest asunder. She forced herself to breathe. She had been a bigger fool than she had previously thought. She loved this man, and he did not love her back. Her grandmother had not warned her against this folly, no doubt thinking it impossible for her cherished, favorite granddaughter to behave with so little good sense, with so little decorum. A lady was not allowed to touch a gentleman who was not her husband, because a lady's heart moved as her body did: in the direction of the man who had kissed her, who had taken her virtue, however much of it she offered him.

In the dim light of that corridor, she saw how badly she had behaved. It would ruin her if anyone ever found out. She drew on her grandmother's pride, since she could not find her own, and met Mr. Waters's eyes.

"I think it best if you leave, sir. I bid you good day. I thank you for your discretion, both now, and in the days to come."

She heard her own voice, and her grandmother's strict tones reflected in it. She saw Mr. Waters flinch from her as if she had struck him, and her heart started to bleed. Still, he was the one who had said they could not marry, who had openly spoken in bald terms of what they both already knew. No further discussion was necessary.

She moved past him and opened the front door. She was deeply grateful for the first time that Jim was not at his post, but busy elsewhere in the house. Where was that warm sense of well-being now, the one brought on by the strange drink Mary Elizabeth had poured over her ice? Whatever warmth she had felt had fled as soon as Mr. Waters stepped away from her and took his hands from her waist.

He stood staring at her now as if she had wounded him. She found she could not apologize. She was glad that perhaps, in spite of that potential hulking wife tucked away in the Highlands, he hurt just a little, too.

He left her then without another word, and she closed the door behind him. She leaned against it, and let her tears come. But she did not weep for long, her grandmother's stricture clear in her mind. No man was worth a woman's tears.

She went upstairs to change her gown, and to put up her hair once more. Her bonnet was a bit crushed, but still serviceable. Much like her heart.

Thirteen

ALEX MANAGED TO GET THE DUCHESS'S GIG HOME before the downpour. He could only imagine what Ian would have to say if he had to replace the leather interior of a ducal carriage with the proceeds of the family's next shipment of furs from Nova Scotia. Best not to find out.

He was out of sorts, fuming at himself for being a cad, and then for handling his caddishness with such a lack of finesse. The girl had kissed him, he had kissed her back, and that should have been the end of it. He should not have drawn her against him. He should have stopped her at the first touch of her lips. She was not that drunk, and he should not have been that foolish.

Or that cruel.

After seeing to the duchess's horses, he let himself in the kitchen entrance of the house. The cook turned from her stove brandishing a large carving knife, but when she saw it was him, she simply smiled and went back to her cooking. The young kitchen maid smiled at him too, but her smile had a bit of a different light in it. His body responded with a jolt, and he realized how aroused he still was from a simple kiss from his angel's lips. He was not one to dally with servant girls though, that day or ever. He nodded at her for politeness's sake and took himself upstairs to find his brother.

Mary Elizabeth found him first as he entered the first floor hallway outside the music room. He heard the lovely sound of Robert playing the fife, and knew that his brother had been at the whisky already—and it wasn't even dinnertime yet. No doubt his brother had fallen into one of his funks from being too long in the south.

"Did you do something to annoy Catherine?" Mary Elizabeth asked, barring his passage into the room where Robert was playing and no doubt drinking.

"No doubt I did," Alex answered. "Why is that any business of yours?"

Mary Elizabeth glared at him. "Alex, she's my only friend in this benighted city, and I won't have you deviling her. You'll go and apologize first thing in the morning, or I'll write to Mama."

"And tell her what? That I'm deviling English girls?"

"That you're annoying my only friend." He saw tears in his sister's eyes then, and he stopped being cruel. It was not her fault he was ill behaved and a rascal and a varlet. Those faults lay square at his own door. She was right. He would have to apologize again, when he and his angel were both less…overwhelmed. And after that, he would have to leave Miss Catherine Middlebrook well alone.

He took his sister's hand gently in his. He watched as she blinked her tears away with difficulty. She hated to cry, but she was a girl after all. Alone in the south, save for him and Robbie, and lost without her fishing, her hunting, and her sword. He leaned down and kissed her forehead, and this time, she blinked in surprise, her tears all but gone.

"I am sorry, Mary Elizabeth. You have my sincere apology. And Miss Middlebrook will have it as well on the morrow."

Mary Elizabeth swallowed hard before she answered. She was not one to hold a grudge. "All right then, Alex. But don't forget. Catherine is important to me."

"I promise you. I won't forget."

As if he could forget her. If Catherine Middlebrook slipped from his mind like an outgoing fog, his life would be the simple, straightforward place it had been less than a week ago—when right was right, left was left, women were for fun alone, and whisky was for drinking. Now, very little made sense. But he did not have to take his own angst out on his little sister.

He kissed her forehead again, as he had when she was small, and sent her upstairs to change for dinner.

"I don't need to change, Alex. This gown is perfectly clean."

"It's not about clean down here among the English, Mary. It's about what's fashionable. It was fashionable to go to Gunter's, and it is fashionable to change for dinner. So that's what we'll do."

She turned to go, but before she headed to her second floor bedroom, she said, "Alex, I am sorry I gave Catherine a tot. Was she ill when you took her home?"

"No, don't trouble yourself over it." Before she

left, he raised a finger at her in warning. "But don't ever do such a thing again. English girls can't handle Scotch whisky."

"Not even the smooth stuff from Islay?"

"Not even that."

Mary Elizabeth sighed and nodded and went on upstairs. Alex did not realize until she was gone that she had not promised anything.

He had more to worry about than his sister. He opened the music room door and found Robbie with his fife in his hand.

The music had stopped and his brother sat brooding, a glass of whisky at his elbow.

"What's her name?" Alex asked, a half smile on his face.

Robbie laughed out loud at that, his usual good humor showing through his rare malaise. "God forbid! I'm not sick with love. I'm sick for home. When are we leaving again, Alex?"

"Tired of the ducal palace that surrounds you already?"

"I'm tired of London, and London dirt, and London coal smoke, and London people."

Alex poured himself two fingers of Islay whisky, the only stuff they drank. "That's quite a list. Anything else?"

"Isn't that enough?"

Alexander raised one dark brow and Robert sighed. "The food's not so good here."

"Don't let the cook hear you say that."

"Oh, she's a good sort, and at least what she makes tastes like something, but every time we eat outside this house, I find I want my mother's bannock, and a slice of decent rye."

"So it's home-cooked bread you're after."

"Don't joke, Alex, this is serious. When can we leave?"

"You know the answer as well as I, Robbie. The day our sister is wedded and bedded to a decent man."

Robert's mouth quirked in a grin. "Only decent? Can't the poor lass hope for a good man?"

"We're among the English, Robbie, don't forget."

His brother laughed out loud at that, as he meant him to. Alex did not join in. He downed his whisky in one gulp and went to pour himself another.

"And what ails you, Brother? Drinking before dinner, and not a head cold or a whore in sight."

"I wanted to go to a whore yesterday," Alex confessed. "I wanted to. I just couldn't."

"Oh, Holy Mary, full of Grace, as Mama would say. What's this, then? Have you lost your keen edge?"

Alexander glowered as his brother laughed at him. When Robbie saw he meant business, he stopped laughing.

"It's worse than that, is it? Though God alone knows what could be worse than that. What the hell's the matter with you?"

His brother's thickening brogue brought Alexander a little comfort. It reminded him of his brother Ian, of his father, of the smell of salt on the open sea, of the taste of clean burn water down from the mountains. It reminded him of home.

When Alex didn't answer, his brother asked, "What's her name?"

Alexander did not dissemble or try to hide his foolishness. He and Robbie were one year apart. They had lived together, fought together, chased women together all their lives. His brother knew him so well that he had only to read his face to know when something was wrong with him. And something was wrong with him now.

"Her name is Catherine Middlebrook."

Robbie smiled. "That sweet-faced girl from Devon? Mary Elizabeth's friend?"

"That's the one."

"Hmmm." Robert contemplated the last of his whisky, then set it aside. "She's a bit young for my taste, mind, a bit grassy green, you might say."

Alexander felt his temper rising like a flash tide, and he caught it before it exploded, but barely. "She is a beautiful girl with everything to recommend her. A good girl, a sweet girl who deserves better than the likes of me, God help her."

Robert examined his brother carefully, but he did not hesitate to say what he was thinking. "She's as poor as a church mouse. I think her sister said she sews her own clothes."

"And what of it? No girl can help what money her father left her, or the lack of it."

Robert squinted at him, becoming even more cautious, watching him as he might watch a ravening beast on a rampage. "True enough, true enough. And you like her well enough to take her from her home, to bring her to the Highlands, to let Mother look after her for the rest of her life among the ice and the heather?"

Alexander knew that despite his brother's glib tone, he was bringing forth real objections. Their mother was English, but she was not a fan of English girls for her sons. She had told them under the strictest terms that they were not to marry themselves off while down south, that she would beat them herself if they did so.

Not that Alexander waited on his mother's opinion in the matter of the fairer sex. He never had and he never would. But he did listen to his brother.

He was listening to him now.

"I am a damned fool," was all Alex said.

Robert grinned and Alexander felt his heart lighten a little. One reason he loved Robbie was that he kept him from being so serious about every single thing on God's good, green earth.

"Well, if you're thinking of marriage, and marriage to an English girl, you've gone a bit mad, that's certain. But you look pretty calm for a madman. Perhaps you're not in love with her after all."

"I have no idea."

It was Robert's turn to raise a brow. "Really? Well, that's the first order of business, isn't it? Before you can do anything else, you'll have to decide. Do you love her, or not?"

Fourteen

CATHERINE DID NOT SLEEP AT ALL THAT NIGHT. AFTER enduring prying looks from her mother all through dinner, she claimed that she had a headache and retired early. Once trapped alone in her room, even Mrs. Radcliffe's latest novel could not distract her from her oppressive thoughts. She ended up blowing out her candle and drawing the bed curtains closed against the firelight in her grate, wishing that she might suddenly sleep, and wake as someone else.

She went back over the events of the afternoon again and again in her mind, as if they were a river flowing through her thoughts that would not be dammed or channeled elsewhere. She remembered the sad old lion, and how she had wished she might set him free. She thought her gaffe in the royal menagerie, and of how Mr. Waters had dealt with it coolly, in a way that had left them both with their dignity intact. Her feelings had been hurt at that point, but at least it was an answer to the question she had been asking herself in her deepest dreams and wildest imaginings: could she and Mr. Waters ever consider a future with one another? And he had answered her with a resounding, quiet no.

If that had been all, she would only have a moment of wounded pride. But she had been schoolgirl foolish enough to accept the odd drink Mary Elizabeth offered her, not knowing how it would make her feel. Warm, and wonderful, as if the world were new, as if she were truly young, and need not fear the lack of money, or her future, or even think of the next moment. She had simply felt the need to draw close to Mr. Waters in that hour after she had taken that drink, and sit with her arm over his, and feel the strength of his firm muscles beneath her hand.

His heated lips on hers had been a revelation. Why had he kissed her back, when he did not want her? She could not understand that. But then, she knew absolutely nothing of the male mind, nothing of his thoughts, nothing of him at all except that he was her friend's brother, and the nearness of him took every sensible thought out of her head and replaced each with folly.

Catherine had never been touched by a man before. She could not believe how easy it had all been, how seamless, as she wrapped her arms around his neck, slid her hands into his hair, untied his ribbon, and pressed herself against the hard, masculine contours of his body, reveling in the touch of every inch of him.

She could not believe her behavior. Even the magical drink that Mary Elizabeth had given her could not excuse such conduct. She could not believe she had done it. How could the calm, quiet, biddable girl who her grandmother had raised possibly have been such a fool?

And yet, she had been. So be it.

Catherine rose from her bed and lit a candle as her grandmother had taught her. Though they were officially members of the Church of England for form's sake and attended services every Sunday at Saint George's when they were in London, she was a good Catholic, as her father's family had always been.

So she said an Act of Contrition from the old religion, and then asked for forgiveness from the Holy Mother simply and without flowery words. She found, as she knelt before the candle on her dressing table, a modicum of peace steal over her heart. Her heart was still wounded, her soul was still bruised, but she was forgiven. Nothing worse had happened. She had sinned, and badly, but she had been spared. She would simply have to take care and follow her grandmother's precepts to the letter, in order to avoid such darkness in the future.

Girls who kissed hulking Scots in their mother's hallways did not make good marriages. And she must marry. She knew her duty, and she would follow it. She would save her family from her mother's spendthrift ways and the loss of their fortune. Her grandmother had been clear: there was no one else to do it. Catherine must put all else aside, and be the woman her grandmother had raised her to be.

She had thought to become a woman on her wedding night. Now, she saw that it was not marriage that made a woman, but the acceptance of responsibility, both for herself and for others.

No matter what the temptation, she would not be a fool again.

After her prayers, Catherine finally slept toward dawn. She woke feeling bleak, and wondered if this was how a woman felt, her dreams discarded, realities taken up in their place.

She told herself to stop whining as she washed her face. She did not call Marie that morning, but braided her hair as she had when she was a girl, and tied it into a makeshift bun on her head. She was vain enough to let a few curls stay loose along her forehead and temples, but she did not spend too much time on vanity, dressing in an old gown from home. She would work in her garden, and receive no one that day. There was nothing like working in good, clean dirt to cleanse the spirit of folly.

❧

Alexander did not take any of the duchess's conveyances but walked the next morning to see his angel. He reminded himself that he could not offer marriage to a girl he had known less than a fortnight. He was bound for the sea in a few months' time, and had to keep his wits about him, and his desire in check, while he was on land. If only desire were the sum total of what he felt for her. But there was something more between them, more than he had ever felt for any woman in his life. Catherine had named it as they stood in the lion's den. She might be young, but she had the wit and the courage to see that what they felt was rare. Not that their feelings changed anything. She was bound to marry a decent Englishman, and he was bound to let her. But he could not leave things as he had the day before. He must smooth things over, if only for Mary Elizabeth's sake.

Of course, as he was a man and not a liar, he knew that he was smoothing things over chiefly for himself.

He could not get the last look on her face out of his thoughts. She had looked as if he had stabbed her through the heart with a dirk—a thin blade, but a deadly one.

When he knocked on the front door, Jim the footman opened it.

"Good day, sir." Jim stood wearing his best officious expression, and said nothing else.

"May I inquire if Miss Middlebrook is at home to callers?"

"No, sir. I mean, yes, sir, you may inquire. She is at home. But she is not receiving."

The young man looked so proud to have remembered that much that Alexander had to swallow his smile. He soldiered on. "Do you know if an exception might be made? It is urgent that I speak with Miss Middlebrook before tonight."

"I am sorry, sir. She is not at home."

"To callers?"

"Yes, sir."

"But she is home."

"Yes."

When Alexander did not speak, but took a moment to gather his thoughts, the footman–under butler closed the door in his face.

If he had not felt like such a bounder, Alexander would have laughed out loud. He walked slowly down the stairs and along the walk, past the back garden. Through the garden gate, he thought he caught a hint of golden hair. He thought for a moment of Mrs. Angel. Her hair was blonde, but fading a little. And Miss Margaret's hair was a burnished bronze, like Robert's. He smiled. He had found his quarry.

Not at home to callers? He would see about that.

Fifteen

CATHERINE WAS MINDING HER OWN BUSINESS, CUTTING lilacs in the back garden when a hulking Scot vaulted over the wall and back into her life.

"I beg your pardon!" she said automatically, idiotically, standing with her pruning shears in one hand and her basket over her other arm. Part of her wanted to toss those shears at him in a fit of ire. But in the next moment, her calm reason asserted itself and she took a series of deep breaths. Blast him, Alexander Waters was still a beautiful man. She had hoped that he might have grown toady warts overnight.

No luck there.

His shoulders, encased this morning in black worsted wool, were as broad as they had ever been. His handsome jaw was just as chiseled, his eyes just as dark. Instead of throwing her shears at him, she turned her back and returned to pruning flowers for the sachets she was making.

"You aren't going to speak to me?" Mr. Waters asked. "I've just leaped over a six-foot wall for you, and you do not even mention it."

Catherine did not look at him but examined her roses for aphids. "It is not polite to leap over walls or to comment on such an occurrence. When you leave, there is no need for such theatrics. The garden gate is well oiled, and will serve."

"You are still angry with me, then." He came to stand beside her, his wide shoulders and broad back blocking the sun. Still, she did not turn to him, but stared blindly at flowers that she could no longer see. What little peace she had been able to cultivate that morning began to slip away. She must work harder, and breathe deeper, for she would be seeing Lord Farleigh at Lady Jersey's ball that night. She must have a clear, serene mind by then. By then, she must be the kind of woman a decent man would wed.

Nothing like the ill-behaved wanton she had been yesterday.

"I don't know what you mean," she said. She clipped a rosebud that was not yet even beginning to turn pink. She would have sworn under her breath at the destruction of such a blossom before it could even open, but she was a lady.

"So you have forgotten my villainous behavior?" he asked.

She turned to him, her bonnet shading her eyes. Her white bonnet was still in her room, Marie cleaning and re-trimming it with silk flowers from one of her mother's discards. She wore her blue bonnet that morning, and a light muslin gown to match. Her heavy gardening gloves, meant to protect her soft skin, made her hands itch. Perhaps it was because she itched to slap Alexander Waters's smug smile off his face.

She could not believe the depth of her anger. Surely it was overdone, and she was overwrought. Surely a true lady would never feel such fury at the mere sight of a man. No lady would wish a man to perdition where he stood.

"I am not receiving," she said.

"So I gathered from your footman."

"And yet, here you are."

"Here I am."

Catherine sighed deeply, setting her shears and basket on a nearby bench. She glanced toward the house, and saw that they were shielded by the great oak that still shaded the house from the summer sun. The oak was in full new leaf, obscuring the sight of them from any prying eyes that might be peering down from the breakfast room or the family parlor.

Thank goodness for small blessings.

"Your behavior, Mr. Waters, was no worse than mine. I ask, on your honor, that we forget the entire afternoon ever happened."

"What if I don't want to forget?"

Catherine stared up at him, wondering what new game he might be playing. Whatever it was, it had to stop, here and now. She must make a decent marriage, and she could not let this man stand in her way.

"I can only imagine what you must think of me," she began, only to be interrupted.

"I doubt very much that you can."

She waved one hand impatiently, then drew off her heavy gardening gloves, casting them down on the bench with her shears. She breathed again, forcing clean air past her stays and into her lungs, so that she might think clearly. This man always did nothing but damage her calm. She must set those feelings aside, just as she must set him.

"Whatever the case, you gave me your word of honor to forget the entire incident. I must hold you to it."

"I gave you my word of honor never to speak to another about what went on between us, and I have not. I will not. But I will not forget it."

Catherine glared up into his face and saw a small smile playing across the sensuous plane of his lips. She remembered what it felt like to have those lips on hers. As her gaze traveled downward, she remembered what it felt like to have his hard body pressed against her, from breast to thigh.

She trembled and turned away from him, moving to her lilacs again, where she bent down and took a deep breath of their cloying sweetness. They had never been her favorite flower. They were her mother's. But their scent drove away any memory of Alexander Waters's body, save for the taste of his lips on hers. No matter what she did, that memory simply would not go away.

"Sir, I beg your pardon, but I have no dealings with married men. No doubt you think to dally with a young girl who knows no better, then return to your wife and children tucked away in the Highlands. But I tell you, you will dally no more with me."

He laughed out loud at that, and she thanked God in His heaven that she had set her shears aside, for she truly would have run him through had they been in her hand.

"I have no wife, Miss Middlebrook, and no children, in the Highlands or anywhere. What put this foolish notion into your head?"

He touched her arm and she flinched away. The heat of his touch moved up her arm and into her heart before she could stop it. She felt tears begin to rise, and she blinked them away. "Yesterday, you stated very clearly that you cannot marry. Your reasons are, of course, your own. I ask only that you leave my presence now, at once, and do not come back."

He simply stared at her, his own breath coming as fast as hers was. She waited, but for once he did not have anything quick to say. Catherine swallowed the tears in the back of her throat, fighting for control. "And do not call me a fool. I am a lady, in spite of my behavior. I will thank you to remember that, until you walk away and never see me again."

"I could not leave you and never see you again, Catherine. So put that idea out of your head."

She felt her ire rise again, and she welcomed it. Anger was preferable to tears. "Get out of my garden."

He raised both of his hands, the black leather of his gloves catching the morning light. She shivered at the sight of those gloves, and cursed herself for a weak and wanton fool.

"I came to apologize, Catherine. And I am making a hash of it, just as I made a hash of our dealings yesterday. I am sorry to intrude on your morning. But I cannot leave this anger between us. The kiss we shared—"

"I beg your pardon? What kiss?" she asked, trying to take a different tack by feigning ignorance.

If he was so indiscreet as to discuss this openly in a garden only ten feet from the street, where anyone might hear, who knew whom else he might tell? She could not admit to the kiss ever having happened. To kiss a man like that and not become his wife made her damaged goods. She could not afford to be ruined. Handsome, ne'er-do-well Highlanders would simply have to step aside.

"Catherine, you cannot pretend to have forgotten."

"I pretend nothing, sir. I remember nothing, because no such kiss occurred. Now, since you will not leave me in peace, as I have requested more than once, I must go inside to my mother."

She left her flowers and gardening things on the bench behind him. She could not risk passing him to pick them up, for she did not trust herself. Even among the sweet spring scents of her garden, she caught the heady smell of bergamot and cedar rising from his skin.

She did not make it far. His hand was on her arm in the next instant, drawing her close, so that all she could smell, all she could see, was him.

"Let me go," she said, her breath coming short. Her body rebelled against her better judgment and sound mind, leaning toward him, hungering for his touch. She shook with the need for him to kiss her as he had the day before. She tried to pull away, but found herself drawn to him as inexorably as a wave is drawn by an outgoing tide.

His lips were gentle on hers as he leaned down and blocked out the sun. All thought fled in that moment, and she was taken up with pure sensation. The sight and sound of the world faded, and there was only him, and the heat of his mouth. He did not draw her too close this time, and she kept her sanity enough not to press herself against him. Still, the taste of him overwhelmed her, an exotic delicacy that she would never get enough of, not if she lived a thousand years. She had been transported to some exotic place, a world where his touch and all the joy it contained were her birthright.

That was a lie. He did not belong to her.

She stepped back then, and he let her go.

He was breathing hard, harder than she was, and his gloved hands were shaking. He reached for her again, as if against his own will, but she took two more steps back.

"This is not over," he said.

"It is, Mr. Waters, I assure you. One more thing to add to the list of all we must forget."

"I am not much for list making. I only know that I will kiss you again."

"You need not trouble yourself. I make excellent lists. And you will never be close enough to me to take a liberty after this morning."

He smiled, and the light of challenge came into his dark eyes. She cursed herself, for her grandmother had warned her about issuing challenges to a man. Men liked nothing better than the thing they could not have, whether that thing be a horse, a fine gun, or a girl. She had just thrown down a gauntlet, and as she watched, he picked it up.

His breathing evened out as if by magic and his smile became a bit arrogant, as if he knew more than she did, as if he knew her better than she knew herself. And there was little doubt that he understood worldly things far better than she ever would. But she was a Middlebrook. She would not be forsworn. If he would not marry her, so be it. She would go about finding a man who would.

"I will leave you now, Miss Middlebrook, by the garden gate. But I will see you tonight at Lady Jersey's ball."

"You may see me, but I would thank you not to speak to me. I think we have said enough."

Alex's smile took on another level of heat, and she felt an answering heat beneath her skin. She took one more cautionary step back, but he did not try to approach her again.

"It is not words I wish to bandy with you."

"You will get nothing else, and not even words will pass between us, if I can help it."

"Indeed, Miss Middlebrook, I will get a dance. The supper waltz will do. Then we can spend another pleasant hour discussing what you will and will not allow."

She straightened her spine, working valiantly to ignore the tingling in her fingertips, and the heat pooling beneath her stomach. She wanted to reach for him more than she had ever wanted anything in her life. She could not see him alone again. She could not think to control herself, though she had no clear idea as to what she would do with him if she put her hands on him as she had yesterday afternoon. She would kiss him, but it seemed she wanted more than that. She could tell by the wicked gleam in his eye that he knew a good deal about the "more" of what she wanted.

"That waltz is taken, Mr. Waters. Now, I would thank you to leave."

He stepped close again, and this time, she stood her ground. She would not be intimidated by a beautiful man in her own back garden, no matter how much he made her flush. She did not feel faint, as a true lady would, but exhilarated, as if fighting him had given her life again after her night of misery and sorrow. Fighting a Scot was much better than pining for him.

"If that waltz is spoken for on your dance card, then that Englishman had better get the deuce out of my way." He spoke low, his voice filled with more danger than if he had raised it in a shout, but Catherine did not back down even then. She met his eyes with what she hoped was cool aplomb, and she would not drop her gaze come Halifax or high water.

She had lied. No one had taken that waltz. But she would hide in the ladies' retiring room for the whole of supper rather than spend it with him.

Alex Waters must have seen something of her defiance in her eyes, for his own flare of temper seemed to cool. For some strange reason, he looked almost proud of her.

"I have done enough to spoil your morning. I will go, through the gate this time. I bid you good day."

"Good-bye, Mr. Waters."

He left without speaking again, and true to his word, he stepped out through the garden gate instead of vaulting over the wall. She pulled off her bonnet as soon as he was gone, fanning herself with the flower-and-straw confection. There did not seem quite enough breeze in the garden, though it was early May.

She collected her things and went into the house,

certain that she would find calm and comfort for her frazzled nerves in the making of her mother's sachets. Her nerves seemed to sing with the joy of battle. She could not tell if she had won or not. He had left her in possession of the field. Perhaps that was something.

When she stepped into the cool of the kitchen, Mrs. Beam was waiting for her, a look of worry on her face. For one horrible moment, Catherine thought that someone might have seen her in the garden with Mr. Waters, but when she saw the missive in the older woman's hand, she felt a sinking in her stomach that only came from financial matters gone awry.

She wondered silently if her mother had managed to run up two awful butcher's bills within a week. When she broke the seal of the letter and read it in the light of the kitchen window, she saw that it was far worse than that.

Miss Middlebrook,

I regret to inform you that the mortgage taken out against your family property in Devon is three months in arrears. Your mother has failed to respond to my previous inquiries, so I am turning to you. Please visit my office at once, with your esteemed mother, so that we might come to an understanding of this debt, that your family might draw up plans to retrench.

Yours sincerely,
Mr. St. John Philips, Esquire

"Miss Catherine, are you all right?"

Catherine realized then what it meant to truly feel faint. She sat down heavily in a spindly chair tucked against the wall, and Cook brought her a cup of ale. She drank it down without bothering to see if it was watered. But there was no help for it. Her senses were keen. She would not faint, nor would she be transported by a bit of ale as she had been by Mary Elizabeth's magic elixir. She would have to face this latest calamity, and the realities of her life with clear eyes, and a clear mind.

God help her.

She finished her ale and stood up, her knees strong once more. She set her mug down, thanked Cook, and with the letter in hand, went to see her mother.

Sixteen

MRS. MIDDLEBROOK WAS SITTING IN THE MUSIC ROOM, listening as Margaret practiced her new Scottish tune on the pianoforte. Margaret did not seem to feel the need to bash at the keys with this lilting music as she did with the Beethoven, but seemed content to master the melody with a bit of finesse. Perhaps Robert Waters had made an impression on her while Catherine was above stairs at the Duchess of Northumberland's house, learning to throw knives.

Catherine wished for a knife now, but it would have been of little use. She could not have simply thrown it to relieve herself of the burden of irritation and frantic energy. She was so angry, she might have actually thrown it at someone—such as her mother.

Margaret brought her Scottish tune to a melodic end. Before she could begin the same tune again, Catherine asked, "Mother, may I speak with you alone?"

Her mother turned to her and smiled, as if she had not a care in the world. Which was more than likely true. The red roses from the unknown admirer still graced the mantel, their hothouse scent lingering in the room like a breath of summer to come. Catherine wondered again which roué had his eye on her mother, and how on earth she was supposed to combat roués and unpaid mortgages both.

"You may speak in front of Margaret, pet, never fear. We are all a family, caught in the throes of life together." Mrs. Middlebrook smiled beatifically, as if the throes she spoke of were mere swells only, and not the crashing tidal wave that Catherine feared.

Perhaps Mr. Philips was mistaken. Perhaps her mother had not taken out a mortgage on the Devon estate, but on the London town house. The effect would still be disastrous, but they could sell the town house without losing her father's legacy altogether.

"Mother, I must ask you about business. Financial business."

Mrs. Middlebrook sighed deeply. "Must you? Very well then. Ask, and I will answer."

"Did you take a mortgage out on the estate?"

Her mother did not answer right away, but rose to her feet and moved to the mantel where her bouquet still bloomed. She fiddled with the flowers, arranging them again, as if they had not been placed in that vase by her own hands and arranged in their current glory that very morning.

"What's a mortgage?" Margaret asked.

Catherine waited, and when her mother still did not speak, she answered her sister. "When you obtain money from a bank, money you did not previously possess, the bank often requires goods or land as collateral. If the money is not paid back, on time, with interest, the bank takes the land or goods as a forfeit to cover the debt."

Margaret may have only been twelve, but she had a much better grasp of reality than their mother did. "Is the bank going to take Papa's land?"

"No, love, no." Mrs. Middlebrook crossed the room and put her arms around her youngest daughter, looking over at Catherine accusingly. "No one is going to take our land. Put that thought right out of your head."

Catherine stood, returning her mother's glare. "Is it true, Mother, or is Mr. Philips mistaken?"

She found the answer she sought on her mother's guilty face. Margaret could not see it, and Catherine did not want to worry the child any more than she already had. So instead of screaming, as she wished to, instead of throwing the letter from their solicitor into her mother's lap, she simply said, "Mr. Philips has requested an interview with both of us present, Mama. I will make the arrangements, if you will be so good as to attend."

Her mother did not answer but looked stricken, as if the horror in her daughter's eyes finally pierced the fantasy world she lived in. Beef cost money, and mortgages, while great fun when they were taken out, had to be paid.

Catherine could not stay in the room another moment. She left her mother and sister sitting together, and closed the door to the music room with an emphatic click behind her.

She stumbled downstairs without a bonnet or a pelisse. She did not stop in her room to pick up either. She had to remove herself from the house, from the environs where her mother lived, without further delay. She could not bear to be there a moment longer. She did not know where she was going; she would discover that when she got there. Her mind was one large bruise.

She stepped into the entrance hall to find Jim opening the door for Lord Farleigh.

She stopped dead in her tracks, wondering why she had chosen that moment to come into the foyer, why she had chosen that day to braid her hair instead of setting curls on the crown of her head in her usual pretty, if serviceable, arrangement. It was too late now, for Lord Farleigh could see her plainly. She met the blue of his eyes even as Jim instructed his lordship that Miss Middlebrook was not at home.

"I beg to differ, my good sir," was all Lord Farleigh said. His eyes lightened at the sight of her, and his usual serious expression lifted into a smile. His lips quirked at the irony of her under butler's gaffe, but Jim stood stock-still, staring straight ahead.

"She is not receiving, my lord."

"Jim, it's all right. Let poor Lord Farleigh in."

His lordship did not laugh out loud, but she saw the light of humor in his eyes, coloring his usually pale countenance with a bit of pink. She felt her own laughter rising, in spite of the terrible hour she had just spent. She felt relief at the sight of him, as she might feel at finally taking a draught of cool water on a hot summer day. Such water was a pleasure, but it was also a necessity. Lord Farleigh might not be dashing, he might not set her heart at a roar, but he was kind.

"Forgive my appearance, my lord. I truly was not at home to visitors today."

Catherine led him into the formal parlor after instructing Jim to send up some refreshments. For once, Lord Farleigh did not refuse her offer of tea.

"You honor me, then, Miss Middlebrook. Thank you for receiving me."

"It is my pleasure, my lord. It is a relief to see you after the morning I have spent."

He sat beside her on the uncomfortable settee. For a moment, she was thrown off a bit by his closeness, but he sat a proper distance from her, and did not reach out to touch her in any way, as Mr. Waters might have done.

"I hope no one among your family is ill."

"No, my lord. I am grateful to say that they are not. We have been spared that, at least."

She closed her mouth on her complaints as Jim brought in the tea tray and set it before her. He withdrew, and she set herself to pouring, giving Lord Farleigh one sugar and a touch of milk, as he instructed. She slipped two lumps into her own cup, and followed it with a dollop of milk as well, not certain how much longer they would be able to afford such luxuries. She repressed a sigh as she sipped the sweet Darjeeling, but Farleigh seemed to hear it.

"You are distressed, Miss Middlebrook. And I am sorry for it."

Catherine forced herself to smile, and to drink her tea. "You are very kind, Lord Farleigh, but I do not mean to trouble you with the nonsense of my house-hold." She tried to suppress her terror and shrug it off at the same time. She certainly could not reveal it to this man. No one spoke of money or the need for it in polite company. She dredged her mind for some decent topic of conversation, and found one.

"The lilacs are blooming well. Perhaps one day I might show them to you."

"You grow them yourself?" he asked.

"I putter around a bit. My mother enjoys their fragrance."

"As does mine."

"Then I must cut you a bunch to take to her before you go, with my compliments."

He smiled, and his light blue eyes took on a warmer depth. She could see clearly that he loved his mother. "Thank you, Miss Middlebrook. That is truly kind. But she is away in the country at the moment. I fear London and its busy environs try her nerves."

"I can understand why."

Catherine spoke without thinking, and then wished her words back in almost the same instant. Lord Farleigh was not the least offended by her candor, but laughed out loud, his pale face brightening with the effort. He was quite handsome when he laughed, like a painting come to life.

"Miss Middlebrook, you are a charming companion over tea and on a drive in the park, but I must not let you change the subject altogether. I find I am quite fond of you, and the thought of something troubling you, troubles me."

Catherine felt her own smile stiffen on her face. She tried to shore it up, but it crumbled in the light of his outspokenness. She tried to build it up again, but found that she could not. She simply was not that good a liar.

"The subject is indelicate, I fear."

He frowned, and looked thoughtful. "And you say it is not illness in the family. It must be money then."

Catherine choked on her Darjeeling, and Lord Farleigh casually reached out and took her cup and saucer from her, setting it back on the tea tray. She fought for control of herself, but he reached out and took her hand.

"Miss Middlebrook, please do not stand on ceremony with me. My mother raised me to be of service to ladies whenever I can. If you would do me the honor of confessing all to me, perhaps I will be able to help."

Catherine regained her breath, and stared at him. She looked into Lord Farleigh's handsome, if somewhat bland face, and wondered what the world would be like if she had a man like this to lean on. Alexander Waters and his broad shoulders rose to block her view, but she dismissed him firmly, turning her mind and her gaze to where she was, and with whom.

"Thank you for the thought, my lord, but I fear there is nothing you can do."

His gloved hand was warm on hers. It did not hold the lightning of the gods as Mr. Waters's touch did, but it was comforting, like the hand of a friend. Catherine had found in the last hour that she needed a friend, and badly.

"Tell me what troubles you, and let me be the judge."

Catherine tried to stop her own mouth, but the words came spilling out, as water from a broken jar.

"I have discovered just today that there is a mortgage on my family's estate in Devon."

She sat still in the hideous silence that followed, hearing only the ticking of the clock on the mantel, and the thunder of her own beating heart. She wished her words back, and even said a prayer that he might ignore them, but Lord Farleigh was a gentleman. He did not ignore her.

"Forgive me for asking an indelicate question, but was it not entailed away upon your father's death?"

"No, my lord, we are not so grand as that. It is a small holding, but it has been in the Middlebrook family for many generations."

"And that ended with your father."

"Unless I am blessed with a son to pass it down to, yes."

Lord Farleigh sat in silence, as if mourning something she could not quite understand. "But as you have no brother, it would be held hereafter under your husband's name."

"Yes, I suppose so. I would bear his name, as would any children of mine."

Farleigh sighed. "That is a true shame, that the Middlebrook name will pass from it."

She thought for a moment that he was missing the point. She was very grateful it had not been entailed away to her cousin Herbert, as the great families disposed of all their properties under the law. She was very fortunate to have their land in Devon as a haven and a home. At least, she had been. Now they might lose it all, if she could not figure out a way to save them.

She could not marry in time for that.

"I fear it will not matter at all now, for the mortgage is in arrears, and we have no way to pay it."

The silence that followed was excruciating. Catherine now knew why her grandmother forbade her to speak of such things to anyone outside the family, much less a man she had once hoped to marry. The humiliation she had experienced at Mr. Waters's hands was nothing to the shame she felt now, with her family's money troubles exposed to a man who was kind, but essentially a stranger. She tried to draw her hand out of his and stand, but his grip tightened. It seemed Lord Farleigh was stronger than he looked.

"I am sorry for speaking of such things," she said.

"You never would have, had I not pressed you."

"Still, it is unbecoming to speak of my private family affairs. You must accept my apology."

"Only if you accept mine for prying."

She smiled wryly, certain that she would never see him again after that day. No man would continue to court a girl who was so reckless in her speech, so unguarded in her manner. Even now, he still held her hand.

Catherine did not try to draw away again but sat in silence, enjoying the comfort of his hand on hers. It was a comfort that would not last, so she drank it down.

"May I pry into your affairs further by asking you the name of your solicitor, Miss Middlebrook?"

"He is a wonderful man, Mr. St. John Philips, of Lincoln's Inn. He worked for my father, and now he does his best to care for us."

"It seems he has failed."

Catherine felt a new flush of shame at the censure in his voice, though she knew it was not directed at her. "He has done his best, I think. All he can do is give advice. My family, I fear, does not always take it."

"And you are left to fend for your family alone, with no man to lean on save a hired lawyer."

Catherine looked down at her lap, wishing she could think of something clever to say. It seemed her thoughts had jumbled themselves into a bunch, and would not come unraveled no matter how she tugged on them, like a skein of yarn that a cat had gotten hold of.

How might her family retrench? They would certainly have to leave London immediately. Perhaps they might sell the town house to pay the debt on the land. Catherine had no idea of how large the debt was. They might have to sell their carriage, perhaps even rent out the family home in Devon and move in with her grandmother. She cringed at the thought of that humiliation, but anything, even that, would be better than losing the land her father loved, the land her father was buried on.

She had almost forgotten Lord Farleigh was there. But his hand was still on hers, and his presence at her side was still a comfort, though a strange and unexpected one. She could not in good conscience expect an offer from him now, but it seemed she had found a friend at least. And that was no small thing.

"I know that you have no man to lean on, Miss Middlebrook."

She raised her eyes and met his gaze, and saw for the first time how serious he was as he looked at her. He looked as if had taken some gauntlet up, though she had not been conscious of laying one down.

"It would be my honor if you would lean on me."

Seventeen

HEAT ROSE IN CATHERINE'S CHEEKS, BURNING HER throat and her chest as well, almost as if she were on fire. She wondered for half a moment if he offered her some indecent proposal, though what that would have entailed, she was not certain. But when she met his eyes again, his gaze was as respectful as it had ever been. There was no heat in his eyes, and no pity, only true concern. The rush of embarrassment began to subside, and she breathed a sigh of relief as she felt it go.

"You are very kind, my lord. I will speak with our solicitor, and I will write to my grandmother. She is a very resourceful lady. No doubt she will think of some clever solution to our current difficulties."

"If she is half as clever as you are brave, Miss Middlebrook, I have no doubt that you are right."

Catherine blushed yet again at the unexpected compliment. Seeing her embarrassment, he rose to his feet, and she rose with him. Her hand was still clasped in his.

"Would you do me the honor of changing our waltz to the second waltz tonight?"

Shocked that he still intended to dance with her,

much less acknowledge her in public, the first frisson of hope rose in Catherine's chest. Perhaps not all was lost.

"The supper waltz?"

"Yes, Miss Middlebrook." He smiled at her befuddlement, and she almost laughed out loud. A fleeting thought of Mr. Waters ran across her mind like a doe pursued by hunters, but she was strict with herself, and forced herself back to the here and now.

"The supper waltz is yours, Lord Farleigh. It is the least I can offer you after you have been so kind to me."

"Then we will dance the first quadrille and the supper waltz, and we will talk of more cheerful subjects than we have this morning," he said.

He smiled on her, and she noticed for the first time how warm his smile was when he was not thinking about serious things, as he so often seemed to do.

He bowed over her hand and kissed it. Unlike Mr. Waters's, Lord Farleigh's lips were cool and self-contained. He did not impose on her person or invade her personal space in any particular way. In every moment of their encounter, save for prying into her affairs, Lord Farleigh had conducted himself as an utter gentleman.

Why did that disappoint her a little?

He left her then, and she sat down again on the uncomfortable settee in the center of the formal parlor. She reached for the teapot, but the Darjeeling had already grown cold. Instead of going downstairs to fetch herself another cup, or ringing for Jim to bring her a fresh pot, she simply sat in silence, wondering where on earth her life would lead her next.

⁓

Catherine did not go into luncheon with her mother and sister, but instead took a sandwich off Jim's tea tray and went to have a nap in her room. There was little chance that Lord Farleigh would still consider offering for her after their encounter that morning, but she may as well do all she could to look her best at the ball that night. She was short on sleep, and feeling a bit hopeless, so a nap might just do her good.

She slipped off into sleep behind the curtains of her bed. In her dreams, she danced not with Lord Farleigh, but with Alexander Waters, who had transformed from a handsome if rakish ne'er-do-well to a young man with prospects who had honored her with serious courtship. The dream was such a joyous one that she woke with a smile on her face. In spite of her fears and terrors, her heart stayed warm for a good half hour after.

If only dreams were real.

Marie helped her dress in the blue silk gown Catherine had sewn herself. It was of the latest fashion, if a bit more modest in the bosom, as befitted a young lady just up from Devon. The scalloped bodice mirrored the scalloped hem, and was trimmed with lace and seed pearls. The pearls were glass, but the lace had been made by her own hand. Her grandmother had taught her to make lace during the long winter months of her childhood, when it had been too cold to go outside and play.

There were more pearls for her hair, real ones this time, in a long strand that Marie wove through her curls. Her grandmother had lent those pearls to her for her London Season. Catherine said a prayer to the Holy Mother that she might marry, save the family, and not disappoint the old woman she loved so much. She sat alone in her room after Marie had gone, and wished fervently that her grandmother were there.

There was a scratching at her door, and Catherine jumped on hearing it. She wondered if her grandmother had heard her prayers and appeared, like a fairy out of some lovely story. When her bedroom door swung open, it revealed her mother, dressed in gray silk trimmed in lavender. Though her father had been dead five years, her mother wore half-mourning still. She had never entirely recovered from his death, and much of her wildness now and lack of care for the future were because she missed him.

That knowledge, and traces of old pain reflected in her mother's light blue eyes, assuaged some of Catherine's anger.

"I have brought you something," Mrs. Middlebrook said.

"Not another note from Mr. Philips, I trust."

Her mother's face fell, and she wished her churlish words back again at once.

"I'm sorry, Mama."

"No." Her mother came to stand beside her, meeting her gaze in the looking glass above her dressing table. "It is I who must apologize. I have put your father's legacy at risk, and your future, and Margaret's future. I did not realize how expensive London would be, how much a Season for you would actually cost."

"I've made all my own clothes, Mama. I wear the flowers grown in our greenhouse."

"You are the soul of economy, sweetheart. I do not fault you. But your gowns are still made of the best silk and muslin, and opening the house in London, even for three months, costs a great deal more than I had bargained for."

Mrs. Middlebrook sighed, sitting with her daughter on the dressing table bench. Catherine scooted over to make room for her. They both fit easily, for her mother was still as slender as a girl.

"We can go home tomorrow," Catherine said. "We can close the house, sell it, and bring the staff home to Devon."

Her mother smiled. "And give up on your strapping Scot? I think not."

Catherine blushed a dark pink at the mention of Alexander Waters. "He is not mine, Mama."

"I believe he is."

Catherine swallowed hard, finding a lump in her throat. "No, Mama. You must trust me."

Mrs. Middlebrook took her daughter's hand in hers and kissed it, getting a bit of lip rouge on her knuckles. "Little one, I know something of men. That one is smitten with you, make no mistake."

Catherine felt tears rising, and she blinked hard to drive them off. She could not weep and spoil her looks before Lady Jersey's ball. Not over the likes of him.

"I fear you are wrong, Mama."

Mrs. Middlebrook smiled with her customary over-confidence. "I guarantee you, little miss, I am not wrong in this. If I were a betting woman, I'd lay a wager on it." Catherine laughed in spite of herself, and her mother laughed with her. "Put your mind at ease, love. I do not bet. I am a matron, after all, not one of those fast, card-playing women, but a decent lady from Devon."

Affection spilled out of Catherine's overflowing heart. She hugged her mother, and her mother hugged her back.

"I know you have quarreled with your Highlander, but hold firm. You will bring him to heel."

Catherine wondered if someone had seen them in the garden that morning after all, but such worries were driven from her mind almost at once. Her mother drew forth a jeweler's box and opened it to reveal one lone, luminescent pearl on a gold chain.

"This was the first gift your father ever gave me," Mrs. Middlebrook said. "He gave it to me on our wedding night, the night we made you."

Catherine could not speak. Her voice had fled.

Her mother stood and unclasped the chain, hanging it around Catherine's slender neck. The pearl nestled in the hollow of her throat. It seemed to gleam with a special luster in the light of her single candle.

"You will wear it tonight, and it will bring you luck, just as it has always brought me."

Catherine did not tell her mother that they needed not luck, but a miracle. She kept her mouth closed and accepted the gift with the same love with which it was offered.

She rose and wrapped her arms around her mother's slender form. She could not remember the last time she and her mother had embraced before this day. Perhaps family crises were partly blessings, too.

"Thank you, Mama."

Her mother kissed her cheek, leaving more lip rouge in her wake. "It will all turn out all right, Catherine. I promise. You will see."

Catherine wished that for one night, she might be catapulted back into her childhood, when her mother's word was law, and always seemed to come true, like a spell she had cast bringing forth good with a simple wave of her hand.

Her mother's blue eyes gleamed bright, and the hope Catherine saw there warmed her heart. Perhaps her mother was right. Perhaps things would turn out well, though she could not, at that moment, see how.

Catherine made a decision, standing there, looking into her mother's bright eyes. Since there was nothing she could do that night to save herself or her family from ruin, she decided to set all thoughts of the mortgage aside until the morning. She would write to her grandmother then. But tonight, she would dance.

Eighteen

ALEX WATERS ARRIVED AT THE BALL EARLY, SO EARLY
that Lady Jersey laughed at him silently as she greeted
him at the door.

"Come to dance with your little Devonshire girl?"
she asked.

"I don't know what you mean, madam. I am here
to escort my sister, as Robert is."

Lady Jersey did not answer him, save to laugh
out loud.

Mary Elizabeth was asked to dance at once, and
flounced off with her English swain in her wake. Alex
knew he should have been paying strict attention,
glaring the man out of countenance, lest he take a
liberty, but he decided to leave the lion's share of
Mary's care that night to his brother. Robbie was
immaculately dressed in a bottle-green coat and black
trousers, with a sober waistcoat of black and gold. He
himself had dressed well for the occasion, thinking
only of his Devon girl, and what he might do to woo
her back. He had rarely been out of a woman's good
graces. He did not know how to respond.

Of course, he had never courted a decent girl before.

Before he could think of the implications of the word *court*, he pushed the thought from his mind altogether and turned his eyes to the door.

The Englishmen he saw enter looked a bit like circus clowns. Many were dressed in dark colors, but their waistcoats sported brilliant hues. Their cravats were tied in such detail that he feared for the sanity of their valets, and the points of the collars were so high that they looked as if they might stab themselves in the eye. Or perhaps someone else, if they leaned too close to peer at a lady's décolletage with their quizzing glasses. A few men wore unrelieved black, with waistcoats of silver or gray.

His waistcoat was the traditional hunting plaid of his clan, a crisscross of soft blues and greens. He wore it with pride, as all Waters men did when they had the chance. Every man and woman he passed stared at him and then at his waistcoat, as if they had never seen a hunting plaid before, but each man who caught his eye immediately looked away. He got the strange if distinct impression that those men were afraid of him.

And he was not even armed.

The women, however, were a different matter altogether. Clearly, living in London did not afford them the opportunity of seeing a real man very often, for they eyed him as he might have looked over a stud at Tattersalls. One or two more flagrant merry widows even went so far as to bat their eyelashes at him with such insistence that he felt honor bound to ask them to dance. He was content to oblige them, for he would never refuse a service to a lady, but even as he moved through the crowd with a delectable woman on his arm, he kept his eyes trained toward the front door.

His angel still managed to slip in without him seeing her. Or perhaps she flew in on frothy wings. Suddenly, she simply appeared at his sister's side, her mother along with her. The two girls were talking animatedly, as though they had not spent the entire afternoon together the day before. He wondered what on God's earth they found to talk about. Then he remembered: his sister liked to teach her new friend bits from her own skill set—how to drink whisky, how to throw knives.

It was then he noticed the coterie of young men that surrounded her. At first, he thought perhaps they were all his sister's conquests, for Londoners seemed to like nothing better than a woman who didn't give a fig for them. But as he watched, he saw more than one young man lead Catherine onto the dance floor. He leaned against a pillar and watched. She moved with grace, no matter how clumsy her partner. He observed from a distance as she smiled and laughed, as if he had never held her in his arms, as if she had forgotten him altogether.

His ire rose with each new song, and each new swain, but he tamped it down. Still, he could feel a muscle leaping in his cheek. He caught the amused gaze of Lady Jersey on him more than once, before she leaned behind her fan to gossip about him with whoever stood beside her.

Why ex-lovers could not contain themselves when watching a man suffer, Alex really couldn't say. He forgot Lady Jersey and her cohorts almost in the next breath, for the first waltz of the night began and his angel danced it with a boy who could not have been older than eighteen.

As Alex watched, the boy caught his eye, and blanched. Only then did Catherine look to see where her suitor's gaze was tending. Only then did she see Alex in the crowd where he stood staring at her, as he had all night.

She did not smile, and unlike her partner, she did not turn a shade of fish-belly white. Instead, she simply nodded, then turned her head and danced on.

Alexander found himself dismissed by a woman for the first time in his life. Not a woman at all but a slip of a girl, a girl who had melted in his arms only the day before.

He had offended her, deeply, and he knew it. He had apologized, but had only gone on to annoy her more during their stolen moments alone in her flower garden. He reminded himself of all these facts, but he found that his fit of temper was as sharp as it first had been. It seemed he could not talk good sense to himself.

She might turn from him here and now, among her own kind, among these English. But he remembered the heat between them even if she did not.

He would enjoy making her remember.

∽

Mary Elizabeth greeted her and her mother as soon as they arrived, kissing Catherine on the cheek as if they were family as well as friends. "You look beautiful, Catherine. Did you really make that gown yourself?"

Embarrassed, Catherine blushed.

"I am sorry," Mary Elizabeth said. "I won't bandy that information about. I know Londoners are a bizarre lot and frown on sewing that actually produces something useful. They'll embroider pointless cushions all day, but God forbid they mend a hem."

Catherine choked on her laughter and Mary Elizabeth smiled at her. "My mother designs all her own gowns, and though she keeps three seamstresses in business, she's been known to put her hand to a dress when she truly loved it."

Young men surrounded them suddenly, and Mary Elizabeth switched tactics, talking with the company about fly-fishing in the Highlands, and how to best cast a reel. She might as well have been speaking Greek as far as Catherine was concerned, but the men who surrounded them seemed utterly enthralled.

Mr. Robert Waters stood close by, looking bored but somewhat vigilant in his role as guardian. Catherine looked about a bit, surreptitiously, but did not see Alexander anywhere. She had caught a glimpse him while she danced with Lord Marlebury, but had not seen him since. No doubt he was sequestered in some dark corner, tempting some woman or other to kiss him again.

That dark thought left her strangely furious, which was a completely inappropriate emotion for a dress ball. So she did as her grandmother would have done, and set him out of her thoughts altogether. As long as she kept her mind on the here and now, the beauty of the gowns, the light of the chandeliers, the laughter and the warmth of the company, she could forget Alexander Waters and all he stood for.

Almost.

She caught a glimpse of her mother on the edge of their group speaking with a man of fifty years or so, his graying hair cut close to his head in the latest fashion. He sported the mustache of a cavalry officer, and when he caught her eye, Catherine smiled at him.

The gentleman took her mother's arm and came to stand beside her. "Mrs. Middlebrook, if you would be so good as to introduce me to your lovely daughter."

For one hideous, sinking moment, Catherine feared that the gentleman had come to her mother only to beg the introduction, and perhaps to court Catherine herself. But she soon noticed the smile on her mother's face. The gentleman in question did not focus his gaze on Catherine, but kept it squarely on Mrs. Middlebrook.

Had she discovered the gentleman who had sent her mother the dozen red roses? As she took in the warm way her mother was gazing at the man, it quickly became clear that the identity of the gentleman had never been in question.

"Mr. Pridemore, may I present my eldest daughter, Miss Catherine Middlebrook, lately of Devon. Catherine, Mr. Josiah Pridemore, just returned home from Bombay."

"Good evening, Miss Middlebrook."

Catherine curtsied prettily, as her grandmother had taught her from the age of three, but she found she could not tear her gaze away from him. Who was this man? Was he courting her mother in earnest, or just flirting? Or was he after something altogether more nefarious?

A fierce protectiveness rose in her heart, and she kept her gaze cool as she took one step closer to her mother.

"Good evening, Mr. Pridemore. What brings you from the wilds of India all the way to Lady Jersey's ball?"

He smiled good-naturedly, and she noticed that his eyes were a dark brown, somewhat like Mr. Waters's eyes. For some reason, this did not incline her toward him in the least.

"I am here with my niece, Miss Eliza Pridemore, whom you see dancing there."

He indicated a very young girl tripping through a country-dance with an even clumsier young man at her side. The girl had a sweet face and soft, blonde hair, and she was laughing at whatever the young man had said.

"I do enjoy a bit of dancing, even at my age."

Catherine had to begrudgingly acknowledge that Mr. Pridemore had a handsome smile as he turned it on her mother. "Will you dance the next set with me, Mrs. Middlebrook?"

Her mother's face lit up, but before she could accept, Catherine said, "Perhaps you will stay with me, Mama. I am in need of a chaperone."

Mr. Pridemore did not contradict her, but she thought she saw a gleam of amusement in his dark eyes before he masked it with polite indifference. She began to think that she might have liked this man, had he not made a target of her gullible, often foolish mother.

They had no money, so he could not be a fortune hunter. Who he was and what he wanted were things Catherine would have to discover on her own somehow, before any more bunches of roses came to the house.

Her mother was not interested in her role of

chaperone, it seemed. She frowned at her daughter, though her voice was still sweet. "Catherine, you are perfectly safe in Lady Jersey's house, among this company of gentlemen. Mr. Robert Waters stands there, looking out for his sister. I have no doubt that he can look after you for the space of one dance."

The new set was forming already, and with that, her mother was gone into the circle of young people who would make up the first quadrille. Catherine opened her mouth to protest, but found her mother vanished and Lord Farleigh standing in her stead.

"Good evening, Miss Middlebrook. I have come to claim my dance, if you will have me."

She expected to be hideously embarrassed after their inappropriate financial talk that morning. But as she looked into his kind blue eyes, she felt nothing but pleasure at his company. It was not the heated joy she felt when she was with Mr. Waters, but it was enough. It might grow into something more, in time.

She chastised herself for her foolish thinking, for no man would seriously court her after discovering the depth of her family's poverty. But even after their discussion that morning, his lordship stood smiling on her. She forced her mind away from thoughts of her fear and thoughts of the future, and placed her hand gently on his arm.

"It would please me greatly to dance with you, my lord."

"The pleasure, and the honor, is mine."

She let her feet carry her into the music then, and found herself smiling as Lord Farleigh led her into the dance.

Nineteen

ALEXANDER WATCHED AS THAT PALE-FACED FOP, LORD Somebody-Or-Other, led Catherine out among the dancers. He had not cared greatly when he saw the other young men dance with his girl, some of whom were too young to know what to do with a woman, much less an angel, were they to find themselves alone with her. But while Lord Somebody-Or-Other might be a bloodless Englishman, he was a man.

Alex cursed under his breath as he watched his angel's face light up at the other man's nearness. He stared the couple down, but neither acknowledged his presence, holding up the same pillar as he had done for the last hour or more. He saw Mary Elizabeth gallop by with her latest suitor in tow, for his sister did not seem to realize that it was appropriate for the gentleman to lead, even in a quadrille.

When the interminable music ended, Alexander shifted his gaze, expecting Lord What's-It to abandon his angel for greener, wealthier pastures. But even as he watched, his lordship did not remove himself from Catherine's side, save to fetch her a glass of punch.

The supper waltz finally struck, and Alexander stalked to her side, cutting a swath through the passel of fops and dandies that filled Lady Jersey's ballroom. They cleared a path for him at once, and stared after him, as he stood head and shoulders above most of them. All save for Lord Whose-It, who faced him with cool aplomb from his angel's side.

"Good evening," Lord Something-Or-Other said. "Mr. Waters, is it? Lately of Scotland, I believe."

"Always of Scotland, my lord." Alexander executed what he hoped was a stylish bow before turning to Catherine.

"I am come to claim my dance, Miss Middlebrook."

His angel did not answer him, but Lord Somebody-Or-Other did. "Indeed? I fear you are mistaken, my Highland friend. Miss Middlebrook has promised this dance, and her company after, to me."

Alexander turned his glare on Catherine, but when she met his eyes, he did not see triumph in their mossy-green depths. He did not find sophisticated amusement over two grown gentlemen arguing over her company. He found honest misery. He may have been angry with her, he may have been angry with himself, but he had not come to the ball to make her miserable. He did not want her to be made unhappy by him or by his actions, there or anywhere.

He recalled his mother's firm hand, and his father's firm birch rod on his backside, the two things that had raised him from a hellion into a man. He drew on his upbringing, and reminded himself that he was a gentleman.

"Forgive the intrusion," was all Alex said. "I must have been mistaken."

Catherine still did not speak, but she looked less wretched. She looked instead a little misty, and he prayed that she would not cry there in front of all those English. He should leave her alone for the rest of the night, leave her in peace among her own kind. But there seemed to be some kind of entreaty buried in the green of her eyes. She seemed to be asking him for something, and he could not turn his back on her. He knew that he never would.

He watched as Lord What's-It drew her into his arms, keeping a decorous distance between them as he whirled her into the waltz. Alexander clenched one fist at his side, his impotence eating away at his spleen. He would not make a scene in front of all those people. But he would not give up yet.

It would take more than one thin lord to keep him from his angel, that night or ever.

⤞⤝

Catherine did her best to enjoy her waltz with Lord Farleigh, but her thoughts, if not her gaze, kept turning to Mr. Waters. She knew he stood on the edge of the dance floor. She knew he watched her even then, for she felt more in tune with him over half a room away than she did with Lord Farleigh who stood just beside her.

Of course, she was no musician, so no tune that might run between them signified. Lord Farleigh was her sensible—most likely her only—choice. His decision to dance with her twice in company suggested that in spite of their earlier, ill-bred conversation, he was still intent on wooing her.

She did not give in to hope. She had promised

herself that for this one night, she would not think of the morrow, and of all the dangers it brought. Still, the two men who pursued her remained strange mysteries to her, mysteries she could not solve. As she whirled in the arms of one man while feeling the gaze of another, she would not try. Let her enjoy the new sensation of being sought by two handsome gentlemen and think about the future tomorrow.

Lord Farleigh made polite conversation about the company and the music as he led her in to supper. There was no formal dining that night, but a great buffet set up where all comers might serve themselves, and seat themselves where they liked among the round tables scattered throughout Lady Jersey's usually formal dining room.

Catherine was grateful for the reprieve from the usual promenade into dinner, in which everyone took his position as his rank dictated. She had read of such things, and her grandmother had drilled her on proper etiquette to exercise at such a time, but she did not trust herself to follow through. Her mother would have been no help, so she simply said a prayer of gratitude and sat where Lord Farleigh placed her while he went to fetch her a plate.

"So you've changed your tastes from strapping Scots to foppish Englishmen in the space of twelve hours."

Catherine did not have to turn to her left to see who spoke to her. She would have known that malmsey-sweet, hot-honeyed voice anywhere.

"I don't know what you mean, Mr. Waters."

"I think you do." He touched her hand once, very lightly, and she turned to face him. He was wearing his black leather gloves again, though the rest of the company wore white gloves of cotton. He seemed always ready to stand out, wanting always to set himself apart wherever he was. She wondered if he was like that in his homeland too, or if he just reacted badly to London society by constantly wanting to be elsewhere.

Though it seemed that night, as his dark eyes devoured her, he did not wish himself anywhere but at her side.

Blast the man.

"Does your fine young Lord What's-It know I had my hands on your person this morning?"

Catherine glared at him. "The gentleman's name is Lord Farleigh. And I do not know of what you speak."

Lord Farleigh appeared at her side then, a plate in each hand. A footman followed with two cups of watered wine. "Good evening, Mr. Waters. You seem to have lost your way. The buffet table is over there. I am sure this fine gentleman can escort you, if you cannot find repast on your own."

Catherine lowered her eyes to the wineglass the footman had set in front of her. Refusing for the moment to look at either man, she sipped at it. If only it were the magic elixir Mary Elizabeth had given her the day before. She could use a taste of oblivion.

"I find I am not hungry," Mr. Waters said. "I think there is plenty of repast for any man right here."

Catherine blushed deeply, then sneaked a look at Lord Farleigh to see if he would simply walk off and leave her in disgust. But it seemed he was the only man among the company who did not feel the need to give the man beside her a wide berth.

Instead of reacting with anger or any sign of displeasure, Lord Farleigh simply shrugged. "Suit yourself. But Lady Jersey's cook has outdone herself this night."

He sat beside her as if Mr. Waters were not even there. "Will you try a bit of this braised quail, Miss Middlebrook? I believe her cook is known for it."

"I thank you, my lord." Catherine took up her gold-pronged fork and sampled it. It was very good. The taste was well spiced, though as she swallowed, the bit of fowl stuck in her dry throat. She drank more wine, and smiled when a passing footman refilled her glass. She drank a bit more wine, and felt a tiny touch of warmth begin to pervade her being.

She knew she should drink no more. Grandmother had warned her away from too much wine, especially at a party, where a young lady might easily make a cake of herself. But she felt a touch of peace and happy warmth from what little she had already taken. Suddenly, being attended on both sides by two attractive men no longer seemed like a burden. "Well, Mr. Waters, you might as well go and fetch yourself a plate," she said. "I like you well enough, but I will not allow you to eat off mine."

Her Highlander laughed then, a low rumble in his chest that she seemed to feel deep in her own body. She ignored her body's response to him and smiled politely, including Lord Farleigh in her regard. Both men watched her as cats might watch a promising mouse hole. Being the focus of such masculine attention made her want to laugh out loud. Instead, she simply ate another bite of quail.

"I will keep your place for you, if you're worried that another gentleman might come to my side and take it."

It was Lord Farleigh's turn to laugh then, and she smiled at him warmly. She could indulge herself by encouraging him without seeming too forward, for his intentions were honest. When she caught the heat from Mr. Waters's dark gaze, she had to confess that she had no idea what his intentions were. Perhaps that was a small part of his attraction, the fact that he simply made no sense, like a puzzle she wished to solve.

She dismissed such a notion at once. She had no time for puzzles or their elusive solutions. She had only this one night to enjoy herself, after all. Tonight, she would eat, drink, and dance.

If two delightful young men intended to spend the evening at her side as she did so, so much the better.

"I will find myself a bit of that quail, Miss Middlebrook. But I hold you to your word. Keep my place."

"As I hold you to yours, Mr. Waters." She sharpened her gaze upon him, and watched as he seemed to gleam with pleasure under it. Of course, that might have simply been the warmth of the wine.

"You hold all gentlemen to their word, I hope, Miss Middlebrook," Lord Farleigh said as Mr. Waters made his way through a crowd of ladies to the buffet. Each woman seemed intent on catching his eye and turning the heat of his gaze on themselves. Many of them went so far as to speak with him as he passed. Catherine saw him smile at each of them, speaking to more than one longer than she would have liked.

She had to stop being a fool. Mr. Waters was a free man who could do as he pleased. He owed her nothing. Just as she owed him nothing in return.

She turned to Lord Farleigh and smiled. "My lord, I find this quail to be braised to perfection. Do you think the cook might be persuaded to part with the recipe?"

Lord Farleigh laughed. "I think she guards all of her recipes with her life, but perhaps I might persuade Lady Jersey to intervene. Would your cook take direction coming from another?"

"I believe she would," Catherine answered. "Though honestly it has never before come up. Always, in our kitchen, Cook has been the teacher and I, the pupil."

Catherine drank a bit more of her wine, smiling down into the glass. She must find out what vintage it was. Perhaps it was something scandalous, like a vintage from France. Somehow the thought made the drink taste even finer.

"You cook?" Lord Farleigh asked. He seemed surprised, if not shocked. Catherine remembered suddenly that most well-bred young ladies did not know how to boil water.

"Well," she said, "my grandmother believes in a woman holding practical skills. She does not approve of an ignorant lady of the manor, but told me that before I ask a servant to do something, I must know how to do it myself, and do it properly."

"Very wise."

She could not tell whether or not Lord Farleigh was simply being polite, but as she finished her second glass of wine, she found that she did not care.

"Is your grandmother Scottish, by any chance?"

Mr. Waters had seated himself again on her left, taking off his leather gloves long enough to cut into his own quail braised with honeyed lavender. He did not savor his food but ate as a military man might, as if it might be taken from him at any moment. Or as if he might be called on to defend the house from invaders, and needed fuel for the fight.

What was it about Alexander Waters that always made her think of fighting? Perhaps it was because he was so large—or perhaps because she always felt safe with him, whatever the odd circumstances. She remembered the vow he had made to protect her, even from himself, as he was dressing her knife wound. No matter how vexing he sometimes was, Mr. Waters would stand for her, and by her, should trouble ever rise.

She turned to look at Lord Farleigh. He was the kind of man who would hire men to guard her, instead of defending her himself. While this was sensible, and gentlemanly, she found herself vaguely dissatisfied by the notion.

She realized then how irrational she was being and resolved to switch from wine to lemonade.

"Do you mean to insult me, Mr. Waters?" she asked.

"Indeed, I do not," he answered. "To have a Scottish grandmother is the highest compliment."

She laughed and found herself filled with joyful well-being, a calm that even encompassed her Highlander.

"Forgive my impertinence, Mr. Waters. I am sure the Scots are a fine people."

"Some of them are. But we have more than one fine dancer among us. May I take you for a turn around the floor, Miss Middlebrook? I believe the second quadrille is about to begin."

She looked to Lord Farleigh as if for permission, but he was not her chaperone, merely her dinner companion and perhaps, if she were very lucky, the companion of her future life. But she had danced twice with him already and could not dance with him a third time, not even if they had been engaged. Still, she looked to him. She felt Mr. Waters stiffen beside her, but she ignored him.

Lord Farleigh, as ever, was the soul of gentlemanly courtesy. "I do hope that you will partake of a slice of cake with me upon your return, Miss Middlebrook. Lady Jersey's chocolate torte is a wonder not to be missed."

Catherine smiled at him. He always sought to make her life easier. What a lovely quality to find in a man. Why had her grandmother not added that quality to the list of a future husband's attributes, along with tolerable good looks and a decent income?

"It would be my pleasure, my lord. I am quite taken with chocolate in all of its forms."

"I will wait for you here then."

Mr. Waters must have heard enough, for he stood, taking her arm, and drawing her to her feet as well. He bowed stiffly from the neck to Lord Farleigh, who offered him a similar bow. For a moment, she feared his lordship would not stand to see them go and offer insult both to her and to her companion, but he bowed to her as he gained his feet, focusing his sole attention on her.

"I do hope you enjoy your dance, in spite of your partner."

Catherine did not know how to politely reply to that, but as Mr. Waters practically dragged her onto the dance floor, she found that she did not have to speak.

Twenty

"GOD'S TEETH, BUT THAT MAN IS AN ASS." ALEX thought he spoke under his breath low enough for his angel not to hear him, but from the glare she tossed his way, she had clearly heard every word.

"Language, Mr. Waters. If you please."

Alex forced himself to smile. He would be charming and reclaim Catherine's full attention, pale fops be damned. "I beg your pardon, Catherine. I am not fond of the shift in your taste in men."

"I am here with you, am I not? And do not call me Catherine."

His smile was genuine then as he looked down at her sweet lips pursed in displeasure. If he could get her alone for the space of five minutes, he could have her smiling again. Well, perhaps not smiling, but definitely sighing and clinging to him.

The fantasy was broken as they were separated by the motion of the dance. He turned his smile on the lady to his right as he drew her through the steps and helped her back to her original partner. He saw Catherine looking at the other man, some boy Mary

Elizabeth had danced with earlier, with undisguised pleasure. The boy looked as if he had been poleaxed. Another conquest for her then. At least he would not have to fight that one off. The boy would run if he only raised an eyebrow at him.

It seemed Lord Farleigh of Who-Knows-Where would not be as accommodating.

But Alex had his hands on his angel again, and this time, he would not let her go. Instead of taking her back into the dining room when the dance ended, he drew her behind a potted palm, which Lady Jersey had kindly set up to block various drafts and to give lovers a place to converse in semi-privacy. Of course, Catherine was not his lover. Yet.

He did not know where that dastardly thought had come from, save perhaps from the rose scent of her hair. He took in the faint shape of her body beneath the modest gown she no doubt had sewn herself, and he wanted her more than he had wanted any woman, experienced courtesan, widow, or bored wife. Pearls gleamed in the soft curls of her hair, and one pearl nestled, not between her breasts, but in the hollow of her throat. If she were his, he would buy her a longer chain and leave the pearl to dangle between her glorious breasts while he ravished her from above. The very thought made him lose his breath.

"I must return to Lord Farleigh," she said. She tried to get around him and leave him flat, but he blocked her with his body.

She drew back from him, her gloved hands coming up to touch his shoulders for the briefest moment, as soft as a butterfly's wings. She did not put her hands behind her back in an effort not to touch him, but left them at her sides. He felt like a villain, and could almost hear his father's sharp bark in his ear, ordering him to stand down. He ignored the teachings of his youth, and his own sense of fair play, and he stepped closer to her, pressing her back against the plaster wall behind her.

"We did not finish our discussion from this morning."

"Indeed we did." Her breath was coming short, as his was. It took all of Alex's willpower not to stare down at her breasts as they rose, almost touching his chest. The two of them were hidden from the room for now, but they could not stay hidden for long. Still, the scent of her lingered like an aphrodisiac. He did not know how he was going to let her go.

"If we were in the Highlands," he said, "I would simply carry you out of here."

Her green eyes were bright with desire, though she no doubt did not understand what that was, nor what to do with it. He would give his soul, and all his tomorrows, to be the one to teach her.

"We do not condone kidnapping in London."

"More's the pity."

He stepped back then, and gave her room to breathe. He offered her his arm. "I will escort you back to your Englishman."

She looked shocked, and more than a little disappointed. "You will?"

He did not reveal his pleasure, but kept his face guarded and neutral. Still, within his breast, his soul was singing. She would be his, come hell or high water.

"It is where you wish to go, is it not?"

She sounded less certain, but she answered at once. "Yes."

"Then that is where I will take you. But I will apologize to you properly. I feel it is only fair to warn you."

She smiled a little at him as he led her back into the ballroom. No one had noticed their disappearance save Lady Jersey, who would say nothing to besmirch a young girl's reputation. For all her faults, his old lover was fair, and often kind.

Before he could return Catherine to the English fop she seemed to fancy, Mrs. Angel descended on them like a whirling dervish.

"Margaret has taken ill!" Mrs. Angel said without preamble. Catherine turned pale at hearing this, and Alex placed a hand over hers to shore her up. She did not seem to notice it, but she leaned on him.

"Ill? Margaret? She was fine when we left."

"A sudden fever. Mrs. Beam sent word."

"Then we must go at once."

Before Catherine could head for the door, Mrs. Angel held up one hand. "No, no my dear. There is no need for your evening to be cut short. I will leave you in the capable care of the Waters family. Mr. Pridemore will see me home."

"But what about our carriage?" his angel asked.

Her mother pursed her lips as if in thought, and Alex started to see which way the wind was blowing. "That is a conundrum. Hmmm... I wish we had a fine, capable man here to advise us."

Catherine frowned at her mother's obvious bid for sympathy, but before she could speak, Alex did—to test the prevailing winds and to confirm his suspicions.

"If it would be convenient, Mrs. Middlebrook, it would be my honor to see Catherine cared for and to convey your carriage home."

Catherine opened her mouth, doubtless to protest, but before she could, Mrs. Angel smiled as if he had solved all the world's ills and thrown a barley cake into the bargain.

"Mr. Waters, that would be perfect. We would be ever so grateful if you might assist the family in this way."

Alex bowed and Catherine's eyes narrowed as she took in her mother and him both. But before she could cry foul—as indeed, foul it was—Lord Namby-Pamby stepped into the group. "May I be of any assistance, Mrs. Middlebrook?"

"Oh, my lord, you are too kind." Mrs. Angel fell short of fawning over the fop, but only just. Clearly she was hedging her bets where her daughter's suitors were concerned. "If you would assist me in finding Mr. Pridemore... I fear I have lost him in all this crush. This to-do has overtaxed my nerves."

"Of course, Mrs. Middlebrook." Lord Namby cast his eyes toward Catherine, who smiled at him valiantly. "You will be all right?" he asked her, as if she stood not in a London ballroom but on a frozen tundra with none to aid her. Alex ground his teeth.

"The Waters family is kind enough to see me home. They are great friends of my mother and sister."

"Friends of the family, you say?" Lord Pamby eyed Alex with a jaundiced eye.

"Practically cousins," Catherine said. Alex heard the desperate tone in her voice, and spoke to smooth it over.

"My brother, sister, and I will see to Miss Middlebrook, if you would be so good as to assist her mother."

Alex hoped that the fop had not heard of the carriage that needed tending. If he knew of Alex's intentions to take her home in a closed carriage, alone, he would not move from her side. Alex was banking on the fact that Lord Namby did not suspect, just as Catherine did not.

A man's intentions were his own business, after all. Lord Pamby must have seen the nervousness reflected in Catherine's eyes, for he bowed to her. "I will call on you tomorrow, Miss Middlebrook. Please give my regards to your other two Scottish cousins as they see you safe home."

"Thank you, my lord. I will."

The fop's gaze lingered on her as if she belonged to him already, as if Alex and her mother did not stand just by. He seemed to want to say something else, but could not in company. Alex did not like the look of that, nor the look his angel gave the fop in return, as if he were a friend she leaned on, a man she could look to in times of trouble.

He wanted to be that man, damn it. He wanted her to look at him that way.

He heard his brother Ian's voice in his head: *Then stop acting like a horse's ass, and behave like a gentleman.*

Mrs. Middlebrook led Lord Namby away then, still giving a good impression of worry over her youngest daughter. As soon as they were lost in the crowd, Alex looked over the ballroom until he found Robbie leaning against a pillar, looking as if he wished for death.

He caught his brother's eye, and gave their signal

from childhood that meant, *Run. The English Watch is nigh*.

Of course, they were not raising Cain in Edinburgh but were in London, surrounded by nothing but English, but the signal still served. Robbie moved fast, wresting Mary Elizabeth away from whatever young suitor she was talking to, and then moving for the door. Alex did not wait but drew Catherine out with him.

He managed to slip by Lady Jersey while she was chatting with another very young man. Perhaps someone she was nicely acquainted with, as she and Alex once had been, for in that moment, she seemed to have eyes for no one but him. Thank God for small blessings.

"Do you think she is very ill?" Catherine asked him as they waited for her carriage to be brought around.

Alex had almost forgotten her sister altogether. Surely her mother could have come up with a different ruse, though he could not argue with the results.

"I am sure you will find her almost completely recovered by the time you are home," was all he said.

He saw Robbie bring Mary Elizabeth into the grand entrance hall, but he did not wait any longer than that. If he let the girls speak to each other, Mary Elizabeth would shout the house down and everyone within a mile would know that he was bringing Catherine Middlebrook home. Alone. Not the done thing.

Though of course, that wasn't going to stop him from doing it.

Twenty-one

CATHERINE SLIPPED INTO HER FAMILY'S CARRIAGE quickly, before anyone could notice that her mother was not there. Mr. Waters slid in beside her, and the conveyance rolled off into the night.

So she found herself alone, with a man, in the dark, in a closed carriage. The wheels turned quite slowly, as their conveyance had not joined traffic that was passing by. Catherine wondered if she should simply slide out of the door and make her own way home. As scandalous as the thought was, she was not certain she could trust herself to stay. The heady scent of Alexander Waters's skin was almost overwhelming.

Before she could talk herself into leaping to safety for her virtue's sake, Alex's hot-honey voice reached out and surrounded her. "Come here, Catherine."

"No," she said automatically.

"I have not apologized to your properly for my earlier behavior. Come here."

"No, thank you," she answered primly. "You might apologize to me while I am sitting just here."

He laughed, and the low sound seemed to travel all

across her nerves, down her spine, and into her belly, where it rested, heating her body as if stoking a furnace. She swallowed hard, and found her mouth still dry.

He did not speak again but moved over to her side of the carriage, blocking her in with his body so that she was trapped between him and the door. She knew she should ask him to move back. If she pressed the issue, she was certain that he would obey her. But the heat of his body was like Mary Elizabeth's magic elixir. It seemed to rob her of her good judgment and her better reasoning. It left her instead with a hunger for something like chocolate cake.

She had missed dessert altogether. Perhaps what Alexander Waters offered her now was something altogether sweeter.

He kissed her then, and she let him. He did not ask permission, but leaned close, plundering her lips like the ravaging, pillaging Northman that he was. She did not push him away, as she knew very well she should. Instead, with the last bit of reason left to her, she took off her cotton gloves and threaded her hands into his long, dark hair.

He did not hesitate, but seemed to take her fingertips massaging his scalp for surrender.

His mouth opened over hers, and his tongue slipped past her defenses, not that she had many left to spare. She leaned against him, and felt the delicious pressure of his chest against her breasts, the heat of his breath on her skin as he pulled back a little, only to trail his lips down her temple, to her cheek, to her throat. He stopped at the top of her bodice, and she pressed against him harder, willing him to touch her beneath it.

She did not consider what a shocking thing such an idea was. She was in a carriage in the dark of night, abandoned to bliss. She would sort out all concerns for the rest later. Tomorrow. Tomorrow seemed soon enough. For now, she would feast.

Except that she could not, for Alex took his delectable lips away from her altogether.

"I thought you were apologizing," she said.

His voice was harsh with his lost breath. He clutched her close, his hands hard on her arm and on her waist. His black leather gloves clenched her gown just above her hip, and the fine silk would be terribly wrinkled. Not that she cared.

"I was apologizing," he said, sounding like someone else altogether. "I am apologizing."

Catherine felt his weakness as he leaned against her. It seemed he was fighting himself. No doubt he wanted to kiss her again, as much as she wished him to, if not more. For the first time in her life, she felt a heady sense of power. She was not the only one brought low by her obsession with him. It seemed that her hulking Highlander was just as obsessed with her.

"Then why do you stop?"

"I am reminding myself that I am a gentleman."

Catherine opened her mouth to argue with him, but save for kissing her twice, he had behaved like a gentleman in all their dealings. He had always been kind, always proper, except for occasionally teasing her. What on earth were they doing together in a closed carriage in the dead of night if he was going to invoke honor in the dark?

She found herself disgruntled. It was an inconvenient time for a surge of conscience. Though as she sat there, she felt her own scruples rising up to taunt her. Her grandmother had not raised her to behave in such a manner.

She sighed and, at last, pushed Alexander Waters away. "You are right, of course. You cannot kiss me, and I cannot let you. It is unseemly, and beneath both of us."

He smiled a little, and did not let her go far. His arms were still around her, though now she had more room to breathe.

"I do not agree."

She opened her mouth to protest, and he kissed her quickly, as if to stifle all argument. She knew she should be angry, but her thoughts were addled by the taste of him lingering on her lips.

He continued as if she had not tried to speak. "Our kisses are a beautiful thing, filled with magic."

She almost spoke again, but he kissed her swiftly, and all she could think of was how happy she was that he was touching her.

Once he had regained her silence, he went on. "You are a lovely girl, and untutored in the ways of the world, as all girls should be, so you must trust me when I tell you—kisses like ours are gifts from the gods, gifts to be savored."

"I have no truck with *the gods* as you put it, or any other pagan nonsense," she said. Her voice was not as stern as she meant it to be. In her own ears, she sounded a bit breathless. She was surprised he had let her speak at all. She'd expected him to kiss her again, but this time, he did not.

"It is a figure of speech. Trust me when I tell you that things between a woman and a man are rarely as they are between us."

"I do not want to hear of your other conquests. I am not, nor will I ever be, one of them." Catherine should have felt affronted that he mentioned other women only seconds after kissing her senseless, but his arms were still about her in the most delicious, warm way, and the sway of the carriage brought their bodies together in glancing blows. If only their journey to her home might last forever.

In that moment, the carriage stopped, and she sighed. It seemed her stolen moment was already over.

"You are not a conquest," Alexander said, still holding her close in the dark, though Jim the footman was bound to come and open the carriage door at any moment. "You are unique in all the world. You must always remember that."

"*Unique* sounds like another word for strange," she said.

"Please believe me when I tell you it is not."

He moved away from her, and she felt suddenly bereft, as if someone had come upon her in her warm bed in winter and ripped her down quilt away. Jim did open the door then, and Alexander climbed out ahead of her to help her down.

She did not speak as he escorted her into her house, his hand solicitously at her elbow. He kept a decorous distance between them. No one looking at them could have believed that only minutes before, she had been in his arms—save for his hair, which had fallen from its ribbon when she'd tugged on it. His long, dark hair now fell around his shoulders in a curtain of black.

She knew that his hair was actually dark brown, but in the light of the candle in the hallway, it looked like a pirate's locks falling around his face.

Jim was used to visits from Mr. Waters by this time, for he closed the front door behind them and left them alone. She needed to remind him to stay present until dismissed, but then Alex's lips were on hers again, and she could think of nothing, not even of how to breathe.

"Have I apologized enough?" he asked.

She smiled up at him, sliding her fingers through the dark mass of his hair. "You might apologize one more time, I think. I am not certain I am completely mollified as of yet."

He smiled back, and a delicious joy curled in her belly, as if their kissing was a game, a game that would never hurt her, a game both he and she might win. He pressed his lips to her one last time, and this time his mouth opened over hers, and she responded, letting him plunder her like a conqueror. She shivered against him, but before she could press herself too close and feel the bliss of his body tight against hers, he pulled away.

"I am a gentleman, and you are a lady, and you are going upstairs to bed."

She wondered why he repeated the obvious. "Yes," she said. "All true. I am not sure why you state it."

"Trust me again when I tell you that to say the words out loud in this moment is necessary."

"You should leave me alone," Catherine said. "You have said you will not marry, and I must marry by summer. We are at odds, Mr. Waters, in everything but this." She pressed against him once, and he caught his breath. She thought for a moment that he might drag her hard against him, but she stepped back before he could.

For the second time that day, his black-gloved hands reached for her, but closed on nothing but air.

"I must see you again," he said,

She swallowed hard, the taste of him still sweet in her mouth. She straightened her shoulders, and told herself to stand firm—both for him, and for herself. "No doubt you will. But this sort of nonsense must cease as of this moment."

"So you keep saying, Miss Middlebrook. And yet, when I touch you, your body tells another tale."

She was shocked that he was so indelicate as to mention her body. Even so, his words brought a shiver along her spine. She wondered at herself, that it was a shiver of pleasure.

"That may be, Mr. Waters, but I stand firm. I am for marriage, and you are not, and there is an end on it."

"Let me woo you."

"To what end?"

"Let us discover that when we come to it."

She scoffed, and opened the door for him. "Good night, Mr. Waters."

"Please, Catherine. At least make this concession. Don't decide on the Englishman until you have spoken again with me."

"I think it best if we forget about each other altogether. You must leave me be, Mr. Waters. We must both get on with our lives."

Though her heart twisted in her chest at her own words, she felt grown-up and sensible saying them.

They were what her grandmother would counsel her to say, if she had been there.

Her heart rose in joy at his answer.

"I will do anything for you, Catherine, but not that."

"Would you indeed?"

"Yes."

The next words were out of her mouth before she thought. "Then discover for me who Mr. Pridemore is and what he wants with my mother."

"You would have me spy for you?"

"Yes."

They faced each other in the dark hallway, and for a moment she thought he might reach for her again. She tensed, though she was not sure if she would flee his arms or run to them. But she did not have the choice, for instead of touching her, he bowed low, his hair falling across his face, so that he had to toss it back over one shoulder as he stood again.

"So be it, Miss Middlebrook. I will do as you ask. But do not marry that Englishman. Not yet."

"He has not yet asked," she said.

Alex kissed her, swift and sure, his mouth like a memory of the pleasure she had found with him in her mother's coach. Then he was gone, off into the London night. She stood staring after him like a fool, until she recalled her good sense long enough to shut the door behind him.

Twenty-two

CATHERINE TRIED VALIANTLY TO SET MR. WATERS OUT of her mind, and mostly failed. He was a puzzle, an enigma. He seemed very forthright and honorable on one hand, but still refused to court her in truth. All the while, his kisses made her forget her reason.

It was a conundrum.

She slept tolerably well, by some strange miracle, and went downstairs to breakfast. Her mother, fresh as a daisy, peered at her from over her demitasse cup of chocolate. Margaret, completely recovered, sat beside her, eating her weight in breakfast bread and bacon. Catherine did not comment on the expensive fare, but focused on the events of the night before.

"Good morning, Mama. Good morning, Margaret. Are you feeling better, Maggie?"

Her sister blinked at her from behind the giant slice of toast and jam she held aloft. She took a huge bite, chewed, and swallowed before she said, "I am quite well, Catherine. I thank you. How are you?"

"You are not feverish? Not ill at all?"

Margaret, always fair, tilted her head to one side

as she thought seriously about her answer. She took another huge, meditative bite of her bread. "Yes," she said. "I am quite well. I would like a pony, however."

"We will see about getting you one, my sweet, so that you might ride in the park."

Catherine glared at her mother but did not contradict her. How they would find the funds to purchase said pony, much less feed it, along with all their other cattle, was something her mother would have no answer for. She pushed aside all thoughts of her mother lying outright the night before simply to leave her alone with Mr. Waters. Mama liked the Highlander, which was well and good, though Lord Farleigh was the only true contender for her hand, if not her heart.

It was best not to think of that inconvenient organ. Nor of the heat in Alexander Waters's eyes that always raised an answering heat under her skin. Such things must be set aside, and realities like mortgages must take their place.

"Mother, I have an appointment with Mr. Philips at ten of the clock this morning. Will you be joining us?"

"Ten of the clock? Good heavens, my dear, that is a bare hour and a half away. I could not possibly be ready in that space of time. My hair alone takes an hour, once my maid has set it. Then I must select a proper gown. I could not be seen in the City any time before two in the afternoon, at the very earliest."

Her mother reached for a scone, and covered it with clotted cream.

"But I don't mean to spoil your fun, my dear. If you wish to speak with tiresome people like our

solicitor about trifles, you must go on and do so. Take
Jim with you. He will keep you safe." Her mother's
eyes widened and her expression turned frighteningly
innocent. "Unless, of course, you wish to bring Mr.
Waters with you. He would make a fine addition to
any law office, no matter how temporarily. It would
do those pale-faced clerks some good to see a real man
in their midst."

Catherine sighed heavily, feeling the cloak of
martyrdom fall on her shoulders. She straightened
her back, and shrugged it off. "No, Mama. I will not
involve Mr. Waters in our financial peccadilloes. I will
take Jim with me, if you are certain you will not go."

Mrs. Middlebrook waved one hand. "The Waterses
will be joining us for tea in the garden this afternoon
in any case. Be sure you're back by three."

Catherine finished her tea and toast, and stood. She
needed to call for the carriage and collect Jim.

"Watch out for pickpockets," her mother said
cheerfully, waving at her with her demitasse cup.

"Excellent advice, Mama. I will endeavor to avoid
them."

Her mother smiled brightly at her, and Catherine
got out of the room before she said something she
knew she would regret.

⁂

Traffic was quite fierce, but John Coachman made it
to Lincoln's Inn with ten minutes to spare. Catherine
was shown at once into Mr. Philips's office, while Jim
waited outside in his under butler's finest, standing and
staring among the clerks. She wondered who would

be answering their front door in his absence. Perhaps Margaret would see to it, or her mother herself.

The thought of that was almost enough to cheer her, but the stones in the pit of her stomach reminded her vividly why she was there. She did not hesitate, but did as grandmother might do, and plunged right in.

"Mr. Philips, as you know, I have come to discuss the mortgage my mother took out against our Devon property. I must know, is it a considerable sum?"

Mr. Philips cleared his throat, moving papers about the surface of his desk in an effort not to meet her gaze. She kept her eyes firmly on his face until he gave up and looked at her over the rims of his half spectacles.

"I'm afraid there has been a mistake," he said.

"A mistake? What do you mean?" Her heart leaped with hope and began to thump in earnest. "There is a mortgage out against our home, as your letter suggested, is there not?"

"Indeed, Miss Middlebrook, indeed. There is a mortgage. I mean to say, there was. It was paid off first thing this morning."

She felt a moment of silent elation, the joy of being freed from the threat of debtor's prison before she had ever seen inside its dreaded walls. Then her mind caught up with her heart and started whirling.

"I do not understand, Mr. Philips. My mother and I have no money to pay."

Her solicitor looked even more aggrieved, and went back to noodling with the papers that covered his desk. He rearranged them twice before he would look at her again.

"There is no question of you or your mother covering the debt," Mr. Philips said at last. His watery blue eyes peered at her from behind his glasses, and a lock of his graying hair fell across his forehead. "The debt has been discharged, with no cost to you."

"But that is impossible."

He smiled for the first time since their interview began. "Indeed, Miss Middlebrook, it is not only possible, but true. In this instance, we must simply thank our stars, and resolve to take out no further mortgages in the future."

Catherine shuddered to think of her mother doing all of this again. She had only known about the debt for a day, and her heart had suffered under the strain, along with her nerves. She prayed earnestly to God that her mother would never do such a thing again, knowing all the time that she had no way to stop her, if she chose to do so.

Perhaps she would marry well, save the family, and her mother would have no call to take out a mortgage to cover the cost of Margaret's first Season.

"If the debt is paid, may I ask by whom?"

Mr. Philips grew even more uncomfortable. This time, his papers were not enough to shield him. He rose from his desk and called for tea, which was quickly delivered in a serviceable earthenware pot. She took a cup out of politeness, and let him play mother, as it was his office.

When he handed her the sweetened cup of Assam tea with a splash of milk, she took a perfunctory sip before she asked again. "Really, Mr. Philips, I must know. Who has paid our debt?"

He met her eyes at last. "I fear the donor to your welfare wishes to remain anonymous."

Catherine felt truly sick. She set her teacup down, and tried to draw breath, but her stays seemed too tight against her ribs. She felt darkness creeping in around the edges of her vision. She ordered herself to buck up and be the man of her family, as she had been since the age of thirteen.

"We cannot accept charity of any kind, especially from an unknown source. Please thank the gentleman in question, but tell him that his money is not needed."

Mr. Philips opened his hands wide. "I am sorry, Miss Middlebrook, but it is already accomplished. The debt is already paid."

"Then we must pay it back," she said, feeling desperate as she grasped at straws.

"Forgive me again, Miss Middlebrook, for being indelicate, but I believe that you know the party in question. Indeed, the gentleman indicated to me that he has a strong interest in your family, and in caring for you and your mother for the rest of your lives."

She felt the door to her future closing then with one heavy, loud slam. She had not known how much she truly wished to bring Mr. Alexander Waters to the point of making an offer until the moment in which she knew she could never in good conscience or honor accept it.

Only one man knew about their debt, save for the man before her. Lord Farleigh had paid the mortgage, and no doubt would offer for her within the week. And she would have to accept him.

She thought of Alex, and the heat of his gloved

hand on her arm, and the other on her waist. She thought of his kisses, of how sweet they were, and of how she would never taste them again.

Tears rose in her throat, and with a great deal of difficulty, she swallowed them down. She had not realized how dearly she valued her choices about her future, as limited as they had been, until the moment when she knew they had been taken away.

The ride home was not as long as the trip to the City had been. Catherine wanted to stare out of her carriage window, but London stared back at her. She closed the leather drape and closed her eyes, willing herself to slip into the oblivion of sleep. Of course, she did not. She thought again and again of the debt that had been paid, wondering all the while how much it had been, and how she would ever be able to begin her married life in good conscience with such a thing hanging over her head.

She had heard of wealthy gentlemen settling large sums on their wives before they wed. Perhaps the debt had not been too much after all. Perhaps the purchase of her future had been at a bargain.

Catherine told herself to stop whining, even in her own mind. Lord Farleigh had made it clear that he wished to help her, and clearly, he had. The fact that she now had no other choice but to marry him was of no matter. She had never truly had any choice. Her time with Alex had simply been a stolen season, a few heated moments that had nothing at all to do with the here and now, or the time to come.

Jim handed her down from the carriage. Instead of going inside, she approached the garden gate, hoping for a little time alone among her flowers before she gave her mother the news that their debt was discharged. She touched her gloved hand to the latch, only to hear her sister shriek with mirth.

She moved quickly into the garden to find Margaret dangling from the window of her bedroom above, clinging to what looked like a hemp rope. The girl swung to and fro along the side of the house, as Mary Elizabeth Waters gave her directions from below.

"You must not make it swing so, Margaret. It is not a toy or a game but something that may well save your life. Come down at once, and let us try again."

Margaret did as she was bid, and clambered the rest of the way down until her feet rested safe on the grass. Catherine felt her throat close over any words she might have spoken. Her day had been too bizarre already, and it looked to become only more strange as it wore on.

"We came early to tea so that I might show you and your sister the use of this rope ladder. It will save your life if ever your house catches fire."

When Catherine said nothing, Mary Elizabeth talked on. "You keep it safe under your bed, and when you wake in the night to find your house ablaze, you secure it to the window frame and toss the ladder down to the ground below."

"Indeed?"

Catherine did not know what else to say. After the morning she had spent, she was simply grateful that she could speak at all.

"Will you try it?"

The look on her friend's face was so open, her smile

so genuine, that Catherine felt her sense of decorum slip away along with the rest of her reality. She had had enough of reality for one day. Let her embrace whimsy then, and take what came.

"Why not?"

Twenty-three

ALEX WATERS WAS BROUGHT INTO THE MIDDLEBROOK house through the front door. Jim did not judge him for having cornered his mistress in the foyer the night before. Alex wondered if the man noticed anything that went on under his nose. That lack of awareness was a rare and wonderful trait to be found in a servant, if it was real.

Jim released him into the back garden as if he were a hound, closing the door behind him. Alex stood, taking in the sweet scent of his angel's garden. It was three in the afternoon, and the sun was slanting gently to the west, bringing out the deep greens and golds among the grasses and flowers. The fruit trees had finished blooming, and now offered a simple light green in their branches that made him feel strangely welcome. As beautiful as his Highlands were, they were never as green as this.

Still, he felt a pang of homesickness twist in his gut like hunger. Suddenly, he wished himself home by the burn that ran cold whatever the season. He would walk there one day with his angel beside him.

He looked for her then among her kin, but did not find her. Mrs. Angel sat on a blanket beneath a greening tree, the last of its pear blossoms falling onto the lawn around her. She drank tea from a china cup, and seemed to listen with bated breath to the man who sat beside her.

Mr. Josiah Pridemore looked quite at home among the flowers and the ladies, though Alex knew him to be a man of action. A man who had helped conquer the Mughals in India, if such a brave and uncompromising people could ever truly be conquered. A man who had given up his place in the army to turn to business, where he now made a great deal of money shipping silks and spices for the East India Company. All this and more he had discovered that day. Only he had failed to acquire the knowledge his angel had sent him for—namely, what Mr. Josiah Pridemore, lately of Mumbai, wanted with Mrs. Olivia Middlebrook. Alex's contacts in shipping could not tell him that.

Alex continued to peruse the garden, taking in the company from the doorway to the house, where he had not yet been seen. His sister, no doubt abandoned among the Middlebrooks by their brother, was peering up at the house as if she would paint the shutters, calling directions to someone he could not see. He smiled. His sister was a managing baggage, but he loved her. Someday soon, he prayed to a merciful God, she would make some poor blighter a loving—if bossy—wife.

Miss Margaret stared up at the house as well, leaping up and down in excitement as she waved to whoever was doing the painting. Alex stepped out of the shadow of the doorway then, and went to his sister's side, so that he might see what amused the two girls so greatly.

As he looked up, he saw his angel swinging from a rope ladder along the side of the house.

He saw a pair of shapely calves encased in thin cotton stockings, tied at the knee with cunning pink bows. Her gown was pink, as was her bonnet. Her white cotton gloves seemed to give her some purchase against the harsh fibers of the rope. He thought to look farther up her skirts, and then remembered that he was a gentleman.

"Blessed Mother! Stay where you are, Catherine. I'll come for you!"

He ran to the rope ladder and caught the end of it, anchoring it against his body so that at least it stopped swaying. She was still twelve feet above the ground, climbing steadily down. She did not heed his voice at all nor the panic in it but continued her descent as calm as you please, until first her calves, now hidden by her gown, and then her hips, were before him. He stepped back then, his hands flexing in an effort not to touch her.

"Catherine, you can't climb rope ladders," was all he could think to say.

She turned to face him then, her sweet face pink with the effort of her descent. She smiled as bright as a summer sunrise, clearly delighted with herself. It would seem that not only young men had a taste for danger. He tried to rein in his tongue so that he would not offend her.

"Indeed I can, Mr. Waters. And indeed I shall, if I so choose. I enjoy a bit of a climb, I find. Who knew?"

"Who knew indeed? And will you climb back up again?"

She looked at him, still smiling in triumph but clearly puzzled. "Whatever for? The object is to escape a burning house, not to climb back into it. I am safe and on the ground now, and not one hair of my head singed. A successful climb."

He wanted to drag her into his arms and check the soundness of her limbs. Another, darker part of him wanted to drag her away from her family, behind a tall bush, and discover what else he might find beneath the frothy petticoats of her skirts. He could not get the sight of her knees and those pink ribbons out of his mind. That view was going to haunt him until he saw more.

He would have to marry this girl, and quickly. He had never thought anything on earth could tempt him to give up the sea, but now he had found it. He would keep this girl safe for the rest of her life. Lord Loverboy might fancy her, but he did not have the mettle to face her down, year after year, and save her from herself.

Alex Waters knew that he was man enough to do it.

The terrifying thought of marrying a woman who never listened to him, who scoffed at every word he said save when she was in his arms, did not give him pause. He was a doomed man, and only now did he accept it. Perhaps he would learn to live with the fact that she would never agree to anything he said for all their married life. Perhaps he would learn to live with the fact that despite her sweet, demure exterior, she was still a girl who scrambled out of windows onto hemp rope ladders twenty feet above the ground, and then climbed down.

His father had warned him that living with a woman was like living with the weather. A man might try to predict what she would do next, but God help him, he would most likely fail.

Alex stared down at his angel, feeling a ridiculous smile spreading across his face. He would doom himself to a life of failure then, and take what came.

Catherine saw his smile and must have noticed that something was amiss. For all her lack of worldliness, she was a clever girl. "What is it?" she asked him, as if her family and his were not standing by.

"I'll tell you later," he said, taking her elbow to steer her away from the blasted rope. He cursed the day Ian had ever taught Mary Elizabeth to climb the rigging of the family schooner. He turned on his sister then, and found Mary Elizabeth squaring her shoulders, readying herself for the tongue lashing she knew was coming.

"Mary Elizabeth Waters, what would your mother say if she knew what you'd been up to?" He heard his brogue coming into his voice, but he could not help himself. His sister responded in kind, her own accent thicker than his.

"And what business is it of hers, I ask you? Am I the one who sent my only daughter to marry among the damned English?" She blinked, and spoke for a moment to his angel. "Begging your pardon, Catherine." She turned back on him at once. "Our mother cannot have a care for me nor for what I do, or she would have kept me by her, among our people, in our homeland. Since I am here, I will do as I bloody please. And you may tell our mother that."

Mary Elizabeth stormed off then, to hide the tears that had come into her eyes. His angel turned on him like the wrath of God.

"Alex, you have made her cry! I swear, if I were your mama, I would thrash you."

His body tightened deliciously at the thought of Catherine with a whip in her hand. He set the happy image aside, for she had slipped away from him and followed his sister into the house. He sighed, and watched her go.

Alex turned to the rest of the company, only to find Mrs. Angel ignoring all that went on, her attention completely taken up with Mr. Pridemore and her tea cakes. Miss Margaret stood at his elbow, looking after where her sister had gone.

She sighed, and blinked up at him. "You had better go after her," she said.

"Mary Elizabeth?" he asked.

"No. Catherine."

The little girl turned away then and went to fetch her own tea and cakes. Alex took her advice, and followed the girls into the house.

❧

Catherine felt her face blazing with a blush, as she always did when she was caught unawares by Mr. Waters. Of course, such a thing had become a daily occurrence, so she ignored it and went to find her friend.

Mary Elizabeth had shut herself in the music room, and Jim stood outside the door, looking perplexed.

"The young lady will not answer my knock, miss. Should I bring tea and cakes?"

"Not just yet, Jim. Let me speak with her a moment. I will ring if we need you."

"Very good, miss."

Doing a wonderful impression of Giles, Jim bowed solemnly and disappeared at once.

Catherine turned and knocked on her own music room door. "Mary Elizabeth? May I come in?"

She heard a sniffle from within. "Not just now, Catherine. I am in the midst of disgracing myself. I cannot let you see me do it."

Catherine was certain she heard her friend crying, and she cursed Alex Waters in silence.

"If you like, Mary, I will thrash him for you. He is a gentleman and as such, he cannot defend himself."

She heard a watery laugh from within, which cheered her. Mary Elizabeth's brogue was so thick, it was difficult to understand her, but Catherine managed. She must be getting used to these passionate, half-wild people.

"It is not Alex's fault," Mary Elizabeth said. Or at least, that is what it sounded like. "My mama sent me packing because she is ashamed of me. It hurts my heart, but there it is."

Catherine felt tears rise in her own eyes, and she blinked them away. At least her mama loved her, as troublesome and difficult as she was.

"Your mama was wrong to send you away. But I am glad you are here. My life would be far too dull without you. You must stay and look after us, or we might all burn to death one night in our beds."

"God forbid," Mary Elizabeth said, opening the door at last.

Alex Waters spoke. "Amen."

He lurked in the hall, leaning against a false pilaster that her grandfather's architect had thought looked smart. He did not smile in his usual smug, superior way, so Catherine did not chastise him. She turned back to his sister in the doorway, and gave her a handkerchief.

"I will launder this and give it back," Mary Elizabeth said, blowing her nose loudly.

Catherine flinched at the indecorous display, but forced herself to smile. "Keep it, with my compliments. I sewed my initials and a butterfly onto it myself."

"Very pretty," Mary Elizabeth said. "Perhaps you might teach me to do that."

"I would be delighted."

Mary Elizabeth nodded to her brother, tucked her new handkerchief into her sleeve, and went back outside to find a tea cake and a sandwich. Catherine was left alone with Alex, his dark eyes boring into her where she stood. For once she did not blush, but turned and stepped into the music room. She pushed away all thoughts of Lord Farleigh, and what she owed him. She walked into the sunlit chamber, knowing that Alex would follow her.

True to himself, he did.

Twenty-four

He closed the door behind them, and for a moment, neither one of them spoke. They stood looking at one another, the heat of a flash fire rising between them. Catherine did her level best to keep her head, to keep her breathing even and her heart calm, but her breathing was quick and light, and her heart thundered in her ears like a runaway horse. She wanted to turn away from him. She wanted to touch him. She did neither. It was Alex who came to her.

He crossed the music room in three long strides and his lips were on hers in the next instant. He had to bend down to kiss her, for he was almost a foot taller than she was. Before she met him, she would have thought such an arrangement inconvenient at best, but he curled around her, succoring her, protecting her from everything in the world but himself.

He smelled delicious, as he always did, and his lips tasted of cider. She wondered where he had been before he came to her house. But then his tongue asked hers to dance, and all her thoughts fled, save for how he felt against her.

She pressed her body to his, reveling in the hard muscles of his chest and thighs against her softness. She tried to burrow closer, but did not know how. It was Alex in the end who kept a clear head. His black-gloved hands took hold of her upper arms, and he pushed her away.

"Catherine, we must stop."

She blinked up at him, all thought gone, knowing only that her prize had been taken from her. "Why?"

"It is my duty to protect you, Catherine, even from yourself. We stop here. You must trust me."

She took a deep breath and felt the thunder of her heart begin to slow, along with her breath. She ached, both in body and mind, though she did not know for what. It seemed there was a great deal she did not know about herself. A great deal it had never occurred to her to learn, save when she was in Alex's arms.

She stepped away from him then, and he let her go. She crossed to the pianoforte and picked out a small tune. She had not the passion Margaret did, but she loved music too, as an amateur might, a girl who had learned to play in the schoolroom and who would never be any good at it.

The bit of Beethoven brought her back to her good sense. She turned back to him. "I lured you in here not for kisses, but for talk."

"More's the pity," he said, shifting where he stood.

She smiled at him, for she heard the laughter in his voice. It was odd that she felt so comfortable with him. She had never dealt with a man like him before, and likely never would again. She would enjoy him for this short while, and remember him always. In so many ways, he was unique.

She felt a pang at the thought of putting him aside, as she knew she must. He stood, wearing a dark blue coat over buff trousers, his boots polished to a high sheen, though she knew he did not keep a man to tend them. His cravat was tied as all men should tie them, without fuss but with a hint of style. His dark hair was drawn back in a ribbon of blue to match his coat, and his brown eyes watched her even now, bemused, as she stood there simply taking him in. She spoke, trying to break the moment between them, and failing.

"You have news of my mother's suitor," she said.

"I would rather speak of us," he answered.

She raised one hand, and felt her heart clench. She knew what she owed to Lord Farleigh. She also knew what she owed to herself, and to Alex. But she could not speak openly of it. She knew she could not bear it.

"No. Please. Not today."

"What better time than now?" He stepped toward her, and she backed away, almost stumbling over the piano bench. He saw she was in earnest then, and the smile drifted away from his face. He took her in, as if trying to read the thoughts behind her eyes. She was grateful that he could not.

"Please, Alex. What of my mother?"

He sighed, staring at her for one long moment—a moment during which she wondered if he would hold his knowledge hostage until she dealt first with him. But he was a gentleman, if occasionally a rascal, and he gave her what she sought.

"I fear I know very little. He is a military man who has now turned to trade, and has done quite well. He deals openly and honestly with all, which bodes well.

He has made a great success of it. Some might call him a nabob."

Catherine smiled at that outlandish term, but would not be distracted. "And what of his intentions toward my mother?"

"Those I do not know."

"Did you ask his butler? His valet?"

Alex laughed outright at that. "Did I ask his servants to spy for me? No, indeed, Catherine, I did not."

"But servants know everything. You would have to pay them, of course. If it is a question of money, I can give you some of my allowance—"

He raised one hand before she could finish her thought. His eyes darkened, along with his countenance, and a strange thrill ran through her. For a moment, he looked almost dangerous. For some reason, that danger did not frighten her, but made her think of delicious things, like hot chocolate, and his kisses.

"I do not take money from women. I certainly would not take money from you."

Catherine felt an odd buzz of excitement underneath her skin, something akin to the way she felt when he touched her. She had to stop herself from smiling for fear of offending him, and perhaps irritating him more. She kept her tone even and her voice cool, though she feared her eyes were dancing.

"And your honor will not allow you to purchase information from servants," she said.

"No, Catherine. Not even for you."

She felt her heart lift then, though she had no idea why. There was something beautiful about this man that went far beyond his good looks, far beyond his soft, dark hair, wide shoulders, and dark brown eyes—all the things that had first drawn her to him. He was a man of honor in a world without, and she found that she loved that about him, more than she would have thought possible.

She loved him.

It did not matter that she could not keep him. Her love was real, and a blessing to her, as all love was.

She felt tears rise in her eyes. She blinked them away.

"You are a good man, Alexander Waters," she said, her heart aching but, at the same time, filled with joy.

He looked bemused, befuddled at the sudden change of topic. He stared at her, as if once more trying to see behind her eyes to her thoughts. She knew that he could not.

"We must talk, Catherine. And not about your mother and Mr. Pridemore."

"About us?" Catherine asked, though she knew the answer to her question already.

"Yes."

"Not today," she said again.

"Tomorrow then?"

"I don't know."

"I must speak with you soon, Catherine."

She did not answer him this time, but crossed the room instead. He followed her and stopped close as he met her in the doorway. She took in the sweetness of his scent, wishing that she might press her face to his linen, that she might tell him her troubles. But she knew that she could tell him nothing. For his part, Alex kept watching her as if he might discover her thoughts among the curves of her face. She knew he would not find them there, or anywhere. They would have to talk, she owed him that much, but not that day. She leaned up, straining on her tiptoes, and kissed his cheek.

"I am going upstairs now," was all she said. "Please give my regards to your sister, and tell her that I will see her tomorrow."

"Tomorrow?"

"We are picnicking in Richmond Park. I believe you are invited."

Twenty-five

SHE LEFT HIM FLAT. SHE DID NOT EVEN GO BACK OUTSIDE to say good-bye to his sister. He watched from her marble foyer as she climbed the stairs, most likely to go to her room.

The room where she slept.

The room that had her bed in it.

As he began to fantasize about whether or not such a room was done in lace or silk, muslin or lawn, he shook himself and went outside into the back garden. Perhaps one day, once they were married, they would come back to this house at the holidays, say, and sleep in that room. He would know then what it looked like. For now, his speculation was pointless and only served to give him pain.

He shifted in discomfort, and strode outdoors to collect his sister.

Mary Elizabeth, fully recovered from her tears over their mother, was sitting with Mrs. Angel and Mr. Pridemore, regaling the company with tales of fishing in the Highlands. As Alex towered over them, he heard Pridemore ask, "And must the line be so long, then?"

"Indeed it must," Mary Elizabeth answered. "The trick is to make the fish at home, until the barb is sunk and you have him in your grasp."

"Then you reel him in," Mr. Pridemore said.

Mrs. Angel clearly could not care less about fly-fishing, but she seemed to be listening to whatever he said, simply because he said it. Margaret was not listening to the adults talk, but was running through the grass, chasing butterflies. He knew that she would have more space to do so in Richmond Park on the morrow. She seemed a sweet girl. Since she was soon to come under his protection, it seemed he had better to get to know her. Did she like to read? Was she fond of sewing, as her sister was? Was she good at math? Was she a clever girl who might one day want to go away to school? Or would she prefer a decent tutor at home?

The last question gave him pause, for they had engaged a tutor for Mary Elizabeth, and look what had become of her.

He pushed all such thoughts out of his head and raised one eyebrow at his sister. She stopped her story of fishing flies in mid-speech, and rose to her feet.

"It is time we were off," Mary Elizabeth said. "My brother Robert is waiting dinner for us. He is a bit bored in London."

Alex winced at that indiscretion. Their brother wasn't bored. He simply hated the city and all the English in it. And as it turned out, there were quite a lot of English.

Mr. Pridemore stood and helped Mrs. Angel to her feet. Margaret stopped chasing butterflies in the slanting light, and they all trooped to the garden gate, where the older couple waved them off.

Alex drove the duchess's open carriage into the busy street. He was grateful that it was the fashionable hour, and everyone who was anyone was already clogging the roadways of Hyde Park.

"You love Catherine," Mary Elizabeth said without preamble. She did not look at him, but took in the greenery of Regent's Park as they passed it.

"I do," Alex answered. He was many things perhaps, but he was not a liar.

"You'd better marry her then," his sister answered, looking at a towering elm to their left.

Alex only grunted.

❧

He found Robbie in the music room. This time he was not playing the fife, but drumming a strange tattoo out on the top of the pianoforte. He would drum, listen to the lingering silence that followed, and then drum again. Alex stared at him for a long time, but finally interrupted him when he realized his brother was not going to stop doing whatever it was that he was doing.

"I don't think you realize what that instrument is for."

Robbie turned back to him, his blue eyes slowly losing their faraway look. Like the old ones, he never wrote down a note of his compositions, but he always remembered them.

"I am working on something for the gathering in August. This thing gives the closest tone to a bodhran." He looked at his brother. "We will be home before August, won't we?"

"Dear God in His heaven, I pray we will."

"Prayers don't get us far," his brother answered. "As men, we have to do for ourselves."

"I suppose we could hog-tie Mary Elizabeth to an unsuspecting Englishman until she agrees to marry him."

"I wouldn't do that to him, whoever he is. Poor bastard."

The brothers laughed together, and Alex poured them both a finger of Islay whisky.

"So you're going to marry her, then?" Robbie said with no segue. His brother always knew what he was going to do, even before he did.

"Aye."

They drank their whisky in silence. Good whisky required silence to be appreciated, a truth Mary Elizabeth seemed incapable of grasping. But then, Alex did not know a woman who did.

"I'm buying a special license tomorrow," Alex said at last. "We'll need to have a Church of England marriage, to make it legal, but I'll marry her in front of a true priest as soon as I get her home."

"You'd best go to Uncle Richard," Robbie said. "The other damned English will make you wait a month."

They never mentioned the fact that their mother had been born an Englishwoman. She was Scottish now, by clan and kin, and by choice, but she kept up with her English relatives, including her brother, the Bishop of London.

Alex grunted in agreement, and finished his whisky. Robbie stood when he did, setting his glass down on the pianoforte he had just been drumming on.

"Does your girl know she's to be married?" Robbie asked.

Alex smiled. "Not yet."

"That'll be a sight, watching you run her to ground."

"You think I'll have to chase her, then? How do you know she won't come running to me?"

Robbie laughed out loud. "Because, *mo bràthair*, the good ones never do."

Twenty-six

CATHERINE KNEW THAT SHE WAS BEING UNCONSCIONABLY rude to her guests, but she could not bear one more moment in Alexander's company. His beauty struck at her bruised heart. She'd had enough for one day. She went upstairs and let him find his own way out.

She went to her bedroom, but the moss green of her curtains and bedding did nothing to soothe her. Nor did the wood violets she had brought in from the garden. A new bouquet from Lord Farleigh rested on her bureau also, a perfectly respectable bunch of beautiful white roses and baby's breath, roses that held just a touch of pink along their edges. Buds ready to open, just as she was.

She found next to the bouquet Lord Farleigh's response to her invitation to Richmond Park on the morrow. Not only was he coming, but he also insisted on driving her mother, her sister, and herself in his open phaeton. It seemed he would also provide the food in a cart that would meet them there. He signed the missive, *Arthur, Lord Farleigh.* The use of his given name was the sign. He was going to offer for her while they ate his cold chicken and drank his white wine.

Her time was up.

Of course, she had known that already. Why that signature made her feel so miserable, she could not say.

Of course, she did love Alex, more than she would ever love another. But full-blown roses were not for every day, and even the most beautiful flowers wilted and died. Much better to cultivate plants that, while less beautiful, offered more green stability and nurturing fragrance. Lord Farleigh was a boxwood plant that would stay green all winter long, and cheer even her gray days with brightness.

One day, she would come to love him. Not as she loved Alex, of course, but a different kind of love. A love that would last into old age, a love that would keep her warm until death.

She thought of the grandchildren she would one day have, watching them frolic on the lawn at her father's home in Devon. She watched them run to her, and saw that they bore not her blonde hair, nor Lord Farleigh's, but Alex's dark locks.

She said half a rosary, but the image of her grandchildren would not change. So instead of dressing for dinner as she knew she should, she climbed the long, narrow staircase to the servants' quarters. There was only one man who could help her.

"Miss Catherine," Giles said. "You must not visit me alone. It is unseemly."

Her family's butler struggled to sit up, but his leg was shackled by its splint. He had five more weeks to go before the doctor said the splint could come off, and he could use a cane to go from place to place. At that time, she would move him into a room on the first floor, so that he would not have to climb stairs, but for now, the only way to get him to stay in bed was to keep him in his usual room. The stairs to the fourth floor were so narrow, only an able-bodied man could navigate them.

"It is perfectly seemly, Giles. Do not fuss."

Catherine left the door standing open behind her and plumped his pillows. She dumped his old water mug out, and poured him fresh from the pitcher by his bed. She was pleased to discover that the water was still cool in its earthenware jar. Mrs. Beam was taking good care of him.

"I find myself at odds, Giles. I have need of your counsel."

The older man nodded solemnly, his bald pate glinting a little in the light from his open window. His view of the back garden was obscured by the tall oak, but the shifting leaves sounded like peace in the early evening air, filtering the last of the sunlight through their green. Catherine took a deep breath of the fresh air, imagining herself home in Devon, and her loved ones with her.

In her imaginings, her father was always still alive. This made her sad, so she stopped thinking of Devon at once. But her sadness seemed to linger in the room between them.

Giles nodded, as if to acknowledge the passing of Mr. Middlebrook through the silent room.

"Your father was a good man. He is still a good man, no doubt, wherever in heaven the Lord has seen fit to put him. I have no doubt he looks in on you, whenever he can. But I know that just as the dead tell no tales, neither do they offer advice."

Catherine smiled wryly. "Indeed, they do not."

"You are torn between two young men," Giles said.

She blinked at him. "How on earth do you know that?"

"You will find that there is very little that happens in this house, or in Devon, that I am not privy to." He smiled a mysterious smile, and Catherine had to swallow a laugh, so as not to offend him. "I know what I know. Let us leave it at that."

"I am torn between two gentlemen. One is calm, reasonable, kind, honorable, everything that is respectable and good."

"And you favor the second one."

Catherine did laugh then, and Giles nodded solemnly as if she had spoken.

"It is a difficult question you pose, Miss Catherine. For all I understand, both gentlemen are equals in breeding and in fortune. One has a title, of course, but that does not signify. Not to a sweet, unspoiled girl like you."

Catherine felt her hated blush rise, and she wished it away. It stayed as it always did, and she looked at the polished wooden floor and took in the edge of Giles's warm, braided rug.

"So there is something else," Giles said. He did not speak again, but waited, knowing that she would answer him, as she knew she must.

"I am bound to one in honor. I am bound to the other in love. I do not know what to do, Giles, or how to choose between them. I tell myself that I know my duty. I must do as honor dictates, but I find my heart does not wish to do it."

"This is a difficult question, indeed, Miss Catherine. One I fear I am not fit to answer."

They sat in silence, and she waited, knowing that he was not finished yet.

"I had the privilege of knowing your father all the years of his life. He grew up in the house while I was under butler, and he was always a man of discernment and integrity. He has raised you to be his equal in this, I think."

Catherine did not answer, for her throat was too tight. Giles nodded and went on as if she had spoken, and agreed.

"I think you do not need my counsel at all, Miss Catherine. I think you came to me only that I may remind you of what your father would say, if he were here."

Catherine felt her tears come then, but she did not swallow them down, or wipe them away. They made tracks on her cheeks, and she let them flow, two tiny rivers of wasted salt.

"I am a woman of honor," Catherine said. "I did not need to ask you. You are right, Giles. I knew the answer already."

Twenty-seven

CATHERINE DRESSED WITH CARE FOR HER OUTING TO Richmond. She wore a soft green walking dress and pelisse that matched her eyes. Instead of one of her two bonnets that blocked her view of the world, she wore her Sunday hat, which perched on her curls in a becoming fashion but left her eyes free to roam.

She wanted all her faculties about her that day, including her vision.

Margaret raced up and down the staircase, happy as a lark to be going with them. Her mother was strangely calm, standing in the foyer next to a new bouquet from Mr. Pridemore, this one a huge, almost funereal bunch of lilies. Mrs. Middlebrook adjusted her hat, fiddling with it halfheartedly to see how it might look best. Catherine wanted to ask her about Pridemore, but did not. She had enough of her own troubles that day without borrowing more.

The Waterses and Lord Farleigh arrived almost at the same time. Robert Waters was nowhere to be seen, but Alex was very much in evidence, looking too huge to fit in the duchess's carriage. He helped

Mary Elizabeth down from her perch and moved to deal with the horses, but not before giving Catherine a smile that told her she was in trouble, and deeply so.

She shook with fear and longing together, drawing her friend away from the others to whisper in her ear.

"I need your help, Mary Elizabeth."

"Anything," her friend answered. "Is there a mouse in the house that needs catching?"

"No. I need you to keep Alexander away from me."

Mary Elizabeth looked at her shrewdly from beneath her own fashionable hat. Her clear maple eyes took all of Catherine in, and seemed to see past her worries into her soul. "I thought you liked him," was all she said.

Catherine felt truly terrible, but she knew there was worse to come. She pushed her pain aside, and hid it in her heart. "I do. But I need to be free of him today."

Mary Elizabeth nodded. "Done. Think no more about it."

"He is very determined, Mary Elizabeth."

Mary Elizabeth smiled at her, and for a moment, Catherine's heart lightened a little as she stood in its warmth. "So am I."

Lord Farleigh was beside her then, and the girls could no longer speak in confidence.

"Miss Middlebrook. Miss Waters. What a delightful day this promises to be. I hope you fancy cold chicken and white wine."

Mary Elizabeth turned her smile on him. "I do, my lord. Will you be so kind as to show us your horse-flesh? Arabians, are they not?"

"Quarter horses, but you have a very good eye."

Lord Farleigh's pale face lit up as he began to expound on horse breeding, crossing lines to get stamina as well as beauty, the differences between racing horses versus driving cattle, and so forth. Catherine did not understand or care about a word of it, but it got her placed gently in Lord Farleigh's high flyer with the lap blanket securely around her waist to keep off the dust from the road.

Her mother smiled over at her as she allowed Alexander Waters to settle her into the duchess's carriage, and Margaret clambered up behind her, talking to Alex nonstop about the baby bird that was roosting at her windowsill.

Mary Elizabeth bowed to Lord Farleigh almost like a man. Once he was secure on the high seat with the reins in his hands, she gave his lead horse a thump on the rump and his matched grays moved quickly off into traffic, leaving the rest of the party behind. "We will see you there," Mary Elizabeth called after them, waving her cream-gloved hand.

Catherine could feel the heat of Alex's gaze piercing her like a blade, but then they turned the corner and were safely out of sight.

"That was neatly done," Lord Farleigh said.

Catherine feigned ignorance. "I beg your pardon?"

"It seems we have at least one ally among your friends and relations. I am obliged to her. I was afraid your—did you say Scottish 'cousin'?—was going to wrest you from me and tuck you up beside him in the duchess's carriage along with your mother and sister."

Catherine could not help but laugh, for she knew that was exactly what Alex would have done, given enough time and opportunity.

"I will bring you to a spot I know close by the river. Richmond is a bit of a drive, but is a lovely place. Have you been there before?"

"Never," Catherine answered, smiling, trying valiantly to put her Scottish "cousin" out of her head, and failing.

"Well, this will be a lovely first then. The place is filled with old trees, oaks, and hawthorns, from the days when it was a hunting preserve for the king."

"Does the King not hunt there now?"

Lord Farleigh looked at her sidelong, and she saw the humor lurking there and found herself smiling in earnest. "I fear our good sovereign is a bit too rotund to be a sporting man."

Catherine laughed out loud again, and did her best to enjoy his company. He was all that was gracious and charming. She knew that she had to thank him for his intervention in the matter of the mortgage, but it was such a beautiful morning, she told herself, *Not just yet.*

&

"Mary Elizabeth, what were you thinking? Sending off Miss Middlebrook in that carriage with a man we barely know?" Alex felt a headache begin behind the backs of his eyes.

His sister, usually so quick to leap aboard any conveyance, noodled about the front of this one, looking after the horses. She petted the nose of the lead horse and gave him a bit of sugar from somewhere up her sleeve. The second horse saw that and jostled for one himself, and Alex blew out a breath so that he would not curse in front of Mrs. Angel. She would not approve of him as a son-in-law if he used florid language in front of ladies in the middle of a quiet street.

"My daughter is headstrong, like your sister there." Mrs. Angel leaned back against the velvet squabs like a potentate, ready to convey to him the wisdom of the world. As long as she spoke of his angel, he would listen. "Catherine doesn't seem overly stubborn, until you cross her," Mrs. Angel said. "But then, watch out."

He looked down at his sister's bent head, where she was now whispering sweet nothings in his geldings' ears. "What would you suggest?"

"Don't take no for an answer," Mrs. Angel said. Margaret listened to her mother solemnly, and for once did not interrupt to talk about birds.

"Mrs. Middlebrook, I am a gentleman."

Mrs. Angel waved one hand. "Yes, yes, no doubt. I'm not saying kidnap her and carry her off to the Highlands—unless you must. But I don't think it will come to that."

"What are you saying, ma'am, if I might inquire?"

She laughed out loud at him, her blue eyes sparkling. "Oh, but you are delicious! If I were twenty years younger, I'd give my girl a run for her money."

Alex felt himself blush beneath his tan. He looked down between the ears of his horses. Mary Elizabeth was now currying their manes with a comb from her reticule.

Mrs. Angel reached over and patted his knee. "Don't trouble yourself, my boy. I have my own kettle of fish to fry." She leaned back once more, surveying the beauty of the day as if she had ordered it from God herself. "What I am saying, young Mr. Alex of Glenderrin, is that for some reason known only to her, my daughter has convinced herself that Lord Farleigh is good for her, the way the nastiness of castor oil is supposed to purge you of all ills."

Mrs. Angel shuddered beside him, and Alex found himself smiling at her.

"She is as stubborn as her father, and once she has the bit between her teeth, you'll have a devil of a time getting her back under control."

"I don't want to control her," Alex answered honestly. "I just want to love her."

Tears came into Mrs. Angel's eyes, and she drew out a lace handkerchief and wiped them away. "You'll do, Alex Waters. You'll do. Just heed my warning. She loves you, or I'm blind and in my dotage already. Now, we had best get on, or they'll have eaten all his lordship's chicken."

"Catherine can't eat that much," Margaret said.

But Alex heeded her mother.

"Mary Elizabeth, leave those horses be and get in this carriage now, or I'm leaving you behind on the street."

His sister must have heard in his voice that he meant business, for she vaulted into the carriage and away they went.

He had an angel to run to ground, and he was burning daylight.

∽

Catherine had never seen such a pretty spot in her life, save at home in Devon. The Thames ran close by, and Richmond Park was filled with towering oaks that seemed to block out the sun. Lord Farleigh stopped in a green clearing, where a pavilion was already set up.

She wondered for a moment if someone grand had been there before them, then realized that the pavilion with its table and chairs had been placed for them.

Footmen in livery served her a glass of wine as soon as her feet touched the soft, spongy grass. She turned to look at the vista that led down to the river. "We will walk there later, if you wish," Lord Farleigh said.

"I would like that," she answered, smiling up at him.

She wished in that moment that it was not the Thames but the river Lethe, that she might drink from it and forget she had ever met Alex. She wished that she might leave all this pain and love behind her as if it had never been. Then she was ashamed of herself. Love was not something one should forget, whatever pain it brought.

Her family arrived. Alex must have driven hell for leather through the country roads, for Mary Elizabeth tumbled out of the carriage at once, leading Margaret toward a great oak while Alex helped her mother down. Her mother winked at her, but then looked over her shoulder at the sound of fresh carriage wheels turning on the gravel road. Mr. Pridemore appeared, roses in hand, driving his own high flyer. He stopped his horses with a flourish, and waved his hat down to her mother, who waved back, a smile of joy on her face.

Catherine was not sure what Mr. Pridemore's intentions were, but he certainly seemed to make her mother happy. Once she was safely married to Lord Farleigh, he could look further into Mr. Pridemore and see to it that his intentions were good.

Somehow, in spite of Lord Farleigh's solicitous regard as he seated her at table, this did not comfort her as she had thought it might.

Alex sat down across the table from her, ignoring the wine the footman offered. Instead, he reached inside his coat and brought out a silver flask lined with leather, a flask that bore his initials. "Good day to you, Miss Middlebrook."

"Good day, Mr. Waters. I do hope you enjoyed the drive."

"Not as much as you did, I gather."

She blushed, looking down at her own half-empty wineglass. She watched in silence as a footman filled it, feeling a strange thrill at the sound of Alex's voice. If she did not know better, she would say he sounded almost jealous. To have such a beautiful, virile man show jealousy over her made her head swim. She took another sip.

Mary Elizabeth joined them, sitting between Alex and Mr. Pridemore. She started a lively discussion of fishing reels that all the gentlemen seemed entranced by, even Lord Farleigh. Only Alex did not listen to a word of it, but ate his chicken like a savage, ripping at the breast before him as if it were responsible for all the world's ills. Catherine watched him surreptitiously, no longer happy with his jealousy but made miserable by it.

She wished before God and all His angels that she did not owe Lord Farleigh the mortgage on her father's land. If she did not, she would run away with Alex that very day, and forget the consequences to her reputation and to her life. She would live beside a cold inland stream in the wilds of the north, freezing near to death each winter. She would even learn to fish if she must, if it would please him.

In that moment of pain, Lord Farleigh leaned over and offered her a bit of bread from the basket. She took it, and the butter he gave her, with murmured thanks. She might wish for the moon, but she would not hold it in her hand.

The man beside her was her future, and she would have to learn to live with that.

Twenty-eight

ALEX COULD NOT GET CLOSER TO HIS ANGEL THAN across the table. Lord Loverboy, on the other hand, seemed always at the ready to ply her with wine, a fresh bite of bread, a tender morsel of chicken—once from his own plate. If Alex had ever seen such a shameless display among decent people, he could not recollect it.

He wished he were the one chasing her so openly. But she would not even meet his eyes.

Maybe Mrs. Angel was right, and Catherine had convinced herself to stay in London for the rest of her life. Perhaps she meant to marry the ingrate. Alex vowed that he would speak to her that very day, that she might know his mind, and thus change her own. He rose after the meal was through to take her on a walk down by the river, but Margaret ran off and Mary Elizabeth after her.

He was distracted for a moment, watching Mary Elizabeth hike up her skirts like any hoyden, and make the leap to the lowest branch of a great oak. The oak grew close to the water's edge. Alex knew she could swim, but even his fearless sister was not immune breaking her neck.

"Mary Elizabeth, come down from there, for the love of God!"

She ignored him, as she always seemed to do of late. Margaret joined her on the lowest branch, after receiving a hoist from her newfound friend in climbing towering trees and descending high windows.

He looked away from his sister and her charge for a moment, searching out his angel. She was standing demurely beside the river, looking at a pleasure boat that was sailing by. It seemed to be piloted by someone Lord Loverboy knew, for he waved and called to them, and the gentleman at the prow doffed his hat and bowed to Catherine, who smiled and waved in return.

Alex took pleasure in the beauty of her body, in the clean lines of the green gown that matched her moss-colored eyes. He knew that she had made it herself. Unlike fool Englishmen and women of the *ton*, he liked a woman who plied a needle to make her own clothes, a woman who had practical skills to serve herself and her household.

As his wife, she would not need them, but the fact that she had them pleased him inordinately. His mother would be pleased as well. She would forgive the fact that he had out-and-out disobeyed her, and married while down south. Born English herself, Lady Glenderrin could surely not fault him for falling in love with one of her former countrywomen.

Falling in love. It seemed a ridiculous notion. Until it happened to you.

He lost sight of his angel as she turned a bend in

the river with her English swain. He was about to go after them, in case Lord Loverly thought to steal a kiss, but he heard his sister shriek, and he looked back to the great oak.

All he could see was Mary Elizabeth clinging to a high branch over the river. This did not concern him, but the odd fact that she kept shrieking did. She pointed down into the water, and it was then he realized that Miss Margaret had vanished.

The girl's head bobbed and ducked with the water's flow. She had not yet been swept into the main, shipping current of the river, the great tide that pulled large ships out to sea. He swore as he leaped into the river to fish her out, ruining a good pair of shoes in the process.

He soon forgot his shoes, for though he was a strong swimmer and the river warm with spring that was quickly moving toward summer, Margaret fought him like a cornered alley cat, not seeming to understand that he was trying to save her. She struggled against him and the river both, and he gave thanks to God that she had enough strength and enough bare ability to paddle so that he had time to reach her.

He was fighting against the current now, and Mary Elizabeth waved to him from the riverbank. She had pulled a length of rope out of the duchess's carriage, weighted one end by tying a branch to it, and tossed it toward him. He swam not for the shore then, but for that branch, Margaret caught secure under one arm. The girl still flailed about, but much of the fight had gone out of her.

And there were fools who said that prayer was never answered.

If he had had only Mary Elizabeth to help pull him in, he would have floated a good ways downstream and out to sea perhaps, but Pridemore had seen the madness and come running. He anchored the rope, pushing Mary Elizabeth out of the way. Between Alex's strong kicks and Pridemore's strong back, they managed to haul himself and Margaret back to shore.

He dropped the branch as soon as he had his feet under him, and carried the girl up the riverbank. He seated her on a dry rock in the sun, and then left her to the shrieking assistance of her mother.

Pridemore handed him a flask, for he had lost his in the river.

"Quick thinking," was all the older man said.

"I was lucky, and you pulled us out."

"I had help."

They drank together in a moment of silence, and Alex took his measure.

"So," he said, "I feel I must ask your intentions." Alex had meant to couch his speech in some measure of politeness, but they were men of action. Pridemore did not shrink from him, as Alex had known he would not. The man simply smiled.

"I might ask you the same thing."

"I'm going to marry my girl, if I can get her alone for the space of a heartbeat so that I can propose to her," Alex answered.

Pridemore's gaze fell on Mrs. Angel, who was even then trying valiantly to pat her daughter dry with her own shawl. Alex saw the other man's gaze soften just a touch, but it was enough.

"I have asked for my lady's hand. She has not yet answered me," Pridemore admitted.

Alex did not speak again, as there was no more need for words between them. He sipped at his new friend's whisky. He wondered if Pridemore was in a hurry to wed, as he was. Perhaps they might make it a double wedding.

He hoped Uncle Richard had sent the special license on from Westminster. The Bishop of London was no doubt a busy man, but never too busy for family.

Mary Elizabeth came to him then, looking as shamefaced as if she had killed a man. Pridemore strode off to comfort Mrs. Angel, and Alex faced his sister down, still dripping with foul river water.

"Alex, I am so sorry."

He saw the pain in her eyes, and he patted her arm. He would have hugged her, but he did not want to ruin her pretty walking dress with his sodden embrace.

"It is not your fault she fell, Mary."

"I should never have brought her up into the tree with me. She never would have climbed, and never would have fallen, had I not been here."

"Well," he said, trying to keep his voice level and calm, to head off the tears in her eyes. He had rarely seen his sister cry, yet she had teared up twice in two days. Could the Apocalypse be nigh? "She had the good sense to fall into the river instead of breaking her neck on the ground. That's something."

"Alex, I told Catherine I would keep you from her this day. That's why I brought Margaret up into the tree. If you had to keep an eye on me, you would not hunt Catherine to ground."

Alex sighed. "And why would you do that, Mary? I thought you liked her."

"I do like her. A great deal." Mary Elizabeth's hazel eyes met his, and he saw the green that skirted her pupils. "I did it because she asked me to."

Alex felt as if another cold, foul sluice of river water had been tossed over his head. But he stood on dry land, and his feet were firm under him. He took out his sodden handkerchief from his coat pocket and wiped his forehead with it. Moving water from one place to another on his person gave him something to do.

"You were being true to a friend, Mary. I will never fault you for that."

Mary Elizabeth hugged him, her thin arms around his waist. She squeezed him hard, as he had always squeezed her when she was feeling down after a fight with their mother.

"I am sorry, Alex."

He hugged her close, and kissed her forehead. "Don't fret yourself, little sister. It will all come out right in the end."

"She loves you Alex. I'm sure of it."

He smiled down at her, feigning a confidence he no longer felt. "Sure and she does. What woman can resist a Glenderrin man?"

Mary Elizabeth laughed, but his heart was still black.

Twenty-nine

CATHERINE THOUGHT SHE HEARD A SHRIEK FROM behind her, but Lord Farleigh did not turn back from their stroll, so neither did she. No doubt it was Mary Elizabeth creating a diversion of sorts to keep her brother happy and out of Catherine's hair.

Catherine wished it were Alex walking beside her, and chastised herself at once for the wicked thought. This man had saved her family's land, and had no doubt saved her family from ruin. It was a kindness and a debt that she would never truly be able to repay.

"I must thank you," she said.

He quirked an eyebrow at her, and for a moment, he looked like a more exciting, rakish man. "Indeed? It is my pleasure to bring you here, and to give your family lunch. Even your *cousins*."

She laughed a little at that, but would not be dissuaded from her course. "No, I must thank you for calling on Mr. Philips."

"You were quite right about him," Lord Farleigh said, taking her arm to assist her over a small branch that lay in their path. "Philips is a good man. I do hope your mother heeds his advice in future, instead of going her own way."

Catherine felt her hated blush rise for at least the third time that day. Her humiliation rose from the ground to swamp her, and she wished the river might swallow her whole. He seemed to sense her mortification at once, and went to work trying to put her at ease again.

"Please do not trouble yourself. I know that you feel at a disadvantage, but please know that I am honored that you leaned on me." He looked down at her, and stopped dead in the center of the well-trodden path. The river flowed beside them, offering a soothing sound that did little to assuage her frayed nerves. She stiffened before she forced herself to relax. It was time.

"I do hope that you will consider leaning on me for the rest of your life."

She stared at him, dumbfounded. Was that a proposal of marriage or not? He tried again.

"Forgive me. This was not at all how I meant to do this. I always thought that I would inquire after my future wife to her father, and then speak to her once the matter was settled. But as your father has gone on before us—" He must have seen the hint of tears that threatened to blind her, for he reached into his coat pocket and offered her a handkerchief.

She took it and wiped her eyes. It should have smelled like bergamot, but it did not. It smelled only of clean, fresh linen that had been dried in the sunshine. A pleasant scent, but not heady, not transporting. Very much like the man himself.

"I must apologize again. I had no notion of making you weep, save perhaps for joy."

She smiled a tremulous smile, knowing that this kindhearted, good man deserved kindness from her. Her pain was her own business.

"Thank you," she said.

"You are not weeping for joy," he said.

Catherine breathed deeply, and her tears receded. She was a woman, and had made a woman's choice. She knew what she had to do. She simply could not bring herself to do it.

"No," she answered.

There was a long silence between them, broken only by the sound of birdsong, and of the river shushing by. Lord Farleigh stared at her a long time, as if waiting for her to speak. When she did not, he did.

"You love another," he said.

The bald truth lay between them like an unsheathed blade. She wished to lie or, at the very least, to deny it with something resembling vehemence, but she did nothing. She did not weep, but stared at the ground, wondering if her future, and her father's legacy, was about to go up in smoke.

She should have known that he would not press her. Instead, Lord Farleigh spoke as calmly as if they were discussing the weather, or something that had happened to someone else.

"You love another, and you cannot have him."

"No," she said. "In all honor, I cannot."

Arthur Farleigh nodded and looked down toward the river. There were willows leaning into the water, their long branches trailing like braids of a woman's hair.

"There was a woman I loved once, long ago."

Catherine's eyes were drawn to his face as if to a lodestone. "And she loved you?"

Arthur did not meet her gaze, but his face softened, and for a moment, he looked like a man who was not always careful, a man who felt deeply. Just not for her.

"She did," he answered. "She loved me better than her own life."

"Where is she now?" Catherine asked.

"Italy, I think. I lost touch with her during the war. I have not seen her nor heard from her for years now."

"Is she dead?"

Catherine saw the pain on his face and wished her words back again. Lord Farleigh swallowed hard, and when he spoke, his voice was muted. "I do not think so. But I do not know."

Catherine touched his arm once, very gently, before drawing her gloved hand away. "I am sorry," she said. "I am sorry for your loss."

He smiled then, and it was a shadow of the calm, bland smile she was used to seeing on his face. "Thank you. I do not tell you this to bring you pain, or to put you off. I tell you only because I understand you. There are times when those we love do not suit us, and we do not suit them. And we must choose whether to cling to them, or to go on."

"You have chosen," Catherine said.

"I have." Arthur Farleigh faced her, and did not flinch from her. "I have chosen to go on. I hope you will do the same, and go on with me."

"I don't know," Catherine said. "I'm not sure I can."

"Believe me when I say that I understand." Arthur

pressed her hand between both of his. His touch was not importunate, nor was it grasping, but warm, like the touch of a friend.

"Do not make up your mind just now," he said. "There is no hurry to have the banns posted. Take the time you need, and consider my suit. I think we would do well together. But it is not my decision to make."

He reached into his pocket and drew out a ring. It was a lovely old piece, no doubt an heirloom—three pearls nestled in a bed of silver. The ring gleamed in the sun, and she watched as if seeing it happen to another as he stripped off her glove and placed his ring on her finger.

"Wear this while you consider my offer. It was my mother's. When I wrote to her of you, she sent me this."

"It is very beautiful," Catherine managed to say. "Thank you. Please tell her thank you from me."

"You will thank her yourself, perhaps," he answered, smiling down on her.

That a grand lady would welcome her into her son's life and family, sight unseen, moved her almost to tears. But she blinked, and did not weep.

Tears would not signify. She had an entire afternoon to get through yet, and then an evening, and then a whole, sleepless night. She would think later of what they had spoken of, of what she still must do. For now, her mind was one large bruise. She could not think again.

She accepted her glove from him and drew it on over his mother's pearl ring. Though hidden, the weight of it dragged down the length of her whole arm.

He offered her his arm as succor. Having no other, she took it, and let him lead her back to the others.

The picnic site was in an uproar. It seemed

Margaret had fallen into the river somehow, and had managed to dog paddle to keep afloat until Alex had fished her out.

Catherine left her almost fiancé and went to her Highlander's side. He was beginning to dry a little in the sun, but his coat and trousers were still wet through, though he was no longer dripping. One shoe was gone, and his stocking, it seemed, had a hole in the toe.

She wanted to take him home, set him by a fire, and give him clean clothes to wear and whisky to drink, while she darned that sock before she sent it to the laundry.

The odd fantasy seemed absurd, and her eyes were watery as she suppressed both mirth and terror at the sight of him. She would have to speak to him as well, but she could not bear to do it that day.

Tomorrow. She would put off all unpleasant conversations until the morrow.

"What's wrong?" Alex asked, surveying her face as if he might find the answer to his question there.

She did not know how to answer him, for she did not want to lie. "I will tell you tomorrow," she said. "Today, I think we need to get you home."

"And into dry clothes," he said, drinking from a small flask that was not his.

"Where is your flask?" she asked him.

He waved one dismissive hand toward the River Thames. "At Tilbury by now, most likely."

She did laugh then, and he quirked a brow at her, his own eyes warming a little. Still he watched her close, dissatisfied with her answer to his question. But he was gentleman enough not to press her, and for that she was grateful.

Thirty

Robbie was home drinking when they got back from their purgatorial picnic in Richmond. He took one look at Alex, shook his head, and poured him a whisky.

"You need to get changed."

"I'm dry by now."

"Don't ruin the duchess's fancy settees."

When Robbie said that, Alex downed his drink and went upstairs to change. When he came back down, a quiet, chastened Mary Elizabeth stayed in her room. Contemplating her sins, he assumed. For the girl to go against the family, in even such a foolish and minor manner, told him how angry she was at their mother and, by extension, at them.

He could not concern himself with his sister at the moment, though she clearly needed a firm hand and more guidance than he had been giving her. He could think of nothing but his angel, and the look on her face when she came back from her walk with Lord Farleigh. Like a woman going to her execution.

It was beginning to look as if he was going to have to save her from herself.

"How long do you think it might take to get from here to the border?" he asked his brother, a fresh whisky in hand.

Robbie stared at him, but answered the question. "Three days, if you change horses every two hours. Why?"

"I might have to kidnap my girl."

"Is she still looking at that Englishman?"

"She is."

Alex swallowed his whisky and set his glass down. He knew he could not take another before dinner and still keep his head. Part of him wanted to drown himself in a vat of the stuff. But they had only brought two barrels, and he was not going to risk running out. God alone knew how long it was going to take to get Mary Elizabeth tied to some Londoner.

God help them.

He put his sister out of his thoughts again. He had bigger fish to fry.

"For some godforsaken reason, she won't let me get close enough to propose marriage myself," Alex said. "And all the while, my girl's trying to get engaged to the bastard."

"While she's in love with you?"

"We've not discussed her feelings, but I am fairly certain. Yes."

Robbie shook his head. "Women."

His brother tossed him the sealed envelope that had come from their uncle that afternoon while he was out. He found the marriage license within. "Special license, my arse," Alex said. "These English are too pretentious to live."

"That must be why we killed so many of them," Robbie said.

Alex laughed in spite of himself.

"You've got the license in hand," his brother said. "You don't need to run to the border."

"If she won't sign it, I might."

"As bad as that?"

"When she came out of the woods after being alone with the bastard, she looked as ill as if she'd swallowed a snake. I fear she may have agreed to marry him already."

Robbie swore. "Do you need to kill him?"

"I doubt it," Alex answered. "He's too thin blooded, and too much a gentleman to offer her insult. But my time is growing short. I must be ready to make my move, if I'm forced to it."

"You know I'm behind you. Father and Ian will be, too. David will laugh his arse off at you, but he'll back you. You've only Mother to contend with, but after you've married the girl, even Mother will have to overlook the abduction."

Alex felt grim. He, the man who had to push women off him most times, was actually contemplating taking a girl away to the border to be wed. The Apocalypse truly was nigh.

"I am not best pleased," Alex said at last.

"I imagine not."

The brothers sat in silence, contemplating the large pianoforte that Miss Margaret Middlebrook had knocked out of tune with her overenthusiastic playing.

"I'll go see my girl tonight," Alex said.

"An evening call?"

"A midnight call, more like."

"If you have to head north, go. I'll look after Mary Elizabeth."

"Something's wrong with the girl," Alex said.

"Something has always been wrong with her. Da indulged her too much, I'd say."

"No," Alex said. "It's more than the usual. I think Mother sending her away has broken her heart. She cried yesterday. And she almost cried today. She would have, and in public too, if I hadn't hugged her."

Robbie swore again, this time louder. "Mother was harsh to her when last they spoke. And sending her south to marry—I would not wish that on a Campbell, much less my own flesh and blood."

"Aye."

"She needs a woman's touch. Your girl's too distracted to be of much help."

Alex smiled. "And when I marry her, she'll be more distracted still."

Robbie laughed, and held up both hands as if to shield himself. "Say nothing more, Brother. Think of my delicate ears."

Alex laughed out loud. His brother was the only one on earth who could always get a laugh out of him, whatever disaster was rising. "And how is Madame Claremont?"

"Still from Cheapside, I warrant. I had an amusing time with two of her girls earlier this afternoon before you came home."

"Not here."

"Do I look like I've suddenly gone daft? No, I kept my whores where they were, happy in their own rooms. I pay so I can leave, you know. Otherwise they'd never let a fine-looking man like me out of their sight."

Alex swatted his brother, and Robbie swatted him back. They were halfhearted, glancing blows that subsided at once. They both went back to silence, each contemplating the afternoon they had spent. Alex knew his brother had had a much better one. But Alex would rather be miserable and in his angel's presence than happy and apart.

He was certainly doomed. But he would go to his own end whistling.

"I'll go to her tonight," he said.

All the advice Robbie offered was this: "Wear black."

Thirty-one

CATHERINE DID NOT SLEEP THAT NIGHT, AS SHE KNEW she would not. She did dress for bed, putting on her night rail of thick cotton edged with lace, its pearl buttons shining dully in the light of her one candle. She tried to read, but Mrs. Radcliffe could not hold her attention. She tried to pray, but it seemed as with King Claudius in Shakespeare's *Hamlet*, her prayers did not to heaven go.

She fingered the pearl her father had given her mother on the night they were wed. She put it around her neck, opening her gown just by its top two buttons so that she could see the pearl gleaming. It was a symbol of her parents' love for each other, love that had been evident every day of her life, until the day her father died.

She raised the pearl ring that shone on her left hand, catching the light of the candle. If she took it off, she might lose it, but it didn't feel right against her flesh. It wasn't a promise of good things to come, but a shackle that tied her to her fate as strong as a chain of adamant. She did not weep, for it seemed her tears had dried up along with her hope. In the end, she could not stand to look at either piece of jewelry anymore, so she added the ring to the chain around her neck, and hid both beneath her dressing gown.

Something rattled against the window above the side yard around midnight, but it might have been a trick of the night wind. At the same time, though, the smell of smoke came from somewhere close. It was stronger than her candle stub, stronger than a lamp in the hand of someone passing in the hall. She looked to the window over the back garden; a glow came from it that was too bright to be a street lamp.

There were no lamps in the garden. The glow was coming from the back of the house.

She opened her window and leaned out, only to find that the kitchen was on fire.

Someone began shrieking then, over and over. She ran from her room to find her mother shaking Margaret awake.

"Catherine, that rope your friend gave you. Where is it? Quickly!"

Margaret woke slowly, but Catherine knew where the rope ladder was. She drew it out from beneath her sister's bed.

She did not hesitate, but opened the window over the back of the house. Smoke blew in from below, and she said a word she had heard Alex use once under her breath.

"Catherine! Language!"

"I am sorry, Mother. The fire is burning below. We must find another way out."

She watched as the servants began to line up in the

back garden, making a sort of bucket brigade from the garden well to the kitchen door. She turned and took her mother and sister by the hand, the rope ladder tucked under one arm.

"Come with me."

Catherine's hands were shaking as she ran with them to the front of the house, where the smoke was bad, but where there were no flames visible. The fumes choked her, and she covered her face with one arm as she tried to go down the staircase to the front hall. Halfway down, the smoke was so thick that she could not even see. She dragged her mother back up the stairs, Margaret sandwiched close between them.

Her heart pounding, she stopped at the second floor, trying to think of what Alex or Mary Elizabeth might do. She opened a window in the formal drawing room. People crowded below, gaping. No doubt the news of this mishap would be one of the talks of the Town come morning. But there was no time to worry about propriety or of what people might think of her. She tossed the rope down the side of the house, securing it carefully to the windowsill.

"Mother, you climb down first, and hold the rope steady for Margaret."

Olivia Middlebrook clutched both daughters close, then climbed down quickly, and with amazing nimbleness for a woman over thirty.

She waved to them from the ground below, and held the rope ladder steady as Margaret scurried down like a monkey.

"Thank God for Mary Elizabeth," Catherine heard her sister say. Thank God indeed.

Catherine tried to breathe in as much clean air from the window as possible, but the smoke was rising and her eyes began to sting. She said a prayer to the Holy Mother and began to climb down.

The hemp scraped against the skin of her palms, and she had a nonsensical thought that she ought to have worn gloves. At least a bonnet was not needed to keep the sun off her face, as it was the dead of night.

A touch of hysterical laughter threatened to bubble in her throat, but she swallowed it down. She was still six feet above the ground when she felt strong hands take hold of her waist.

"Let go of that blasted rope, Catherine. I've got you."

Alex Waters's voice sounded in her ear like a voice from another life. He drew her down and into his arms, and she clung to him like a cocklebur. Once her bare feet touched ground, she found that she was shaking.

"What are you doing here?" She heard the tears in her voice before she felt them on her cheeks. He held her close, not showing any sign of letting her go.

"I am here to see you. I didn't think to find you climbing down to the street, your house on fire."

She laughed a watery laugh. Her mother was quietly fussing over Margaret, who was standing close by, none the worse for wear, swathed in Alex's oversized coat. The sleeves dangled far past her hands, and she kept trying to push them back, and failing.

"Come into the garden," Alex said. "They are trying to put it out. I've got to help them."

A chill of horror ran along her spine, cold down her back like the fingers of a corpse. "Giles," she said. "Did someone think to get Giles out?"

"I have no idea," Alex said. "Is he your dog?"

"He's the butler," Catherine said, her voice rising with the hysterics she was trying so hard to repress. She took a deep breath. "He is on the fourth floor, up a narrow stair. His leg is broken."

Alex suddenly looked even more grim, soot beginning to line his face. She wondered how ghastly she looked, having climbed out of their house, if he looked like that from simply standing too close on the street.

Catherine turned to go back inside, but Alex held her fast.

"What do you think you're doing?"

"I must help him. He'll suffocate up there. The smoke is rising!"

Alex's touch was soothing, but she could not budge the strength of his arms. He drew her with him into the back garden, so that they were at least off the street. The kitchen was still burning, the fire an almost merry blaze. Half of the lower floor was gone; how could the building still be standing? Surely it was going to collapse.

Margaret and her mother stood in the back of the garden, as far from the flames and smoke as possible. The wind was shifting in their favor, but the flames were a tide that would not yet be stemmed. Catherine looked frantically at the servants gathered to haul water and watched as her mother went to join them, after giving Margaret strict instructions to stay where she was.

There were Jim and William, and the young boot-black, Charlie, who was a sort of boy of all work. She saw Marie, still dressed in her maid's blacks, carrying bucket after bucket, as Mrs. Beam did the same. Her mother's French maid was helping, but without a great deal of efficiency. But Giles was nowhere to be seen.

"Dear God, Alex, he's not here."

Alex kissed her once, fiercely, as if to silence her. The touch of his lips on hers grounded her, and her hysteria began to recede. He did not speak but turned and went into the house through the back door, heedless of smoke and flames, his white shirtsleeves bright in the light of the fire.

This fire was her punishment for her sins of wickedness. She had loved one man while allowing herself to be courted by another. All this was God's judgment. She could feel it in the hollow of her bones.

If Alex died trying to save her people, she would never forgive herself.

It seemed an eternity as she paced in the garden, trampling down good grass as her nightgown grazed her lilacs. She had said almost an entire rosary before Alex appeared again, this time rounding the house from the front, carrying a disgruntled Giles on his back.

A cheer went up from all the household, and tears wet Catherine's cheeks again. She did not wipe them away, but went to the bench where Alex set her butler down, and threw her arms around the man who was the last link to her father.

Giles stopped grousing that he was man enough to walk on his own, and patted her back. "There, there, Miss Middlebrook. No need to fret. It is just plaster and paint. We will build again."

"I am not weeping for the house," she said. "I am weeping for you."

"Well, as you can see, there's no need for that. If you want to be useful, go help your mother put the flames out."

Alex stood by, getting his breath as Margaret began fussing over Giles. Catherine looked up into his soot-smeared face, more tears running from her already sore and reddened eyes. "Thank you," she said.

"You might as well thank the sun for rising," Alex answered her. "Wherever I go, and whatever I do for the rest of my life, will be done in your service."

She wanted to put her arms around him again, but he turned away to help the bucket brigade. She followed him, and stayed, even when he tried to send her back to Margaret and Giles. She kept crying all the while she was carrying buckets. If only her tears might be of use, and put out some of the flames.

The fire went out without the help of her tears, though, and soon even the smoke began to clear. It rose away on the night air to mingle with the smoke that hung thick in London's skies. Catherine sat down in the grass alongside Marie, exhausted. She heard Cook say, "It was the kitchen chimney. We've not had it cleaned in a donkey's age, and look what it's come to now."

Catherine could not feel even a hint of horror at the thought of such a loss coming from a foolish oversight. She simply lay back on the grass and let the early morning dew begin to wash her clean.

❧

"Catherine! Get off that wet lawn at once!"

Her mother's voice woke her abruptly from whatever

bit of sleep she had been able to snatch. It could not have been later than one in the morning, but despite her moment of sleep, Catherine felt as if she had been awake a year. She stood at once, before Alex could offer her his hand to help her up.

His face was covered in smoke dust, as no doubt hers was as well. She looked at the house her great-grandfather had built, and sighed to see the mess the fire had left behind. She would have to inquire in the morning of Mr. Philips, that he might send someone to see if the structure was sound. The thought of all that the morning would bring weighed on her like a curse. Her shoulders slumped under the heavy load.

Alex took her hand, his black leather glove soft and tempting against her skin. "Whatever it is, don't think about it now. Come home with me and sleep. We will deal with your burdens tomorrow."

His dark eyes warmed her from the inside out, even as the heat of his touch warmed her palm. She wished fervently and forever that she might lay her burdens on his shoulders, that she might tell him all and cast her future and her life in with his. But she knew her duty. She knew what her father would say, if he were there. And she would hold to honor, for the last vestige of what he had taught her would keep him still alive, if only in her heart.

She squeezed Alex's hand once, and then let him go.

Thirty-two

MARY ELIZABETH GREETED THEM IN THE FOYER OF THE Duchess of Northumberland's house with cups of warm cider. There was a maid apiece to lead Margaret and their mother up to their guest rooms, which Mary Elizabeth already had prepared.

"You are welcome to stay as long as you like, as long as you must, and beyond," Mary Elizabeth said, her brogue coming out, whether from exercising hospitality as was fit for a Scottish woman, or from exhaustion due to the late hour, Catherine could not say.

Mary Elizabeth went on. "This house is like a museum or a tomb, it is so big and silent. What's that grand tomb those heathens built in India, Robbie?" she asked her brother.

"The Taj Mahal," he replied, sleep rumpled but handsome.

"Aye, whatever that may mean. It's a great big place that looks like a palace, but it holds only one dead woman. This house is like that. So welcome." Mary Elizabeth hugged Catherine tight, and took Mrs. Middlebrook and Margaret into her arms as well.

Mary Elizabeth brooked no argument as they were ushered up the staircase to their separate but adjoining rooms. After the scare they'd had, Catherine had no doubt that they would sleep in the same bed. She did not mention that to Mary Elizabeth, who seemed pleased to have at least three more rooms in the empty house filled up.

All the servants had been taken in as well, save for Jim, who stayed with the house to keep looters away. Catherine felt herself taken up and comforted by Mary Elizabeth's busyness, but even so, she felt Alex's eyes on her, and she wondered how she was going to sleep even a moment in the same house as he. Her earlier exhaustion had fled as soon as they entered the grand house. The heat of his gaze followed her, and made her light-headed and lighthearted all the way up the staircase.

She bathed in one of the three bathing rooms in the house, all of which had heated water flowing down from a cistern in the roof. Catherine had rarely known such luxury, but she did not savor it, bathing quickly.

The soft soap in the duchess's bath smelled like jasmine, the fragrance heady and almost overpowering. She smoothed the scent over her skin, washing away all soot and dirt. And she thought of Alex, and how his hands might feel on her skin.

She shocked herself with this line of thought, but her night had taken on a truly unreal quality, as if she had stepped somehow outside of time, outside of her life. She knew that she must marry Lord Farleigh. And she did not have the strength to wait, to have a decent, sensible engagement with its rounds of parties and two weeks of dressmaking, and then a formal wedding with Margaret as bridesmaid. She must leave Alex Waters behind, and begin a new life. She would go to Lord Farleigh, to Arthur, as soon as the sun was up and ask him to run away with her.

His mother would no doubt disapprove if they fled to Gretna Green, but once wedded and bedded, the scandal would subside in the light of Lord Farleigh's staid, calm ways. Indeed, a runaway marriage might even impress some of his friends, and show them that he was not always the boring man they no doubt thought him to be. She knew that if she asked, Lord Farleigh would take her to Scotland and marry her over an anvil, no questions asked.

She had first liked him for that very biddableness. Though Alex had shown her that she had a taste for another kind of man altogether, her personal tastes did not signify. She would marry Lord Farleigh, and he would care for her and hers for the rest of their lives. Their debt to him would be paid, and all would be as it should.

All of that would happen in the light of the new day. Catherine dried herself with the duchess's thick bathing sheets. She would shirk no longer, and that was a promise. Come morning, she would run away from Alex and all the temptation he offered, and flee to Gretna Green with Lord Farleigh. With Arthur.

But the notion of the calm, quiet marriage she would soon build with Lord Farleigh brought a strange devastation that shook her to her core. She pushed that devastation aside. Like all grief, it would fade in time to something less horrible. But if she had something to live on for the rest of her days, something to remember of Alex that went beyond a touch of his hand on hers, that went beyond a few stolen kisses…

She took off her mother's pearl and Lord Farleigh's ring. She slipped them into the bag Mary Elizabeth had given her that was filled with underthings, a pair of stays, a nightgown, and a pressed day gown that no doubt now was rumpled. She slipped on the night rail and braided her hair as if going to sleep. But she would not sleep. Not that night, perhaps not ever again.

Her blood sang as if she were going into battle as, with bag in hand, she knocked quietly on Mary Elizabeth's bedroom door.

"Are you frightened from the fire?" Mary Elizabeth asked, still wide-awake from tending to her guests.

"No," Catherine answered. "May I come in?"

"Of course."

Facing her friend, Catherine found her voice gone. She cleared her throat and took a sip of the cider offered her.

"I am going away in the morning," she said at once.

Mary Elizabeth frowned. "But you've only just arrived. You truly are welcome to stay as long as you'd like. I wish you'd never leave, truth be told. This mausoleum needs livening up, and we are just the two ladies to do it."

Catherine laughed at the loyalty and sweetness reflected in Mary Elizabeth's face. "I've never had a friend before. I am grateful for you."

"Well, it's high time you did. Now, what is this nonsense about going away?"

"I am running away in the morning. With Lord Farleigh."

Catherine watched as a shadow crossed her friend's face. Mary Elizabeth clearly wanted to ask about Alex, and about her feelings for him, but out of loyalty to Catherine, she did not.

"And where will you go?"

"Gretna Green," Catherine said, her voice growing stronger with the telling. "We'll marry across the anvil."

"Running to the Lowlands to be wed," Mary Elizabeth said, raising one brow. "I had heard you English did such things. But why not marry here? There are plenty of priests about."

"The marriage laws are strict."

"But not in Scotland?"

"No."

"I had always thought a handfasting with a priest to bless it was sufficient for any woman and man, so I suppose that's what you'll have when you cross the border." Mary Elizabeth straightened her shoulders and gave Catherine a swift, sure hug. "I don't understand your choice, but I'll support it. I'll look after your mother and sister as if they were my own. Robbie will only laugh at the foolishness of English girls, but Alex might take offense. He's taken quite a shine to you. I think he'll come after you."

"We'll be gone just after dawn," she answered. "He won't be able to catch us."

Mary Elizabeth did not look convinced, but she did not voice any more objections. She took out a leather sheath that held half a dozen throwing knives—the small, light kind that she had taught Catherine to throw in the duchess's ballroom what felt like a lifetime ago. She wrapped three in a heavy bit of flannel and handed them to Catherine.

"Keep one of these in your reticule at all times, and one in your boot. It's best if you hide the third somewhere in the carriage where you can get at it easily."

"Thank you, Mary, but I don't need knives."

"Aye, and you do. Your man looks to be a good sort, but I doubt he'd be good in a fight. You'll be wanting speed, so he won't be bringing outriders with him, as any sensible man should when traveling among the English. Lowlifes and ruffians abound on the North Road, and none mean to do you good. You'll take these knives and keep them by you, so you've got some defense, if some evildoer looks to harm you."

Catherine tucked the knives into her leather satchel, and slipped on the half boots Mary Elizabeth handed her. She did not lace them, but found that they fit.

"The rest of my clothes will fit you, too. My stays lace up the front, because I can't stand to have a woman dress me. You'll get used to them, and it looks as if you'll need them where you're going. I don't suppose your man will bring a lady's maid along on his honeymoon."

Mary Elizabeth laughed at that, and Catherine wondered what she thought was funny, but did not question her. But dawn was coming in less than three hours, and she had one more stop to make.

"Thank you," she said, kissing her friend on the cheek.

She left Mary Elizabeth, and stood for one long moment in the dark hall outside the bedroom door. She should go to the guest room only two doors down. She needed to rest a bit, if not sleep, before she dressed for the day ahead. But she did not. Instead, she turned the other way.

She walked down the corridor to the room she had dreamed of too many times. She had been in it only once before, but she found it with ease, like a lost pigeon coming home.

Catherine did not knock, but when she found the door to Alex Waters's room unlocked, she turned the knob and stepped inside.

Thirty-three

Once he watched Catherine walk up the stairs ahead of him, Alex went to take his own bath. Sadly, all three bathing rooms were occupied, so he stood outside the one that held his angel and listened to her splash.

He would go to the kitchen, wash himself off in the sink, then take an urn up to his dressing room and finish washing himself there. He did not need warmed water, for it was his soap that would get him clean. The water down south would never run as cold as the burn next to his father's castle, not if a new ice age came and froze the world.

Still, he lingered outside her bathing room, feeling like a cad and a bounder. He stayed and listened, thinking of her smooth skin with the water running off of it as she stood up in her bath. He left then. The pain in his loins was a good enough punishment for his thoughts. He would never touch her. Not until he had his ring on her finger.

Which, from the size of the pain he was in, had better be soon.

He did not sleep after washing up, of course, but

listened to the sounds of the house finally settling down. He stared at the wooden canopy above his bed, at the crest carved into the walnut. He supposed some Northumberland duke had commissioned it during Elizabeth I's reign, to remind the guest in question whose house they slept in. He sighed and wondered how much longer he would have to wait before he could marry his girl, and go home.

And that was when she walked into his room, the firelight gleaming on the pure white of her borrowed dressing gown, and he could no longer think at all.

"Catherine, why are you wearing my sister's boots?"

It was the only thing that Alex could force himself to say. His tongue was cleaving to the roof of this mouth, and he thought for a moment that he might choke on it.

His angel looked down at her footwear, her borrowed wrapper and nightgown still tight about her. Her soft, clean hair was braided, and his blood-deprived mind thought that he could sense a touch of jasmine on the air, much like his mother's favorite soap. He focused on that scent, but instead of dampening his ardor as it surely should have done, his ardor transformed the scent into something altogether new, something that had nothing to do with any woman save this one standing before him.

He would have her, and he knew it. He would make love to her, then marry her and ask God for forgiveness afterward.

He sat up, careful so that the bedclothes would not fall too low and frighten her away. As it was, she looked up at him, her eyes as round as saucers, taking in the expanse of his bare chest, where it shone in the dark above the bedclothes. She seemed to want to pull her eyes away, as any decent young lady would, but she didn't do it. Alex watched the pulse jump in her throat like the sudden leap of a rabbit in the garden. He needed to say something soothing, so she wouldn't flee.

"Why don't you step into my sitting room, Catherine, and I will be out in a moment."

His angel swallowed hard, her eyes still on his body. He almost took her under him then and there; it was clear she wanted him. But he was a gentleman, and she a lady, and they had more than one thing to settle still between them.

She, who was usually so graceful, stumbled a little over her unlaced boots as she slipped into his parlor. He did not take long, but drew on trousers and the shirt he had left by for the laundry woman, and walked out to her barefoot.

But his girl was brave as well as bold, for she sat where he had first set her in that room, on the settee close by his favorite chair. He sat beside her, so that she might get used to the scent of him, and accept his nearness before he touched her. She stiffened in fear at first, but when he did not reach for her, as he so often had in the past, she relaxed against the cushions behind her and sighed.

"You should be sleeping, Catherine. Why are you up and about, wandering the duchess's house in a wrapper and boots?"

"And a bag," his angel said, gesturing to a leather satchel that sat oddly by his door. "I'm going away tomorrow, but I wanted to tell you good-bye first."

He loved the singular turn of her mind, and the odd fancies she gave herself over to. He knew that he would love exploring those turns of mind, and talking her out of her fancies, for the rest of his life.

Now that he had her alone in his room, half-dressed, he would never let her go. He would be pleased to escort her to his Lordship of Love's house on the morrow, that she might set him down easy, and explain things to him. And if she did not wish to do so, Alex would visit the young lord himself, and put him at his ease. He would call on the Waterses's charm of Glenderrin fame. With any luck, the man wouldn't get too hotheaded and try to shoot him with a dueling pistol, or brain him with a walking stick.

Alex looked at the curves of his angel in the fire-light. The man would be right to brain him and steal her for himself. Of course, as a man and a Scot, Alex would not allow it. Still, he had a bit of sympathy for the English bastard, now that he had won.

All this passed through his mind in an instant, and then he rose slowly from the settee so as not to frighten her, and knelt beside her feet on the plush carpet.

She looked alarmed in truth then, and he realized that the rutting bastard must have proposed to her that day in the woods, kneeling down much as he was now. He set such an unpleasant thought aside, and smiled up at her. At the sight of his smile, she relaxed a little, and he started talking.

"I am sorry to hear you're going," he said. "But you're not leaving this instant, are you? Not in my sister's best dressing gown?"

"I—I suppose not."

Catherine looked down at her attire as if seeing it for the first time. She drew the top of the robe together tighter under her chin, which served only to draw the fabric close against her magnificent breasts. She was not wearing stays, and he could see the outline of her softness pressed against the cotton and silk. He swallowed hard and managed to keep his voice even, though it had grown a bit raspy.

"Well, take your rest awhile here. Have a sip of cider with me." His hand slid down her leg, from her knee to her toes, and she did not jump away, but shivered. He looked up at her and saw the heat in his eyes reflected in her own. He did not speed up his movements, though, or pull her down to him on the carpet as he so sorely wished to. He would make her first time a time of pure bliss, if he was lucky enough to get permission to touch her.

Had she been any other woman, alone in his room with him in the dark of night, he would have been sure of the outcome. But it was his angel sitting here beside him. He never knew with any certainty what she might do. She might fly into a fit of irritation suddenly if he moved too quick. She might flounce out, leaving both boots and bag behind.

As she took a deep breath, and her breasts rose and fell above him, he knew he could not bear it if she left him flat. Not this time.

For the moment, he settled for slipping his hand over her ankle. "Might I help you remove your boots, at least while you're here?" He slid his hand beneath her gown, up to her bare knee, and back down again. She wore no stockings, and all he could feel was the soft give of her firm calf beneath his fingertips. She shivered again, and it seemed to him that her mossy-green eyes grew darker.

She did not answer, and he suppressed a smile of triumph. So far, it seemed he was winning. But his girl could turn on a farthing, so he kept his face smooth of the passion he felt, though his own breath was coming hard and his heart pounded in his ears like the hooves of a runaway horse.

"Or should I lace them for you, as we have no maid present?"

His angel laughed then, even in the face of her own desire. "I suppose we can take them off, for a little while at least. They are uncomfortable without the laces done. And I have no stockings on."

"So I see." Alex tried to stop himself, but he found his hand moving up to her knee again beneath the cotton of her nightgown. His other hand traced the curve of her leg, stopping—with difficulty—at the knee. He wanted to trace higher, and feel the soft skin of her inner thighs beneath the calluses of his palms. As it was, her eyes had grown heavy-lidded with wanting, but she tensed beneath his hands, so he took them away again.

"Are your feet cold?" Alex said. "I have a thick pair of wool socks that might suit you."

She laughed at that too, her body relaxing against the cushions behind her once more.

"It's May, Alex. I'm warm enough, I think."

He drew her boots off, one at a time, caressing her instep as he did so. She was not ticklish it seemed, or at least not under his hands. He began to massage her feet and she sighed deeply.

"You're tired, Catherine. Perhaps you should leave your journeying for tomorrow."

"No," she said, her voice dreamy with pleasure as his large hands encompassed her small feet, soothing the tension and soreness out of them. "I have to go soon," she said. Her voice trailed off, and she moaned a little.

The sound went straight to his loins, and he had to swallow the lust that rose like a beast inside him. "But not yet," he managed to say.

"No," she answered. "Not yet."

He was sure she would sleep then, no matter what she said, but when he stopped rubbing her toes, her eyelids fluttered open and she smiled at him. "Thank you, Alex. I don't know why I feel so at ease with you. So safe. It is not right, but there it is. I feel as if I have known you for much longer than we have, as if we grew up together in the same house, under the same roof, since I was a girl."

Alex did not move, for fear he might break the spell. He stared up at her, taking in the soft golden strands of her braid as it fell over one shoulder, crossing her breast. He took in the sight of her sweet face, relaxed in a sleepy smile. He would make it his life's work to make her feel this safe and happy, and to keep her that way for the rest of her days.

If she had been a more experienced woman, he would have raised her foot to his lips and kissed her instep, trailing his mouth and tongue up her leg slowly, to discover other pleasures. As it was, however, he simply kept his hand over both her feet where they rested on the fancy ducal carpet.

"You will always be safe with me," he said. "Every day of your life, from this day forward."

Catherine seemed to hear the vow within his words and she frowned a little, a shadow crossing her beautiful face. "Alex—" she began.

But he raised one hand and smiled at her. "Don't trouble yourself just now, Catherine Middlebrook. Take another sip of cider with me before you go, either to bed down the hall or on your journey to back of beyond."

She relaxed at his odd compliance, and he almost laughed out loud. How on God's blessed earth she could think that he would ever let her go after she had clung to him in the midst of the fire, after she had come to his room in the dark of night, he could not say. Still, he would never know the all workings of this woman's mind, and he supposed he did not need to. He need only love her, and honor her, and all the rest would follow.

Thirty-four

His hands rubbing her feet had made her almost fall asleep. But the pleasure was too great, so Catherine stayed awake.

When he vowed to keep her safe for the rest of her life, her heart almost burst in her chest. His touch was so gentle, so tender for such a large man. She should leave him. She should go to her room and change, then sneak out to find Lord Farleigh. She knew this, but she still had hours until morning, hours until full light. She wanted to keep these stolen hours, and spend them with him.

What would happen if she kissed him?

She was a bold, wanton woman. She had known this since she first touched him in her front hallway. And now she sat with him, alone in the middle of the night, in the middle of his sitting room, thinking about how it would feel to have his lips on hers again.

She drank the cider he brought her. He warmed it over the fire in front of her, and then handed it to her as if it were tribute, and she, the Queen of Sheba. She took a sip and the taste of sweet apple slid down her throat, warming her insides as much as his smile did.

"Cider is the one thing the English do right," he said.

She smiled at him, feeling coquettish. "I must remind you again that I am an Englishwoman."

"Do remind me." He sat down beside her, his big body a wall of heat. He sat close this time, so that his thigh rested against the softness of her gown. The strength of him was like a bulwark against the world, and she wished again, and fervently, that she might be free to choose him, and take shelter with him for the rest of his life.

He knew nothing of her thoughts, nothing of what she owed to another. He ran his fingertip along her jaw, pushing one blonde curl gently back from her cheek. "You are from Devon, are you not?"

His lips brushed her temple, and she almost dropped the mug she held. He took it from her in one deft motion, setting it aside she knew not where, for her eyes were closed, that she might feel only the heat of his body and hear only the honey warmth of his voice.

"Yes," she said, her voice sounding breathless in her own ears.

"I have it on good authority that Devon is practically Cornwall, and Cornwall is practically civilized."

His lips were on hers then, moving with the soft insistence that she remembered from her dreams. The taste of him was sweet and salt together, the feel of his tongue on hers a temptation she could not turn from. He kissed her deeply, his mouth covering hers with a hunger that rose like the flames of a flash fire, threatening to consume her. She let her reason go, and gave herself up to the way his lips felt on hers. If she was to have this bliss only once, let it be tonight.

Just as that wicked thought filtered through her mind, he drew back, taking his warmth with him, leaving her unsatisfied.

She ached deep in her belly. Her throat was dry and all she could think about was the way he tasted—and that she wanted that taste on her tongue again.

"Catherine," he said, his voice rasping against her skin, though he now sat a foot away, reclining backward on the cushions of his bedroom's settee. "My angel, we must stop. You must go to bed. We will speak in the morning."

Catherine knew that she might live to be a very old woman. She might live out her life in Devon, or wherever Lord Farleigh's seat was, and never be touched by a man like this again. No. She would never be touched by this man again.

She knew now why her mother was so loud and despairing. Her mother despaired because she had once had a love like this, and lost it.

That would not be Catherine's fate. She would not grow wild as her mother had, but once she lost Alex, a part of her heart would fade away from disuse. Her children would have her heart; her husband would have it. But there was a piece of her that would always be in this room, sitting in the firelight with Alexander Waters of Glenderrin.

That part of her deserved something to take with her when she left.

"All right," she said, standing. Her legs were weak beneath her, but they held her weight. The look of surprise that crossed Alex's face shored her up as well. She might be young and inexperienced, but she had seen this man cut a swath through the ladies of the *ton*. She knew he was not a man who was used to women walking away.

But she did not leave the room, taking her bag with her. She walked into his bedroom instead, without looking back.

She stripped off her dressing gown and laid it over a chair. She did it carefully, laying it down precisely, as if she were in her own room. She heard him in the doorway then, and she turned to smile at him.

Alex was not smiling.

"You can't sleep here," he said.

"I don't mean to sleep," she answered.

His voice was strangled. "What do you mean to do then?"

"I don't know," she said. "I had hoped that you might show me."

He walked out, and she felt the first flash of humiliation slide up from the ground, burning through her body. She felt her hated blush, and prayed that the horror might consume her as the heat from his touch had threatened to do. But it did not. Her blush subsided, for she saw him step back into the bedroom with her bag in hand. She watched as he closed and locked the door behind him.

He held up the key. "I have locked the outer door. As you can see, I have locked this one."

He tossed her bag down and held the key aloft. He laid it on his open palm and offered it to her.

"The servants cannot come in now and catch us. I am giving this key to you. But in return, I would ask for your pledge that you won't leave this room without me."

Her heart pounded in her ears. She shook with the need to touch him, but she held her ground. She would not lie to him, and she did not.

"I promise, Alex. I will not leave by that door, not unless you walk beside me."

He nodded then, and laid the key on his dressing table where it gleamed in the candlelight. He did not come to her, and she realized that he was still waffling, no doubt wrestling with his honor.

She would have to go to him herself.

Catherine pushed all thoughts of Lord Farleigh, of duty, of her grandmother's teachings, out of her head. She would forget them all, and be with this one man. She would think about all the rest later. This hour, and all the wonders it held, was for her.

She stepped toward him, and stood close until her breasts brushed the white linen of his shirt.

"I still think you should go, Catherine. But if you stay, know that you'll be mine. Not just tonight, but always." He looked into her eyes, searching her face as he had down by the river. She hoped he could only see her love for him, and not her real plans for the future. She hoped that he saw the desire that matched his own, the heat she did not know what to do with, but which she wanted finally to indulge in with him.

"I am yours already," she said. "Now kiss me."

Thirty-five

ALEX USUALLY DID NOT NEED TO BE TOLD TO KISS A woman. Usually, he did not need to be led to his own bed as a lamb on a rope. But this was no ordinary woman. This was the woman who would bear his sons, the woman who would lie by his side in that bed, and every other, for the rest of his life. It was a heavy moment, full of portents and of the future. Still, his body raged on, his lust like the background music of an opera, when all he wanted to do was stand and take in the beauty of the woman about to open her mouth to sing. His songbird stood before him, waiting. In the end, it was she who once again stepped close, rose on the tips of her toes, and kissed him.

She had learned a bit since the last time. Her knowledge seemed to grow by what it fed on, and now her lips danced over his with their own innate rhythm—not the steps he had taught her, but new ones, entirely her own. He could taste her desire and her innocence together, a heady drug.

She pressed herself against him and he could feel the soft contours of her breasts against his chest. His arms went around her in spite of his better judgment. He knew he would have to choose: surrender or send her away. But he also knew himself. He had locked both doors, not just to keep her in, but to keep the rest of the world out. He intended to have her, and to make it such a night that the priest's blessing to come would seem like an afterthought. This was their true wedding night, and he would vow himself to her before he took her under him.

He pulled back from her, and when she moaned in protest, he pressed his lips to hers once, swiftly, in consolation. "I must speak, my angel, before we go on."

"Must you?"

She wriggled against him, trying to give her hungry body solace, trying to find a way to assuage the need she felt. But she rubbed hard against his nether region, and he felt desire spike in his blood and in his chest like a lance. He took a deep breath, thanking God he was a man, and in control of himself.

He looked into her fevered eyes. The mossy green had burned away, and brightly lit emeralds had taken their place. He almost said to hell with it and kissed her again, but this moment between them was sacred. Impatient as she was, she would thank him for it later.

"You must know that I have a special license. We will be married tomorrow, by my uncle, the Bishop of London, quietly. Your mother and sister will attend, as will Robert and Mary Elizabeth. You may even have Mr. Pridemore there, if you prefer."

The last was a sad attempt at a joke, but his angel did not think it was funny. He could see that he was dampening her ardor with all this talk of planning. She pressed herself against him again, no doubt in an effort to distract him from his folly. He swallowed hard, his lust beginning to rise like a flash tide that would never go out.

"But this night is our wedding night, for all that a priest has not blessed us yet. My uncle is Church of England, and good for little other than to circumvent English law. But I will marry you again in the Highlands, at Glenderrin, with both our families present, before a true priest of the Church." Alex realized he'd been issuing orders as if she were his valet. He swallowed hard, and watched the firelight as it played over the gentle planes of her face.

She was as still as a rabbit in his hand, a rabbit who hoped to deceive the hunter into passing on.

"Will you marry me, Catherine Middlebrook?"

She swallowed hard and kissed him, fiercely. She looked into his eyes. "The day we find ourselves before a true priest of the Church, I will wed you, and bless the day as the best of my life."

He quirked an eyebrow at her. It was an odd way to agree to be his wife, when all she had to do was say *yes*, but nothing was easy with his girl.

"All right, then," he said.

It seemed that there was a shadow in her eyes, dimming the emerald brilliance. But she pressed herself against him as if she were drowning at sea and he was the last rock in the world. He kissed her then, and wondered how he was going to coax her nightgown off without frightening her when she wriggled out of his arms and walked away.

❦

Catherine could not bear one more moment of talking about a marriage that would never be. She knew now that she would be breaking his heart as well as her own. Once she was safely wed to another, she would write to Alex and explain all she had done, and why. No doubt he would curse her, and all the love he felt for her now would turn to bitterness. Catherine knew that she was selfish. She should leave him where he stood, even now. The key waited for her. All she had to do was pick it up, and turn it in the lock. But she knew that she would not do it.

She walked to his bed and climbed up on it. She was no siren, and had no way of knowing how fashionable ladies got their husbands to come to them when they were reluctant. She would have to simply be herself, and improvise.

She drew her borrowed nightgown up and over her head, tossing it down on the thick rug. She felt a blush rise, but for once it was not from embarrassment. Alex's jaw went slack from shock, his eyes darkening almost to black with desire. A sudden wave of triumph broke over her, and she felt drunk with power. That she could make the man she loved look at her like that by only taking off a cotton gown was a miracle.

Next, she undid her braid.

He did not move to her side but watched her as a cat watched a mouse hole. Something new and strange seemed bound to happen when he leaped on her as that cat might. She had no doubt that he would make sure that she enjoyed it.

She knew a little of what went on from watching the birds dance and the sheep cover each other in the fall, but she was not ready to turn her back on him and let him mount her yet. As much as she wanted his body on hers, she wanted to keep looking at him even more.

Her hair fell about her shoulders and down her back like a curtain. She sighed at the feeling of the softness of her own hair against her skin. Her hair was always up, except when she brushed it out. She had never felt it against her naked skin before. She rolled her neck back and forth and her long hair moved with it, sliding over her back and shoulders like a blessing. She almost forgot about Alex for a moment of sensual pleasure, but he was beside her then, reminding her of his presence.

"You are the most beautiful woman God ever made," he said. He placed his hand gently against her cheek, leaning down to kiss her. He did not devour her, as she wished he would, but skated his lips across hers, then down her cheek, to her throat, where his mouth caressed the beat of her pulse.

He laved his tongue there against her skin, and she shivered, grabbing on to him. She rose up on her knees, trying to draw him closer. But he was much bigger than she was. There was no doubt from the moment he touched her who was in control.

She let him draw her down onto the bed, the soft sheets and blankets cushioning her as she fell. She smelled the scent of bergamot all around her then, both from the heat of his skin and from the sheets beneath her head, and she knew in that moment that she had come home.

He lay down on top of her, and she moaned as his

lips closed over her nipple. It had never occurred to her that a man might do such a thing, but she was so happy that he did. His other hand closed over her other breast, so that she was assaulted with pleasure on all sides.

She tried to keep her eyes closed, so that she could concentrate on nothing but how it felt to have him touch her, but she could not stop looking at the way his dark hair fell against the white of her skin, reveling in the feel of his lips on her body. She started to tremble beneath him, and he smiled up at her.

For one awful moment, she thought he might stop what he was doing, but he simply kissed her over her heart, then leaned down and went back to his work on her other breast.

His lips closed over her and his tongue twirled in some magical way across her flesh. When he bit down, once, very gently, she cried out from the pleasure, and he did it again. There was a wicked gleam of triumph in his eyes when he looked up at her.

She was breathless, but she found she could still speak. "Don't be too full of yourself, Alex Waters. You're getting too big for your britches."

He laughed out loud at that, and she felt the delicious vibration of it all the way down her body. "I am definitely too big for my britches at the moment, sweet Catherine, but that is all your doing."

She was not sure what he meant, until he pressed his hips to hers and she felt the swelling of his manhood against her. Catherine took a deep breath, reaching for her courage even as she ran her hand over him through the thick wool of his trousers. She was well rewarded, for Alex groaned, then hissed between his teeth. She liked to watch his face change as she ran her palm over him. Her hand was small, and he was large, but her ministrations seemed to bear fruit, for when he opened his eyes again, all the laughter had been burned out of them.

For one moment, she felt a thrill of fear, much like she had when she'd told him he might take money from her. His face was all hard planes at that moment. With his long, dark hair falling around them, he looked more like a warrior bent on plunder than a gentleman.

Thank God for that.

She knew not where that irrational thought had come from, for it fled just as quickly. For he stood up and left her. She opened her mouth to protest, but he started undressing, and she found that her breath was gone.

He stood over her supine, naked body, his eyes running over her skin from her toes to her face. She closed her mouth and took in the beauty of him as he stood above her, his wide chest dusted with a coating of dark hair. As he leaned down to strip off his trousers, she reached up and ran her hand across his chest, very lightly, to see how that hair felt against her skin. Her palm warmed from his scented flesh and his hair felt soft and prickly at the same time. She was about to tell him this when he fell on her again, his great body one large, heated brick against her.

She wriggled in pleasure at the warmth of it, knowing now how Scottish women stayed warm through the depths of those long, cold winters.

Alex looked down into her face, and she felt the pleasure at his warmth taking second place to the pleasure his lust brought her. He spoke then, and she felt tears of joy come into her eyes.

"I love you. I will love you all my life, and beyond, if the priests are right. I want you to know it."

She pressed her hand against his heart, and felt it thundering above her. She leaned up and pressed her lips where her palm had been, the wiry hair of his chest soft against her cheek. She kissed him, then rubbed her face against him like a cat.

"I love you, Alex. And I always will."

He lowered himself to her, and she shivered as she felt all of his weight come down on her. His manhood was high against her belly, but she could not reach down to touch it, because he had taken both of her hands in one of his. He raised her wrists above her head so that her breasts stood at attention close to his mouth. He blew on them with his heated breath until the nipples peaked, calling to him. She wriggled and moaned, but he did not move to give her relief.

"You are mine, Catherine Middlebrook. Don't forget it."

His lips sealed this promise by pressing over hers just as his chest pressed down on her breasts. He let her wrists go then, for his hands smoothed their way down her body, rising to cup her breasts in a heated caress, and moving lower over her thighs.

She left her hand above her head in abject surrender as he lowered his mouth to follow his hands all the way down her body, from her breasts, across her belly, to between her thighs, where at long last, he kissed her.

Thirty-six

HER NETHER LIPS SMELLED LIKE JASMINE, WARM woman, and desire. He laved his tongue across the folds of her flower until it opened beneath his mouth. He plundered it, searching for the sweet spot that would bring her the most bliss. He found it almost at once, for she was the most responsive woman he had ever had the privilege to touch.

He had primed the well, for she was at the brink of pleasure when he put his mouth on her. It took very little to coax her over that edge.

She cried his name and fell apart in his arms. He held her down and his mouth did not stop moving over her, his tongue running over that place between her thighs until she bit her lip, as if trying to suppress her own noise—and almost succeeded.

She fell silent finally, hoarse and trembling. He felt her soft hands on his hair, and he raised his head to smile at her.

"What was that?" she asked him, her breath still gone.

"That was fun and pleasure both," he said.

She laughed a little at that but tapped him on the

crown to let him know he had better answer her, and quick.

"It has a Latin name, but I've never been over fond of Latin. Let us simply call it kissing the quim, and leave it at that."

"Quim?" she asked, looking thoughtful.

"Yes," he answered, raising himself on one elbow so he could better enjoy the play of her thoughts as they crossed her face.

"Hmmm…" she said.

He leaned down and hummed against her belly, making her writhe. "Hmmm indeed," he said.

She laughed again, as he had meant her to.

"I am still hungry," she said.

"I'll sneak down stairs and get you a snack," he said, his body protesting fiercely as he started to rise from the warmth of hers.

"No," she said, smacking him lightly again, as if he were an unruly schoolboy and it was the only way she could get his attention. "My body is still hungry for you. How can that be?"

He raised himself to meet her halfway and kissed her lips gently. "Your body is still hungry because we are not done yet."

Her eyes widened and he almost laughed at her sweetness. He was about to take her innocence, and gladly, but there was a great deal about it he would miss. Of course, the compensations would more than make up for the loss.

"I love you, Catherine Middlebrook. Don't forget it."

Tears came into her eyes, and when one rolled down her temple, he kissed it away.

He smoothed his hands down her body, feeling the supple curves and the softness of her skin beneath his hand. She shivered under his touch, and the desire rose again behind her eyes, rising off her flesh like the heat from a peat fire. He leaned down and kissed her lips, and when he drew back, he met her eyes.

"If you wish to turn back, tell me now."

She smiled at him, her eyes still bright with tears and lust together. "I don't want to turn back."

She wriggled then, so he gave her room and let her get her bearings. But she did not rise from their bed. Instead, she turned her back to him and rose on her knees and hands, presenting her beautiful, rounded derrière for his view.

He kissed her bottom, running his hands over it. "My angel," he said, "what are you doing?"

"I'm presenting my backside," she answered pertly, "so you can mount me."

He bit his lip hard so that he would not laugh at her. He coughed instead, and moved to the cup of water that sat by on the bedside table to take a sip from it. She looked at him over one shoulder, puzzled, and he offered the cup to her. She shook her head, but her eyes were beginning to lose their gleam of lust and take on the light of embarrassment.

"Catherine," he said. "I will take you that way once or twice in our married life, I warrant. But not this time."

Her look of embarrassment began to fade, and intrigue began to take its place. "There is another way?" she asked. "I have seen the horses and the pigs and the sheep do it like this."

"As man, we are closer to God, and as such, we have other options. Why don't you let me lead, as if we were waltzing, and let's see where we end up?"

She turned back and sat next to him, as trusting as a foal. Her breasts pressed against his side, and the scent of her jasmine skin filled him with light. He was overwhelmed with love for this girl, and thanked God for her, even as she sat there. She took the cup from his hand then and drank the cool, clear water that had come up from the duchess's well.

"You had better lead," she said. "I don't know what to do, other than what I've seen at home in the barnyard."

He smiled and pushed her blonde curls out of her eyes, pressing his lips to the corner of her mouth. "Why don't you come sit in my lap, and see what you find?"

She looked down at his burgeoning manhood and smiled at him. It had subsided a bit while he was struggling with laughter, but the sight of her naked, pressed against him, beautiful and innocent, made his lust rise again.

She crawled into his lap and wrapped her arms around him. She sat on him as she would a horse, sidesaddle, with her legs dangling down. That would not work for their purposes, but he did not mean to take her that way her first time at any rate. He let her sit as she would while he kissed her, trailing his lips down her temple, over her cheek and jaw, and down her throat.

"Alex," she said, her breathing not as ragged as he had hoped it might be, "this is lovely. But might we lie back down and do it your way?"

He laughed and kissed her full on the mouth. "You'd like me lying down then, would you?"

"I like it when you lie down on top of me," she said. "I feel safe from the world."

"And so you are."

He lingered over her lips until her tongue joined him in the dance. When he drew back, her breath was short at last. His hand caressed her breasts, first one and then the other, until her nipples were hard against his palm. Catherine arched a little, writhing on his lap, brushing against his manhood while pushing the softness of her breast deeper into his hand. He had made her wait too long already.

He ran his hands over her body, from her breasts to her quim, and back again. She pressed her hips against him in earnest, and as she trembled, he felt her lust catch fire. He lay her down then, not wasting time to chat or canoodle any further. He laid his body over hers, just as she had requested, and instead of trembling and closing her knees, her thighs fell open instinctively to cradle him between them.

"I love you, Catherine," he said again. The words had become his new catechism, and he repeated them so that she might not forget.

Her response filled his heart with joy even as she wriggled beneath him, trying to get closer. "I love you, Alex. Now, show me what to do."

He laughed low, pressing his lips to her heart so that she could feel the vibration of it in her breast. She shivered, and he laved her nipple one more time, his questing hand seeking her warmth and wetness. She was damp and ready, and he could wait no longer.

He had been as much a gentleman as he might. When they rose from that bed, he would place his ring on her finger, the ring he had purchased yesterday. But now he let all else go, and rested his body and his mind on her.

"I will do my best not to hurt you," he said.

"No more talking, Alex," she said. "I need you."

He slipped his manhood between her thighs and pressed inside her relentlessly, in one smooth motion. He felt her maidenhead give, and she tensed beneath him from the pain. He stopped moving and kissed her temple. "I'm sorry, *leannan*. It won't happen again."

"It won't?" she asked, looking horrified and wounded at the same time.

He kissed her lips. "The pain won't."

She relaxed beneath him when he said that, and her passage made way for his intrusion, as if she had begun to learn his dimensions already. He was a big man, and she was a good deal smaller, but her body fit him like a well-tailored glove. He moved in her a little, raising her hips so that he might brush over her secret place within. He knew he had hit the spot when she gasped. "Alex!"

Once found, he moved against it relentlessly, ruthlessly ignoring his own needs and focusing solely on hers.

She came apart in his arms as she had when he kissed her nether lips, but this time, her screams were so loud that he had to kiss her to silence her. She shook beneath him as if she had been taken over by an earthquake that affected only her, though her passage tightened around him so that he had to breathe deep to keep from losing the last vestige of his control. But he was not a man and a Scot for nothing, and he managed to bring her to the peak of bliss not once but twice before he gave himself up to the way her body felt around and beneath him.

He lay on top of her afterward as if slain by a giant, struck down by a force greater than himself. He had taken his first lover at fifteen. He enjoyed women, all of them, whether he had them or not. But if he needed more proof that this woman was different, he had it as he held her in his arms after their mutual climax had passed. Unlike before, he did not want to flee. He was not thinking of where he needed to be on the morrow, what he needed to do or what tasks needed to be seen to. He thought not of how to ask her to leave, but how to get her to stay.

But then he remembered: he had locked all the doors, and Catherine had sworn not to pass beyond the door without him. This time, his girl would not walk away from him. This time, he had her.

He kissed her and brushed her hair back from her face. "Are you all right?"

She was weeping quietly, as some women were wont to do after their pleasure had passed. He kissed her tears away, but they fell too quickly, so he reached for a handkerchief and wiped her eyes for her.

"I hope these are tears of joy," he said.

She kissed him then, and he tasted her sorrow. Perhaps she was worried about what Lord Loverboy would say, or her mother, or how the world would look at her from that day on. Since they were to marry in the morning, the world had better keep a civil tongue in its head. He had no interest in letting anyone speak ill of his wife, that day or ever.

"I love you, Catherine. My angel, do not weep. You hurt my heart."

She stopped then, and sniffled against his chest. She lay quiet against him, and he held her close until her breathing turned even, and for many minutes after. When he knew she was asleep, he allowed himself to drift off as well.

They lay together on that borrowed bed, as if adrift on an island in a silent sea. All he could hear was the sound of her breathing, and the sound of the wind as it blew against the house. The tree next to his window rattled a bit against the glass, but the sound was soothing, for she was in his arms, as if she had always been there, as he knew she always would be.

Thirty-seven

THE MAN SHE WOULD LOVE ALL HER LIFE SLEPT THE sleep of the just beneath her. She watched him sleep, his face relaxed as she now knew it rarely was. When he was awake, he was always watchful, always taking care of everyone around him—Mary Elizabeth, his brother, and her.

Catherine kissed his lips, feathering hers lightly over his face and across his eyelids. He shifted in his sleep but did not wake. Her stolen season, as beautiful as it had been, was over.

The knowledge of the mortgage money she owed Lord Farleigh bore down on her soul like the weight of the world. And now she would have this to hide from him, too—not only that she had lost her maidenhead, but that her heart would always belong to another.

She thought of her mother, of her sister, of her grandmother. She thought of her father, buried in the family chapel, and of how her mother would one day want to be buried there beside him. She could not renege on this deal, unspoken as it was. Lord Farleigh had bought back her childhood home, and now her future was his.

She kissed Alex one last time, then disentangled herself from his embrace. He was strong, but he was gentle, for when she pulled away, after the first reflexive clutching of her person, he seemed to remember his manners even in his sleep. Alex was never a man to hold a lady against her will, locked doors aside. Even in sleep, when she asked it of him, he let her go.

She dressed quickly and quietly after she used the chamber pot and washed herself clean. She smelled of bergamot soap after, and she savored the scent, though it also brought her pain. She filched the bar that sat by the washbasin, slipping it into her borrowed bag. She would return everything else to the Waterses once she was wed, but not that. The soap Alex used was something she would keep.

The window was silent and well oiled, which was to be expected in a duchess's house. Catherine raised it above her head and cast her borrowed bag down into the garden below. It was a good throw, for the bag landed far away from the house and did not ruin even one flowered bush.

She reached below the bed and drew out the hemp rope ladder that she knew she would find there. Mary Elizabeth had stowed such rope ladders all over the second and third floors of the house. When Catherine returned, she would tell her friend to stow some on the fourth floor, so that the servants might escape a fire if the duchess's house were to have the bad manners to burn down in the night.

She took one last look at the man she loved, sleeping peacefully where she had left him. He slept on his stomach now, with a pillow clutched close. Tears rose

in her eyes, but she told herself to stop being a fool.
She was a woman now, making a woman's choice.
She had no more time or use for tears.

The rope ladder held steady as she climbed down
the side of the Duchess of Northumberland's house.
The wind was fierce and rising, but the great oak
beside Alex's window sheltered her as she descended,
just as he would have done if he had been there. Her
feet touched the ground and she stood for a long
moment, looking up at the room, at the life she had
left behind. She said a prayer for Alex Waters, and all
his kin, before she picked up her borrowed bag and
left the ducal garden, where climbing roses of red and
white were just beginning to bloom.

※

Lord Farleigh lived just two squares over, close by
Hyde Park. She walked all the way, her steps slowing
even as she approached her goal. The sun was rising
through last night's coal smoke, and she could see a
hint of blue begin to light the sky. It was going to be
a beautiful day.

The pain in her heart stole her breath. But even so,
she felt more alive than she had ever felt, save when
she was in Alex Waters's arms.

In spite of the day and the night she had just spent,
she was not tired. She felt instead as if it were her last
day on earth, and every ounce of energy she possessed
must go into memorizing the beauty of the day, the
blue of the sky, the song of the lark from a nearby elm.
She stood in front of Lord Farleigh's door. Once she
knocked, her life would change forever.

She reminded herself that her life had changed for the worse the day her mother took out the mortgage on their family home, and again on the day she spoke of the debt to Lord Farleigh. The die was cast, and now she must pay the croupier.

"Good day, madam."

Lord Farleigh's butler could not have shown more contempt if he had refused to open the door to her altogether. He stared down at her, his eyebrows rising, taking her in as if she were a fallen woman. Which, she supposed, was what she was.

"Might I inquire if Lord Farleigh is at home?"

The man drew himself up straight to an even more impressive height. "His lordship is at home, but he is unaccustomed to receiving visitors at such an hour."

"Billings, let her pass, for the love of God. That is my future wife."

The butler straightened his back even more, if such a thing were possible. His look of disdain did not waver, but his voice was bland and all correctness as he bowed to her slightly. "Very good, my lord. My felicitations, miss."

He stepped back and let her inside, then closed the door behind her. Lord Farleigh stood at the foot of the staircase, dressed in riding clothes.

"Forgive me," she said. "I have come too early."

He smiled. The warmth of it was like a sunrise, and did a little to warm her bruised and battered heart. She had hurt herself, and badly, for few wounds bleed as much as self-inflicted ones. In Arthur's presence, she felt a slight lifting of her spirits. He was not dashing. He was not beautiful, as Alex was. But he was her friend.

"Bring tea and toast into the drawing room, Billings."

"Very good, my lord."

Arthur took her arm and hefted her bag. "You look as if you've run away," he said, the smile on his face betraying how foolish such a thing would be.

"I have," Catherine answered him. "I was hoping you might run away with me."

Arthur's handsome face was marred with a frown as he seated her in a comfortable chair. The fire in the grate had not yet been lit, so he bent down with a flint to light it instead of calling for someone else to do it.

"Catherine, I am afraid I do not understand."

"Yesterday, you asked me to marry you. Do you still wish to marry me?"

Arthur looked at her gravely as he stood before her. "I do."

"The answer to your question then is yes. But with two conditions. I want to elope to Gretna Green, and I want to leave today."

"You want to leave this morning," he said, gesturing to the bag he had set down close by the hearth.

"Yes." Catherine was amazed at herself. She did not blush, nor did her hands shake. She faced Arthur squarely without even feeling pain anymore. The pain would come back, but for now, all she could feel was the need to be gone.

"I must ask you first about your Scottish cousin," Arthur said.

Catherine felt a pang of dread, and could not stop herself from foolish obfuscation. "Mary Elizabeth?"

Arthur smiled at that. "I think you know who I mean."

She looked down at her hands where they were

folded demurely in her lap. She realized for the first time that, in her haste to be gone, she had forgotten gloves and a bonnet.

She cleared her throat, and met Arthur's eyes. "I suppose you know he is not my cousin."

Arthur sat down beside her. "I had gathered that."

"I love him," she said.

He waited patiently, and did not rise to his feet in anger, nor did he speak.

"I love him," she said. "But we do not suit. I am going to marry you."

Arthur was silent for a long time. The room was so quiet that she could hear the ormolu clock ticking from its place on the marble mantelpiece. The fire burned cheerfully, and she kept one eye on it, feeling a little fearful that it might leap the hearth and catch her bag, and the rest of the house, on fire. It was irrational, but she had never wanted so badly to be gone from any room in all her life.

"Are you certain, Catherine? The choice you make is a grave one, and once done, it cannot be undone." Arthur took her hand in his. "You are not wearing my ring."

"It is in the bag there."

He smoothed the skin of her hand with his fingertips, then kissed it. "If you come with me now, know that you may turn back, even as we stand together over the anvil. I will honor your choice, whatever choice you make, between him and me. I am not the most handsome man in the kingdom. But I am a good man, and a steady one, who will care for you and yours the rest of your life, if that is truly what you wish."

"Yes," Catherine said. "I know it. And I honor you for it. It is why I have chosen you."

He kissed her then, and his lips were chaste, like the touch of a cool stream on a windless day. He drew back from her almost at once, and rose to his feet.

"Eat a bit of toast and jam. Drink the tea Billings will bring. I will call for the carriage, and have the horses put to."

"You will take me north then?" She felt a strange feeling of relief, coupled with a sorrow that she knew she would bear for the rest of her life. Arthur smiled at her, and she felt a little of the sorrow ease.

"Of course we will go to Gretna Green. If you are certain you wish to wed, I will see it done." He turned to leave, but stopped at the door. His smile widened, as if he just realized that he would soon see his wedding day. "I am sorry you wish to flee, but there is no other woman I would rather run north with."

He bowed to her like the gentleman he was, and she was left alone, with the dratted fire burning close beside her. She stood and moved her bag farther from the flames, wishing all the while that she did not feel as if she had thrown herself into a fire of her own making.

Thirty-eight

ALEX WOKE TO THE SCENT OF JASMINE.

He stretched and smiled in his sleep, knowing even before he woke that the scent of jasmine meant that his love lay close beside him. He did not open his eyes but reached for her, and found only a soft pillow upon which her head had lain the night before. His eyes opened, and the room was bare.

"Catherine?"

He woke all at once, and was on his feet. The window stood open to the morning light. Someone, perhaps that damned Englishman, had somehow climbed in through the window and taken her.

Then he saw Mary Elizabeth's hemp rope ladder clinging to its place on the sill where his sister had driven nails into the duchess's expensive wainscoting. He swore, loudly and eloquently, for a full minute. Then he got possession of himself, and dressed in clean riding clothes.

He managed not to shriek like a fishwife in the middle of the ducal household, but walked all the way down to the breakfast room before venting his wrath.

"Mary Elizabeth," he said, his voice cold. "You will tell me where she is, and you will tell me now."

Robbie swallowed hard, almost choking on his toast. Mrs. Angel sat sipping her oversugared tea, regarding him passively. Mary Elizabeth was the only one who would not meet his gaze. His sister looked down at her plate, which held a single slice of barley bread with honey. She seemed fascinated with her favorite breakfast all of sudden, but he knew her well, for he had been foiling schemes of hers all her short life. As he watched, her thoughts flitted across her face as sunlight over a pane of glass. His sister was willful, headstrong, and difficult, but she was not a liar.

"She has gone to meet her Englishman," she said at last. She faced him without flinching, her maple eyes showing no remorse, but a certain level of pity.

"God have mercy," Mrs. Angel said. "That girl is determined to ruin her life."

Alex did not speak, for he could not find his voice. Mary Elizabeth found hers, as she always seemed to. "Alex, she loves you. I'm sure of that. But that Englishman has some hold over her. She feels bound to him, though I know not why."

"She has not told you?" His question sounded like the grinding of broken glass.

"She has not confided in me," Mary Elizabeth said. "All she told me is that she and her Englishman will be going to Gretna Green this day."

"The folly of youth," Mrs. Angel said at last. All the young people in the room turned to stare at her, but none of them contradicted her assertion. "Heaven save us from it."

She lowered her teacup and filled it once more with the duchess's finest Darjeeling. After she had over-sugared it and added three generous splashes of milk, Mrs. Angel looked at him as if he were a simpleton.

"Why are you still standing here?" she asked him.

Alex did not know what reply to make, so he made none. She spoke on.

"There is only one road to the north, is there not?"

Alex blinked at her.

"Why are you not on it?" Mrs. Angel asked.

"I beg your pardon, ma'am?"

"I have told you more than once, dear boy, you must protect my daughter from herself. Kidnap her if you must, throw her over your shoulder if you will, but by all means, do not let her marry that man. It will be the ruination of her life and the devastation of her soul. If you love her, as the look on face suggests you do, hire the fastest horse you can, and lead on."

"They can only be three hours gone," Mary Elizabeth said.

His sister was right. His angel had slept quiet in his arms not three hours ago. They had not much of a lead at all. He would catch her and deal with the Englishman when he did.

He could not think of the bandy-legged bastard offering her more than a touch of a gloved hand. If he did, he would forget himself for the second time that morning when what he needed was his wits about him. He checked his waistcoat pocket and found the special license his uncle had sent still warm against his side.

"Are you armed?" Robbie asked.

Alex always wore his dirk, even when down south

among the English—especially down south. "Of course," he answered.

"Take a pistol, too," Mary Elizabeth offered helpfully.

"Dear God, young man, don't shoot him. Just fetch my daughter back."

He glowered at Mary Elizabeth and spoke politely to Mrs. Angel. "I will not shoot him."

"He might stab him though," Robbie said. "It all depends on what he finds when he catches up to them."

Alex turned his glare on his brother. Robbie did not wilt under its heat but sipped at his coffee before freshening it from the silver ducal pot.

"Whatever you do, you must find her before nightfall," Mrs. Angel said. "Otherwise, a bad situation will only become worse."

"And then you will have to kill him," Robbie said with good cheer as he buttered a fresh slice of toast.

Alex ate the buttered and honeyed slice of barley cake that Mary Elizabeth thrust into his hand. She kissed him, offered him coffee, and he drank it down in one gulp. When he had his own household, his coffee cups would be large enough to hold more than two swallows.

"Ride fast, but be careful," his sister instructed him. "Watch out for robbers. The English are everywhere."

~⁂~

Catherine had never been in as comfortable a chaise carriage as Lord Farleigh's. Arthur said nothing, and neither did she, allowing silence to descend. She had thought she might want to fling herself out of the carriage as it left London, but instead she fell asleep within half an hour. She found herself drifting almost at once, for she knew that while he was not her heart's choice, kind Lord Farleigh would look after her.

As she slept, she dreamed that Alex and her father stood together like friends beside the river Thames, where Alex had saved Margaret's life. Both men turned to her in her dream, and though they did not speak, the weight of their sorrow touched her.

She woke hours later, her heart heavy with the pain of loss, and the sorrow that she had disappointed her father, and left the love of her life behind. Dread threatened to overwhelm her as she blinked to get her bearings. She could not live with choice she had made, not for another moment, much less for the rest of her life. She had made a terrible mistake.

"Arthur," she said. "Lord Farleigh," she corrected herself. "We must stop the carriage at once."

"Do you need the necessary?" he asked bluntly. "Fear not. We are close to the outskirts of Oxford. I took a first in literature at Queen's College, so I am quite familiar with the town and the university both. There is a place we might stop and refresh ourselves shortly— the Maiden and the Unicorn. Quite a lovely place…"

"No, my lord. We must stop now."

"You've changed your mind, then?"

"I'm sorry, my lord. But I have."

Lord Farleigh smiled at her and pressed her hand. She was not sure, but she thought that her runaway would-be bridegroom looked relieved.

He was a good man, to suffer her madcap ways with such patience. His blond hair was perfect, as were his traveling clothes of charcoal gray. Catherine felt foolish and rumpled beside him. She did not know how she would repay him, or how she would survive the complete and total loss of her honor. But she must climb out of that carriage within the next moment, or suffocate in its stifling confines.

As if by magic, the carriage stopped of its own accord.

Catherine had enough presence of mind to know that carriages did not stop on their own. Someone had stopped it. She reached into her reticule and closed her fingers around a throwing knife.

The driver shouted at someone outside, his voice filled with fear. Lord Farleigh looked not in the least perturbed, but merely curious, as if the idea that anyone might have the audacity to stop his conveyance without his consent was simply beyond the pale of thought.

She would have only one chance. She drew her knife out, and saw Lord Farleigh's eyes widen even farther. "Miss Middlebrook, please, put that away."

She did not heed him or even look at him again, but kept her eyes on the door. As she heard the sound of the knob turning, she let her knife fly.

Unfortunately, the opposite door was the one that opened.

Her knife buried itself in the still-closed door across the carriage, while Alexander Waters filled the other with his Highland bulk.

She had never been so happy to see him in her life. A smile of unadulterated joy broke over her face, and she reached for him, but he shrugged her off. He did not look at her at all but hauled Arthur from the carriage unceremoniously, like a sack of grain.

"Alex!" she said. "Don't!"

She was not sure he even heard her. She climbed out after him, only to find Arthur up against the side of his lacquered coach, Alex's dagger at his throat. The driver had his gun drawn by this time, and had it trained on Alex's head.

"No, please!" she said, raising one hand to the driver in supplication. He did not heed her, so she drew out a second knife, ready to throw it at him. She was not sure she could even hit his shooting arm, much less strike before his bullet hit home. She started to pray.

Alex noticed neither she nor the driver nor the gun in the driver's hand. He only had eyes for Arthur.

"Did you touch her?" he asked, his voice strangely calm for a demented Scotsman.

"I beg your pardon," Lord Farleigh said. "I don't know what you mean."

"Yes, you do. Did you touch her?"

Catherine prayed then that Arthur would have the good sense to omit the chaste kiss he had given her in his drawing room.

"I handed her into the coach," he said.

"With gloves on?"

"I am wearing them, as you see. She came to me this morning without gloves and a bonnet."

"I didn't ask anything about her."

"Mr. Waters, I am baffled. Why are you holding a knife at my throat? I had planned to escort Miss Middlebrook to Gretna Green, at her request, but she has since changed her mind."

"She changed her mind, you say? How can you tell?" Alex asked.

Lord Farleigh smiled in the face of the angry Scot and his knife. Clearly, he had more courage than she had known. "She told me so just now."

Alex dropped his knife hand, and slid the wicked-looking blade back beneath his coat. The driver did not lower his weapon, so neither did Catherine.

Alex looked to her then, and saw the blade in her hand. A smile flitted across his face. "Do you mean to skewer me, angel?"

"No," she answered. "It is for him."

She nodded to the driver, who still did not waver. Alex took him in, along with his gun, and just as quickly dismissed him. "Put your knife away, angel. I can't have you stabbing men over me."

"Indeed not, Miss Middlebrook. There is no need for anyone to be stabbed." Lord Farleigh turned to Alex. "You say you wish to marry Miss Middlebrook?"

"I do."

"And you have her mother's consent?"

Catherine was beginning to respect Lord Farleigh more as each moment passed, but Alex's face darkened. "I do. Which is more than I can say for you."

"Mr. Waters, you are in the right. True love is a rare and precious thing. It is time I retire from the field, and leave you to your fiancée." Arthur Farleigh bowed to her as if they stood in her mother's drawing room and not in the dust of the roadside. "Miss Middlebrook, may I be the first to wish you happy."

"Thank you, my lord."

She reached into her reticule, slipped in her borrowed knife, and drew out his mother's ring. The pearls and silver gleamed in the sunlight. Lord Farleigh stepped forward, bowed from the neck, and accepted his ring back.

"I thank you," he said, his hand closing around the ring convulsively, as if he was secretly glad to have it back. Catherine did not know him well, but there seemed to be a newfound joy in his face, as if he had just been released from prison. She wondered if she should feel insulted, but he smiled at her and she knew that she had found a friend. She would pay him back for the mortgage money somehow. Alex and his family would help her. Then she would set herself to finding the right girl for him—one who could make him forget his lost love as she had not. Perhaps Mary Elizabeth had some ideas of a girl who might suit.

Lord Farleigh seemed to remember Alex at last, for he nodded to him as well. "I bid you both good day."

He climbed back into his carriage as if no one had drawn a knife on him in his life. His driver, satisfied at last that all was well, put his gun down and called to the horses. Catherine was covered in road dust as the carriage pulled away, heading still toward Oxford town. No doubt Lord Farleigh would take his ease at the Maiden and the Unicorn, and soundly curse her name.

"I must write him a note of apology," she said. "And his mother, too."

"And what of me, Catherine? By God, I told you last night you are mine, and no other's. That did not mean until the sun rose. That meant until the sun sets on my life."

She stepped toward him, and pressed her hand against his heart. He did not stay still under her palm, but picked her up, much as he had Lord Farleigh. He swung her into his arms as if they were a sling, one behind her knees, another at her back, and hoisted her high onto his horse.

He did not speak again, but climbed up behind her, and turned his horse's head not toward London, but up the North Road, following in Lord Farleigh's carriage's dusty wake.

Thirty-nine

A<small>LEX</small> <small>COULD NOT REMEMBER A TIME WHEN HE HAD</small> been more incensed. When he caught their carriage and forced it off the road, he had thought that he was angry with the Englishman. But now he saw that he was furious with her.

Not an auspicious beginning to a wedding day.

He rode into Oxford with his angel on the front of his horse. Her borrowed bag was long gone, headed who knew where by now. All she had were the clothes she stood up in, which was all he had as well, so they were even.

The pearl she had worn at Lady Jersey's ball still gleamed at her throat. It was all she had taken from her burning house in London, save for the nightgown she had worn when she clung to him in her yard, the gown that had been ruined by smoke. He took pleasure in the notion that all she had, all she wore from that day on, would come from him.

Perhaps they might find a dressmaker tomorrow, and have something fitted for her. As it was, he had no intention of closing his eyes again until she was his wife in the eyes of the law as well as in the eyes of God. The license burned a hole in his pocket. Like a madman, he kept checking to make certain that it was there, that he had not lost it along the road.

But he needed to have a chat with his little wife first.

He wound through the narrow streets of Oxford until he came to the wide gates of the university. No one stopped him, so he did not have to show the letter his uncle had given him. The chapel was exactly where his uncle had said it would be. Just because his mother's brother was a bishop of the English church, that did not mean he did not know where his rivals were to be found.

Hidden deep within the beautiful stone confines of Magdalen College, Alex found the jewel he searched for. The tiny chapel shone brilliant in the sunlight of the evening, the stained-glass windows catching the rays of the slanting sun. Alex stopped the duchess's gelding in front of the church, and the horse stood as steady as a post. It was a good steed, one he was tempted to buy from Her Grace, for it had served him well this day, on the most important errand of his life.

The object of his quest leaned silent against his heart. She did not try to bolt or flee again, though he was wary of her now. He needed to know what had possessed her to go back on her word to him, to let him have her as only a husband might, only later to leap from a three-story window to escape him.

His heart had never hurt so much in his life, and all from a blow from one girl. It was humbling. But she was his girl, whether she knew it or not. He supposed that was why she had the power to wound him so deeply, as no one else on earth could.

He climbed down and patted the horse's flank. He loosened the girth that bound the saddle so that his mount might breathe a bit easier, for they would be there for at least an hour or more. Only then did he reach up for Catherine, who sat straight in the saddle, waiting patiently for him to tell her what came next.

He was not deceived. He had thought she had given herself over to him the night before, and he had been wrong. This day, he would be certain of her mind, and bind her to him with the blessing of a true priest before the sun set on them again.

He spotted a tiny wren of a man wearing the black robes of a Dominican friar. He did not approach, but stood waiting for them on the chapel steps, for all the world as if he had been expecting them.

"I received word from the Bishop of London this morning that you might find your way here," the priest said.

Alex drew Catherine down from the horse's back. He removed the bridle and left his mount free to crop the grass by the church door. He kept his arm around her waist, in case she might find her angel wings and take flight.

"And how did my uncle summon you, Father?"

The priest smiled, his eyes warm with love and faith together, as well as a dose of humor, a combination of traits that all true priests seemed to possess. "By carrier pigeon."

Alex laughed at that, and held his girl closer still.

"You have come here to be wed, in the eyes of the Church as well as in the eyes of the law?"

"We have, Father. But I must speak with my wife first."

The priest nodded as if this sort of chat before a wedding was a common occurrence. Perhaps a man and a girl often rode up out of nowhere to this obscure chapel everyone save a handful of Catholics had forgotten even existed.

"You may speak in the vestry," the priest said. "I will prepare the Host and wine. Come into the chapel when you are ready. Christ and I will be waiting."

Catherine smiled at that, and Alex had never seen such a beautiful woman in all his life. Her hair was mussed, falling from the braided bun on the top of her head in strands of gold, her borrowed pink gown crumpled beyond repair, and her mossy-green eyes showed the promise of all the springs in his life to come.

He leaned down and kissed her as soon as the priest turned his back. She did not resist him, but leaned close, as if he were a wall and she, a bird taking shelter in a storm. His lips were firm on hers, and hers were soft, yielding, so that he forgot to be angry and simply drank in the sweet taste of her. In spite of her time in the Englishman's carriage, she still smelled like jasmine.

"I am sorry, Alex. I hope you can forgive me. I was wrong to leave you, and more wrong still to leave you as I did. I have made a complete muddle of this day. If I had it to do over, I would change it all."

"I would change nothing," he answered. "For now you are here, and with me."

"I will be with you every day for the rest of my life," she said.

"I love you, Catherine Middlebrook. I will love you every day for the rest of my life. I will give up the sea, and all the work I once thought I might do on it, so that I can be with you."

She trembled in his arms, as if shivering in a cold wind. Alex drew her close, and kissed her.

"I love you too, Alex."

He thought to stand there in silence, holding the woman he would soon make his wife. But there was one more question he had to ask. "Early this morning—why did you leave me in bed alone?"

Catherine sighed heavily, and he kept his eyes on hers so that she would not falter and try to hide anything from him again. "We owe Lord Farleigh money."

"What?"

"My mother took out a mortgage against my family's property in Devon. The note came due, and we could not pay. Lord Farleigh paid it for us."

"And he expected you to marry him to answer the debt."

His estimation of the Englishman had risen slightly that day, but now it plummeted again. He felt his rage rising, and he gritted his teeth against its onslaught.

"No," Catherine said. "He did not. It was my decision. I thought I knew what my father would have me do, if he were here. But then I realized that my father would wish me to be happy."

That last statement was a hodgepodge of explosives, so Alex did not touch it. He kissed her forehead at the mention of her father, then asked, "How much does your family owe, Catherine?"

She blinked at him, as if he had asked her to

calculate in her head the worth of the moon. "I don't know."

Alex breathed deep once, and then released it again. He tightened his grip on his girl, and she wriggled closer to him still. She laid her head on his chest, as if she were listening for the beat of his heart. That she had been willing to sell her life and her future for an undisclosed sum did not concern him. That she had not even bothered to ask the amount did. She might have ruined her life and his for a paltry fifty pounds.

"Who may I ask, Catherine, to discover this sum?"

"My father's lawyer, Mr. Philips. He is in the City."

Alex filed that information away, and then let it go. He had more pressing matters before him. However much it was, Ian would help him pay it, over time if necessary. The Englishman would see reason. He seemed, indeed, like an eminently reasonable man.

"Catherine, hear me, for I will only say this once."

She looked up at him, her green eyes rimmed with flecks of gold. He did not allow himself to be distracted, but talked on.

"I will find out what this debt is, and I will pay it. Will that suffice to make your time with Lord Loverboy lie behind us?"

"Lord Loverboy?" Her lips quirked in a smile. He wanted very much to lean down and bite her pillow of a bottom lip, but he did not.

"Catherine."

She must have heard the warning in his voice that he was in deadly earnest. She sobered, and turned to press her body full against him. The feel of her breasts and the cradle of her thighs against his almost shook him free of his reason, but he held on by a fingernail and listened to her speak.

"Lord Farleigh is behind us, and forever, whether the debt is paid or not."

He kissed her then, plundering her mouth as a pirate might a horde of gold. She opened to him and met him in the dance, her own passion as heated and ungoverned as his. It was he who remembered himself, where they were, and why. He drew back from her only to find his new horse staring at them both, as at a play.

"What is his name?" Catherine asked.

"Jerrod."

"It does not suit him. I wonder if he might answer to Zeus?"

The horse heard his new name, and seemed to nod in acceptance before he leaned down and cropped the grass at his feet.

"Zeus it is then," Alex said.

He drew back from her and pulled a ring out of his pocket. It was a peridot in a bed of gold, and it shone in the sunlight like the moss green of her eyes. "It is not the biggest ring they had, nor the finest, but it suits you well."

"It is beautiful," his angel breathed, reaching out to take it from him.

He closed his hand over it, hiding it once more in his fist. "No indeed, Miss Middlebrook. I have seen what you do with gentlemen's betrothal gifts. We will take it to the priest inside and make it your wedding ring."

"But we must post the banns," she said. "How can we marry today?"

"As I told you last night, when perhaps you were not attending…" She blushed and he kissed her before he went on. "I have a special license, which will please His Majesty's government. I have procured a priest, which pleases God. Now all I need is your consent. Catherine, will you step inside and marry me?"

Her green eyes shone with tears that she did not shed. She faced him alone, with none of her kin beside her. In her eyes burned the message that she would love him for the rest of her life, and beyond, if the priests were right.

"Yes."

Forty

CATHERINE HAD OFTEN THOUGHT OF HER WEDDING DAY as a child. She had dressed her hair in summer flowers and had mocked walking down an aisle, imagining her father at her side. In the last few years, she had thought of what kind of dress she would make for the day, what color it would be, what kind of cloth, wondering always if it would be silk or damask or muslin. She had thought to have Margaret attend her, and her mother looking on from the front pew of the village chapel.

On her true wedding day, she wore a borrowed gown of light wool that was rumpled from being stowed in a satchel, donned in the half dark of early morning, and creased beyond repair from having been slept in while she had ridden in a jouncing coach. Her mother and sister were both a half day's travel away, and instead of tucked away in the village church of her childhood, with the people she had known all of her life looking on, she stood at an altar in Oxford with a priest she had met just that hour standing before her.

But none of that mattered. For this day, Alex Waters stood beside her.

Every thought she had ever had, every fantasy she had ever cherished of her wedding, faded as the phantoms of dreams at morning. All that mattered was that the only man she had ever loved, the only man she would ever love, stood beside her. His hand cradled hers as if he would cherish it, and all the rest of her, for the rest of his time on earth.

The fading light of day slanted through the chapel's stained-glass windows. An older lady had come to replace the altar flowers, and she watched as Alex and Catherine faced each other before the priest.

Catherine was glad the stranger was there, so that there was a second witness to her happiness. She felt for an otherworldly moment as if she had entered a dream, but then Alex smiled at her, and she knew that smile was real.

The words of the priest were short, his blessing sweet. He wrapped their hands in a stole, and admonished them to remember their vows, and that they would last into the hereafter. Alex put the ring he had shown her on her finger, and it fit. It did not slip or slide across her knuckle; it did not feel like a shackle on her hand. If anything, her hand felt lighter with the symbol of his love upon it.

The green of the stone shone like grass and growing things. It seemed to her that their love would not stay as it was in that moment, but would keep growing, like the great oak with its unfurled leaves that stood on the village green back home.

When their vows were made, and the stole removed from their hands, the old lady and the priest left them alone at the altar. Catherine knew that they must leave. They must go back into the world and return to London, where her mother and sister, where his brother and sister were waiting. But as she stood looking into the dark eyes of the man she loved, she could not think of anyone or of anything else.

"We should go home," she said, knowing her duty, and all the music that had to be faced.

"To the Highlands?" Alex asked, a teasing smile playing at the corners of his mouth, lighting his eyes with the fire of mischief.

"Later this summer," she answered. "I meant, home to my mother."

"Your mother knows where you are," Alex answered her. "She knows you are in my care. She probably even knows that we have married."

"Is she clairvoyant, then?"

Catherine wished her words back, for she did not want to start the first five minutes of her marriage with annoyance. But Alex did not take offense. He slipped his arm around her waist, for all the world as if he truly thought she might escape him again.

"She sent me to fetch you back," Alex said. "But I think she will understand if we do not go today."

"Where will we go?" Catherine asked, worried.

Alex kissed her deeply, and her mood suddenly improved. "Come with me a little ways, and I will show you."

❧

They went first to an office tucked away among the curved streets of Oxford, where they were married under the law by a curate of the Church of England.

This ceremony was short, and had only two witnesses. Catherine understood the necessity of it, and she took pleasure in making her vows twice, though she was married already.

After that strange interlude, Catherine rode on the front of his saddle as they wended their way along the outskirts of town, along the river. She thought for a moment that Alex was lost, but then Zeus stopped in front of a small whitewashed cottage with a trellis of roses climbing up the side. The roses were pink and white, and some of their blooms were just beginning to open.

"How lovely," Catherine said. "Whose house is this?"

"For this night, it's ours," Alex answered.

"You can procure a house and a priest and a vicar, all at a moment's notice?"

"Give me a day, and I'll furnish you with a new gown and a coach and four as well."

Catherine laughed, as she knew he had meant her to, and then lost her breath as he swung her down from Zeus's back. He drew her close, so that she slid down the length of his hard body. He kept her against him, so that her toes barely touched the ground. He did not kiss her, but leaned close, taking in her scent from her hair, along her temple, down to her throat.

"You still smell of jasmine," he said. "I would never know that you were with that Englishman."

"I wasn't *with* him," she corrected. "I was riding in a carriage with him."

"On your way to marry him, if I recall."

Catherine frowned at him and watched as he relented in front of her.

"I am sorry, angel. I promise you, I will not bring him up again."

"It is a new day," she said. "We are married now."

His smile shifted, and his eyes took on a light of reverence, the same light they had held in the stone chapel as they spoke their vows. "It is a new world," he answered.

He kissed her, and his lips tasted of sunlight and coffee. She drank him in, grateful to God that she was in his arms, that she would be in his arms for the rest of her life. She shifted against him, her body growing hungry as it had the night before. She wondered how soon they might go to bed and whether decent married people ever made love in the sunshine of a borrowed garden.

She knew the answer to that, but a girl could dream.

Her dreams were shattered by the rumble of her stomach.

Alex pulled back from kissing her and looked down at her, one eyebrow raised. "When was the last time you ate, angel?"

"I drank that cider you gave me last night," she said. "I didn't each much dinner before the fire. I was too worried about you, and what I was going to do."

"Well," he said. "Let's see if Father Patrick has stocked the larder."

She did not let him go when he made a move to leave her. She clung to him like a limpet, pressing herself hard against the burgeoning manhood she could feel rising against her stomach.

"Alex," she said, remembering the night before with sudden vivid clarity, the way his lips had felt on her, the way his body had felt inside her. The memories came back to her like a flash tide, leaving her gasping. "I don't want food. I want you."

He kissed her hard, wrapping his arms around her and enfolding her in an embrace that felt unbreakable. She shivered with joy and need together, wriggling against him in a futile effort to get closer. He groaned and kissed her again before he came up for air.

"Mrs. Waters, I will feed you before I have you again."

"Why?" she asked plaintively, her stomach rumbling a second time.

"My first duty is to see you cared for, and that's what I'll do."

She smiled up at him through her lashes, the way she'd seen her mother smile at her father, long ago. He seemed to falter for an instant, but then he laughed. "You won't get around me on this with your feminine wiles, you little minx."

But his hand lingered on her derriere in a manner that said he longed for her body as much as she longed for his. She took that as her due, and strolled off ahead of him to investigate the house where they would spend their wedding night.

The house was small, but clean. The parlor stood open to the garden in the back of the house, and the kitchen was well stocked. She did not go upstairs, but began to rummage in the pantry, finding a nice wheel of Cambray cheese and a bottle of red wine from France. A fresh loaf of bread was swathed in towels, and no mice had eaten at it yet, so she declared it sound.

There was even a crock of butter tucked between cool stones by the pantry door, so she thanked her stars and got to work slicing and buttering. Alex came in with a jar of butter pickles, which he had found who knew where. He saw her preparing their meal, crossed the small room, and took her bread knife from her.

"My love, I said I would feed you."

"And so you have. Look at all this bounty." Catherine beamed up at him, and relinquished the knife to his grasp.

"Since our meeting in the coach, you must understand why I want the knife in my own hand."

She laughed out loud at that. She had never thought to have such a joy-filled wedding night. She said another prayer of thanksgiving even as she baited him. "I did not know it was you, Alex. Mary Elizabeth warned me of highway robbers, and I was prepared."

"You threw at the wrong door, Catherine."

"That was only my first try."

It was his turn to laugh as he sliced delicate hunks of cheese and arrayed them with pickles on a plate. He set the thick slices of fresh bread in a basket on the table and started buttering the ones she'd missed.

"I will prepare your meal this night, wife. You've had enough excitement for one day. Take your ease there, and let your husband work for you."

Catherine laughed, for she did not have to be told twice. "I think I can stand a bit more excitement, Alex."

He quirked a brow at her, and the heat in his eyes made her want to push the food out of the way and crawl across the table to him. As it was, he came around to her side and sat with her on the simple wooden bench. He sat close and offered her a bite of white bread with sweet butter on it, which he fed to her from his own hand.

"This is crude fare, wife, but I will make it up to you. I'll do better tomorrow."

"It's a feast fit for a queen," Catherine answered him. "And I would not wish myself anywhere but here."

Catherine had hoped to explore the upstairs with him, but after they had wrapped up the remains of their meal, Alex led her outside to take in the last of the sunset, and a stroll down to the river. It was not yet late, and she was not even slightly tired. Her body hummed with energy at his nearness until the very waiting seemed to soothe her senses as well as enflame them. Alex was in a talking mood, telling her of his home in Glenderrin. She liked to hear him talk, so they walked down by the river and looked at the irises that bloomed in beds of green close by the willow trees.

"The Thames is beautiful here," Catherine said, her hand clasped firm in his great one.

He quirked a brow at her, and she caught the light of humor in his eyes. "I like it a sight better than at Richmond."

"Did I thank you for saving Margaret?" she asked. "Let me thank you now."

She rose on the tips of her toes, and he leaned down to meet her. She kissed his lips, exploring the contours and the taste of him, the taste of bread and butter and spiced pickles with cheese. And the scent of him—his favorite soap and his musky smell of man and horse. She lost the thread of her intent, which was only to tease him, and lost herself along with it. She found herself in his arms on the damp ground, his hands beneath her skirt and her hair falling from its pins behind her.

"I love you, Catherine. I will not have you for the first time as my wife in the damp grass of a borrowed lawn."

"Will we do this on our own lawn then one day?" she asked him coyly.

He laughed, as she had meant him to. "It's too cold to take our ease by the burn near Castle Glenderrin. But if we are in Devon in summer, I will consider it. Have they a river there?"

"Yes, the river Culm. I will show it to you, if you promise to teach me how to fish in your burn."

He pressed his lips to her temple. "You need not learn to fish for me, angel. I love you as you are."

"I'll try it once. Mary Elizabeth sets her heart by it," Catherine answered, snuggling close against him, taking deep draughts of his scent as if she might never have him by her again. But she would have him by her every day of her life. She had the ring and the paperwork to prove it.

They did not spend much more time talking about fishing or family. He helped her up from the grass, and she noticed in the failing light that her borrowed pink gown now had grass stains on it. She laughed a little. "I'll have to buy Mary Elizabeth a new dress."

"We can buy her a dozen."

Alex did not linger, but took her hand and led her back to the house as dusk was rising from the riverbank, making all the world turn as indigo as the sky where the first stars of the night had already come out.

Forty-one

ALEX LED HER BY THE HAND ALL THE WAY UP THE stairs. He stopped in the kitchen and poured a glass of red wine. She did not protest that he poured only one, for she had already had one glass, and it had made her feel light-headed. Wicked French wine was known to do that.

He brought her into a little room that was almost completely filled with a great four-poster bed. The bed curtains were drawn back, as were the lace curtains on the windows, so that as Catherine stood there in the light of one glowing lamp, she could see the moon rising over the river below. She did not think she had ever seen anything so beautiful.

Alex brought her fingers to his lips, and kissed them. "Wife, I think I need to see you naked now. Is that shocking?"

Giddy laughter bubbled up inside her and spilled out, as champagne overflowed a fluted glass. She leaned up and kissed his lips, a brief, glancing butterfly of a kiss. She stepped back deftly out of his reach before he could draw her close and under him.

"Very shocking, husband. And I have a shocking confession to make as well."

"What confession might that be, wife?"

Alex's voice was even, but she could see the banked heat rising in his eyes. She shivered as she stood under his gaze and started undressing, freeing her breasts from the modest gown Mary Elizabeth had lent her. His eyes glazed over as her breasts peeked out at him, their nipples hard, from beneath the filmy lawn of her shift. Her skirt fell next, and she felt the first hint of delicious power.

She stepped out of her gown, where it lay on the floor at her feet, and stood before him in only her shift and stays. The stays fell away next beneath her hands, and he moved toward her, forgetting her confession, the light in his eyes brighter, and full of desire. She took one more step back, and eluded him.

"My confession, husband, is that I like those black gloves you always wear. You were wearing them the night I first met you, if I recall."

"My gloves?" Alex's eyes clouded over for a moment in confusion. "I'm happy you like them, wife, but what has that to do with us, here and now, on our wedding night?"

"I want you to wear them," she said. "I want to feel those gloves against my naked flesh, with nothing else between you and me but that black leather."

He swallowed hard, and closed his eyes as if to ward off her words. But when he turned and left her without another word, she knew he was not repulsed. She listened as he stumbled in the dark downstairs, looking for those gloves.

"You left them on the kitchen table," she called to him down the narrow staircase. "Between the crock of butter and the bread knife."

She listened for a moment longer as he found them in the half dark below. "Don't take off another stitch of clothes," he called up the stairs. "Not until I get there."

"I make no promises," she said, though she did not move to take off any more of her under things. As she listened, she could hear Alex moving stealthily along the hall downstairs, and his boots as they sounded on the wooden staircase.

He burst into the room, only to find her where she was, without her having moved a muscle. This show of obedience seemed to please him, in spite of his breathlessness from rummaging downstairs. He had his leather gloves clutched in one fist, and the sight of them made her lose her breath.

She did not relinquish control to him, as she had the night before. She was enjoying herself far too much for that.

Her voice sounded rough in her own ears, deeper than it ever was, and slightly more musical, if the music were played by a bassoon. "Husband," she said, "I fear you are wearing far too many clothes."

He tossed the gloves down on the bed. "Indeed, wife." He started to strip, but she stopped him as he tossed his waistcoat aside. She moved close to him, and slipped her hand over his broad chest, taking pleasure in the heat and the muscled firmness of it beneath her hand, the thin lawn of his shirt the only thing between them. She had been so overwhelmed the night before that she had not thought to touch him. But she was a married woman now, and less overwhelmed—so far, at least. She reached down and drew his shirt from his breeches.

"Alex, let me help."

She slid her hands beneath his shirt, drawing it up to his shoulders. She was too short to pull it over his head, so he did that bit for her, tossing the shirt away onto the borrowed floor.

His hair curled in tight furls that surrounded his nipples. His chest hair was as dark as the hair on his head, but curly and springy. She moved close and rubbed first her hand over it, then her cheek. He moaned when she leaned up and suckled him, his flat, taut nipple rising a little to meet her questing tongue.

"Catherine," he murmured, his usually precise English crumbling into the lovely brogue she had heard in his voice when he'd taken her to bed the night before. That was true music in her ears, for she knew that he wanted her as much as she wanted him.

She did not take pity on him, but ran her hand down his flat abdomen to his breeches, where she began to work at the placket. The first two buttons came undone easily, but his manhood was swelling beneath her hand and she could not get the other two buttons free. She simply began to move her hand over him with the wool of his breeches between them. He stopped her then, cupping her hand in his great one and drawing it up to his mouth, where he planted a kiss in her palm that made her shiver.

"Catherine," he said, "I'll finish stripping for you now."

She smiled at him, pleased that he was so amenable to her suggestion, but when she saw the hot light of desire in his eyes, she shivered. His tongue flicked out and caressed her palm. She remembered what his tongue had done to her body the night before, when he had kissed her between her thighs, and she wondered if he would do that to her again. She had asked for the gloves. Maybe she could ask for that, too.

She felt daring and brave as she stood in front of him in her thin, almost transparent chemise. She also felt completely protected and cherished. She had found a safe harbor in the world for the first time since her father had died, perhaps for the first time ever, and she was giddy with the joyous feeling of freedom it gave her. She might do anything, and Alex would love and care for her anyway.

It was a heady thought.

His breeches hit the wooden floor then, and his smallclothes followed, along with his boots and stockings. Catherine found herself staring at his manhood, something that looked altogether too large to fit into her tiny sheath. Perhaps it shrank inside her. Or perhaps her sheath was larger than she thought.

She pondered this question, running her fingers gently over the head of him. He groaned out loud as her fingertips fondled him, and she stopped moving, checking his eyes. His face was a mask of what looked like pain.

"Does it hurt you when I do that?" she asked, worried for the first time that night.

"No." His voice sounded a bit like broken glass being driven over by a slow coach. He swallowed hard, and she touched him again, making him moan. "It is overwhelming pleasure, angel, that threatens to undo me."

She took her hand away, and smiled up at him. "We can't have that," she said. She turned to find his gloves where they rested on the bed. She looked at him coyly over her shoulder as she bent down to pick them up. She felt the short hem of her chemise rise across her derriere and felt as well as saw his eyes follow the curve of her behind. She even wiggled it a little, to tempt him, and he laughed.

"Minx, you are going to kill me. Can I touch you now?"

"Not just yet," she said. As soon as he touched her, she would lose all reason. She was enjoying the game they played, though she saw from the growing heat in his eyes and the way his hands had started to shake that she did not have much time left. The thought made her shiver almost as much as the sight of his beautiful naked body.

"You look like a statue from one of my father's books," she said, admiring him even as she slipped the gloves over his hands. "Not the Roman ones but the Greeks."

"I don't have much truck with the Greeks, angel."

He smiled to himself, as at a jest, as he helped her in her progress. Alex flexed his fingers into the taut gloves, drawing them on for her with a manly, practiced grace that made her tongue suddenly cling to the roof of her mouth. She watched his one gloved hand for a long moment, her mind distracted, along with her body. A great well of heat and want was rising inside her, and she had no idea what to do with it.

Thankfully, he did.

He took the second glove from her nerveless fingers

and drew it on, never once taking his eyes from hers. The power inherent in his form, the latent potency of his gaze, made her forget language altogether. She simply stood and watched him, his beauty all but overwhelming her. And then he smiled his wry smile, and he was Alex again.

"I'm the only one naked, my beloved. I don't think that's at all fair. Do you?"

She still could not speak, so she shook her head. He stepped close to her then, so close that his body was like a raging furnace that she wanted to press herself against, a heat she wanted to warm herself on for the rest of her life.

His hands, gloved now in the black leather she loved, slid slowly down her arms, leaving goose bumps in their wake. Her heart started to hammer, and she gasped for breath as those hands flirted with the edge of her chemise along the tops of her thighs before he very slowly, very carefully, drew it off and over her head.

Her body was on fire from the glancing touch of his leather on her skin. He did not touch her again right away, but took her hand and seated her on the high mattress with an almost courtly gesture.

"Are you teasing me, Alex, now that your gloves are on?" she managed to ask.

He smiled down at her and leaned close, his lips the only thing touching her temple. They grazed her skin, and he took her earlobe between his teeth. "As you teased me, stripping me of my clothes one thread at a time? Aye, lass, I might at that."

She laughed then, and his lips were on hers, his tongue delving into her mouth as she opened to welcome him. He devoured her, but drew back almost at once, very much in control of himself. She wanted him to lose that control—on top of her.

She shook with need for him, and was gratified to see that his hands shook also as he knelt before her, his black leather drawing one of her silk stockings off, slowly. She raised one foot and caressed his bare thigh with it.

He quirked a brow at her and smiled, bringing her foot to his mouth even as he leaned down to meet it. His breath was hot on her sole, and her second stocking disappeared under his hands. His mouth moved back over her arch, to the secret place behind her knee, to her inner thigh.

When he was that high on her body, she fell back on the mattress, stretched out before him, not certain if he pushed her down or if she melted onto the bed of her own accord. But he rose over her, his breath hot between her thighs. "I would kiss you there," Alex said. "But I can't wait. May I have you now, and kiss you after?"

She shook with the need for him. "I need you inside me, Alex. Hurry." She heard the tone of command in her voice, and she thought to soften it, if belatedly. "Please."

He laughed and joined her on the bed. She sighed in pleasure as he raised his knee to part her thighs, and she wriggled against his heavy muscled leg. He kissed her deeply, running first one hand and then the other over her body, covering her breasts with his black leather palms. She shivered at the touch of that leather on her skin. It was far more delectable, far more wonderfully sinful than she had thought it would be.

"You must always wear these in bed," she said.

"I'll get a special pair, just for this," he answered.

"No," she said, "I like these."

He groaned as one of his leather-gloved fingers played between the curls that rested between her thighs. She felt herself heavy and damp with wanting him already, and when he touched her with two fingers, she almost flew off the bed. He smiled a wolfish, pleased smile, and added a third to the brigade set to torment her with pleasure. She did not rise off the bed again, for he put his whole weight on her, and she was crushed by the delicious feel of him all the way down her body. He whirled his fingers against her one last time, and she came apart in his arms, screaming his name.

She trembled as the pleasure crested a second time under the heavy press of his palm on her body. She shook and thought that she might lose the ability to speak at all, ever again. Not that she cared.

She watched as the pleasure spiraled away from her, going back to the magic realm from whence it came. But, in spite of her sated joy, she was still unsatisfied.

Catherine did not recognize her own voice in that moment, it was so deep and throaty. "Alex, I need you inside me."

Her husband needed no more encouragement. He slid inside her in one smooth motion. As big as he was, her body took him in greedily, as if it had been waiting for him since the moment he had left her that morning. She shuddered with a new pleasure as her body drank him in, and she milked him as he moved inside her.

He tried to hold on to his usual calm, his usual focused patience, but then on impulse, she tightened her inner muscles around him and he groaned long and loud. "Witch," he said against her hair.

She laughed. "You love it, Alex."

"I do. God help me."

"Keep moving, Alex. I still need you."

Catherine raised her hips against his and squeezed again. He shook hard, and for a moment, she feared she had lost him. But he rallied and plunged into her, over and over, as a man possessed.

Catherine gasped under the onslaught of his passion, her body accommodating him without her consent, without her conscious thought. She could no longer find the focus to press him with her inner strength, for he was battering away at her as the high waves pummeled the rocks during a storm. She shook beneath him, her pleasure building again, this time from a deeper place inside her, a place where all the joy in the world seemed to live.

She screamed his name again, but this time he did not heed her, so bent was he on his own pleasure. It was his turn to come apart in her arms, and she clutched him close, one hand at his back, the other at his shoulder. Her legs went around his waist in an effort to draw him still closer to her. She cradled him with her slight body, her own pleasure beginning to recede, as the tide after a storm was through.

She sighed against the softness of his hair, which had come undone from its queue and fell around them both in a dark curtain. "I love you, Alex Waters."

She would have thought that he had died, but he still breathed heavy against her. She did not expect a response, but it seemed he was not as far gone as she thought.

"I love you, Catherine Waters. I will love you all my life and beyond."

"If the priests are right," she said.

He smiled, and she felt it against the soft skin of her cheek. He whispered in her ear, "They are."

Forty-two

ALEX WOKE TO THE SOUND OF BIRDSONG THROUGH the leaded glass windows across from the bed. The curtains had never been drawn, so the morning light filtered in gently through the diamond panes. His sleep-addled mind had a moment of fear that she had left him again, but then he felt her move beside him, and his fear receded.

He had not taken the precaution of locking her in with him the night before, for he had been too sleepy to bother. Their lovemaking had also left him with the certainty that they were bound now together, for good or ill, for the rest of their lives. She would not leave him again. He was almost completely sure of it.

He had also come to the conclusion that no lock would keep this woman in. He would have to keep her by his side with other methods—by loving her so well that she was too tired to leap from three-story windows. And someday, God willing it be soon, tie her to him with the children they would raise together in joy, far away in the Highlands.

Thoughts of home led back to thoughts of Robbie and Mary Elizabeth, and what might befall them alone among the English. Now that he had his girl in hand, he knew his duty. He must return to them as soon as he might. No doubt his angel wished to see her mother and sister as well.

His wife mewled a little in her sleep, like a kitten, and pressed against him as she stretched, waking slowly beside him. Her moss-green eyes opened, lit from within with what looked to be joy. "Good morning, husband."

He smiled at her, his hands finding her curves beneath the bedclothes. "Good morning, wife."

She stretched beneath his hands, and he thought to draw her under him again, but she had duties of her own, and it seemed she had remembered them. Their idyll, as brief as it had been, was over.

"We must go home to Mama and Margaret," she said. "I don't know what they're doing about the house."

"I have no doubt that Jim is reporting to Giles daily as he sees to the refurbishing of it," Alex answered her, sitting against the bolster and drawing her up with him to lean against his chest. Her ear rested against his heart, and the warm weight of her was a delight he knew he would never grow tired of. "Giles is a grand man. I'm glad I saved his life."

Catherine kissed him. "I'm glad you saved him, too." A frown marred her beautiful face, clouding her moss-green eyes. "I fear he will be displeased with me."

Alex thought it odd that she might worry about

her butler's good opinion, but he knew better than to voice such a thought. "Why would he be?"

"Because I ran away."

"Ah."

Alex stroked her hair where it fell in long, golden tangles down her back. She settled at his touch, relaxing again almost to the point where he thought she might have fallen asleep. He spoke low, in case she had slipped off. "I think Giles will understand that a young girl, alone in the world with no one to defend her, might occasionally make a wild gesture or two."

She leaned back and smiled sleepily at him. "I'm not alone in the world now."

He kissed her gently, with no desire between them, only love. "Not anymore."

He raised himself up from the bed, taking her with him, for he knew himself well. He had not long to linger before the heat that always flowed between them rose again to block his reason, and to shatter his reserve. He wanted her home, in a place he could keep her safe. Since he could not yet take her to the Highlands, he would take her back to the duchess's house. In the south, it was the next best thing.

"It's time we go home," was all he said.

❧

The gown she had borrowed from Mary Elizabeth was salvageable by a decent lady's maid, but since one was not present, Alex took his new bride into Oxford and bought her a new gown. He watched as the seamstress his uncle knew dressed his wife from the skin out in new finery, the soft lawn of her under things competing with the soft sprigged muslin of the gown she wore. The pelisse was some shade of green that went well with his angel's eyes. Catherine was happy with a new bonnet and gloves on, which was all he cared about.

With his new wife respectably clad once more, Alex hired a coach and four to get them to London as quickly as possible. He left Zeus resting comfortably in a decent livery stable, eating his weight in oats. The horse had served him well, and he would send a man to fetch him back on the morrow. After the madcap ride the gelding had carried him on the day before, the mount deserved a respite.

Alex wished he might take a long, well-deserved respite with his hard-won wife, but he had not forgotten that her town house needed rebuilding, her mother and sister needed looking after, and Mary Elizabeth needed to be married off. Please God, before the summer ended.

Alex pushed that last duty out of his mind, for he had no idea how on God's green earth he was going to accomplish that. Though the men of the *ton* seemed less frightened of her than the men in Edinburgh had been, no one had made an offer for her. Not yet.

As they drove up to the duchess's house, it was Mary Elizabeth who ran out to greet them. "Thank God you're home!" she said. "Mrs. Middlebrook has run away!"

Alex sighed as his well-laid plans for a peaceful evening between his wife's thighs evaporated like so much mist.

✦

Catherine stood in horror outside the Duchess of Northumberland's town house. All of her hope and joy seemed to drain out of her feet, just as the color drained out of her face. Had her mother fled in fear of the mortgage? Or was she on some wild chase with Mr. Pridemore? Catherine felt her nausea rise as Alex took her arm to support her.

"Don't look so stricken, angel. We'll find her."

He meant that he would find her, for other than to chase down the North Road toward Gretna Green, Catherine had no idea of where they might look.

She let Alex lead her into the house, grateful that she actually had him to lean on. She was not used to the luxury of a man at her side, but it was a good thing he was there, for her mind simply would not function. Like one of the great machines of the north after a Luddite had been at it, her mind had shuddered to a stop.

Margaret ran to her in the middle of the grand entrance hall, her arms going around her waist.

"She didn't even leave a note," Margaret sobbed, trying to suppress her tears and failing. "The footman saw her leave in Mr. Pridemore's carriage yesterday."

Catherine forced herself to rally, and to set her own fear aside. "I am sure Mama meant to leave word," she lied. "No doubt the note got lost in her reticule, and she only realized it once she had left London."

Margaret sniffled and wiped her eyes on her embroidered handkerchief. "Do you think so?"

Catherine heard that her own voice was firm and warm, and hid all of her fear that was swiftly turning to anger at the sight of her sister's pain. "I have no doubt of it."

"Do you think you might take a cup of tea, Miss Margaret?" Mary Elizabeth asked. "We have some sandwiches and cakes set out in the music room."

Margaret looked to Catherine, who nodded. "Go ahead and eat a little something, Maggie. I will be there directly."

Alex had been conferring in whispers with his brother Robert across the hall. Catherine turned to him as she drew off her gloves. Mary Elizabeth saw her wedding ring then, and before Alex could speak, his sister threw her arms around her. "Welcome to the family! I knew he would persuade you."

Catherine hugged her new sister back, and took the hand that Robert Waters offered. "You're a brave lass to take this family on, mostly sight unseen. Mary Elizabeth may be wild, but she is nothing to our brothers Ian and David."

Alex laughed. "Not to mention our mother."

Robert and Alex laughed together for a bit. Catherine accepted her new brother's kiss, but her annoyed gaze stayed on Alex.

"Thank you for the kind welcome," she said before she turned to Alex. "Why are you standing about and laughing? My mother is God alone knows where, and I must find her."

The front door opened and her mother stood framed in the doorway, a fur muff on one hand though it was almost June.

"Darling, I'm home!" Her mother swept in with Mr. Pridemore behind her, carrying bags and packages. Two footmen followed behind as well, both their arms loaded down. "Put all those things upstairs," she said. "The housekeeper can tell you where my room is." She smiled at her gentleman friend as he relinquished her luggage to another two servants. "Staying with a duchess, no less."

"It is no less than you deserve, my dear."

Catherine heard that endearment and bit her tongue so that she would not scream in ire.

At the sound of her mother's voice, Margaret was in the hall like a shot, her arms wrapped around Mrs. Middlebrook as if she would never let her go.

"What is all this? Why all these tears?" Mrs. Middlebrook asked.

"You left no word. Where were you?"

"Darling, I was only on a trip to Devon. Did the maid not tell you where I was?"

"Which maid?" Margaret asked.

"The tall one who changes my bed linens."

"That would be Claire," Mary Elizabeth said. "I fear she speaks only French." She shrugged one shoulder. "The duchess hired her to save her from Napoleon, or some such. Her English is still fairly poor."

"I am sorry, sweetheart." Mrs. Middlebrook kissed her youngest daughter and led her into the music room as if she were in her own house, and not a borrowed one, once removed.

Catherine thought that her head might implode. All the goodwill and joy had gone out of the day for her. All she could think of was getting her hands around her mother's neck, and throttling her with every ounce of strength she possessed. Before she followed them to berate the erstwhile Olivia, Alex held her back.

"*Leannan*," he said, in the gentlest voice she had ever heard. "I know you are angry, but take a breath. Look at me."

She did as he asked, and she found in the depths of his brown eyes enough love and compassion to assuage all she had never gotten from her mother, all she had not received daily since her father's death. She knew that her mother loved her. She also knew that most of the time, her mother was thoughtless, if never intentionally cruel. She breathed deep and leaned against him.

"I want to do her violence," she said.

He laughed a little. "She took your disappearance with much more equanimity," he said. "She was the one who sent me after you."

Catherine looked into his eyes and saw that he was not trying to persuade her to change her mind, but only telling her the simple truth. "She did that, for me? She wasn't angry? She didn't condemn me?"

"On the contrary, angel. She seems to know you as well as she loves you. She's just a headstrong woman with no man to guide her."

Catherine rolled her eyes at that, and saw his smile.

"Come and listen to her tale before you judge her."

Catherine did as he asked once more, and followed Mary Elizabeth and Robert into the music room.

Olivia Middlebrook met her eldest daughter in the center of the room. She took her hand, and when Catherine left her hand in hers, she bent to kiss her. "I am sorry to trouble you, Daughter. I have apologized to the little one, too."

"She was worried and weeping, Mama."

"I know—as you would have been, if you were

here. I should not have left at dawn with no warning. I should have left a note at least."

"Or taken me with you," Margaret piped up, a scone doused in cream clutched in her hand.

"I will remember that in future. Girls, come here." Mrs. Middlebrook led Catherine by the hand to sit close to her sister, placing herself between them on the duchess's brocade settee.

"Girls, I went today without you to visit our home. Mr. Pridemore has been kind enough to pay off our mortgage with the bank. He has also been kind enough to ask me to become his wife."

Margaret said nothing, and neither did Catherine. She looked to Alex, who nodded to her from behind the tea tray as he poured a cup of Darjeeling, mixing sugar in. She took comfort in his presence, and felt her shoulders relax even as she looked at him.

"The mortgage was paid by Mr. Pridemore," she said.

"It is," her mother answered. Mrs. Middlebrook patted her eldest daughter's hand. "I am not a complete ninnyhammer, love. I would never let our family's land go to a stranger."

"But now you must marry him," Catherine said. She got control of herself, and nodded to Mr. Pridemore, who was adding a tot of whisky to his tea. "Begging your pardon, sir."

The gentleman smiled at her. "No offense meant, and none taken."

Alex caught her gaze again, and she held her tongue.

Olivia Middlebrook continued as if nothing had been said. "I want to marry Mr. Pridemore. I went home to ask your father's permission."

Tears came into her mother's eyes then, and Catherine pressed her hand as Margaret set her scone down, and leaned against her mother's arm. Mrs. Middlebrook spoke on. "I found after a hard journey drawn by six fast horses that your father was not there. It was just a stone in the chapel floor, with his name carved on it."

Catherine felt tears rise, and she swallowed hard.

"He has gone on to heaven, Mama," Margaret said.

"Indeed, he has. So I have concluded that it is all right for me to go on here on earth." Mrs. Middlebrook drew off her kidskin glove to reveal an emerald engagement ring. "We will marry in Devon as soon as may be. I had thought of St. George's chapel here in London, but I would rather be married at home."

"I'd be happy to arrange St. George's for you, ma'am, if you change your mind," Mary Elizabeth said. "The Duchess of Northumberland's name is good for something, I warrant."

"A great deal," Robert said. "Like launching a wild Highland girl onto an unsuspecting Almack's."

Alex coughed to cover a laugh, as Mary Elizabeth shot her brothers a look that promised death, or at the very least, a nasty bruise.

Her mother turned her blue gaze on Catherine, ignoring their hosts' antics. "And you are married already, Daughter, I suppose?"

"I am." Alex crossed the room and brought her the cup of tea he had poured for her, with a splash of milk and two sugar lumps added in. She took his hand in hers. "We are."

He smiled down at her. "I am sorry to be so hasty, madam, but your daughter is impetuous."

Mrs. Middlebrook smiled. "I believe she inherited that trait from me."

"I wanted to be a bridesmaid," Margaret said, frowning.

Alex laughed, and Mrs. Middlebrook patted her hand. "Fear not, sweet. When I wed in one week's time, you will stand up with me."

"Will I have a new dress?" Margaret's eyes lit up as with a sunrise.

"Indeed you shall. And a bouquet of flowers tied with ribbons."

Mr. Pridemore stood then, setting his teacup down. He spoke loud enough that all could hear him, but it was Catherine and Margaret he faced. "Girls, I swear on my honor that I will never carry your mother away again without telling you."

Catherine stood, setting aside her own half-finished tea. "Thank you for saving our land, sir. We can never repay you."

He smiled, and she felt her heart lighten. "Mrs. Waters, I can tell you that keeping your mother company for the rest of my life is thanks enough."

Mrs. Middlebrook turned pink with pleasure, but Catherine was not done with him yet.

"And you will care for Margaret, and guard her as if she were your own?"

"I so swear, in front of God and all these witnesses."

Catherine held out her hand. "Pax, then," she said.

He shook her hand as a man from Manchester might, a businessman who had just closed an auspicious deal. "Pax."

"Well, thank God for that," Robert said. "Your town house refurbishment continues, Catherine, under the eagle eye of your Mr. Giles. It seems my brother has caught you and trussed you up good, as Pridemore has caught your mother. Now we have only Miss Margaret to see to."

His blue eyes lit with laughter, and Catherine wondered for a moment if Margaret would take offense, thinking that he was mocking her. Her sister simply tossed an expensive cushion at his head, which he caught deftly in one hand.

Robert sobered a bit. "In all honesty, I think we might need to leave Town. Mary Elizabeth drew a sword on Lord Grathton in Hyde Park this afternoon."

"I thought he was stealing that woman's purse," Mary Elizabeth answered, pouring herself a fresh cup of tea.

"Reticule," Robert corrected her.

"Whatever the English call those little bags that their women keep their hartshorns in," Mary Elizabeth rejoined.

Catherine almost choked on her own tea. She was grateful she had sat down again, for she had heard of Lord Grathton—a powerful man in the House of Lords, he was a Yorkshire man and not to be trifled with.

"What were you doing with a sword in Hyde Park?" Catherine managed to ask.

Mary Elizabeth addressed her as if it were a serious question. "I always keep my broadsword tucked under a blanket on the floor of the carriage whenever we leave the house. It is England, after all, Catherine. Brigands are everywhere."

"Oh, how thrilling!" Mrs. Middlebrook exclaimed. "I am so sorry to have missed it!"

Robert smiled. "Hearing of the spectacle went a long way toward cheering up Miss Margaret, at least."

"And did you rescue the bag?" Catherine asked, ignoring her husband's look that was telling her to drop the subject at once. Married only one day and she was already able to tell when he wished for her to hold her tongue.

Well, a man might keep on wishing.

Mary Elizabeth smiled at her, quite pleased that someone had picked up what was, in her opinion, the most salient point. "Indeed, I did. The Lady Cecelia was a bit embarrassed, I think, but pleased to have her bag back. Once I realized my mistake, I apologized to Lord Grathton. I had no idea he was the lady's fiancé."

Alex drew a flask from his pocket, and drank straight from it without even pouring the whisky into a teacup. Catherine ignored him, as did everyone but Robert, who elbowed him in an effort to get him to share. The men passed the flask back and forth between them, and even Catherine's mother paid them no mind. For a moment, Catherine thought that Margaret might ask for a sip, but when none of the other ladies even acknowledged the presence of the flask, Margaret followed suit.

"The day was saved by a quiet mouse of a lady who stepped up and intervened before Grathton called me out," Robert said.

"Don't be ridiculous, Robbie. If his lordship was going to take up arms against anyone, it would have been against me," Mary Elizabeth said. This time, everyone, including Catherine, ignored her.

"The lady looked to be a bit down on her luck. I've asked her to come by and have a chat with our Mary here, to see if she might suit as a companion," Robert said.

"A lady you say?" Alex asked, raising one eyebrow. There seemed to be some significance in his glance that the gentlemen and her mother understood, but which went over Catherine's head, as well as the heads of both the other girls.

"A true lady," Robert said. "You'll meet Mrs. Prudence tomorrow and then you'll see what I mean. She's a widow of five years who still wears gray. She was even wearing a veil, for God's sake."

"Language, Robert, if you please," Mrs. Middlebrook said. "No taking the Lord's name in vain in this house." No one seemed to notice that it was not her house, but the Duchess of Northumberland's.

Robert had the good grace to appear properly chastened. "Begging your pardon, ma'am."

"I'll look her over tomorrow before we leave for Devon, and I will be the judge," Alex said.

"I looked her over today, and I tell you she is a lady. She might just be the answer to our prayers."

Mary Elizabeth looked at Robert with a narrow-eyed stare, but spoke pleasantly enough to Catherine. "She seems like a woman of sense." She turned back to her brothers. "But I do not need a keeper."

Before the moment could escalate into a full-scale Scottish riot, Catherine stepped in. "Mary, a companion might be a lovely addition to your household. I, for one, would welcome another woman's company once we return from Mama's wedding. And as you say, this house is large enough for an army."

"True. I suppose we might invite her and see how we all get on."

Catherine smiled. "Splendid. Another lady will be just the thing. Perhaps she'll even have a good influence on Robert there."

It was the first time Catherine had ventured to tease her new brother-in-law, and she could tell that he did not know how to take it. A gentleman, he simply chose the safest course, and said nothing in reply.

"Indeed. A widow just might," Robert said at last.

For no reason Catherine could fathom, Alex shot his brother a look that should have struck terror into his heart. But Robert did not even blink. He simply smiled at his brother as if accepting an unspoken challenge.

"May I play your pianoforte?" Margaret asked. Clearly she had grown bored with the talk of widows and claymores.

"Of course you may, child. Your playing delights us all," Mrs. Middlebrook said.

Robert reached for the whisky flask, and Alex smiled as Margaret began to play a jaunty Scottish tune. It was a new one to Catherine's ears, and she would have stayed and listened had her husband not taken hold of her hand, and drawn her to her feet. He escorted her to a painting by the parlor door, as if to show her the merits of the art. He pitched his voice so quietly that she almost could not hear him over the deafening music.

"I think we should retire directly after dinner, wife."

Catherine felt breathless, the heat of his body making her shiver as he stood close beside her, the family and the room around them all but forgotten. "Might we play one of the games you taught me, husband?" she asked, feeling her blush rise unbidden. It seemed now that when she blushed for her husband, she no longer hated the color in her cheeks.

"Kissing the quim, perhaps?" he whispered low, careful that no one else might hear them over the sound of Margaret's thundering pianoforte.

Catherine pressed her forehead against his shoulder, sure that her mother could read her thoughts from across the room. But Mrs. Middlebrook was happily chatting with her own fiancé, as Mary Elizabeth and Robert argued in undertones over Alex's silver flask.

"Yes, Alex."

"I want you right now," he said. He took her hand and drew her from the room. For one delicious, exciting moment, she thought he might drag her into a closet, and take her against a wall. Instead, he stopped in the entrance hall, the place where in her own home she had first kissed him.

His lips were on hers then, a promise of carnal bliss to come. But he was gentle, and did not enflame her senses, with both their families in the next room. He simply held her close, and she leaned against him, taking in the scent of bergamot on his skin.

"I will love you all my life, Alex."

"And beyond," he answered, an echo of his words the night before. "If the priests are right."

She drew back so that she might see his chocolate eyes smiling down at her, their depths filled with the joys her future held. "And so they are."

Read on for a sneak peek at the second book in
the Broadswords and Ballrooms series

How to Wed a Warrior

London, 1820

LADY PRUDENCE WAS LATE FOR TEA WITH MISS
Harrington when she passed a young lady drawing a
sword on the Earl of Grathton.

Prudence had deliberately chosen Hyde Park over
the vulgar, newer part of London so that she might
walk in quiet and remember better times. In only one
day more, she would complete arrangements with the
Harringtons of Bombay to become their daughter's
companion, and the last remnant of her old life would
be swept away. She never anticipated that as she
strolled, her peaceful contemplation would be shattered by the glint of a long blade…or by the hulking
form of an exasperated Scot.

"Mary Elizabeth, what in God's holy name are
you doin'?"

The fine man stood beside the sword-wielding girl,
glaring at her, his brogue thick and almost musical.
Save for his height, which was almost six feet, and
his broad shoulders, which were almost bursting from

his dark blue coat, the Scot looked almost civilized.
His curling, auburn hair was a bit longer than fashion
dictated, touching the edge of his high collar and his
simply tied cravat. But it was the gleam in his eyes
that made her think of mayhem, and the steel in his
furious gaze that made her certain that, if she did not
intervene, he would murder the young lady standing
with him in the middle of the Promenade Hour.

The slight, slender girl was still holding a large
sword with what looked to be bizarre comfort and
ease, aiming it in the direction of Lord Grathton's
stomach, while Lady Cecelia Wellington cowered
behind him.

Pru did not think of self-preservation. She did not
think of her carefully constructed disguise of the past
five years, or of the fact that, as her brother's best
friend, the earl would be able to see right through it.
She simply stepped between the girl's sword tip and
Lord Grathton, certain that it would all come out right
in the end.

As it must. Or so she always told herself. Surely,
someday, at some point, things would come out all right.

She held tight to that belief yet again and cleared
her throat. "Good day, my lord. It seems you are
having some difficulty picking up your fiancée's reticule. Might I be of assistance?" For the young blonde
girl with the blade had placed herself protectively over
the small bag that Grathton's companion, Lady Cecelia
Wellington, had dropped in the verge.

Upon hearing that the owner of the bag was Lord
Grathton's companion, the lovely girl brandishing the
overlarge sword blinked twice and lowered her weapon.

"I beg your pardon, sir. I thought you were a robber." The girl's sword gleamed in the light of the late afternoon sun. She did not move to put it away, but stood staring at Lord Grathton as if expecting him to speak to her without an introduction after she had threatened his life.

The large Scot stepped forward to intervene at last. Pru placed herself discretely between him and the earl, hoping he would follow her lead, even though men rarely did. Still, a woman might live in hope.

"If you will excuse us, Lord Grathton," Prudence said. "My companions and I are a bit confused at this late hour. Too much sun, and a desperate need for a cup of tea. I do beg your pardon."

Grathton did not seem to be listening to her words, but to the sound of her voice. He stared into her face, trying to peer beyond her glasses, beyond the chasm of years that separated them. She had not seen him since the summer her brother had been lost at sea, taking her family's fortune with him—the year she had disappeared from polite society altogether. She prayed for a miracle, that Grathton might not remember her, but she saw the moment when the flint of memory sparked and caught fire.

"Pru?" Grathton asked, his voice filled with wonder and with something else she would rather not remember. Five years was not long enough, it seemed, for him to have forgotten. Pru would have sworn silently to herself had she not been the remnant of a lady.

"I beg your pardon, my lord. We must leave you and your lady in peace."

The Lady Cecelia stared down her long nose at Pru,

who was a head shorter than she was. The lady's cold, blue gaze took in her frumpy dress and the hideous bonnet perched over her curls. Pru felt color rise to her cheeks, and she was catapulted back to the time when the *ton* had turned their backs on her en masse, and had ceased to receive her family altogether.

Pru rallied, reminding herself to leave the past behind, and tapped the young blonde's arm. Without having to be told twice, the Scottish girl slipped away, making an oddly graceful curtsy, the hilt of the long sword still clutched in both fists.

"Good day," the girl said to no one in particular, attracting the icy glare of Lady Cecelia as she slipped toward a carriage that waited by the side of the road. The girl did not seem to notice or care that she was the focus of so much censure. Pru was glad to have the lady's stare removed from her person, but could feel the heated gaze of both Grathton and the hulking Scot take its place. She swallowed the lump that had risen in her throat.

"Forgive the intrusion," Prudence said to Grathton. "Good day."

She thought to slip away and perhaps hide herself behind a convenient bush until she could find a way out of the park, but the Scotsman stepped up and took her arm, bowing to Lord Grathton. "Good day, my lord."

Grathton did not speak. His fiancée, however, did. "My word," Cecelia drawled, speaking to Grathton as if no one else were there. "What a bizarre episode. I cannot understand why foreigners are even allowed in the park, much less among civilized people. What is

Town coming to?" Her acid tongue drew a flush to Prudence's skin as if the woman's vitriol was directed at her.

Lady Cecelia did not wait for Grathton to answer but glanced over her lover's shoulder to the path beyond to see who might be watching. She saw a boon companion driving by, and waved to her, dismissing Pru and the two Scots as if they had never existed.

Pru remembered the chill of that cold shoulder from the ladies who had once been her mother's bosom friends. Once the family money disappeared, society's interest in her family had vanished as well. Except for Grathton. When she had been cast out into utter darkness, he had tried to help, though to stand by her would have meant his own ruin. He looked as if he wanted to help again now, no matter what the cost to his reputation. She could not allow that.

She took the Scot's arm and propelled the man back toward his waiting coach. "Hoist me up," she told him, and he obliged, lifting her above the tall wheels of the carriage. The young girl had hidden her sword away again, or perhaps had tossed it behind a tree, for now she sat as demure as you please, her skirt arranged around her neatly on the carriage seat and her gloved hands folded neatly in her lap.

"The claymore is under the seat," the girl said, blithely answering Pru's unspoken question.

The Scot rose up beside them on the high seat. Pru did not address the girl beside her, but the man. "Drive."

And he did.

❧

Why on God's blessed green earth Robert Waters had chosen to listen to a single word the slip of a woman said, he did not know. Not only that, he found himself obeying her as she ordered him around as if he were her bootblack. Perhaps it was the blue of her eyes that did it, an indigo that was a sea for a man to drown in.

No, not that. Robbie didn't care a fig for a woman's eyes.

Perhaps it was her neat, curved figure, currently swathed in an abundance of sickly gray worsted wool and pale cream lace. He never noticed a woman's clothes, but these were just ugly enough to repulse him, had they not contained the soft breasts and rounded behind of a woman of quality. How he knew she was quality, he could not say. Perhaps it was the snap in her eyes that had joined the snap in her voice when she spoke to him.

Whatever the reason, he'd found himself standing back and allowing her to rescue his sister from herself in the middle of Hyde Park, in the middle of the fashionable hour.

When he found his tongue again, Robert did not ask the name of the impressive lady who now sat so primly beside him, for he was not at all sure that she would relinquish it. Instead, he used his reclaimed voice to browbeat his sister.

"Mary Elizabeth, for the love of God, the English are going to burn us out! You benighted fool, how could you draw a blade on an Englishman in the middle of a London park in broad daylight?

And not just an Englishman, but one of their lairds? Christ wept, Mary, you'll get us all run out on a rail."

"Don't be dramatic," Mary Elizabeth answered, resting herself, as relaxed as you please, against the soft cushions of the fancy carriage seat. "The English won't burn us out. We're staying with the Duchess of Northumberland and they won't touch the house of one of their own."

"They might kill us in the street the next time we chance to get your ices at Gunter's," he groused.

"You might lower your voice a trifle, sir," the lady said. "You seem to be attracting more unwanted attention."

Robert did not give a tinker's dam for what the English thought of him, but he caught himself before he shouted again. He could smell the bossy, curvy woman beside him, and her perfume was making him even more irritable. She smelled of hyacinths and heather. He would swear, if he had not known better, that she smelled of home.

He cursed himself for a fool and focused his mind where it belonged. Not on some spinster virgin who was trying to hide her beauty for some mad reason, but on his sister, who was certain to drive him to drown himself before the week was through.

"What will Alex say when he hears you've drawn a sword in public?" Robert asked.

Mary Elizabeth shrugged one shoulder, looking out over the traffic and the houses as they passed them. People had stopped nodding to them ever since Mary Elizabeth had shown them her steel, and now simply stared as though they were apparitions or demons risen up from hell. Robert swore, out loud this time, and the bossy woman spoke.

"I would thank you to keep a civil tongue in your head, if you please, sir. Pull over here," she said, for all the world as if she paid him five pounds per annum as a servant boy.

Robert looked at her, his eyebrow rising, but did as he was told. His mother had drummed into him the simple stricture: never hold a lady against her will. His gaze wandered along the front of the woman's hideous gown, sussing out the sweet curve of her breasts beneath. Now, if she were a widow woman, or a woman of ill repute, there might be some negotiating to be done.

Robert loved the company of women almost as much as he loved leaving them behind once they began to become tedious. But this one was tempting him to forget his good reason, and why he had come to London at all. No woman had ever tossed his bad manners back in his face before. He found that he liked it.

He thought of the money he had set aside, that he barely needed and almost never touched. It would be easy enough to dip into that money and set this little baggage up in her own parlor, with a quiet back stair that might lead to a bedroom he also paid for. He thought of the delights he and this little bit of fluff might find there, and he found himself smiling.

The *bit of fluff* seemed to read his thoughts and where they were tending. She met his eyes, and her blue gaze filled with the Wrath of God. Had he been a lesser man, he would have been singed where he sat. She was anything but fluffy, it seemed. He merely smiled once more. If he had ever seen a woman besides his mother face him down like that, he could not remember it.

"I would thank you to hand me down to the street, sir. I believe we have made our escape."

"And now you hope to make yours," he answered.

Mary Elizabeth frowned at him. "Don't mind my brother. He has the manners of an ape. Thank you for helping me. I'm afraid I stepped in it quite badly back there."

The lady turned her eyes away from him, and as soon as she did, her face softened into a smile. "No thanks are necessary, miss. But I must warn you not to draw on Lord Grathton again. He is a crack shot. And while he would never call out a lady, he might call on your brother here."

Mary Elizabeth laughed. "God help him. Robbie's a fury with his fists and with a sword. The laird might have his work cut out for him."

For some mad reason, Robbie felt himself swell with pride at his sister's casual description of him. He was indeed a fury on the field of battle, wherever that field might lie, but he had not expected his sister to know it. He looked to the lady beside him, but she did not seem impressed. She did not even look his way, but sniffed.

"Well," she said. "That's as may be. But please keep your weapon sheathed when out in polite company in future."

Robbie thought of one or two choice things to say to that, but he held his tongue.

"I thought he was robbing her," Mary Elizabeth said.

"At such a time, a lady must allow a gentleman to intervene," she said.

If he or his brother Alex had offered such sage advice, Mary Elizabeth would have ignored them both. But she listened to the woman and nodded, as if by stating the obvious, she had revealed a deep mystery, and solved a puzzling riddle.

"Indeed," Mary Elizabeth said. "I might consider that."

Robert climbed down and offered his hand, wondering how he was going to get this woman's name, and learn where she lived. He needn't have worried. With her best friend Catherine now run off with their brother Alex, Mary Elizabeth was ripe for a new conquest.

"You must come and take tea with us tomorrow," Mary Elizabeth said. "We live at the Duchess of Northumberland's house. I am Mary Elizabeth Waters, and this lout is Robert."

Robert sketched a bow, and the lady raised one eyebrow. She did not curtsy back.

"Good day," she said to him, before turning a much friendlier gaze on his sister. "And I am Mrs. Prudence Whittaker. It is a pleasure to make your acquaintance."

"Why were you walking alone?" Mary Elizabeth asked.

Robert wanted the answer to this question himself. He smiled down at the fine, honey-brown curls that were trying to escape from beneath the ugly straw bonnet she had clapped over them. She ignored him as if he were not there.

"As a widow, I often have occasion to stroll in the park without a maid," she said.

Robert knew that this was considered barbaric even among the heathen English, who had no better care for their women than he had for a stray sow, but he did not question her. He wanted to see what outlandish thing she might say next. It hit him then, the word she had spoken, the most important word in that sentence.

Widow.

"We'll see you tomorrow afternoon at four then," he said. "Shall I come and pick you up in the duchess's carriage?"

He saw the light of battle flare in her eyes before she tamped it down. It seemed this Mrs. Whittaker was a feisty bit. He was looking forward to finding out how feisty she could be, and how often.

"I thank you, Mr. Waters. But I will find my own way there." She smiled at Mary Elizabeth before she strode away. "Good day."

Two

PRU DID NOT KNOW WHAT POSSESSED HER TO AGREE to take tea at a duchess's house with a broad-shouldered Scot and his wayward sister. Perhaps it was the way his blue eyes had seemed to hold her still, like a butterfly under glass. A part of her simply could not catch her breath when he looked at her. Even though she had been strict with herself, and kept her eyes from him except to frown, she had felt his gaze on her. It lingered like the warmth of a sun she had never felt before.

Perhaps she had simply run mad.

So the next day, she set aside her misgivings in her borrowed room in the house of her aunt, and dressed in her ugliest gown. Aunt Winifred Whittaker, whose last name Pru had adopted, looked her over, inspecting her disguise for flaws, as she always did before Pru went out into the world. Her aunt's unswerving gaze always on her was one more reason she was finally seeking employment as a companion. Out in the world, no matter how odd or unpleasant the family she ended up with might turn out to be, no one would watch her as her mother's sister did—always searching for a defect.

"It will serve," Winifred said at last. "But I think that bonnet could do without the flower."

Pru glanced at the wide glass above the mantel that served to reflect both sunlight and candlelight across the room, making the small sitting room brighter. The tiny white rose she had tucked into the brim of her ugly bonnet was out of place. No doubt of it. She was not even sure why she had plucked that rose from the hedge in the yard early that morning, or why she wore it now. Five years ago, when her brother had died and her family had fallen into ruin, she had given up beautiful things. The sight of that one rose was not pert or pretty, but sad.

"No doubt you are right, Aunt." But Pru did not move to throw it away.

"Well, I think you might better serve God and your fellow man by living here and working for the poor with me," Winifred said. "But as you have your heart set on serving in some nabob's house, there is little I can say in the matter."

Pru's heart was bent not on service, but freedom. She did not tell her aunt that, however.

"Miss Harrington seems quite well brought up for a tradesman's child. She needs a bit of polish, but I think I will be able to see her married within the year."

"Not in society, surely." Winifred's cold tone was colored with a touch of genteel horror.

"Nabobs have their own society, Aunt. I am sure the girl will make a very good marriage among her father's peers."

Winifred sniffed. "Indeed. As long as they don't delude themselves into thinking she might marry quality. As you might have done, had you not been so foolish."

Pru sighed. It never took long for her aunt to bring up and disapprove of her past choices. A marriage without love was a marriage without honor. Her father had taught her that. Never one to move in society herself, her aunt had never fully grasped how complete Pru's ruin was. And now, as a twenty-five-year-old spinster securely on the shelf, with no money and no family name to speak of, she was better off on her own. Pru would leave her aunt's house and make her own way in the world. Nabobs' daughters were kinder than quality, and their fathers paid better.

The brass clock on the mantel struck the hour. "I must go, Aunt. The Harrington family is waiting."

She had not mentioned her invitation to the Duchess of Northumberland's town house. Winifred would have protested that such an invitation from Highland barbarians was a dishonor in itself, but she also would have insisted on coming along if only to see the duchess. Lying to her aunt was easier than dealing with her for the entire afternoon.

"Don't let their commonness rub off on you, Prudence," her aunt said, unable to let her leave in peace. She seemed to relish the nasty parting words that would ring in her niece's ears for the rest of the day. "Never forget, no matter how foolish you behave, that you are an earl's daughter."

Prudence swallowed her ire, closing her mouth on words she longed to say. For the sake of the memory of her mother, she held her tongue until she could speak with respect. "Indeed, Aunt. I never do."

❧

With Alexander safely married and on the way to Devon with his young bride, Robert could breathe easier. The problem of what to do with his wild sister was still unsolved, but he thought he might see a solution glimmering in the distance, like a pearl gleaming in the depths of the sea.

"A companion?" Mary Elizabeth said. "What for?"

"For company," Robert answered. "Alex and Catherine will be in Devon with her mother and sister for a fortnight. You'll be bored here all alone. Having the Englishwoman about might do you a world of good."

"Don't insult her by calling her English, Robbie."

"She is English, Mary."

"If she were a hunchback, you wouldn't tell her to her face, now would you?"

"No, I suppose not."

"Then leave her Englishness out of it."

Robert held his tongue. In spite of Mary Elizabeth's usual tirade against the benighted English, she seemed to be considering what he had said. Since the first time they had been ordered south by their mother, she might actually take his advice.

He wished for a moment he had his brother Ian's way of giving a woman an idea and making her think it was hers all along. But Robert was a plainspoken man, if charming in his own way. He'd have to rely on Mary Elizabeth's long-buried good sense, and a bit of luck.

He had good luck in abundance.

"I'll ask her," Mary Elizabeth said. "She's a true lady, so she might refuse."

Robbie agreed with that. The delectable widow who hid her glorious curves under ugly gowns had the manners of a lady. A lady he would like to unwrap, like a present on Twelfth Night.

"She is a lady. But she helped us yesterday. She might help us again."

Mary Elizabeth's blue eyes were sharp on his face. "I don't need her help."

Robert could feel his advantage slipping, so he lied a little. "She doesn't know that."

The fancy ducal butler scratched on the parlor door, and Robert felt his neck prickle at the sound. "God's breath, but he sounds like a cat in sand."

Mary Elizabeth shot him a quelling look, but she was smiling. "Come in," she called, as Robbie couldn't be bothered to encourage the duchess's servants in their odd English ways.

The butler, Pemberton, stood glowering in the open doorway. "There is a lady to see you."

He did not address Mary Elizabeth or Robert directly, but spoke to the room at large, as though his mistress the duchess might be hiding behind the wainscoting, or be tucked away behind one of the heavy velvet drapes.

"Thank you, Pemberton. Please send her in, along with the tea tray."

"As you say, miss."

The butler bowed from the neck, and in another silent moment, the enticing subject of their conversation was standing in the doorway, as if she was confused as to how she had gotten there at all. She blinked behind the thick lenses of her spectacles, and Robbie felt his pulse quicken inexplicably.

It did not occur to him to inquire as to why he had a sudden taste for widows in ugly bonnets and brown wool. He had never been a man to reflect overmuch on his sexual tastes; rather, he preferred to spend all his time fulfilling them. He watched the woman step into the room and accept his sister's outstretched hand. He wondered how long it would be before he might sample this one.

His sister and the lady were making some feminine conversation, none of which interested him in the slightest. He simply stood at attention, watching the rise and fall of the lady's breasts as she spoke.

When both girls turned to him, as if expecting some answer, he blinked. "Yes?" he asked at last.

Mary Elizabeth frowned at him. "I told you he has the manners of an ape," she said.

The Englishwoman stared him down, as if measuring him for a birch rod, so that she might take him over her knee. He shifted uncomfortably at that thought and, before he could follow that flight of fancy, reminded himself that his sister was in the room.

The tea tray arrived, rescuing him from whatever his sister and her new friend had recently concocted. The butler left the tray unattended by the settee, closing the door unceremoniously behind him.

The imperious lady raised one eyebrow at the rudeness of the duchess's servant, but had the good grace not to comment on it. "Well," she said at last. "Shall I pour?"

Three

ROBERT WATCHED AS MRS. WHITTAKER SANK ONTO the purgatorial settee beside his sister and started pouring tea. Mary Elizabeth did not seem to think it odd that their guest had just taken over as hostess, but then, what in their lives was not odd? If that was the strangest thing to happen all afternoon, he would count himself lucky.

He sat across from the two girls, wondering how he was going to bring up the matter of companionship for his sister while still keeping himself from panting too openly over the tempting widow in her unsightly brown gown. Happily, Mary Elizabeth solved his problem for him.

"I take two lumps and a splash of milk," she instructed. When the lady handed the Sevres china cup to her, along with its saucer, his sister said, "Thank you, Mrs. Whittaker. Would you be so kind as to add only lemon to my brother's cup? And might you consider taking on the role of companion to me?"

Mrs. Whittaker paused for the barest moment, raising one eyebrow as she handed him his tiny cup. He reached into his pocket for his flask. When he drew it out, though, her censorious look made him freeze in place before putting the flask back where it had come from. Perhaps he would take his tea without his traditional tot of whisky. Just this afternoon, of course.

To keep the peace.

The lady's eagle eye turned from him almost reluctantly, as soon as she saw that he had silently obeyed her stricture to keep their teatime a civilized, whisky-free affair. She smiled at his sister, poured her own tea without adding milk or sugar, and took a meditative sip.

Mary Elizabeth kept talking. "My brother and sister-in-law are in the country, and I am staying in Town. My brother Robert here is a decent sort, but not fit company for a lady."

Robert snorted. "I'll thank you for that, Mary."

His sister's eyes widened at him over the Englishwoman's head as she bent to add a touch more tea to her cup. He saw then that Mary Elizabeth was simply trying to reel the lady in by calling once more on her protective instincts, and he held his tongue.

Mrs. Whittaker did not even glance at him, but met his sister's eyes. "You are the lady in question."

"Of course I am."

Robert felt his ire begin to rise at the hint of censure in the woman's voice. He might call Mary Elizabeth all manner of hoydenish names, but he would be damned if he sat by while someone from outside the family criticized her.

"Forgive my rudeness, Miss Waters. I have no doubt that you are a lady. But as you know, the *ton* is more than a little set in their ways. They have not quite taken to opening their doors to foreigners, and as you are from the north, they might be found especially reticent."

"I would have thought so," Mary Elizabeth answered, "but they do as the duchess tells them."

"The Duchess of Northumberland is not in residence, is she?"

"No. She's at home, trying to bring her wayward son to heel. He refuses to marry and continue their line. More's the pity. I don't know what's wrong with the man."

Robert did not point out that she was just as stubborn as the reclusive duke they'd never met, but his sister had the bit between her teeth, so he held his tongue.

Mary Elizabeth went on blithely. "The duchess could not come south for my Season, but she has sponsored me."

"Which is why you were received everywhere. Until you drew a weapon on Lord Grathton."

Mary Elizabeth frowned, her blue eyes looking troubled. "Was he that offended, then?"

"I think the earl is a gentleman who would overlook even such folly. But the women of his family, and the women of the *ton*, are far less forgiving."

Mary Elizabeth's frown deepened. "I did not think. I just acted."

The imperious lady softened slightly as she bent forward and took his sister's hand. It was odd to see a near stranger offer comfort, and for Mary Elizabeth to accept it so readily. Mary Elizabeth did not turn away as Robert thought she might, but sat still and listened to the woman speak.

"Have you received a great many invitations this Season?"

"I have," Mary Elizabeth answered.

"And have you received any yet today?"

There was a long, uncomfortable silence, in which Mary Elizabeth sat very still, looking suddenly miserable. Robert had the almost overwhelming need to run the whole stuck-up, mincing mass of London's elite through with his own sword for putting that sorrowful look on his sister's face. The sons of whores.

"No." Mary Elizabeth's voice was low. Mrs. Whittaker had not yet let go of her hand.

"I think perhaps it is time to retrench, Miss Waters. If you chose to take me on as a companion, it might behoove you to listen to my advice and, wherever you can, to heed it, so that you can continue as a success."

Mary Elizabeth still looked dejected. "I can try, Mrs. Whittaker, but I am myself, always. I don't know how to be anyone else."

The lady smiled then. Her smile was warm and sincere, her eyes shining from behind her thick glasses, cutting past them as light after a storm.

"Of course you must be yourself. I simply suggest that we might plan a manner of attack on society that would make you welcome for all your own stellar qualities, and not just because of the duchess's influence."

"Stellar qualities?" Mary Elizabeth looked doubtful. "What are they?"

Mrs. Whittaker leaned close and patted his sister's other hand. "I think we can take a week or two to explore them, don't you think? And then launch you back into society a new woman."

"But as I said, I am always my own woman," Mary Elizabeth answered. "I can be no other."

"And we will find a way to show that woman off to advantage, in a way that will not frighten the lords and ladies of London."

"I think I'd rather go home."

Robert swallowed hard, but before he could remind his sister of the folly of that, Mrs. Whittaker spoke for him.

"You will no doubt go home, and to great approbation. But first, do you not think it might be fun to wow the *ton* a little?"

"Wow them?"

"Shock them with what a lady you are."

Mary Elizabeth mused. "I am a lady already."

"Of course you are."

"And if I get a good report from her friends down here," his sister said, "Mama might welcome me home."

Robert felt his heart squeeze, but as he watched, Mrs. Whittaker did not waver. "You will make your mother very proud."

Mary Elizabeth squared her shoulders, and the light of battle came into her eyes. "How do we start?"

❧

Pru was sure she had offended Miss Waters and her hulking brother past bearing by speaking so plainly, but by the time she rose to take her leave, the girl seemed eager to begin her new regime. There was no way to be certain that such a regimen would take, but if she could keep her new charge from drawing a blade in public, she would have accomplished something.

Mr. Robert Waters did not comment. Indeed, he said almost nothing all afternoon, which worried her a bit. Of course, if he simply held his tongue for the few months it might take to bring his sister into shape, it might be best for them all.

Though, even if she never had to hear his deep, lilting voice again, she had no idea what to do about his blue eyes. Or his curling, overlong hair. Or his broad shoulders. Or the way he smelled of cedar.

Pru told herself not be a fool. She had turned away men much better bred and much richer than Mr. Robert Waters. But none of them had given her a shiver down her spine whenever they entered the room. Or spoke. Or sat in silence.

It seemed that she had a taste for Highland men that, until now, she had been unaware of. Damn and blast it.

Pru rose to put on her gloves and curtsied, watching as Miss Waters curtsied back very prettily to her. The girl was graceful, no mistake. She would take Mary Elizabeth through her paces, and see if they might find some charming, ladylike skill with which to woo the *ton*. Pru wondered if she might even have to call on Lord Grathton to ask for his help in setting the girl to rights with the cats of society.

She prayed not. That part of her life was over, and forever. She could not very well ask such a favor of him after all this time, and not expect consequences.

John Vaughton, Earl of Grathton was well on his way to being married to someone else. Perhaps he had already set aside all memory of her, and continued to move on with his life.

Pru was not sure what it was about the young Miss Waters that had convinced her to abandon a perfectly lucrative year with Miss Harrington of Bombay. Miss Harrington and Miss Waters were so different. Miss Waters was a child of privilege and wealth, much as Pru had once been. But there was a fire and a joy in Mary Elizabeth that Pru could not remember having, even when she had been safe and warm, tucked away in Yorkshire in her father's house.

Pru adjusted her bonnet and moved to the front door, taking in the cool nod of the butler, who seemed slightly mollified to see an English lady in the house. Mary Elizabeth did not accompany her into the entrance hall, but Robert Waters did.

"Forgive me, Mr. Waters. Did I forget something?"

The Highlander smiled down on her, and she felt a hint of hot lava move straight to her nether region. She swallowed hard and forced herself to stand very still as Robert Waters stepped close to her—too close for propriety's sake. She tried to find her breath, and failed. She could not seem to find her tongue either. How on God's loving green earth was she was going to live with this man for the time it would take to see his sister married?

Perhaps she had made a mistake.

"Indeed you have forgotten something, Mrs. Whittaker. Something a bit more important than the tea and crumpets we've just shared."

Pru could not find her voice, so she simply stared at him past the annoying rim of her ugly brown bonnet.

His breath was warm on her cheek as he leaned close. For one delicious, horrifying moment, she thought that he might kiss her there in the entrance hall of a ducal mansion, with the stern butler standing by. But instead of his lips, it was one broad fingertip which rose to her cheek, and brushed a curl back. It had come loose from its pins, threatening to fall into her eye. Robert Waters stood close and let her hair curl around his finger, as if it loved him, as if it wished for him to stay close. Pru knew that she must say something, anything, to set this man down. But her reason had deserted her along with her voice.

"What shall we be paying you then, Mrs. Prudence Whittaker? What price would you put on my sister's marriage?"

Pru blinked at him, frozen like a rabbit that had scented the hunter. She wished fervently that her good sense would return from wherever it had gone. She also wished that he would touch more than just a stray curl.

When she still did not answer, Robert Waters smiled at her, looking down her body as he might at a horse he wished to purchase at market. His eyes seemed to linger on her breasts, hidden as they were beneath the brown worsted of her gown. He met her gaze again, and she felt her cheeks flush.

She opened her mouth to give him the dressing-down he deserved, but she felt as if he were laughing, not at her, but at himself. There was such a light of good humor tucked away behind the blue of his gaze that, for the moment, her anger vanished like smoke. She almost laughed herself. He was a charmer, of that there was no doubt. She would have to guard against that charm, along with everything else.

"I suppose twenty pounds per annum will suffice, Mr. Waters, paid each quarter."

"Only twenty pounds? Great God, Mrs. Whittaker, you hold yourself too cheap. I don't think you realize the monumental task you have set yourself. We'll be paying you twenty pounds per month, and that only to start. If you manage to marry her off, I'll throw in a five hundred pound bonus, which ought to set you up for life."

It was difficult to understand him, and Pru couldn't be sure whether it was the fact that he was still standing so close, or that his Scottish burr was clouding his words, making her have to listen hard, and longer. But before she could object to such an outrageous sum— far more than the Harringtons had been willing to pay—Mr. Robert Waters had taken her arm, just like a gentleman, and had led her down the town house steps to a waiting open carriage.

"I must go and fetch my things from my aunt's house," she managed to say at last. "I'll return before dark."

"Aye, that you will. For I'll be driving you."

He did not hand her into the carriage, but raised her bodily onto the seat. His hands were hot on her waist. She could feel the sweltering effects of his touch through her thick gown and stays. She clutched her reticule, desperate to take herself in hand.

Sudden wealth and overwhelming attraction after years of poverty and loneliness might seem like gifts from heaven, but she knew she could not allow herself to fall into the blue of Robert Waters's eyes and ruin herself. No matter how much she enjoyed his touch, she was still a lady. A widow might indulge herself in frolics between the sheets, but gently reared virgins could not, even at the ripe old age of twenty-five.

Or so she told herself as she watched Robert Waters vault into the carriage, sitting so close to her that his thigh pressed against hers. She took in the warm, crooked smile he sent her way and felt her heart shift along with her breath. She was in for more trouble than she had bargained for.

God help her. God keep her from seductive Highlanders. God keep her safe from herself.

Acknowledgments

As always, whenever I have the privilege of writing a novel there are a lot of people to thank. I want to begin with the usual suspects, my mother, Karen English, my father, Carl English, and my brother, Barry English, for a lifetime of your love and encouragement. Thanks to my godparents, Ron and Vena Miller, as well as my dear friends, Amy and Troy Pierce, Laura Creasy, and LaDonna Lindgren for the years of love and unwavering support. My affectionate thanks also go to Trilby Newkirk and Marianne and Chris Nubel for their sympathetic ear, and for always making me laugh just at the right moment. And I have to thank Mike and Jennifer Peace as well as Ellen and Andy Seltz, not just for the years of friendship, but for raising four of the best girls ever to walk the face of the earth.

I also want to thank the incredible team at Sourcebooks Casablanca. Without my amazing editor, Mary Altman, the Waterses and all their antics never would have seen the light of day. Many thanks to Rachel Gilmer and her stellar team, as well as Hilary for her timely and thoughtful insights, and to Amelia Narigon for getting the word out. And I have to thank the design team for the beautiful cover.

A heartfelt thanks to you, the readers, for spending time with me and my Highlanders.

About the Author

Ever since Christy English picked up a fake sword in stage combat class at the age of fourteen, she has lived vicariously through the sword-wielding women of her imagination. A banker by day and a writer by night, she loves to eat chocolate, drink too many soft drinks, and walk the mountain trails of her home in western North Carolina. Please visit her at www.ChristyEnglish.com.

When a Rake Falls
The Rake's Handbook
by Sally Orr

❧

He's racing to win back his reputation

Having hired a balloon to get him to Paris in a daring race, Lord Boyce Parker is simultaneously exhilarated and unnerved by the wonders and dangers of flight, and most of all by the beautiful, stubborn, intelligent lady operating the balloon.

She's curious about the science of love

Eve Mountfloy is in the process of conducting weather experiments when she finds herself spirited away to France by a notorious rake. She's only slightly dismayed—the rake seems to respect her work—but she is frequently distracted by his windblown good looks and buoyant spirits.

What happens when they descend from the clouds?

As risky as aeronautics may be, once their feet touch the ground, Eve and Boyce learn the real danger of a very different type of falling...

❧

Praise for *The Rake's Handbook*:

For more Sally Orr, visit:
www.sourcebooks.com

50 Ways to Ruin a Rake

Rakes and Rogues
by Jade Lee

Mellie Smithson has a plan

Mellie Smithson is trapped in the country with no suitors and no prospects on the horizon except, perhaps, the exasperating—although admittedly handsome—guest of her father. Unwilling to settle, Mellie will do anything to escape to London…

Trevor Anaedsley has a problem

Trevor Anaedsley's grandfather has cut off his funds until he gets engaged. Beset by creditors, Trevor escapes to the country—ostensibly to visit his old tutor Mr. Smithson—where he meets Smithson's lovely daughter Mellie. The obvious solution is suddenly before him—but will this fake engagement go as Trevor and Mellie plan? Or will they find that even the best laid plans often go awry?

Praise for *What the Groom Wants*:

"Sensual, suspenseful, and satisfying, [Jade Lee] delivers on all levels." —Eileen Dreyer, *New York Times* bestselling author

"Lee spins an intriguing tale." —*RT Book Reviews*

"Highly entertaining…Jade Lee knows how to write an explosive scene." —*Fresh Fiction*

For more Jade Lee, visit:
www.sourcebooks.com

The Rogue You Know

Covent Garden Cubs

by Shana Galen

❧

She's beyond his reach...

Gideon Harrow has spent his life in London's dark underworld—and he wants out. A thief and a con, he plans one last heist to finally win his freedom. But when everything goes wrong, he finds himself at the tender mercies of one of Society's most untouchable women—Lady Susanna Derring.

...and out of her depth

Susanna has spent her life in London's glittering *ton*, under the thumb of a domineering mother—and she wants out. When a wickedly charming rogue lands at her feet, she jumps at the chance to experience life before it's too late. But as she descends into London's underworld, she finds that nothing—not even Gideon—is as it seems. As excitement turns to danger, Susanna must decide what price she's willing to pay...for the love of a reformed thief.

❧

Praise for *Earls Just Want to Have Fun*:

"Pure Galen: a lively pace, wonderful repartee, colorful dialogue, and a marvelous cast of characters."
—*RT Book Reviews*, Top Pick, 4 1/2 Stars

For more Shana Galen, visit:
www.sourcebooks.com